A Heart to Call Home

What Reviewers Say About Jeannie Levig's Work

Threads of the Heart

"What a beautiful and moving story about five women learning invaluable lessons about love, self-awareness, cause and effect, consequences, betrayal, trust, truth, relationships, friendships, family…and life."—*2015 Rainbow Awards*

"[The main characters'] individual stories were interesting on their own but the interaction between the characters really makes this novel great. …The steamy scenes were so well written and extremely hot—in fact the best I've read in a long time. They were very varied and inventive. I thoroughly enjoyed the book and was so sad to finish it. I wanted it to go on and on!"—*Inked Rainbow Reads*

Embracing the Dawn

"*Embracing the Dawn* by Jeannie Levig has to be considered one of the best books of 2016 and one of the best audiobooks of 2017. We also see a lot of the relationships with secondary characters, and how important those friendships are to the growth and happiness of our main characters. Levig handles all of these relationships with a deftness that is truly a joy to read, and reread. The story is well plotted, the characters have depth, and the story sucks you in and keeps you turning pages."—*The Lesbian Review*

"*Embracing the Dawn* was written beautifully and it has slipped straight into my Favorite and Must Read Again shelves. It was so raw and honest. The story was very believable and I think that's what has stood out from most books I've read recently. Bold Stokes Books have really upped the ante recently with their authors. This was a fantastic novel. I was gripped from the beginning." —*Les Reveur*

"Seldom have I read such a passionate and insightful love story as this. Ms Levig's novel flows like a magnificent river, sometimes roaring other times meandering but always effortlessly and impressively moving gracefully on."—*Inked Rainbow Reads*

Into Thin Air

"Two things are apparent to me after reading Jeannie Levig's three novels. 1. She is an absolutely fantastic writer. 2. She is anything but formulaic. Every single one of her books has been good, but all so different. This writer knows how to draw emotion from her readers. …Levig challenges you with this book. This story is like a pendulum of emotions, so well crafted that you can't stop. This is a really fantastic book, you haven't read anything like this one, I promise."—*The Romantic Reader*

By the Author

Threads of the Heart

Embracing the Dawn

Into Thin Air

A Heart to Call Home

A Heart to Call Home

by

Jeannie Levig

2018

A HEART TO CALL HOME

ISBN 13: 978-1-63555-059-7

This Trade Paperback Original Is Published By
Bold Strokes Books, Inc.
P.O. Box 249
Valley Falls, NY 12185

First Edition: February 2018

Credits
Editors: Victoria Villasenor and Cindy Cresap
Production Design: Susan Ramundo
Cover Design By Tammy Seidick

Acknowledgments

First, a huge and heartfelt acknowledgement and thank you to Jamie Patterson, my Ideal Reader, my soul sister, and my best friend. Thank you for reading every word I write and for your invaluable feedback. I doubt I would be writing the acknowledgements for my fourth book if not for your constant love and support—and occasional kick in the butt. Thank you for being such a big part of my life.

As always, at the top of my list of blessings that I count each and every day are my amazing family, my spiritual circle, and my friends who give me their unwavering love and support in everything I do. I couldn't walk this path without each and every one of you. Thank you.

Immeasurable appreciation and admiration for the amazing team at Bold Strokes Books. To Radclyffe for creating and tirelessly leading this publishing house that is so dedicated to making sure every book is of the highest quality and all of its authors are fully supported in their growth and development as writers. To Sandy Lowe for everything you do on a daily basis to help keep BSB running smoothly and for always being available with insights and suggestions to make my books stronger from the very start. To my editors extraordinaire, Victoria Villasenor and Cindy Cresap. Vic, thank you for giving so much of yourself, your brilliance, your knowledge, and your heart in our work together. Your support, encouragement, suggestions, and humor have made my initial experiences with editing a fun and treasured learning gift. I will miss you. To Cindy, I am so grateful for your impeccable copy editing and everything else you do in the production of my books. And a huge thank you to all the behind the scenes people at BSB committed to excellence in publishing.

Finally, my deepest gratitude to all the readers who buy my books and share these stories with me. This is all for you. And always feel free to drop me a note and say hi through my website at www.JeannieLevig.com.

Chapter One

Jessie Weldon collected the last two essays as her seventh period class filed from the room. She straightened the stack of papers, then fastened them together with a large clip and dropped them onto her desk. *No question what I'll be doing tonight.*

"Ms. Weldon?" someone said from the doorway.

Jessie tensed and looked up, knowing exactly who she'd find. She'd recognize the voice anywhere.

"Jessica Weldon?" Dakota Scott flashed her cocky grin, her legendary confidence evident in the way she rested one forearm high on the doorjamb, her other hand splayed across her hip. Her long, dark auburn ponytail flowed out the back of a Clearwater Springs High School baseball cap. With that stance and her athletic build, she looked every inch the formidable girls volleyball and basketball coach she was reputed to be.

Jessie smiled pleasantly, despite the tightening in her shoulders and the queasiness in her stomach. It wasn't hearing Jessica, the name only her father had once called her, that gave her pause. She was getting used to that, since she'd started using it when she'd accepted the long-term substitute position that made her far more visible in her return to her hometown than if she'd stuck to her original plan. She'd only intended to stay a couple of months to reconnect with her foster father and regroup following her divorce from Shelly. It was this face-to-face with Dakota Scott that unsettled her, but she'd known, as soon as she'd decided to stay longer and had taken the job at the high school, it was inevitable. "Yes?"

Dakota strode across the room and extended her hand. "Hi, I'm—"

"I know who you are," Jessie said far too quickly. *And I know why you're here. I'll stay focused on that and deal with the rest later.* Her long buried conflict where Dakota Scott was concerned began to uncoil in her depths, but she intended to hold her ground, no matter who Dakota was—or who she'd once been in Jessie's mind. She'd known this moment was coming, had even tried to prepare for it. She shook Dakota's hand. "I mean, you're a Scott, right?" She laughed dismissively. "Who in this town doesn't know the Scotts?"

"Oh! Thank you." Dakota's tone was surprised—feigned, no doubt, since her expression wasn't. Of course, she was used to everyone knowing who she was, even if—as now—she had no recollection of them. "It's nice to meet you."

Jessie inclined her head in acknowledgement. Despite everything that linked them, this *was* the first time they'd actually met. "What can I do for you?"

"Well, first, let me welcome you to the school." Dakota pulled a student desk from the end row and sat on its top. She planted one sneakered foot in the seat, while keeping herself balanced with the other on the floor.

Jessie would have reprimanded a student for sitting on the desk that way, but she refrained with Dakota. They had dirtier floors to mop. Instead, she tried to ignore the muscles of Dakota's obviously toned thighs working beneath the relaxed fit of her black leggings, tried not to notice that the bright green of the baseball hat was the exact shade of Dakota's eyes. An old—yet, amazingly, still familiar—flutter tickled Jessie's stomach. She'd always liked looking at Dakota, even long ago when she'd been too young to understand what it meant. *But damn it, this is now.* She focused.

"Are you settling in?" Dakota asked.

"Yes, thank you. I'm starting to feel a little more acclimated." Jessie had taken over Jim Anderson's eleventh grade English classes three weeks earlier when he'd fallen from his second story roof and severely injured his back. He'd be out for at least the remainder of the school year, perhaps permanently. "It's been a bit of a challenge figuring out another teacher's system and then shifting it to my own, but it's coming along."

Dakota nodded. "That's kind of what I wanted to talk to you about."

"No, you want to talk to me about Melinda Jenson's grade." Jessie wanted to cut the chitchat and get to the point. She had no idea how long she could be in the same room with Dakota this first time without the full past flooding in. Besides, she wanted to make it crystal clear she wouldn't be played where a student's grades were concerned.

Dakota's lips parted slightly, and she arched an eyebrow. "Well…yes. That's exactly it."

"What would you like to say?" Jessie toyed with the ankh pendant at her throat but kept her gaze on Dakota.

"I wanted to ask why you gave her an F." There was a hint of condescension in Dakota's tone.

Jessie bristled inwardly. "Because they won't let me give her a G." Her confidence returned. She was on solid ground with this topic.

Dakota hesitated, surprising Jessie with a flicker of uncertainty in her expression, but it vanished as suddenly as it had appeared. She let out a humorless chuckle. "That's very funny. I'll have to remember that one. But seriously, there was no indication on Mel's mid-quarter progress report that she was falling behind."

"I wasn't here for the progress reports, so I can't speak to that." Jessie held her voice steady. At forty-five, she'd taught high school English for twenty years and knew what was going on here, knew what some coaches occasionally asked of academic teachers. It saddened her that someone she'd once admired—granted, it'd been idol worship and a childhood crush, but still—was the one doing it now. She was aware of Dakota's arrogance, however—the arrogance of all the Scotts—and she remembered her own mother's bitter words from years earlier. *The Scotts can get away with anything.* She shook away the thought with resolve. *Don't worry, Mom. She won't get away with this, at least.* It wasn't much, but it was something. "All I know about Melinda's actual grades is that there were none recorded prior to my arrival, she failed the two quizzes *I've* given since then, and she hasn't turned in a single homework assignment. Hence, the F."

Dakota paused, clearly reassessing the situation, then flashed that grin again. "Look, Jessica…May I call you Jessica?"

Jessie almost rolled her eyes, an occupational hazard from being around teenagers every day, but nodded her acquiescence.

"Jessica," Dakota said again, "Jim and I had kind of an arrangement you might not be aware of, concerning a few of our mutual students."

"I suspected as much, given Melinda's attitude and the fact that she's the star of the girls volleyball team." In truth, Jessie had figured it out very quickly. "But that was an arrangement you had with Jim. Not with me."

A soft chime sounded, and Dakota retrieved a cell phone from the pocket of her zippered hoodie. She glanced at the screen. "If you knew about it, couldn't you have said something to me before the quarter grades came out?" She stuffed the phone back into her pocket.

"I addressed it with Melinda," Jessie said flatly. "*She's* my student."

"Maybe you don't understand how important it is that she keep her GPA at least a 2.00."

Jessie couldn't help but laugh. "Coach Scott, I—"

"Please, call me Dakota." The grin again.

Jessie shook her head in amusement. "Coach Scott, I assure you, I understand the importance of an athlete maintaining a 2.00 grade point average. The difference between you and me, however, is that *I* understand that it's up to the athlete. Not the coach. And *certainly* not the teacher. And I have no intention of honoring the arrangement you had with Jim."

Dakota's jaw tightened, and she studied Jessie. "Okay, I get it. You've made your point. But if you were aware of an arrangement you weren't going to honor, a conversation with me might have been in order. That would have been the caring thing to do, so maybe we could have worked out something else."

Jessie opened her mouth to speak.

Dakota held up a hand. "I'm not finished," she said, her expression hardening. "For some of these kids, an athletic scholarship is their only chance of going to college. Mel's family doesn't have a lot of money. Maybe you don't *get* that not everyone has it easy. And now, since her recorded quarter grade is an F, she's ineligible to play for the rest of the season. And in order to have a shot at a scholarship, she needs to play."

A hot gust of anger blew through Jessie. Her inclination was to launch into a diatribe of exactly how well she understood such a scenario, how hard she'd had to work even to get to college, never mind stay there long enough to earn her teaching credential. But she wouldn't defend herself, or Melinda Jenson, to anyone, especially not to someone like Dakota Scott who came from money, privilege, and entitlement, someone who didn't have a clue what the hell she was talking about. She reined in her emotions. "I am very aware of the fact that not all families have the finances to send their children to college, and of the importance of an athletic scholarship in some cases. I'm also aware of the importance of a student having more than one option and of the responsibility we have as teachers to ensure that they do, if possible. You aren't doing Melinda, or any other students for whom you've made *an arrangement*, any favors by teaching them that their athletic ability is their only value."

Dakota bolted to her feet, her eyes narrowed. "I don't—"

Jessie halted her with her own raised hand. "My turn." She kept her tone professional. "What happens when they get the athletic scholarship and get to college but they can't put a sentence together to write a paper in the classes they have to pass in order to stay eligible *there*? Worse—because there will most likely be a coach like you there as well, who'll make an *arrangement* for them—what happens if they get injured and can no longer play sports? If they haven't learned anything else, what are they supposed to do then?"

Dakota glanced away. She pressed her lips together, then stalked to the window and stood with her back to Jessie. "You should have talked to me."

"As I mentioned," Jessie said coolly. "I spoke with Melinda. If she wasn't comfortable talking with you about what I offered, that's between the two of you."

Dakota shot a glare over her shoulder. "She talks to me." Her voice rose. "I'm her coach. She talked to me this morning."

"Yes, and I'm sure the conversation went something like this." Jessie did a hair flip. "Oh, Coach Scott," she said in a high-pitched Southern accent. "That mean new teacher gave me an F, and I have no idea why." Then she shifted to her best John Wayne stance and lowered the timber of her voice. "Don't worry, little lady, I'll take care of it."

Dakota's mouth quirked. Her cell phone chimed, and she took it from her pocket again. She frowned at the screen and shook her head. "Fine," she said, returning her attention to Jessie. "What did you offer her?"

"What?" Jessie had been expecting an angry response to her mockery, or at the very least, a mild rebuke. She kind of deserved one. The ridicule had been uncalled for, even if it did feel good.

"You said, if she didn't tell me what you offered. What did you offer?"

Jessie gathered her thoughts. "Since I know she plays basketball as well as volleyball, I offered to work with her outside of class to help her raise her semester grade so she can play basketball when the season starts. And I suggested that perhaps you could put her on academic probation now, so that as long as she's making progress, she can still finish out the volleyball season."

Dakota tilted her head. "You know a lot about how this works."

"I've been teaching high school for twenty years. I know how a lot of things work," Jessie said with derision.

Dakota paused, a question in her eyes. "Mel has practice after school," she said, obviously sidestepping Jessie's comment. "She can't meet with you then."

"I didn't say anything about after school." Jessie turned and began tidying her desk. "She can come in before school—I get here at six forty-five—or at lunch. Or I can meet with her in the evening." She powered off her laptop. "I'll meet with her at midnight if she shows any intention of taking it seriously."

"You'd do that?" Dakota asked, her surprise evident. "Work with her on *her* schedule?"

Jessie turned to face her again. "I care about my students, Coach Scott. Even the pampered ones with attitude. But I won't waste time. It won't do anyone any good for me to care more about her grade than she does. However, if she's willing to work, I'm willing to work with her whenever she can."

Music blared from Dakota's jacket pocket—the chorus from the old rock song "Little Miss Can't Be Wrong." She let out an obviously exasperated sigh and rolled her eyes. "Excuse me," she said as she turned away and put the phone to her ear. "What is it, Tina?"

Jessie resumed finishing up for the day, packing several stacks of essays into her briefcase. She remembered Dakota's little sister, Tina. She'd been a year ahead of Jessie in school, much closer in age than Dakota's four years, and had been one of those pampered teenagers with attitude about whom they'd just been speaking. Perhaps not much had changed if the two previous texts had also been from her, and if the ring tone was any indication.

"I'm still at work," Dakota said. "Just deal with her."

"She won't listen to me." Tina's voice was shrill, the words clear as they spilled into the quiet classroom. "She'll only listen to you when she gets like this. You need to come."

"I'll be there when I can." Dakota glanced at Jessie. "I'm busy right now."

"Dakota!" Tina drew the "o" into two syllables. "You promised you'd—"

"I'll come when I'm done." Dakota ended the call and turned back to Jessie. "Sorry." She shrugged, looking embarrassed. "Family. You know."

Jessie didn't know. She hadn't known *family* for a long time, and one of the reasons was standing right in front of her. A wave of exhaustion overtook her. This meeting had claimed more energy, opened more emotional doors, than she'd anticipated. She'd thought she'd stayed focused on the subject at hand, but apparently some ghosts from the past had slipped through. She needed to be away from Dakota Scott. "Are we finished?"

Dakota cocked an eyebrow. "I suppose we are." She walked toward the door. "I'll talk to Mel, and we'll get back to you on when she can meet."

"Make sure it's her," Jessie said to Dakota's back.

Dakota turned in the doorway. "Excuse me?"

"It should be Melinda who gets back to me," Jessie said, making an effort to soften her tone. "She's the student. It's her responsibility. Not yours."

Dakota fixed her gaze on Jessie, her expression unreadable. She didn't answer for a long moment, then she nodded and left.

Jessie heard "Little Miss Can't Be Wrong" drift back into the room from the hallway, then Dakota's irritated, "I'm on my way." She dropped into the chair behind her desk and sighed. She'd done it. She'd gotten through her first encounter with Dakota Scott. With as much as she'd been dreading it and as conflicted as she'd felt about it, she was glad it'd caught her off guard. She hadn't had time to freeze up, or worse, panic over whether Dakota might know who she was. She wanted to keep that card concealed until *she* chose to play it.

She understood this would be far from the last meeting, especially since they'd both be monitoring Melinda Jenson's progress, but at least now she knew what she'd be dealing with. She could no longer deny that she still blamed Dakota for what had happened and that she held resentment for Dakota's status and position in Clearwater Springs. And, ridiculously, remnants of her childhood crush still lingered in conflict with everything else. But this was good. After all, wasn't facing her demons the reason she'd decided to stay longer? And Dakota was one of those demons. If Jessie could come to terms with the person who'd killed her sister, she could most likely handle the rest.

Chapter Two

Dakota settled into the driver's seat of her SUV and stared unseeingly out the windshield. *Who is that woman? And what just happened?*

Dakota was used to getting her way. People usually responded to her positively, flattered by the hint of flirtation she added to many conversations. Everyone loved her. *No, not everyone, not anymore—not around here.* Some in Clearwater Springs held the past over her—the very reason she'd stayed away so long—so she made an extra effort with newcomers. She could never be certain who someone new to town had already talked to, what rumors they might have heard and been tainted by. What had happened had taken place decades ago, but it still ranked high on the list of the town's unofficial highlights. She'd never understood what people got out of gossiping about the misfortune of others.

Some of the older townspeople still avoided her, believing ancient accusations of wrongdoings swept under the rug because of her family name. Even after all these years, it still stung that a faction of the close-knit community had turned on her, but she always played the role of her younger self—unaffected, confident, even cocky. She never exposed her soft underbelly.

Had Jessica Weldon already heard all about the night that had changed Dakota forever? At least, heard the other version of it? Dakota's twin brother, Drew, had pointed out more than once that *that* version was all anyone had to talk about, since she'd never shared anything about that night and had forbidden him to as well. Their father had given a public statement addressing the issue, but Dakota had only ever spoken of it with a couple of therapists in the years since, and with one girlfriend, Diane, who had come with her when she'd returned to Clearwater Springs ten years earlier from San Francisco. Diane had since ended the relationship, though, and moved back to the Bay Area. She'd said small-town life didn't suit her, but Dakota wondered how much of a role the town gossip and judgments, and maybe even Dakota's guilt in the matter, had played in Diane's decision. And then there was Dakota's family—the responsibilities, the drama, the demands.

Speaking of which. Dakota started the engine. *Duty calls.*

As she maneuvered her Grand Cherokee—one of the indulgences she'd allowed herself for returning to Clearwater Springs, that and a house in town—through the quaint streets, her thoughts drifted back to Jessica Weldon. Something about her had drawn Dakota in. It might simply have been her looks—those smooth curves beneath the cocoa colored dress that seemed to make her olive skin glow, the dark golden hair that gently framed her face, enhancing the thin gold band that ringed her rich brown irises, her full lips. Everything about her was soft, everything except her demeanor. Even that, though, had captured Dakota's attention.

Jessica hadn't flinched once and had held her ground through their entire disagreement. As much as Dakota liked an unequivocal win, she respected someone who took a stand for a cause. *And her attempt at a John Wayne impression.* Dakota chuckled out loud in the solitude of her Jeep. *How cute was that?*

Dakota had gotten a ping off Jessica, and her gaydar was usually pretty accurate. In another place and time, she would have asked her out in a heartbeat. She would have been all over her, but that was the Dakota of old who didn't wonder if beneath every conversation lay hidden judgments and blame. She wasn't confident and cocky anymore. Not since she'd returned home. That was a well-practiced façade. She was uncertain and felt far more vulnerable than she was comfortable revealing.

Diane had been the last person she'd shared even a fraction of her true feelings with, and Diane had left. Alone, she'd had to figure out who in her hometown was still really *with* her and who wasn't. In all honesty, though, Diane's departure hadn't been a surprise. Dakota had been expecting it since the first day they'd unpacked, maybe even since the day she'd explained to Diane that she had to return home and why. Diane wasn't cut out for emotional baggage and a haunted past. She'd fallen in love with Dakota Scott, nationally known and respected NCAA coach of a championship women's volleyball team, an admired and unencumbered partner—not Dakota Scott of the Clearwater Springs Scotts, who'd fallen from grace and still carried the scars.

Dakota turned off the main road and stopped to punch the code into the security keypad. When the gates swung open, she passed under the archway that read Ghost Rider Ranch and made her way down the long, landscaped drive to the family ranch house. It was hardly a true ranch house, though. It was, in reality, a small mansion, but it had been built on the same site as the original rustic wooden structure her great-grandfather had built almost a hundred years earlier, and over time, everyone had continued calling it the ranch house.

The front twenty of the ten-thousand-acre spread had been converted into more of a compound over the past few decades, providing homes for grown children as well as the families of a few longstanding foremen and some indoor staff. Crystal, Dakota's older sister; and her husband, Paul; had lived in one of the houses until they'd agreed to move into the ranch house to oversee the care of the matriarch of the Scott family, Dakota's mother. Her twin brother, Drew; and his wife, Selena; had raised three children in the residence near the bunkhouse on the edge of the actual ranch, their youngest graduating from high school this year. And Tina and her soon-to-be fourth husband lived in the guesthouse that shared the pool and tennis courts with the main residence. Dakota had long ago given the home deemed hers to Drew's other romantic partner, Randy, having no interest whatsoever in living on the ranch again and figuring if Drew, Selena, and Randy could work out the complications of their twenty-seven-year relationship, they deserved all the support she could give them. Kudos to them. *She'd* never been able to sustain even a traditional relationship for more than a minute and a half, comparatively. Diane had been her longest-standing girlfriend, and they'd lasted only six years.

As Dakota parked in her usual spot outside the kitchen entrance, Tina shot out the door and was on her before she got one foot to the ground.

"You have to talk to her." Tina grabbed Dakota's arm and pulled her from her seat. "You have to stop her."

"Hi, Tina," Dakota said, letting herself be dragged into the house. "Yeah, my day was pretty good, except for my star player failing English and a new teacher who's a stickler for protocol. But thanks for asking. How are you?"

"You can see how she is," Ada, the Scotts' long-time cook and house manager said from where she stirred the contents of a pot at the stove. The lines around her eyes crinkled as she flashed a broad smile. "She's been like this all day."

"Oh my God," Dakota said, peering into the pot. "How'd you stand it?"

Ada laughed softly. "Same as when she was seven. I tune her out."

Dakota inhaled the savory scent of Ada's homemade chicken soup. "Mmmmm, I'm staying for dinner."

"You know you're always welcome." Ada squeezed her hand.

"Dakota!" Tina's shriek filled the kitchen. "Go!"

Dakota winced. "I'm going," she said emphatically, then turned back to Ada. "Where is she?"

"Hiding in her room. Do you blame her?"

Dakota laughed and headed up the back stairs. She tapped on the door to the master suite. "Mama?" She turned the knob and peeked inside.

Her mother sat at the window, gazing out into the fading afternoon light. Her white hair was tied back with a loose ribbon, and she was impeccably dressed in a silver and blue designer jogging suit. Not that she jogged. She just liked comfortable clothing. At seventy-five, she was relatively healthy and exercised regularly in her home gym but didn't spend much time outdoors. She hummed quietly, evidently lost in thought.

Dakota touched her shoulder. "Mama?"

Her mother startled and turned wide eyes to her, then her expression softened. "I'm glad you're not Tina."

Dakota mimed wiping her brow. "Phew. Me, too. Can you imagine what it's like to be her?"

Her mother laughed.

Dakota loved the sound. She'd always savored it during the times her mother was lucid and interactive so she could recall it during the bad times. She kissed her mother's cheek, then sat beside her on the loveseat. "So what's going on between you two?"

Her mother scowled. "She doesn't want Captain Red to escort me to her wedding."

"Captain Red?" Dakota searched her memory. She vaguely remembered a Captain Red in the cast of characters that traveled the dark twists and turns of her mother's damaged mind.

Vivian Scott had been diagnosed with schizophrenia when Dakota was eight. The two years between the onset of the disease and its identification had been terrifying. Dakota had watched and felt the mother that had previously adored her and beamed every time her children entered a room transform into a stranger, unpredictable in her emotional states, behavior, and treatment of her family. Their father had noticed some of the changes, but merely told the kids their mother was simply going through a tough time, and she'd be back to her old self soon. His focus, during those years, had been on building his veterinary practice, and he counted on his wife to hold things together at home. When everything came to light, he'd begged for their forgiveness.

Dakota had awakened in the darkness more than once to find her mother standing over her, staring down at her in bed, murmuring about danger and killing. One memory could still reduce her to trembling at times. She'd never told anyone of the incident, afraid her mother would be taken away if anyone knew. But that had happened anyway, several months later, when Dakota had walked into her parents' bedroom, the very room they sat in now, to find her mother holding a sobbing, five-year-old Tina out the third-floor window, arguing with some voice only she could hear, about killing the children. Thank God she'd been present enough to argue. Tina, to this day, had no recollection of the event, but Dakota recalled it vividly.

She hated her mother's sickness for stealing her from them—from Dakota—and for the tragedy it'd caused. At times, she even hated her mother, and she could be consumed by guilt for that, if she weren't careful. But she loved her. There were the good times, too. *Right?*

Dakota stifled a disappointed sigh. *Is she heading into one of her episodes? Is she messing with her meds again?* "I'm sorry, Mama," she said, looking into her mother's eyes, so much like her own. She was like her mother had been in many ways. She remembered being afraid all through her twenties that she would be like her in the onslaught of delusions and hallucinations, and had only let go of that fear when she'd hit her thirties. "I'm not sure I know Captain Red."

"Tina thinks just because he's a pirate he won't know how to behave properly," Dakota's mother said without acknowledgment of Dakota's comment.

"Have you seen him?" Dakota asked, dreading the answer. A knot tightened in the pit of her stomach. "Has he spoken to you in the past couple of days?"

"Like most people, Tina thinks that all pirates just sit around drinking rum and making people walk the plank. But Captain Red used to be a gentleman. He—"

"Mama," Dakota said, a little more sharply than she'd intended.

Her mother blinked at her. "Yes, dear?"

"Did the captain actually talk to you?" Dakota asked again.

"Well, no. Tina brought him up. She said no one like him could be at her wedding. But then I remembered the last time she got married and I attended with that nice young man, Richard..."

Dakota breathed a sigh of relief. Richard had been one of the personal assistants from the home care service providers they contracted with to help with her mother. As long as Captain Red hadn't actually made an appearance, her mother wasn't likely headed into one of her dark times. *But what the hell is Tina thinking, bringing him up?*

"Captain Red said then that he wanted to escort me to the next wedding. I thought the next one might be yours and Diane's, but I haven't seen Diane in a long while. Is she well?"

"Yes, Mama, she's fine." Dakota leaned back into the plush loveseat. "Remember, she moved back to San Francisco?" She relaxed, knowing the Captain Red conversation was most likely over and forgotten. Unless, of course, Tina brought it up again.

"Did she?" Her mother looked perplexed as she always did when the subject of Diane came up. "Hm, I thought she might be *the one* for you." She took Dakota's hand as she rested her head on Dakota's shoulder, returning her gaze to the panoramic view of the ranch lands through the expanse of windows.

Dakota pressed her cheek to the softness of her mother's hair. "No, Mama. Not the one." When she was younger, even into early adulthood, she'd liked listening to her mother's romantic ideas of true love and the story of how she and Dakota's father had found each other, but now, on the brink of fifty and with her father married to another woman, Dakota didn't think she believed in *the one* anymore. She still wanted to—desperately—but just couldn't dredge up the idealism. Her sister Crystal had found her *one* in Paul, and Drew had actually found *two*. Maybe since he and Dakota were twins, he'd ended up with hers as well. And Tina… Well, Tina found *the one* every time she went out on a date. Even their father had found Rowina, and though she might not be his true love, he seemed happy with her in the house he'd built for them on the grounds of his veterinary hospital.

"Don't worry, sweetie." Dakota's mother patted her thigh. "It just means your true love is still on her way."

Dakota had serious doubts. At this point, she wasn't even sure she wanted to be in a relationship. Since Diane had left, she'd been surprisingly content on her own. As though summoned, the image of Jessica Weldon executing the hair flip rose in front of her again, and she frowned. *Not going there.*

She sat in the quiet with her mother, taking in the beautiful rolling hills of the ranch, until she felt her mother relax against her as she did when she'd drifted off to sleep. Dakota eased her down on the loveseat, covered her with the afghan from the foot of her bed, and slipped out of the room.

"What did she say? Did you talk her out of it? Did you tell her the imaginary pirate friend can't come to my wedding?" Tina's barrage of questions hit Dakota like a battery of cannon balls from Captain Red's ship the instant she stepped back into the kitchen.

"It's all fine, Tina. *She's* fine. She said you're the one who brought it up," Dakota said, suddenly annoyed with the wasted trip out there and the sullen mood that had overtaken her from the conversation about *the one*. "Captain Red isn't even around. She was just remembering something he'd said the last time you got married."

"I wish you wouldn't talk about him like he's real. It's creepy." Tina returned to the chair at the table in the breakfast nook she'd leapt up from at Dakota's entrance. "She agreed, though, right? You made her agree?"

"She can't agree to something four months away." Dakota leaned against the counter beside Ada. "She's going to come up with a thousand brand new things to get you all frantic and crazy between now and then, if you react to them. She's already forgotten about Captain Red, and he'll probably stay forgotten, unless *you* bring him up again. So don't."

"This is my wedding," Tina said with a huff. "I don't want anything going wrong."

"This is your *fourth* wedding," Dakota said with equal irritation. "And if you want everything in your life to go perfectly and without drama, you're in the wrong family. This is the family in which nothing takes place without drama, including a perfectly nice Wednesday afternoon, like this one had been." *Until Jessica Weldon. That's where it all started today.*

"What's going on?" Crystal asked, coming into the kitchen from the dining room entrance. She dumped her purse and a stack of mail onto the table in front of Tina. "I could hear you two all the way from the foyer."

"Dakota doesn't think I should ever get married again just because my previous marriages didn't work out." Tina slouched in her chair and hugged herself tightly.

"I don't care how many times you get married." Dakota folded her arms across her chest. "I just don't see why you have to subject everyone to a huge wedding every time. We're not really designed for public affairs."

"Well, what am I supposed to do?"

"Get out your phone," Dakota said.

Tina glared at her suspiciously but did as instructed.

"Google this." Dakota could feel Crystal watching her. "E-l-o-p-e. I'm sure you can find some instructions on how to do it."

Tina gasped and tossed her phone onto the table.

Ada let out a soft chuckle.

Crystal glared at Dakota, her lips pressed into a firm line. "Dakota," she said, her tone admonishing.

Dakota had expected it. When their mother had been committed to an institution for treatment until her symptoms could be brought under control—and maybe until her children were old enough to understand that the mother they'd once had was gone forever—Crystal, at age eleven, had all but become Tina's mother. And she'd spoiled her beyond recovery.

Dakota held up her hands in surrender. "I'm just saying."

Tina turned on the tears that usually got Crystal's attention.

"And here come the waterworks." Dakota shook her head in disbelief. "I'm done with this." She pushed away from the counter and strode out of the room.

On the balcony off the formal living room, she watched the final vestiges of the sunset be swallowed like prey by the encroaching twilight and the pool light and patio lanterns spring to life below her. She felt, more than heard, a soft movement behind her and knew it was Crystal. "I'm sorry," she said, certain Crystal would understand the apology was for her, not Tina.

Crystal moved up beside her and handed her a glass.

Dakota knew it'd be filled with citrus water. Her favorite. "Thanks," she said, but didn't take a drink. "I know you hate it when Tina and I fight."

"Hate's a strong word." Crystal rested her forearms on the railing and held her own glass over the edge. "Maybe it just dismays me."

Dakota cringed. "Oh, God, not *dismay*."

Crystal let out a quiet laugh. "You know me. I've always wanted all of us to simply get along. But as you said, we're a family made for drama. None of us would know how to act if *something* wasn't going on at any given moment." She sighed. "And it usually involves Tina in some way."

Dakota cut her a sideways glance. *And whose doing is that?*

Crystal tilted her head in evident acknowledgment, then shifted her gaze down to the pool. "You, me, and Drew…We had Mom for a while before she got sick. We knew what it was like to have a mother. And you and Drew had each other. You've always had each other. But Tina…" She pursed her lips, looking thoughtful. "I know I overcompensated."

Dakota watched Crystal in the gathering moonlight that glinted off the white streaks in her auburn hair. Only three years older than Dakota, Crystal was still striking, but more of life creased her features, no doubt because she'd borne far more family responsibilities than Dakota had. For that, Dakota admired her. "Crys," she whispered. "You've done so much for all of us. I don't mean to be critical. I'm sorry."

Crystal turned to her and smiled. "I don't think you're being critical. Tina can be frustrating. Believe me, I—of all people—know that. I really came out here to make sure you're okay. You seemed disproportionately upset. Is there something else going on?"

"I'm fine. Don't worry about me."

Crystal studied her for a moment, then nodded. "Are you staying for dinner? I think Drew and his clan are joining us."

Dakota considered it, remembering she'd already told Ada she would, but she still felt unsettled. Not about Tina, even though there was almost always something that could annoy her when it came to her younger sister. But no. Something still lingered from her conversation with her mother, the reminder of Diane, the talk of weddings, the concept of *the one*. The last thing she wanted tonight was to be a third wheel, or a fifth, or whatever odd number she'd be in a roomful of people who shared their lives with one another. Maybe she'd grab a pizza on the way home. "Thanks, but I have to get going." She downed half of her water and handed the glass back to Crystal.

"Okay." Crystal's voice held a note of disappointment. "Maybe this weekend? Paul would love to see you. It's been a while."

"Sure, the weekend sounds good." Certainly, by then, she'd be fine. She pressed a kiss to Crystal's forehead, suddenly eager to be by herself. As she turned to leave, though, she found herself wondering how Jessica Weldon was spending *her* evening and if she'd found *the one* in her life.

Chapter Three

Jessie finished entering the grades from the vocabulary tests she'd given on Friday into her computer, then glanced around her classroom.

Fourteen students sat in silence, all but one reading or with their heads bent over a binder or notebook, writing. Ian Langston slouched in his seat, legs stretched out, arms clamped across his chest, his jaw set. A dark bruise shadowed one side of his face.

Vice Principal Thornton had told Jessie Ian had been in a fight. This was his first day in early morning detention.

Ian's clothes were torn in a couple of places and raggedly mended in others, but they were clean. His shaggy blond hair desperately needed a cut, and his cotton plaid shirt that hung open over a slightly wrinkled grayed T-shirt seemed woefully inadequate against the chilly autumn morning.

Jessie shivered. She remembered how deeply the cold cut without a jacket, even this early in the fall, and the long wait for the warmth from the school heater to chase it fully from her bones.

Ian glared out the window in obvious defiance of the instructions she knew he'd received for his time in her detention.

The seven thirty-five bell rang, signaling the students to start heading to their first period classes. Everyone began collecting their things. Ian jerked to his feet and took a step toward the door.

"Mr. Langston, may I see you for a moment?" Jessie asked just loudly enough to be heard over the increasing clamor of voices, books slamming shut, and backpacks being zipped.

He shot her an insolent glance.

For a split second, she thought he might ignore her request. She met and held his gaze, keeping her expression calm but firm. It was a look she'd perfected years earlier. *Don't do it.* She waited.

Finally, he moved around the row he'd been sitting in and strode to her desk.

She never lowered her eyes, but kept them fixed on his, even when she had to tilt her head back to do so as he stood in front of her. He was a good head taller than her. She knew if she wavered, she'd lose him.

She had a tender spot for kids like Ian. In her experience, the tough, defiant, seemingly unreachable kind were trying to protect a soft inner core. Their outward expression was really a call for someone to notice them, to care that they might be hurting, or lonely, or scared. She also knew, though, that before she'd have the slightest chance of him letting her in, she'd have to earn his respect.

"It's my understanding that you chose early morning detention over being suspended." She kept her voice low so as to honor his privacy, though many of the students in the room had made the same choice. "Is that correct?"

His jaw tightened, but uncertainty flickered across his face.

Again, she thought he might not answer.

He nodded.

She retrieved a sheet of paper from her desk and held it up. "It's also my understanding that your counselor gave you this list of instructions for my detention, number two of which is 'Bring homework to complete or a book to read.' Is *that* correct?"

He shifted his gaze past her. His eyes narrowed.

"Mr. Langston?" Jessie hardened her tone ever so slightly.

He looked back at her. "Yeah."

"So am I to assume you've changed your mind, that you'd prefer suspension after all?"

Ian swallowed, his only movement, but a light flush touched his cheeks. "No."

"Oh. All right then," Jessie said, returning the paper to her desk. "Since your detention was to start today and part of the agreement was to do some work while you were here, you can make up the time at lunch."

His eyes went wide, and he opened his mouth.

"Please bring something to work on," she said before he could protest. "Or I'll have to let the vice principal know you've changed your mind about the suspension."

"Pshhh." He shook his head. "Can I go now?"

"You may." As she watched his retreat, she caught sight of Dakota standing just inside the doorway, her features striking in the bright sunlight streaming through the windows and her styled jogging suit draping the subtle curves of her toned body in all the right ways. Tingles gathered in Jessie's abdomen. She swept them aside and focused on old anger instead.

Dakota, closer to Ian's height and carriage, held her ground briefly before stepping aside to let him pass.

Jessie suspected Dakota felt her position and reputation at the school and in the community carried more weight than that of a brand new substitute teacher, and the thought brought her temper to a simmer. She'd never needed anyone to fight her battles for her. "Coach Scott," she said in a cool greeting. "How may I help you this morning?"

Dakota kept her attention on Ian an extra few beats as he made his way down the hall. "That kid's trouble."

"He hasn't been for me." Jessie wanted to make it clear she had things under control. "How may I help you?" she asked again, collecting her notes for her first period lecture on the commonalities in mythologies.

"I just stopped by to see how it went this morning with Mel." Dakota's demeanor lightened, and she came farther into the room.

"It didn't go at all," Jessie said. "I haven't seen her."

"What do you mean? She told me she was going to start working with you today."

"She told me that, too, but she didn't show up." Jessie hadn't been particularly surprised at Melinda's absence that morning. When she'd spoken with Jessie the previous Friday, she still had attitude. Melinda had chosen the time before school, but only, it seemed, as a last resort.

Dakota planted her hands on her hips and looked thoughtful. "Something must have come up. She knows this is important."

Jessie wasn't sure what to say, so she said nothing.

"I promise she'll be here tomorrow."

Jessie hesitated. She knew this was all new to Dakota, having to comply with someone else's rules. How far should she push her? She might as well go all the way. As important as it was for Ian Langston to respect her in order for her to be able to offer him something, Dakota's respect was just as necessary in order for Jessie to be able to help Melinda. Melinda would be taking her cues from Dakota. "So that means she'll be sitting out volleyball practice this afternoon as well?"

"What?" Dakota looked genuinely perplexed.

Jessie stifled a smirk. She had to admit, she did enjoy poking at Dakota. "If there's no consequence for not taking her tutoring seriously, why would she? A practice for a tutoring session seems fair."

Dakota stared at her. "She can't miss practice."

The matter-of-factness of Dakota's response sucked Jessie in momentarily, as though Melinda Jenson missing a practice could possibly bring on the apocalypse. "Well," she said, considering other options, "I've already given up my lunch today. She can come in then."

"Great. I'll tell her." Dakota grinned. "I'll bring her in myself if I have to." She eased onto a nearby desktop, making it clear she wasn't leaving just yet.

Jessie winced. She wished Dakota wouldn't sit that way. If she kept doing it, Jessie knew she'd have to say something. It was one of her pet peeves.

"So how'd you end up being the prison warden?" Dakota asked. "One of the penalties of being the new kid on the block?"

"Excuse me?" Jessie had no idea what she was talking about.

"Early morning detention." Dakota waved her hand, motioning around the room as though the students were still there. "No one wants that job."

Jessie considered her answer. She knew how it would sound, but to be honest, she wouldn't mind taking Dakota's position down a notch or two, even if it was only her own opinion. "I requested it in exchange for not having to take tickets or chaperone the concession stand at any of the athletic events."

Dakota studied her as though she couldn't quite believe what she was hearing. "Because having to attend a football game or volleyball match would be a fate worse than death?" she asked finally.

"Not at all." Jessie offered her a satisfied smile. "Having to attend a tractor pull would be a fate worse than death. Working a football game or volleyball match would simply take up an evening I'd rather spend doing something else."

Dakota nodded. "I can understand that. Especially since the football games are on Friday nights. Perfect date nights and evenings to spend with your husband or boyfriend. But, you know, you could bring him to the games."

Jessie blinked in astonishment. Was she hearing correctly? Was Dakota actually fishing for information about her orientation and relationship status?

Jessie, of course, didn't need to fish. Everyone in Clearwater Springs knew Dakota's orientation, ever since she and her twin brother had double-dated to their sophomore winter formal—Dakota with Marci Simmons and Drew with Randy Bradshaw. It'd been the talk of the town for quite some time. For Marci, it'd merely been her fifteen minutes of fame in the spotlight with the Scott twins, and she'd long since married an accountant—a male accountant—that worked for her parents. For Dakota, Drew, and Randy, however, it'd been a true coming out; Dakota and Randy as gay and Drew as bisexual, apparently, since he now also had a wife.

Regardless of what Jessie knew, though, Dakota's sexual orientation was moot. She would never get involved with Dakota, never even entertain the idea of a fling or a hookup. In fact, she wanted Dakota to know who she was, wanted to see the look on her face when she found out Jessie's last name used to be Brogan. *That* would almost certainly put a halt to Dakota's flirting and fishing expeditions. Wouldn't it?

What if it doesn't? Jessie took in a shallow breath. *What if she doesn't even remember the name?* The thought of it meaning so little to Dakota made her feel ill.

Several students hurried in from the hall and dropped into seats nearby.

Jessie forced a smile. "If you'll excuse me," she said to Dakota. "I need to finish preparing for class."

"Yeah." Dakota leapt up. "And I've got to get to the gym. I'll see you at lunch." And before Jessie could answer, she was gone.

Jessie spent the rest of the morning with that disturbing question in the back of her mind. *What if she doesn't even remember?*

At the beginning of third period, Dakota stood on the top step outside her office and watched the girls file into the locker room. When she saw Mel, she motioned her up. "What happened this morning?" she asked as she settled behind her desk and gestured for Mel to close the door. She made sure her "coach" face was in place.

Mel lifted a shoulder. "I guess I overslept."

At least she hadn't pretended not to know what they were talking about. Dakota hated that. "You overslept? That doesn't sound like you. You've never overslept for a morning practice or an early departure for an away game. Try again." Dakota leaned back in her chair.

Mel glanced around the office, avoiding Dakota's direct gaze. "I just…I don't know how to do all that English stuff."

"That's the point of working with Ms. Weldon. So you can *learn* how to do it." Dakota paused. "And so you can stay on the team."

"I was on the team before and I didn't have to do it." Mel's tone held a mixture of challenge and inquiry.

Dakota lightly drummed her fingers on the desk. "That was my fault," she said, recalling Jessica's accusation about teaching her players that their athletic ability was their only value. To cut herself some slack, she *had* already been planning to end her practice of making special arrangements for certain students, but she hadn't figured out how to handle the several juniors and seniors—like Mel—who were used to it. She knew now, though, that was a big juicy rationalization. *This, right here, is how. Just do it.* Why had it taken Jessica Weldon to get her moving? "Things are going to be different. To stay on the team, you need to keep your grades up, and Ms. Weldon is going to help you with that. End of story."

Mel sighed.

"And it's going to start today like we agreed."

"But I already missed today," Mel said.

"She said you can come in at lunch." Dakota pulled her roll book from her desk drawer and started rummaging for a pen. "It's either that or miss practice today, and I don't want you missing, especially since we're going up against DHS this week."

"What's with this new teacher?" Mel asked with a frown. "Why is she calling all the shots?"

Dakota snapped her head up and pinned Mel with a glare. "*She* isn't calling the shots. *I* am," she said in her sternest coach voice, at least for indoor use, reserved for moments just like this one. She wasn't about to have any of her players think she wasn't the one in charge. She'd lose their respect, and then she'd be useless as their coach. "So you'll be in her classroom at lunchtime, and you'll do whatever she says. Understood?"

Mel shifted uneasily. "Sorry, Coach."

Something in Mel's expression caught Dakota's attention. She softened a little. "What's the problem with this? Why are you making it such a big deal? You go work with her a few times a week, learn some grammar and how to write an essay, and then life goes on."

Mel shrugged. "It's just…I just haven't had to do it before, that's all."

"Yeah? Well…Things change. Now you do."

"And…" Mel looked to the floor, then back at Dakota.

"And what?" Dakota waited, aware that her class needed to start soon.

Mel hesitated.

"And what?" Dakota asked again, trying to sound more patient than she felt. She had to admit this whole thing had her irritated, but Jessica Weldon held the higher hand here.

Mel pressed her lips into a firm line and shrugged. "She scares me a little."

Dakota stifled a chuckle. *Yeah, I can see that.* She remembered the way Jessica had stood up to the kid in detention who'd towered over her this morning without so much as a blink, the way she'd confronted Dakota last week, even mocking her. She *was* a little scary. And Dakota could only imagine how she came off in class. "She's offered to help you instead of simply letting you be kicked off the team. She cares…even if she is a little scary," Dakota added under her breath.

Mel bit her lower lip. "Will you go with me?"

Dakota couldn't hold back a laugh. "Seriously?"

Mel smiled, but the question lingered in her eyes.

What would it hurt? At least for the first few times, until Mel felt more comfortable. It would give Dakota an idea of what Mel was working on in case she needed some help, and… Dakota thought of Jessica's dark golden hair that looked like it'd be silky to the touch, and the gentle contours of her body. Maybe, if she went with Mel to the first few sessions, it would not only put Mel at ease, but also allow Dakota a new beginning with Jessica, maybe smooth out the bumpy start they'd gotten. Who knew? Maybe she could even invite her for coffee, or…

"Coach?" Mel's voice interrupted Dakota's thoughts.

"Okay, fine. I'll go with you." Dakota didn't know if there was a possibility of anything there with Jessica, or if she even really wanted there to be. She did know, however, she wanted to be around her more. She liked talking to her. And if it'd help Mel, and maybe a few other of her players… She stood. "Get dressed out. And hurry up. I don't want to hold up class."

Chapter Four

Jessie hurried toward her classroom, weaving through the remaining students that lingered in the hallways at lunch. She hadn't had time to get to the cafeteria to pick up something to eat. She'd barely made it to the restroom. She wanted to be back when Ian and Melinda got there, and she scooted into her doorway just as she saw Ian round the corner at the opposite end of the hall. She was glad to see he carried a book and a notebook in one hand.

Okay. Message delivered and received. She'd made her point. Now, if Melinda Jenson showed up, Jessie could claim the day as hers.

She grabbed her own book from her desk and began writing notes for her fifth period class on a section of the white board that covered the walls.

Ian ambled into the room in that lazy walk Jessie had noticed he used, as though defying anyone to rush him or make him do anything he didn't want to do. He was there, though, *with* something to work on. That was all that mattered.

"Mr. Langston." She smiled at him over her shoulder as she continued writing. "Take a seat anywhere you'd like."

He looked around the room, as though this might be the most important decision he'd have to make all day, then sat in the row closest to the door. He stretched out his long legs beneath the desk, leaned back, and opened his book. Without a word or another look her way, he began to read.

That was easy. After their confrontation that morning, Jessie had to wonder if this newfound compliance was a trick of some kind. She finished her notes and glanced at the clock. The lunch period was ticking away, and no Melinda Jenson. She couldn't claim the day as her victory yet. She might have to stay after school a bit, go down to the gym, and pull the girl out of her volleyball practice before she could do that.

"So your timing is the most important thing to work on if you're going to be able to consistently get on top of the ball." Dakota's voice drifted into the room, announcing their arrival.

Melinda carried a cafeteria tray holding a hamburger, bag of chips, small box of cookies, and a soda. And nothing else.

"Sorry we're a few minutes late," Dakota said, holding an insulated lunch bag that said *Keep your eye on the ball* on the side. "Mel needed to get something to eat."

Ian lifted his gaze and looked at the tray—or probably more accurately, the burger, since its savory aroma wafted in the air—then quickly returned to his book when he noticed Jessie watching him.

She remembered how long the days could be with an empty stomach, how difficult it was sometimes to concentrate during the later periods. She forced her attention back to Melinda. "Why don't you have a binder and something to write with?"

Melinda froze, mid-step. "Uh…" She looked at Dakota.

Dakota opened her mouth as if to speak, then closed it. She nodded toward the nearest desk to Melinda.

Melinda scurried to obey.

Dakota continued to where Jessie stood. "Look, I'm sorry. That was my bad," she said, her voice lowered. "We just got focused on lunch. She'll be fully prepared from now on." Clearly, Dakota knew what Jessie's first response would normally be. She'd seen it that morning.

Jessie held her expression firm. "It's not your responsibility."

"I know. But this *is* my fault, as you so succinctly pointed out last week. Because of how I've fixed things for her, she really

doesn't know what's expected here, but I'll make sure she does from now on." Dakota watched Jessie, waiting. "Please?"

Jessie felt her eyebrows shoot up. Was this happening? Dakota Scott was begging? Okay, maybe one please didn't constitute begging in the true sense. Imploring, perhaps?

"Come on," Dakota said. "Give us a chance to catch up."

Jessie sighed and retrieved a fresh notebook from her cupboard, along with a pencil from a box of spares. She set them beside the tray on Melinda's desk. "You have half an hour left. I'd like a writing sample from you. It can be on any topic or in any form, but see if you can get at least two pages."

Melinda looked up at her, the proverbial deer in the headlights. "Two pages? What do I write?"

"Anything," Jessie said again. "You can write about sports, or other hobbies, or your family and friends…It doesn't matter."

"Why can't I use one of the computers?"

"Because I want to see what *you* know, not what spell and grammar check know," Jessie said, reminding herself to be patient. What Dakota had pointed out about Melinda not understanding what was expected of her might be true.

"But I thought you were supposed to help me," Melinda said with a challenge in her voice.

"Before I can do that, I need to see what you already know so I can see where to start." Jessie tapped the notebook. "Let's not waste any more time."

Ian sniffed a laugh from a couple of rows away.

Melinda glared at him. "What's he doing here, anyway? I thought I was supposed to get private tutoring."

"I never said anything about private," Jessie said to Melinda while wiggling a finger at Ian's book and arching an eyebrow at him.

He returned his gaze to the page.

Jessie looked back to Melinda. "Any more questions?"

Melinda thought for a moment. "Can it be a story?"

Jessie tilted her head in surprise. "Yes. It can be a story."

Melinda nodded, her expression going distant, obviously already in thought.

Who would have known? The spoiled athlete with the attitude likes to write stories? This was one of the things Jessie loved about teaching—the discovery, and hopefully nurturing, of what lay beneath the surface of what otherwise appeared to be the stereotypical teenager. "Do the best you can so we don't end up covering things you already know. Let's get you a dictionary in case you need one. Coach Scott, would you please…" She turned to catch Dakota jerking her gaze from Jessie's legs to her face.

Dakota blushed. "I'm sorry, what?"

Jessie smirked. "Never mind." She crossed to the cupboard and pulled out a dictionary and started back to Melinda's desk.

Still in thought, Melinda unwrapped her burger and started to take a bite. She halted when she saw Ian staring at her. "What are you looking at, loser?"

Ian immediately averted his gaze, his unbruised cheek flaming red.

Before Jessie could respond, Dakota was on her feet. "Mel." Her voice filled the room, and she closed the distance between them in three long strides.

Another surprise! So the star player *could* do wrong in the coach's eyes. Jessie obviously wasn't needed in this scenario. She placed the book in front of Melinda and returned to her desk, while Dakota had a muffled, and very brief, conversation with the newly subdued Melinda.

When Dakota returned, she pulled a chair up beside Jessie. "I'm sorry," she said, her tone low. "About Mel's comment to the kid. She'll be running some laps after practice tonight. And she'll apologize."

"His name is Ian," Jessie said, her own voice barely above a whisper.

"What?"

"*The kid*," Jessie said admonishingly. "His name is Ian."

"Right. She'll apologize to Ian."

Jessie had planned to do some grading for the rest of the period, but Dakota was way too close. Why was she so close? *Why is she even staying?*

"I'm also sorry about…you know…"

Jessie flinched. *Sorry about what? My sister?* Had Dakota figured out who Jessie was?

Dakota glanced down at Jessie's crossed legs.

Jessie heated with embarrassment. *What an idiot.* Of course Dakota wasn't apologizing for Jackie's death. Even *if* she were inclined to do so, she wouldn't do it here. Not now. Irritated with herself, Jessie tugged the hem of her dress down from where it was hiked higher in her seated position. "I don't think an apology counts if you offer it while doing the same thing again." This time she did whisper.

Dakota returned her attention to Jessie's face. "You're right." She cleared her throat. "I'm sorry. Again."

Jessie eyed her. "Coach Scott, is there—"

"Can you please call me Dakota?"

There was that word again, and this time, there was a slight emphasis on it. "Coach Scott," Jessie said with a little emphasis of her own. "Is there a reason you're still here? I'm sure I can handle these two."

"Oh, yes," Dakota said as though just remembering it herself. "I have this fabulous meatloaf sandwich." She opened her lunch bag. "My older sister makes the best meatloaf on the planet, and I went out to their place last night for dinner." She retrieved a foil packet. "And before I left, she made me this sandwich for my lunch today, which I'd be more than happy to share." She made a show out of spreading the unwrapped foil into a square plate.

Jessie smiled. "That's so nice of you." She mimicked Dakota's exaggerated tone.

Dakota grinned that grin. "And," she said, reaching into the bag, "there's some of Ada's homemade cheese biscuits…"

Whoever Ada is.

"…and some to-die-for potato salad." Dakota used a plastic fork to scoop some of the latter from a container onto the makeshift plate. She added a biscuit and slid the meal in front of Jessie.

"That does look delicious," Jessie said, opening her side drawer. She pulled out a bottle of water. "And, again, it's so nice of you to share. Thank you."

"My pleasure." The grin softened into a genuine smile.

Jessie pushed away from the desk, made a slight production of uncrossing her legs, then took the meal to Ian.

When she placed it in front of him, he looked up at her, eyes wide and mouth slightly agape. She almost heard the *Really?* that accompanied the expression. She smiled.

He grabbed the sandwich and took a huge bite.

Jessie returned to a sheepish looking Dakota.

"Okay, I feel like an ass," Dakota said under her breath. "I should have thought of that."

Jessie looked into Dakota's face and saw that she meant it. She wasn't playing a role as she seemed to have been doing when they'd first talked the previous week, or even that morning. There was sincerity there. A wisp of hair lay across her forehead where it'd fallen a few minutes earlier, and Jessie found herself wanting to brush it aside before it slipped into Dakota's eyes. But, of course, she wouldn't. "You thought of sharing it. That's enough."

Their gazes held for an extra beat, and there seemed to be a plea in Dakota's, a request.

For what? Jessie looked away. "If you'll excuse me, Coach Scott, I'd like to get some grading done so I don't have to stay up so late tonight."

"Sure." Dakota's voice was hoarse. "Why don't you take the rest of this? I have some chips and nuts in my office I can munch on." She slid the other half of the sandwich in front of Jessie.

Jessie wanted to argue, to refuse. But she wanted some distance from Dakota even more. Was this going to happen whenever they were in the same room for any length of time, this pull that made Jessie feel…What? Like she was being sucked into some parallel universe in which she and Dakota weren't who they were? They *were* who they were. Nothing could change that. She needed to tell Dakota who she was. *That* would keep her away.

Jessie had come home to make peace with the past, but she needed space. She couldn't work through everything with Dakota so close, popping in all the time, sitting next to her, and looking into her eyes. She couldn't do it with Dakota wanting something from her. She glanced at Melinda and Ian. She couldn't tell Dakota here and now, though. Not in front of students. "Thank you," she said and took the sandwich. *Now go.*

And with a nod, Dakota did. She stopped by Melinda's desk and murmured something, then she was gone.

Jessie stared after her. What had happened in that moment between them? What had Dakota been asking for? What could she, of all people, need from Jessie?

When the bell ending lunch period rang, Jessie looked up from the vocabulary test she was grading.

Melinda was coming toward her with the cafeteria tray in one hand and some papers in the other, but she stopped beside Ian's desk in route. "You can draw?" she asked, looking down at what he was doing.

He barely gave her a glance. "Obviously."

"That's really good." Melinda moved in for a closer look.

"Thanks." The word came out as more of a grunt.

Melinda straightened, then paused. "Hey, I'm sorry for what I said before. You know, calling you a loser."

Ian went back to his drawing. "Whatever."

Jessie watched the exchange, saw the disappointment in Melinda's eyes at Ian's dismissal. Is that what Jessie had done with Dakota's apology—dismissed it? Dismissed her?

Melinda's expression hardened. "Yeah. Whatever," she said, then made her way to Jessie's desk. "It went over two pages. I hope that's okay," she said to Jessie. "And could I have it back after you read it? I think I'd like to finish the story."

"Of course," Jessie said, startled. Who was this new girl?

Melinda smiled hesitantly. "And would it be okay if I came in to work with you at lunch instead of before school? I don't think I want to be in with the detention kids."

"As I told you..." Jessie took the papers from her. "Whenever you want."

Melinda's smile broadened. "Can I keep working on that story when I come back?"

Melinda's new spark touched Jessie. This day was turning out to be a victory after all. "Sure, we can incorporate it into what we're doing. But there will also be your vocabulary each week and the class essays."

"Okay. Thanks."

When Melinda was gone, Jessie walked over to where Ian still sat hunched over his sketching. She looked down at his work and was amazed at what she saw. Two large wolves sat side by side, watching over two young boys at play.

Ian frantically shaded in the fur of the darker one.

"You're quite talented, Mr. Langston." Jessie sat sideways in the desk in front of him so she could speak with him more easily. "Are you taking art?"

He stopped what he was doing and shook his head. He glanced up at her. "You have to have good grades to get into those classes."

"Really?" Jessie hadn't heard of that.

"Yeah."

"Where did you learn to draw then?" she asked.

"I didn't. I just started doing it and figured it out." He sat back and looked at his sketch, then started shading in another section.

Jessie picked up the book he'd been reading. "Ah, a *Game of Thrones* fan." It was the graphic novel, but at least he was reading. "So that's why your wolves are so big. They're dire wolves?"

"Yeah."

"And the children then must be Bran and Rickon Stark, since they're so young."

Ian eyed her. "You like *Game of Thrones*?"

"I do." Jessie remembered the entire month she'd lost several summers earlier when she'd discovered the *Song of Ice and Fire* series by George R. R. Martin, and had gotten so sucked into it, she'd done nothing but sit on the couch and read until she'd finished all five books. There were supposedly seven planned in the series, and she'd been waiting, not so patiently, for the release of the sixth for years. She could easily grumble about it, if given the opportunity, but she didn't think Ian needed to hear her complaints. "I've only read the books. I haven't seen the series on TV."

"Me neither." He was watching her now.

She flipped through the pages. "Your sketch is better than these." She came to the inside cover where the name Richard Stein was printed. Richard was in her second period class. She doubted he and Ian were friends.

"Thanks."

She handed him the book. "Well, you should get going. You don't want to be late for your next class." She walked him out, but just past the doorway, he stopped.

"I heard you tell Mel she could come in at lunch," he said, not meeting her gaze. "Could I do that, too? I mean, do my detention then instead of in the morning?"

Jessie wondered what his reason was but decided not to ask. They'd had a moment, a connection, through their conversation about *Game of Thrones* and his art. She didn't want to blow that. And she'd be in her classroom at lunch with Melinda anyway. "That would be fine, if that works better for you," she said, looking at him even though he still didn't meet her eyes. "The same rules apply, though, as in detention."

He gave a quick nod and started down the hall.

As Jessie greeted a couple of students in her fifth period class, she noticed him turn around and head the other way. She glanced in the direction he'd been going and saw three boys in lettermen jackets watching him and laughing.

Melinda stood with them, but when she saw who their attention was on, she slapped one on the arm, then turned and stalked away.

What was that about? Jessie studied the boys a moment longer. She wondered if it had to do with the bruise that all but covered half his face. She made up her mind to find out more about the fight he'd been in.

Jessie spent the rest of the afternoon with the two teenagers on her mind—Ian and Melinda. She thought she'd made some headway with Melinda and had felt a definite link with Ian. She'd had the opportunity to glance at Melinda's writing sample and had actually been fairly impressed. The beginning of the story she'd written was creative and engaging, and her writing wasn't half bad. She'd need to focus on some points of grammar and most likely needed to learn how to write an essay in order to pass the proficiency test and for any college entrance exams, but other than that, she was doing okay, in spite of Dakota's ridiculous way of handling her athletes.

But what about Ian? What was his story? Jessie doubted he had college to look forward to. What would his path be? She'd always tried to help kids like him and had managed it periodically, but there had to be a way to do more, some kind of program that had the potential to reach a larger number, to prepare them for whatever their futures held.

And then there was Dakota, flitting in and out of Jessie's thoughts. Jessie didn't have a clue what was going on there. Whatever it was made her uncomfortable, though. There was a softness to it that shouldn't be there under the circumstances. When Dakota had looked at Jessie in that moment, she'd seemed so vulnerable. It'd affected Jessie, made her want to reach out to her, and that wasn't supposed to happen. Jessie was here to put the past to rest for herself. Nothing more. Her reaction had to be rooted in that dammed schoolgirl crush she'd had on Dakota from the first time she'd seen her, when Jessie was ten and Dakota was fourteen. That's all it was. But it was ridiculous now, just as, in reality, it'd been then.

Dakota had *never* known who Jessie was. Jessie was merely one of so many little girls, and older ones too, she supposed, who idolized Dakota, who wanted to be like her, and some who—along with all the boys—wanted to be *with* her. Jessie remembered the one time she'd thought Dakota had noticed her. She'd been about twelve, Dakota sixteen. It was at the end of a high school girls softball game for which Dakota had hit a fly ball to deep center field for a win for Clearwater Springs. Jessie had waited outside the locker room with a throng of others to cheer for the team as they came out. Dakota had burst through the door first, of course, and was carrying the game ball that had been presented to her by the coach. As she'd sauntered past, waving at everyone, she'd made eye contact with Jessie, grinned that Dakota Scott grin, and tossed her that ball. It'd taken Jessie's breath—the spark in Dakota's vibrant green eyes, the smile that felt like it was just for her, and the gift that she'd cherished. At least for a year and a half. Until that night. Until all the talk.

Jessie hadn't wanted to believe what some of the townspeople said about Dakota, what Jessie's mother was saying, but the only alternative was the story Dakota's brother had told the police. And *that* was unthinkable. The idea of it had all but destroyed her mother, and even now, in this moment, Jessie couldn't possibly consider it. Instead, she let herself wonder about that ball. She had no recollection of what had happened to it.

After school, when Jessie stepped through the back door of the home where she'd lived her last two years of high school, she found her foster father bent over in a coughing fit with an open can of Chunky beef vegetable soup sitting next to a pot on the stove. "Curtis!" She rushed to him and helped him to a chair. "What are you doing? You should be in bed. I'll make you some dinner that will be way better for you than that." She felt his forehead. "You're still running a fever."

He'd had a nasty bug for the past few days. "I know," he said, still sputtering. "But Janice called in with the same thing today. Ray covered the office for the afternoon, but he's got his kids tonight. He can't stay past five."

"Well, *you* can't work like this," she said, rubbing his shoulders. "Let me make you something to eat real quick, and I'll go in. Does Margie come on at ten?"

Curtis slumped in the chair and coughed again. "Yeah, but you already worked a full day."

Jessie laughed. "I could have worked thirty-six hours straight and I'd still be in better shape to handle the desk than you are right now." She stepped away and opened the pantry. "You need to get back to bed and rest." She scanned the contents. "How about that garlic broccoli pasta you like so much? That would be soft on your throat."

Curtis groaned. "You're an angel, shrimp." He'd started calling her shrimp when she was eight and still did when he wanted to lighten the mood.

"Yeah, and don't you forget it, old man." She loved teasing with him. After all, he was the one who'd taught her how to do it. She'd begun calling him *old man* way before he was close to being one, but now he was getting up in years, which saddened her.

Almost seventy, he was still strong, but his once thick, dark brown hair was thinning and gray, and his hands were speckled with age spots. The lines on his face had deepened since his loss of Laura, his wife and love for four decades, five years earlier.

He and Laura had given Jessie's mother a job a few years after Jessie's father was killed in a car accident, leaving her with two young girls to raise on her own. Prior to that, she'd only been able to get odd jobs here and there. She'd started out cleaning the rooms and doing the laundry at the Triple M—the Midnight Moon Motel—and they were accommodating with her hours. They hadn't been able to pay her a lot as they were just getting the business off the ground, but the work was consistent. They'd let her bring Jessie and her older sister, Jackie, to work with her if necessary, and Laura would entertain them in the office while Jessie's mother worked. They'd been the benefactors of many a Christmas dinner over the years and always made sure the girls, as well as their mother, had gifts on their birthdays. When Jackie was killed, they'd continued providing paychecks during the months Jessie's mother had been too depressed to get out of bed on many days, and when she'd died of a heart attack two weeks before Jessie turned sixteen, they'd given Jessie a home.

Once she'd gone away to college, she'd returned to visit Curtis and Laura as much as she could bear, but to her, Clearwater Springs had become the place that had taken her entire family from her. Her foster parents had understood and had always been happy for her regular telephone calls, and they'd come to see her periodically, when they could afford it.

Jessie loved Curtis and Laura, but when her mother had died, it felt as though something died in Jessie as well. Curtis had said her mother had died of a broken heart after losing her husband and a daughter. Jessie hadn't ever told him how much it hurt her to know *she* wasn't enough to live for. It wasn't until nine months earlier when Jessie was seeing a counselor to figure out why her marriage to Shelly wasn't working that she realized she'd given Curtis and Laura the exact same message, and she'd carried her hurt and resentment into every relationship she'd had since.

It'd been too late to mend things with Shelly, who had already moved on to someone else, and Laura was gone, but Jessie wanted to reconnect with Curtis. That's when she'd decided to make a brand new start in her life, to heal her past and begin again. She started by not renewing her contract for the teaching position in Boston she'd held for twelve years, and coming back to Clearwater Springs to spend the summer with Curtis, to face her past and heal. Then she could see what possibilities lay before her.

Now, here it was two months into a new school year, and in some ways, she'd just begun doing what she'd come here to do. She was okay with that, though. She'd spent the summer and early fall almost constantly with Curtis, helping him in the motel and with some redecorating in the house. They'd cleared out the remainder of Laura's things, something he hadn't been able to bear doing by himself, and now, with the long-term sub position she'd taken, she had the time—and, apparently, ample opportunity, since Dakota seemed so omnipresent all of a sudden—to take on the rest of her task.

Jessie set two plates of pasta on the table, then poured a couple of cups of herbal tea and sat down.

"Thank you, Jessie girl," Curtis said, affection in his hazel eyes. He covered her hand with his and gave it a squeeze.

Jessie smiled softly. "Someone has to watch over you. You take care of everyone but yourself."

He chuckled and began to eat. "I hope I didn't ruin any plans you had for tonight."

Jessie almost laughed out loud. She seldom had plans in the evening. "I was only going to grade papers. I can do that while I cover the desk."

"I just hate to ask you to do that." Curtis took a deep swallow of hot tea, then sighed. "That feels good."

"You didn't ask," Jessie said between bites. She checked the time on the wall clock. "But you could have, you know. Nobody should work when they feel as lousy as you do. Besides, you look awful. You'd scare people away if anyone showed up to check in."

Curtis laughed. "Well, I'm grateful. I don't know if I could've actually made it till ten."

"And now you don't need to. You can go back to bed and not worry about a thing." Jessie watched him to make sure he was eating. "Maybe you should hire some part-time help or sign up with a temp agency to help out in a pinch."

"You know how the off months are. We just get by without laying anyone off."

Jessie knew how loyal Curtis was to his employees. He'd do anything he could to ensure they got full paychecks, and he'd much rather one of them get a little overtime than hire someone part-time to come in.

"What I need sometimes is free help. Like you." He smiled and took another bite.

"You know I don't mind." The words came out of Jessie's mouth, but her thoughts had shifted in another direction. "What about a junior or senior who worked for you in exchange for learning the skill set involved in running a motel? Like an internship," she said pensively.

"An internship?" Curtis rested his forearms on the table.

"Yes. A student helps out in exchange for training. And as they learn more, they can handle more responsibility." She followed the thought down the line. "And by the time they graduate, they've learned some marketable skills, and you've gotten some help without it costing anything."

"Hmm." Curtis chewed a bit of pasta. "There'd still be some cost. I'd have to add them to my insurance policy if they're working on the premises in any kind of official capacity, even if they aren't getting paid. And...I don't know." He shook his head. "Do kids today work for nothing? I'd feel like they should get something."

Jessie could tell he'd moved into the brainstorming process with her, and she loved him for it. She never remembered a time when he'd simply shut down an idea. "Okay." She let her mind wander. "What if we got a subsidy from somewhere?"

He looked at her closely. "A subsidy? Somehow, I don't think we're talking about just getting me a little help around here anymore. What *are* we talking about?"

Jessie sat back in her chair. "I met this boy today. I don't know anything about him, but I think he has potential. He struck me as coming from a family who doesn't have much, and I don't know if there's support at home."

"This kid have a name?"

"Ian Langston," Jessie said, hoping Curtis might be able to give her some information.

"Oh, yeah. He lives with his grandpa out in the trailer park." He squinted, obviously in thought. "No, they don't have much. He came to live with Isaac a year or so ago. I'm not sure where his parents are."

Jessie remembered the mended holes in Ian's clothing, an earnest attempt at making them last longer by either a teenage boy or his grandfather. "I've tried over the years to come up with some way to help kids like Ian to get some practical skills they can use to make a living when they get out of high school."

"Like a vocational training program?" Curtis wiped his mouth with his napkin. "Yeah, I see where you're going with this. And if you could get the program some financial backing, you could make it more enticing for small business owners. It's worth thinking about." He nodded.

"Yes, it is." Jessie gave him a bright smile. "Thank you for talking it through with me. Now," she said sternly, "you get to bed, and let me get over to the office and relieve Ray."

At ten o'clock, Jessie said good night to Margie and wished her a good shift, then started across the gravel lot to the house behind the motel. After a full day of teaching and an evening of double duty, grading papers, and taking care of the needs of the guests at Midnight Moon, she should have been exhausted, but her mind was filled with competing thoughts: possibilities for a program for kids like Ian, the look she and Dakota had exchanged, Melinda's story, her moment with Dakota at age twelve, that damned baseball. *Where the hell is it?* Recollections of all that Curtis and Laura had done for her mother and her and the ache that could still twist her heart at the loss of her family. There was no way she'd be able to sleep. Maybe a walk would clear her head.

She stopped by the house long enough to find Curtis sound asleep in his bed. She grabbed a jacket, then set out into the quiet town. The air was cold, the temperature still dropping, and clouds hid the stars. The night reminded her of countless others just like it, of lying in the darkness of her room, cuddled against Jackie for warmth.

After her father's death, even after her mother went to work for Curtis and Laura, they hadn't been able to afford a lot in terms of living accommodations, so Jessie had grown up in the Colby Cottages, named for the street they were on. They weren't really cottages, though. They were tiny, one-bedroom shacks, with thin walls and windows that didn't close tightly. Jessie thought back to winter nights throughout which she shivered, even with a roof over her head. Sometimes, when she couldn't sleep, and sometimes just because, she'd lie in bed and stare out the cracked bedroom window at the Scott mansion high on the hill outside of town and make up stories about life there. Once, after one of the few times her mother had let Laura come over, they'd suddenly had more blankets to crawl beneath. As she'd felt the joy of being warm drifting off to sleep, she'd wondered if that was what it was like to be rich.

Jessie shook the memory away and focused on the here and now. As she did, though, she found herself standing under a streetlight on Colby Way, right in the middle of the high-end housing tract that had been built in the field where the cottages once stood. She considered the irony of these upscale homes being built directly on top of the demolished cottages, wiping away the traces of the desperately poor, as though they'd never existed. She steeled herself against the sadness that threatened to overtake her. Her family *had* existed, and so had many others who'd lived there over the years. What had happened to Wynona Blanch and her three little boys, or old Mr. Archer who sometimes shared the tomato soup he made from hot water and ketchup? Were they all gone and forgotten, their lives buried with the first turn of the soil in the building of these new homes? But who was Jessie to judge? She'd left this place at a dead run without looking back, until now.

She pulled her jacket more snugly around her as a chill ran through her, and she looked up at the Scott mansion. She couldn't help but wonder what Dakota was doing inside, then chastised herself for caring, even for a minute.

Chapter Five

Dakota shuddered and put down the lesbian romantic thriller she was reading. The creepy guy lurking in the shadows of the neighborhood of the woman he'd kidnapped as a child and was now stalking as an adult was giving her the heebie-jeebies. She knew better than to read that kind of book after dark, but in her defense, it hadn't been dark when she sat down with it. She stared into the glowing embers in the fireplace and wondered how long she'd been absorbed in the story.

When she'd gotten home from practice, she'd needed something to escape into, something to focus on besides the recurring thoughts of lunch period from earlier that day. Not so much the thoughts, but the feelings. She'd been so embarrassed that she hadn't considered the kid in Jessica's room might not have anything to eat. She should have. And then to make such a production of sharing her food with Jessica. She didn't think Jessica had thought much of her prior to that, but now...Dakota felt like such a jerk.

What really nagged at her, though, was why she even cared what Jessica Weldon thought of her. And what about that look Jessica had given her—right at the moment Dakota had felt the worst? It'd been so tender Dakota had thought Jessica might reach out and touch her. *Crazy.*

Dakota stirred the fire and dropped another log onto the awakening flames. She went to the kitchen to rummage up something to eat. The refrigerator yielded nothing that resembled dinner, even by her loose definition, and the cupboard bore the same result. She had to go shopping. She pulled a box of Cheez-Its from the top of the fridge and scooped out a handful, then picked up the phone and ordered a pizza. As she hung up, she glanced out the front window, and her heart leapt into her throat.

A hooded man stood beneath the streetlight in front of her house, staring at the house across the street—exactly like in the book. She looked harder. Okay, maybe not *exactly*. This figure wasn't hooded, wasn't in the shadows, and certainly wasn't a man. Dakota shook her head at her runaway imagination. She studied the woman. She could only see her from the back, but there was something familiar about her. She wore jeans and boots and a fleece-lined black bomber jacket pulled tightly around her torso, setting off the flare of her hips, and her hair shone a dark gold under the illumination of the streetlamp. *Jessica's hair.*

Dakota blinked. What the hell was Jessica doing outside her house? Could it possibly be someone else?

Dakota watched her, taking in every detail, every curve, the way she held herself. Dakota's breath stilled. Her abdomen tightened with the stirrings of arousal. It was definitely Jessica. Had the powers that be given her yet one more chance to start fresh with her?

She slipped into her Uggs and pulled on a jacket, then stepped out her front door. She waited, but Jessica hadn't heard her, or at least, she didn't turn around. Dakota moved down the walk. She didn't want to scare her, wanted to keep it light. "Are you stalking me?" she asked, loudly enough to be heard, but hopefully not loud enough to frighten.

Jessica spun around, clearly startled despite Dakota's attempt not to do that very thing, then her expression relaxed with obvious recognition. "I was taking a walk."

"Really? Isn't it kind of late?" Was it? Dakota didn't know what time it was.

"You know what they say, there's only the now." Jessica gave her a curious look. "What are you doing here?"

"I live here," Dakota said, feeling on somewhat firm footing with Jessica for the first time since she'd walked into her classroom the previous week.

"You live *here*?" Jessica's surprise was evident.

"Mm-hm. Right there. In the very house we're in front of." Dakota tilted her head. "Hence, my question. Are you stalking me?"

Jessica looked at the house as though taking in every detail.

"You know, you didn't have to come all the way over here to ask me out," Dakota said, teasing her. "You could have looked up my number in the faculty directory." She hadn't known those words were going to come out of her mouth, but since they had, in a second she might have the answer to one of her questions about Jessica.

Jessica parted her lips, but only a sputter came out. Her cheeks, already a bright pink from the chilly air, darkened to red. "I didn't come over to ask you out."

Okay. She didn't say she isn't gay. That was the first thing straight women said when a lesbian hit on them—*if* they weren't interested, that is. That was something. "Why did you come over, then?"

"I didn't." The pitch of Jessica's voice rose slightly.

"You're here." Dakota shrugged and slipped her hands into the pockets of her jacket.

"Well…yes," Jessica said. "I came over. But I didn't come over to ask…I mean, no. I didn't *come over…*"

Dakota watched her struggle. She was enjoying having the upper hand for a change.

"I was just taking…like I said…" Jessica waved her hand in the air as though that explained everything.

"Maybe you came over in hopes that *I'd* ask *you* out, then."

"What? No. I didn't" Jessica's voice rose.

"Are you sure?" Dakota winked at her. "Maybe subconsciously*?"*

"No!" Jessica said firmly. "I told you. I didn't come over for *any* reason. I *didn't* come over."

"But you're here."

Jessica clenched her teeth and looked at the sky. She released an obviously exasperated sigh.

"So what are you doing now?" Dakota pushed a little further. "You know, since you didn't come over to ask me out or to get me to ask you out, even though you're in front of my house?"

"What?" Jessica looked confused.

"You said you *were* taking a walk." Dakota glanced up and down the street. "But you're not walking."

Jessica hesitated. She still looked flustered. "I…just ended up here." She glanced around the neighborhood.

"Really. What a coincidence." Dakota smiled.

Jessica considered her as though pondering something, then regained her customary composure. Her expression settled, a decision obviously made. "No, not a coincidence. I used to live here."

Dakota faltered in shock. "In Clearwater Springs?"

"Yes." Jessica cleared her throat. "And here." She gestured around them. "Right here."

Dakota followed the motion of her hand. "In this tract? Do you now?"

"No, I'm staying across town at the Triple M."

The nickname had been given to a little place called the Midnight Moon Motel by the townspeople years ago. It'd been there Dakota's whole life. She'd passed it every day of her childhood on her way into town to school. She'd been intrigued with the sign—a big, full moon set against the background of a starry, indigo sky, with Midnight Moon Motel swirled across the face in a wispy script. When she was in elementary school, she thought that was where wizards and sorceresses stayed when they came to town, until Crystal told her that was ridiculous.

"I lived here a long time ago," Jessie said, something changing in her tone.

At that, Dakota knew *she* was being messed with. She supposed she deserved some kind of retaliation for her teasing. "This tract wasn't here a long time ago. It's only been here about ten years." To be accurate, it was built ten and a half years earlier, right before Dakota and Diane had bought the home that was now Dakota's.

"No," Jessica said as her gaze shifted to the houses across the street, then went distant as though not seeing them. "This was mostly an empty field then. There were only some tiny houses right over there, along the edge. You might not remember them."

Dakota went cold. She got a flash—two rows of little blue shacks, a long dirt drive, the rattle of a thin door as she'd knocked. She'd only known one person who'd lived there, hadn't really *known* her, but had never been able to forget her.

Dakota had balked when the real estate agent had brought them into this development for a showing. It was the newest in town, though, and Diane had loved the house. Besides, the neighborhood didn't look anything like it once had, and those horrible cottages had been torn down a long time before, so Dakota had blocked the memory, as she had so many others from back then. She sure as hell wasn't going to revisit that place now. She scrambled for a change in subject. "Why were you surprised I live here?" It was lame, but it was something.

Jessica cut her a sideways glance. "I thought you lived up there." She lifted her chin toward Dakota's childhood home on the hill. "I thought all the Scotts lived there."

Disappointment swept through Dakota like a dust storm on a dry day. She hadn't realized how much she wanted for Jessica to know little of her family and their standing in the community. Of course Jessica knew, though. She'd said so in their first meeting. That was one of the things Dakota had loved about living somewhere else for all those years. She'd counted on it. When she met a woman she was interested in, she could let them get to know her gradually, dole out what information she wanted them to know and at her own pace. She hadn't been newly interested in a woman for a long time. Not since she and Diane were introduced. And with that realization, she had to admit she was interested in Jessica.

Jessica leaned against the lamppost and returned her attention across the street, but now, Dakota knew she wasn't looking at the house in front of her, but at the mansion, at several illuminated front windows, at the lights that lined the long driveway from the main road.

"When I was little, I used to lie in bed at night and look up there." Jessica's voice went soft. "And sometimes, it looked like it does now, quiet, like people are getting ready for bed."

Dakota followed Jessica's gaze and could see what she meant. The ranch house was a mere shadow except for the few lighted windows, against the rise of the mountain that jutted skyward behind the foothills of the ranch. She could imagine Crystal in her favorite chair in front of the fire, finishing one last chapter in whatever book she was reading, Paul already in bed, their mother in a hot bath.

"But sometimes," Jessica said, continuing with a far away expression, "all the lights were on. Not only inside, but all over the grounds as well. They were so bright and covered so much of the property around the house itself, it seemed like I should be able to see people moving around. But, of course, I couldn't, so I imagined what might be going on, why there were so many lights."

Dakota's stomach twisted, but she let Jessica continue. She wanted to hear what the young Jessica made up, knowing she couldn't possibly know the truth.

"I imagined a big party. All the men in tuxedos. The women in long, flowing gowns and sparkling jewelry. I could see them in my mind, dancing, an orchestra playing on a brightly lit gazebo in the middle of a big grassy area. And I wondered what it must be like to live there." Jessica paused, as though considering not going on. Then she added, "To be a Scott."

Dakota thought again of the tiny houses, the rickety door, the roach she'd seen scurry across the step. She knew now what it meant to live in a place like that, even if she hadn't thought about it back then. She knew the dichotomy between living in one of those little blue houses and living at the Ghost Rider Ranch, understood a child's romanticizing of the latter. Things weren't all bright and sparkly at the ranch, though. Things weren't what many people thought. She studied Jessica's profile under the streetlight. She looked so wistful, and a shadow of sorrow veiled her rich brown eyes.

Dakota leaned against the other side of the lamppost and fixed her own stare on the mansion. She'd been so engrossed in Jessica's childhood memories, she now felt like the little girl *she'd* once been. "Some nights *were* quiet," she said, her voice low in the night. "But on the ones when all the lights were on and everything seemed so bright and shiny to you, my mother had gone off her meds and gotten confused by voices only she heard. She has schizophrenia. Did you know that?" *Of course she knows that. Hell, everyone knows that.* But few knew what it was like to live with it.

Dakota missed Jessica's answer, if she'd given one. "And when that happened, sometimes she'd wander out of the house and onto the acreage. And she'd get lost." She swallowed a lump as she relived each time she'd heard the panic in her father's or Crystal's voice. *Mama's missing. We have to find her.* "And that's when all the lights came on. And everyone in the family and all the staff and wranglers would go out searching. And if it was winter, we had to hurry, because she could freeze. But even in the summer, she could come across a pack of coyotes or fall into a ravine." Dakota stared blankly at the mansion, remembering those nights, then she remembered *that* night—the phone call for her and Drew to hurry home, the race along the back roads, the darkness. But she never talked about that, so she remained silent. She became aware of Jessica watching her, seemingly rooted in the moment, her eyes wide.

A huge droplet of water splashed against Dakota's ear, then trickled down her neck. Another hit the top of her head, then another, and another, bringing her back to the present. She looked up, and rain splashed her face. She shook her head, slinging the moisture aside. "Come on," she said, grabbing Jessica's hand and pulling her toward the house. "Let's get inside."

The clouds let loose, and the rain soaked them before they reached the door.

In the house, Dakota stripped off her jacket and hung it on the coat tree in the entryway, then helped Jessica with hers. "We can dry the collar of this in front of the fire. Boy, that really hit fast." She crossed to the dining area and pulled a chair over to the hearth, then draped the jacket over the back.

Jessica stood just inside the door, her wet hair plastered to her scalp. Rivulets trickled from the ends and down the cable knit of her forest green sweater.

"Let me get you a towel," Dakota said in a rush. She hurried to the bathroom. "Come over here where it's warm," she said when she returned. She gestured Jessica to the fireside.

Jessica complied but still said nothing. She gave Dakota a measured look as she took the towel and began drying her hair.

"Are you okay?" Dakota asked, squeezing the length of her ponytail in her own towel. The intimacy of the moment on the street, the sharing of childhood experiences, lingered between them.

Jessica nodded. "I'm fine." She rubbed the towel over her head. "I never knew…I never would have known…How often did that happen…with your mother?"

Dakota stiffened, suddenly realizing what she'd shared. "Oh," she said slowly. "Uh…I don't know. It was a long time ago."

Jessica's demeanor shifted, and despite her casual attire and soaked hair, despite how adorably flustered she'd been by Dakota's teasing such a short while ago, she was the Jessica of her classroom again. "So you don't remember anything from that long ago?"

Dakota wanted the other Jessica back, the one who couldn't seem to find words to explain herself, the one who'd blushed. She wanted this woman standing in front of her in jeans and a bulky sweater that made her look so cuddly to be the one speaking. She wanted the expression Jessica had worn when she'd first stepped through the door, the one that seemed to hold a hint of wonder for some reason. She wanted to touch Jessica. But *this* Jessica was the one who was a little scary.

How can I get the other one back? Dakota grinned. "Here, let me help." She turned Jessica around by the shoulders and tousled her own towel over the back of her hair.

Jessica finished the front, then faced Dakota once more. "Thank you," she said, sounding awkward. "That's fine."

Dakota laughed, taking in the tangled mess. "You don't want it to dry this way." She ran a hand over the top of Jessica's head, smoothing her hair back, then finger combed the sides. It was so fine, so soft, even though it was wet.

Jessica tilted her head ever so slightly. Her eyes fluttered closed, then quickly opened. She lifted her gaze to Dakota's.

The rain on the skylight and the crackle of the fire were the only sounds.

Her fingertips still in Jessica's hair, Dakota grazed her temple with her thumb.

Jessica drew in a breath, then stepped away. "I should go." She reached for her jacket.

"Wait," Dakota said, grabbing her wrist. "You can't walk home. It's pouring out there. I'll drive you, but I ordered a pizza. I need to wait for the delivery."

Jessica glanced out the window, then eased from Dakota's grasp. "Or maybe it will let up."

"Yeah, maybe." Dakota relaxed. She hadn't been aware of how much she'd wanted Jessica to stay. She pulled her hair free of its ponytail and finished drying it. "Can I get you something to drink?" she asked as she moved toward the kitchen. "A glass of wine?"

"No, thank you." Jessica turned and held her hands out to the heat of the flames. "But don't let me stop you."

"Beer?" Dakota asked in an attempt to ease the tension that had crept into the room. "Something stronger?"

Jessica looked over her shoulder. "No, really," she said in that same tight tone. "I'm fine."

"I know." Dakota stopped in the kitchen doorway and wriggled her eyebrows. "A cup of hot cocoa. Is that your weakness?"

Jessica's lips twitched, as though she was trying to hold back a smile. Then she laughed.

"I knew it." Dakota slapped the doorjamb. "A steaming hot cup of cocoa, comin' right up." *Now, if I only have milk. And cocoa.* In about five minutes, she strode back into the living room with two mugs, feeling pretty proud of herself for accomplishing the task. She offered one to Jessica.

Jessica took it, still looking at a framed snapshot of the four Scott children, not as children, but taken only five years earlier in front of the Christmas tree. Beside it on the mantel sat another in which Crystal was thirteen, Dakota and Drew ten, and Tina only seven, in the very same spot, in front of another decorated tree.

"Those are my siblings," Dakota said. "My older sister, Crystal, the maker of magic meatloaf; me and my twin, Drew; and my little sister, Tina." She pointed to each image in turn.

A smile touched the corners of Jessica's mouth as she took a sip of her drink. "I know who you all are."

"Oh. Yeah." Dakota paused. "Because you used to live here."

Jessica nodded. "I did."

"I'm sorry," Dakota said, unable to believe she couldn't remember her. "I don't know why I can't place you."

"I wouldn't expect you to be able to." Jessica turned to face her, her gaze sharp. "You're a Scott. The Scotts only notice what matters to them."

"Ouch." Dakota pressed a hand to her chest. "That's a little harsh."

Jessica considered her. "Perhaps," she said more mildly. "But is it not true?"

Dakota thought for a moment. Maybe it was. Wasn't it true of anyone, though? Didn't everyone see only what pertained to them, what affected them? "I'm sorry," she said again, hoping to avoid going any farther down the rabbit hole of what it really meant to be a Scott. Besides, she'd rather get to know who Jessica was today and find out if, just maybe, Jessica might like that, too. She looked into Jessica's eyes. There was so much there—strength, compassion, a little defiance. And beneath that, sadness and longing and anger.

And way down deep, behind everything else…Was that a spark? A flicker of interest, of attraction, of connection? Dakota brushed the sweep of Jessica's bangs from her forehead. "I've noticed you now. Can we start fresh?"

Jessica's expression softened. "Coach Scott, there's something—"

Dakota groaned. She dropped her hand to her side and stepped back. "Really? Still with the Coach Scott?"

The flustered Jessica was back. "I—"

The doorbell rang.

"Pizza's here," Dakota said brightly, hoping the distraction would deflect whatever distance Jessica was trying to keep between them. She really wanted a chance to get to know her better. She paid the delivery boy, a skinny teenager with glasses who seemed to know her but whom Dakota didn't recall ever seeing before. Maybe Jessica was right about her not noticing people enough. She pushed the thought aside and carried the pizza into the kitchen. She expected Jessica to follow, but she remained alone. She could see her through the opening above the bar, still by the fire. She dished up a couple of slices, then deposited them and the box holding the rest onto the dining table. "Join me?"

Jessica simply looked at her, then slowly crossed the room. She studied the pizza as though the decision was equivalent to choosing a life career.

"It's still raining," Dakota said, hoping to convince her. "I can take you home now, but I'm starving. Maybe we could eat first?"

Jessica looked into Dakota's face. She seemed to be searching for something. There was an intensity in her eyes that drew Dakota in and caused a flutter of sensation in her center. "Jessica?" she said quietly.

Jessica didn't respond. She kept staring into Dakota's eyes. "It's Jessie," she said finally.

"Jessie." Dakota smiled at the resonance. It was so much softer, more intimate. "That's nice."

Jessie continued to watch her, intent and probing.

Without thinking, Dakota slid an arm around Jessie's waist and pulled her close. She twined her fingers into her hair, then slowly brushed her lips across Jessie's.

Jessie's hands came to Dakota's shoulders.

Dakota covered her mouth with her own.

Jessie went rigid, then melted into her, her lips parting.

Dakota slipped her tongue into the opening and deepened the kiss. Jessie's curves were soft against Dakota, her hair silken between Dakota's fingers, her mouth supple, warm, inviting in response to Dakota's claim. Everything about her caressed Dakota's desire. Dakota shifted against her.

Jessie's tongue touched Dakota's and she moaned quietly, then she stiffened. She pushed hard against Dakota's chest and broke free. Her hands flew to her mouth, her eyes wide. She backed away. "Oh, my God," she whispered.

Dakota stood, her mouth open, the kiss still burning on her lips. "I'm sorry," she said, breathless. "I thought..."

"Oh, my God. What have I done?" Tears welled in Jessie's eyes. She spun around, her back to Dakota.

"What? I'm sorry. What's wrong?" She touched Jessie's shoulder.

Jessie whirled around again, her eyes clear once more. "I can't...I don't..." Her chin quivered, then she tightened her jaw, her lips pressing together in a firm line. That hint of defiance that shone in her eyes earlier flared into a hot flame. "This can't happen. My name is Jessie Brogan," she said, her voice hard. "Jackie Brogan was my sister."

The words hit Dakota like a fist in her gut. She stared in horror. She couldn't breathe. She couldn't speak. The image of Jackie Brogan's face against her windshield filled her vision. The spider web of cracks dissecting her features, the gush of blood from her nose, flooded Dakota's memory. She gripped the edge of the table. It'd taken her years to lock that picture away, and now, here it was, fresh and clear, like it was yesterday. She had to think of something else, *go* somewhere else. *A sister?* She steeled herself. "I didn't think...I didn't know she had a sister."

Jessie squeezed her eyes shut, moisture seeping from beneath her lids "And I…" She touched her lips. "I can't believe I…How could I?"

Dakota fell into one of the dining room chairs.

With one last look at Dakota, Jessie raced to the fireplace and grabbed her jacket.

Dakota slumped forward as the front door slammed behind her. *Jackie Brogan's sister? Christ! Will this nightmare ever end?*

Chapter Six

Jessie ran from the house. Down the street. Around the corner at the intersection. She slouched against the fence of a side yard to catch her breath. The rain had let up some, and the thick umbrella of branches of a nearby pine tree shielded her from the remaining drizzle.

What did I do? How could I? How could I kiss the woman that killed Jackie? She hadn't meant to, hadn't seen it coming. She began to cry. She'd been so focused on telling Dakota who she was, watching for any signs of recognition, of recollection.

A car pulled up to the stop sign.

Jessie drew in a sharp breath and looked up. Had Dakota followed her? Was she looking for her? She shrank into the shadow of the fence. The car, a sedan, turned left and headed downtown. No, Dakota drove a SUV. *A Jeep, maybe?* What if it *had* been her, though? What if Dakota did come looking for her? She couldn't face her after what just happened. She had to get home.

She wiped her eyes, her nose, and pulled on Curtis's old bomber jacket. She glanced the way the sedan had gone. If she went that way, Dakota would be sure to find her—if she came looking. She scanned the road in the opposite direction. It was a much longer route, around the outskirts of town, but one less likely to be followed. Besides, it would give her time to clear her head. She checked her watch. Eleven forty-three. She grimaced. But what did she expect? She hadn't left the motel until after ten. She pulled the jacket tightly around her and started walking.

The night was colder than it had been earlier, but at least the rain had stopped. Only the slightest mist lingered in the air and whispered across her face.

What the hell am I doing here? Why had she come back to this town? She hated it here. She'd come because she'd wanted to heal her past, to be free of the feelings of loss and being alone in the world that had haunted her since childhood. Thanks to years of therapy, she knew that wasn't true. She wasn't alone, at least not unless she chose to be. She'd had Curtis and Laura. She'd had friends in college and anyplace she'd worked since then. She'd been in romantic relationships here and there—even lived with a few women and finally married one—until she'd found a reason to leave. Somewhere deep down inside, though, there was always the question. *What's the point? Why get close to anyone when life's so fragile?*

And now, here she was, back where the most significant people in her life, those who were supposed to always be there to come home to, to turn to—her family—had been taken from her. One by one. First her father, run off the road on his way home from work by a drunk driver. Jessie had only been six when it happened. Then Jackie, hit and killed by Dakota one night on the same road—the same exact curve—where their father had died. *Coincidence?* That old, nagging question poked its head up. Jessie squashed it back down, as she always did, unwilling to consider the possible answers. And finally, her mother, who'd simply given up. Never mind the fact that she still had a daughter. Never mind that Jessie had been only fifteen and still needed help finding her place in the world. Never mind anything else.

Jessie knew that people with depression weren't capable of thinking about anyone else, even those that depended on them. There were other parts of her, though, those unhealed parts—that little girl who'd lost her father and hadn't really understood where he'd gone, the thirteen-year-old who'd sobbed as the casket taking away her sister was lowered into a dank hole, the stoic teen who'd stood in the same cemetery two years later without a tear left to shed for her mother… Those parts of her didn't understand at all why she hadn't been enough to keep her mother's heart beating.

And now, as though her being back in Clearwater Springs wasn't complicated enough with all of that to resolve, she'd *kissed* Dakota Scott. *What the hell is wrong with me?*

Her phone rang from the pocket of her jacket, the assigned ringtone, "Friends in Low Places." *Sandy! Thank God! Thank God! Thank God!* "I kissed Dakota!" she blurted when she'd answered the call.

A pause.

"I need more information." Sandy's voice held its customary steadiness and composure.

She and Jessie had met their freshman year at UMass Amherst in a lesbian bar over several games of darts and way too many buttery nipples. There'd been an instant connection. Their backgrounds were similar, both having grown up with very little, and as it turned out, their hometowns were only a few hours apart in California. Each had ended up in Massachusetts in an attempt to get as far from the past as possible and still be in the same country. Sandy called them trailer park twins, even though Jessie had never lived in one. They'd slept together once and decided it was something that should never happen again and had been best friends ever since.

"I *kissed* her!" Tears filled Jessie's eyes again.

"Jess." Sandy's tone was patient. "Just because you say something twice doesn't make it *more*. Tell me what happened."

"I don't…" Jessie ran her hand through her hair. A definite mistake. They were Dakota's fingers she felt. "I don't know what happened. We were in the dining room, and I'd told her about living here and the cottages, and she asked if I wanted pizza and said she liked my name and it was raining, and—"

"Jessie, focus." Sandy's voice was calm but stern.

"And she kissed me," Jessie said in a rush. "And then…I was kissing her back." She hiccupped and fought back fresh tears.

Sandy was silent—which rarely happened—then she said, "Wow."

"No! Don't say *wow*. It's not wow."

"Okay, okay. I'm sorry." Sandy sounded sheepish. "But it's not the end of the world. Come on. We're the trailer park twins.

We don't fall apart over a kiss. The TPTs don't take no shit," she added in her mock drill sergeant voice left over from her venture into ROTC. "Remember?"

Jessie's short laugh through another hiccup turned into a snort. Sandy's voice, her tone, the strength in it, began to calm her.

"It's okay. And not all that surprising, if you think about it." Sandy was winding up for a full-on pep talk. "You said you could still feel that crush thing from when you were a kid. You knew it was still there. This was just a mistake. We've all kissed someone who was a mistake."

Jessie wanted to be consoled by the words, but she knew they didn't apply here. She'd felt that kiss in her bones. "No, Sandy." She squeezed her eyes shut. "This wasn't a childhood crush kiss. This was..." She couldn't even finish the sentence.

"You can still put it behind you. It doesn't have to happen again or alter anything." Sandy sounded so certain.

But Jessie wasn't sure. She could still feel Dakota's mouth on hers, still taste it, still hear her own soft moan as their tongues touched. She was afraid it *would* alter things if she couldn't make herself forget it. She had to get a grip. She listened as Sandy went on, not to the words so much, but to the calming presence Sandy had always been for her. She drew in a deep breath.

"It'll be okay...didn't do anything wrong...just a moment that can be moved past...it'll all feel different in the morning," Sandy was saying. She was soothing, reassuring. "As soon as she knows who you are—"

"She does," Jessie said with a sniffle.

"What?"

"I told her after the kiss. I just blurted it out." Jessie felt her face heat with embarrassment.

Sandy hesitated. "What'd she say?"

Jessie had to think. She wasn't sure she even remembered. "She said she didn't know Jackie had a sister."

"That's it?" Sandy asked, clearly incredulous. "That's *all*?"

Then Jessie recalled Dakota's face, her expression. "She went pale, Sandy. She looked at me like I was Jackie's ghost, not her sister." Jessie sickened. Had that been what she'd wanted? A part of her did. The part that still missed Jackie so much, that still felt robbed of her and didn't understand what happened that night, wanted to know she wasn't alone in it. She wanted to know that it still affected Dakota, still haunted her as well. It'd always infuriated her to think that Dakota just forgot it all, like Jessie's mother insisted had happened when Dakota left for college. That look in Dakota's eyes, though, the horror, made Jessie reconsider. Did she really wish her own pain from that night on someone else?

"Jess?" Sandy's voice cut in. "You there?"

Jessie sighed. "I'm here. I'm a terrible person."

"You are not." Sandy scoffed.

"I shouldn't have dumped it on her like that, then just run out." Jessie wondered what Dakota was doing, what she was thinking. Had she recovered from the shock?

"So you'll apologize for that," Sandy said. "And probably for the kiss, knowing you."

"What do you mean by that?" Jessie felt her defenses go up. That was ridiculous, though. This was her bestie she was talking to.

"It's just what you do. You almost always take the high road, so you'll apologize for the kiss, even though she started it."

Jessie replayed the situation in her mind. "She didn't know who she was kissing. I did," she said finally.

"See, that's what I'm talking about. Regardless, once the apology is made, you can both put it behind you, and you can get to your task of reconciling yourself with your past in Small Town USA and get home. I miss you," Sandy said tenderly. "You can check Facing Dakota Scott off your bucket list. I'd say kissing her counts as facing her."

Did it? Jessie didn't know. It felt like the events of tonight had opened a door between them—not only the kiss but what Dakota had shared about her mother, and the intimacy of being in Dakota's house. All of it had felt like a beginning, not the closure of something that could now be checked off of a list. Maybe Sandy was right, though. Maybe once Jessie got some time and distance between tonight and the light of day tomorrow, it would feel different. And an apology could go a long way. As for the reveal of who Jessie was… She wasn't sure, now that it'd happened, what she'd wanted from it. If it'd simply been to know Dakota remembered, well…Dakota definitely remembered.

"Yoo-hoo. Where do you keep going?" Sandy asked.

"I'm sorry." Jessie laughed softly. "Maybe you're right. I'm probably making more of this than it is."

"Of course I'm right. You should know that by now."

A low murmur drifted through the phone.

"It's okay, honey. Go back to sleep," Sandy said, the words muffled.

More murmuring.

"Well, now I have to go," Sandy said. "I woke up Bethany."

"Wait. What did you call about?" Jessie asked quickly.

"I don't know. I just woke up and knew I needed to call you." Sandy yawned. "Let me know what happens."

When Jessie returned her phone to her pocket, she looked around to get her bearings. She'd been walking the whole time she and Sandy had been talking and wasn't sure where she was. Wasn't that how she'd ended up in Dakota's neighborhood? She had to start paying closer attention.

Many of the back roads around Clearwater Springs looked the same, especially in the dark. Two lanes, shrubbery and trees along the shoulder, twists and turns. Jessie wasn't worried, though. She knew them all like she knew her own name. She didn't remember turning off the main road, but she must have, because she was heading west. Could she be…She rounded a curve, and there it was, that place from her past, that bend in the road—Brogan's Bend.

It'd been dubbed that when she was in high school through no one's fault but her own. She'd started going out there, sneaking out after her mother was asleep, on nights when she felt so deeply alone she couldn't stand it. At first, she merely wanted to see it—the place where both her father and her sister had died—but she'd felt such a sense of peace there, a sense of closeness to those she'd lost, she kept coming back. She could sit there for hours, gazing at the stars and the moonlit meadow across the road, listening to the night. It'd surprised her that the place didn't bother her, didn't bring up images of the two accidents, but maybe since she didn't actually know much about how either had happened, there wasn't anything to picture. She'd wondered sometimes, but mostly being there soothed her soul.

Then one night, when she'd been sitting in the shadows among the trees, a car had come around the bend and skidded to a stop. She'd recognized it as belonging to the quarterback of the football team. Several boys stumbled out, staggered toward some bushes as they'd unzipped their pants, and started to relieve themselves. She'd hated them for their disrespect and irreverence, then realized this place was only sacred to her. As quietly as she could, she'd risen and tried to make her way down the side of the road.

"Oh, fuck! What's that?" one boy said, his speech slurred.

"Christ! Let's get outta here," another one said.

In seconds, they were back in the car and speeding off. By lunchtime the next day at school, Jessie had heard about the ghost out on Hightower Road, where *that Brogan girl and her father both died.* Because every haunted spot needed a cool name, it'd quickly become Brogan's Bend, where kids dared their friends to go face the ghosts. Jessie had been spotted as the ghost a couple more times, but usually she kept herself hidden if anyone arrived. She wondered if kids still came out there.

She walked slowly up the road to where it curved. Hands in her jacket pockets, she stood and stared across the pavement, through the gap in the trees, and over the tall grass of the meadow, silver tipped in the moonlight. She hadn't been out here since she'd returned, but it had hardly changed—the underbrush was thicker, the trees a little taller in the sky—but for all intents and purposes, it could have been thirty years earlier. She'd always thought it strange that a place of such tragedy could be so beautiful. Shouldn't it be marked somehow, marred with some symbol of what had happened there? A charred tree, split by lightning? An ugly, bare patch of ground where nothing would grow? But here it was, as gorgeous as ever.

Jessie crossed the road, ducked through the shadows of the undergrowth and trees, and found the wide, flat rock that she used to sit on. The moment seemed frozen in time. She settled onto it and lay back. The overhead branches were thicker than they used to be, obscuring the view of the stars beginning to peek through the parting clouds, but she could still appreciate the beauty. Just like it had been in her teens, everything fell away, all of life's problems and questions, all worries and concerns. Solace surrounded and engulfed her.

Maybe it was the presence of her father and Jackie she felt here that comforted her. She knew *she* was the only ghost that had ever actually been seen out here, but perhaps some remnants of her father's and Jackie's essences lingered where they'd spent their last moments and touched her in some way when she made herself available to it. She didn't know. All she knew was that she felt something here that she'd never felt anywhere else. She closed her eyes and allowed it to overtake her.

When she heard the rumble of an engine, she had no idea how long she'd been lying there, if she'd fallen asleep or simply let her mind wander. The car moved slowly, creeping onto the shoulder of the road, loose rocks and tree debris crunching beneath its tires. The flutter of Jessie's eyelids opening was her only movement. She listened.

A car door opened. Then another. Whispers. The scuffling of feet.

A voice. Female. A teenage girl. "This is too scary. I want to go back."

"Shhh." Someone else.

Jessie frowned, irritation wriggling through her like a baby snake. She wanted to lie there just a little longer in her solitude, in the comfort of this special place she considered hers, before she had to start thinking about the next day, her lesson plans, a meeting after school, an apology. But the suspension of time and thought that always seemed to rule here had been shattered. She was back in the physical world that demanded a response. It was time.

She sat up, her muscles stiff from lying on cold stone, the seat of her jeans wet from the rain water she'd ignored when she'd sat on the rock. She knew all she had to do was stand up, maybe make some rustling noises in the underbrush, just enough to draw the attention of the intruders. Then they'd look her way, see her silhouette in the moonlight. There might be a scream and certainly a mad rush back to the car, and then they'd race off into the night, leaving nothing but a cloud of dust and a story to tell. Jessie almost smiled through her annoyance. *They should be home in bed anyway.*

She rose and let the scene unfold exactly as she'd known it would, then started the long walk back to the reality of her life.

Dakota rubbed her eyes. They burned from interrupted sleep and tears she'd failed to fight back. She'd dumped a half bottle of Visine into them earlier that morning in hopes of clearing out the redness, but it hadn't done the job completely. She'd considered calling in for a sub but needed the distraction of work to ward off the memories of the previous night as well as those of thirty years earlier. She flipped on the lights in the gym and adjusted the thermostat, then returned to the locker room to wait for her first period class to dress out.

Some of the girls were still filing in, others already changing clothes. All were chattering like wild monkeys. Locker doors clanged open and shut.

Dakota's head pounded. She took the four steps up to her office in two quick strides.

"Hey, Paige," someone called above the din. "Did you hear that Jeff, Cameron, and Madison saw the ghost last night?"

Dakota jerked to a stop to listen, her heart racing.

"No way," Paige yelled back. "Jeff's full of it. There's no ghost."

"He swears. Madison, too." The other girl was Lisa Hamblin, always instigating something. "Anyone want to head out to Brogan's Bend tonight and see for ourselves?"

Dakota cringed, then clenched her jaw at the pithy moniker that had been given to the place that'd had such a devastating impact on her life. "That's enough." Her voice boomed out over the space.

The locker room went silent. All the girls stared at her, wide-eyed.

She knew the kids went out there sometimes, and she hated it. She'd always ignored it, though. That's what she should have done now, but she'd already started this, so she had to finish somehow. They were all waiting. She had to say something. "And if I hear of *anyone* being out there, I won't even ask for names. Every single one of you will be running laps all next week." Okay, that probably wasn't the best thing, but it was out now. She'd have to back it. *God damn, Jessie Brogan.* What the hell was she doing here anyway? Clearly, she'd been gone for decades. Why couldn't she have stayed gone? Dakota stomped into her office and slammed the door.

She flopped into her desk chair and rested her head in her hands. *Brogan's Bend. When the hell had it been nicknamed that?* No one had called it that before she'd left for college, but then, she'd only been in Clearwater Springs for another year, her senior year, after the accident. And when she came home for visits, she never went anyplace where she would have heard it. When she'd moved home, though, all the kids called it that—because of the ghost. *Christ!* Why hadn't someone warned her? Drew or Crystal, at least. *Because you won't let anyone talk about that night or its events.* A gentle reminder from her inner voice diluted some of the anger.

And why now? Why today? Why couldn't she have gotten through the day without having to deal with anything else to do with that time in her life? She'd managed to avoid Jessica Weldon when she'd gotten to school this morning. *Jessica Weldon.* Maybe she could go back to thinking of her as Jessica Weldon, and put that other name out of her mind.

It's Jessie. The caress of Jessie's voice in that moment whispered through Dakota. She remembered how warm it'd felt.

But had there really been warmth, or had Jessie simply been laying the groundwork for the final blow? *My name is Jessie Brogan. I'm Jackie Brogan's sister.* She chilled at the impact of those words.

What about the kiss, though? Sure, Dakota had started it, but Jessie had responded. And what a response. Dakota hadn't been able to form a thought with Jessie's mouth moving against hers, Jessie's body molded to her. In that moment, would she have cared that it was Jackie Brogan's sister she was kissing?

A rap sounded on the door.

Dakota waved her first period class assistant into the office.

"Coach Scott?" Kylie was also one of Dakota's volleyball players. "We're lined up. Do you want me to take roll?"

"Yeah," Dakota said, her tone still sharper than she wanted, but she couldn't seem to help it. She pulled the attendance book from her top drawer and tossed it across the desk. "I'll be out in a second."

The morning dragged like a bad movie. Dakota ignored any minor infractions, like the three students that lingered way too long at the drinking fountain in deep conversation and the girl in second period who wore flowered shorts instead of the required solid green, so as not to bark out another ridiculous consequence she'd have to follow through on. At the end of third period, Mel showed up at Dakota's office door and tapped lightly on the jamb. "Are you okay, Coach? You don't look so good."

Dakota hesitated. She couldn't deny the obvious. "Just a rough night. I didn't sleep well." She waited. "Is there something you need?" There it was again, that sharpness. She winced inwardly. *Damn Jessie Brogan.*

"Oh, uh. I just wanted to tell you I brought my lunch today, so we won't be late to Ms. Weldon's room."

Dakota felt like she was sinking into the floor. *Ms. Weldon's room. Lunch. Shit.*

"You know, so she won't be mad again."

"Yeah, okay." Did she have to do this, too? Mel was sixteen, for God's sake. Did she really need her hand held just to get some tutoring? "Look, Mel—"

"Coach, you promised," Mel said in a rush, obviously reading Dakota's thoughts.

Mel was right. Dakota had promised she'd go with her for a while, at least until Mel was more comfortable with…*Jessie? Ms. Weldon.* Yes, Ms. Weldon. She had to think of her as Ms. Weldon. *It's Jessie.* Dakota flinched. "All right. I'll meet you at the end of the east wing."

Mel sighed with evident relief. "Thanks." She smiled. "See you later."

Right. Later.

At the beginning of lunch period, Dakota waited at the designated spot. She hadn't bothered with food for herself. She doubted she'd be able to eat anyway.

The kid from the previous day—what was his name—the one with no lunch, rounded the corner and swerved past her. His gait caught as he looked down the hall.

Dakota followed his gaze to three football players standing at the midway point. She knew them from the school athletic league. They seemed all right. She met Justin Byrd's eyes, and in an instant, he turned and walked the other way, his friends in tow. *Odd.*

The kid—Ian, that was it—glanced at her.

She gave him a nod. "Something going on there?"

Ian shook his head and continued on his way, but she didn't miss the relief in his eyes.

Dakota had heard about the fight that'd taken place the previous week in the boys' locker room, but had only started putting the pieces together as to the participants when she'd seen the result on Ian's face in Jessica Weldon's room. She'd assumed he was the loser of the altercation. Now she knew the winners, although, from the stitches in Dale Simpson's lip and Randy Damian's black eye, it seemed Ian had gotten in a few good licks as well. Supposedly, he'd started trouble with the three and paid the price for it, according to the head football coach. After witnessing this current exchange, though, Dakota doubted it. How stupid would Ian have to be to pick a fight with three linebackers?

"Hey, Coach," Mel said, a little breathless as she trotted up beside Dakota. She carried a lunch sack.

Dakota shook off the question about the boys and took a deep breath. *Let's get this over with.* "Hey, yourself." She draped an arm around Mel's shoulders, and they followed Ian.

Dakota steeled herself as she stepped into the classroom, then came up short. Mrs. Dennison, a regular and well-liked substitute, sat behind the teacher's desk. Where the hell was Jessie? Jessica? Ms. Weldon? *Damn it! What the hell am I supposed to call her now?*

"Hello, Coach Scott." Mrs. Dennison smiled.

"Hi, Mrs. Dennison. How are you?"

"I'm well, dear."

Dakota knew a little more chitchat might be in order, but she didn't have it in her. "So Ms. Weldon isn't here?" She sounded like a moron. *Of course she isn't here. Ergo, the substitute.* "I mean, is she sick?" She certainly wasn't sick thirteen hours ago. Apprehension crept in with a new thought. *Did something happen to her walking home so late?* Dakota tensed. *I should have driven her.*

"I'm not sure. I just got a call this morning asking if I could cover her classes," Mrs. Dennison said. "And, Mel." She held out some papers. "She left instructions for you to continue working on your story. She read through what you wrote yesterday and made some corrections and comments she'd like you to take into account in your work today."

"Okay," Mel said, her tone relaxed. She took the pages and settled into a seat across from Ian.

Well, nothing too bad could have happened to her if she'd prepared for a tutoring student in addition to all of her classes. So why wasn't she here? Had the events of the previous night been so terrible she couldn't come to work? Dakota had come to work, and that had been no picnic for her either. And Dakota had endured the anxiety and anticipation of their first face-to-face with this new revelation between them—what to say, how to act, what it meant—and Jessie wasn't even here. *Jessie. Shit. Jessica Weldon.*

And what did *she* have to be upset about anyway? *She'd* known who she was. And she'd known who Dakota was all along. She wasn't the one who'd been blindsided. She was the one who'd brought the past crashing in.

Mrs. Dennison was saying something. Was she talking to Dakota? "I'm sorry, what did you say?"

Mrs. Dennison chuckled. "I said that Mel will be busy working on her story the whole period, so there won't be anything you need to hear. Ms. Weldon said you wouldn't need to stay."

Oh, Ms. Weldon said that, did she? Dakota was being dismissed by someone who couldn't even be bothered to show up. She seethed. "Fine." She glanced at Mel.

Mel reached into her lunch bag, then leaned across the aisle and set a sandwich on Ian's desk.

Ian eyed it, then Mel.

"Just take it and say thank you," Mel whispered. She turned her attention to her own lunch and the papers in front of her.

Dakota did a double take. *What the hell?* Had the whole world changed overnight? At least Mel's change was for the better. Dakota wasn't sure about her own. "I guess I'll take off," she said to Mrs. Dennison, but her mind was still on Jessie. Why wasn't she here? And why was Dakota so mad about it? She shoved her hands into her pockets as she stalked out the door. And why the hell couldn't she get those two soft words out of her head? *It's Jessie.*

Chapter Seven

When Jessie had finally gotten home the night before, it'd been close to three in the morning. She'd tried to sleep, but each time she'd closed her eyes, she was back in Dakota's house, back at Brogan's Bend, her thoughts and emotions in a whirl. The composure she'd managed to grasp while talking to Sandy was suddenly slippery and amorphous, as though she were trying to sculpt a statue from a glob of pudding. She kept seeing the vulnerability in Dakota's expression when Dakota had shared about her mother, kept feeling Dakota's fingers in her hair, Dakota's lips on her mouth, their bodies pressed to one another. Her conflict kept resurfacing—the memory of feeling so drawn to Dakota in that moment, while at the same time, trying so desperately to maintain her distance. To do what she'd promised herself she'd do—tell Dakota who she was. And then, the horror and pain in Dakota's eyes when she'd done that very thing had shocked her.

Then there was Jessie's doubt. It'd seemed so important to make sure Dakota knew she was Jackie's sister, knew the part she'd played in Jessie's painful past. After seeing the raw ache in Dakota's eyes, though, Jessie wondered. *Why had it been so important?* What had she thought it would do?

Exasperated, she'd flung off the covers, lurched from bed, and stalked to the kitchen to whip up some fresh cinnamon rolls as a surprise for Curtis and the motel guests when they woke. Then she'd settled at the table in the warmth of the kitchen to enjoy one with a cup of tea. Her mind wouldn't settle, though. Her thoughts shifted from Dakota the previous night to facing her in the light of morning. *What will I say?* What would either of them say? She dreaded the awkwardness of the moment. Eventually, her exhaustion had caught up with her, but by then, it was time to start getting ready for work. Instead, she'd uncharacteristically called in for a sub, emailed her instructions, and crawled back into bed—for sleep, of course. She wasn't avoiding Dakota. She simply needed some rest.

When she'd awakened at three thirty in the afternoon, she did feel rested, but almost wished she'd gone to work that morning. That way, she would have already faced Dakota, and however things were going to be between them would be established by now. As it was, the anticipation and anxiety of that moment of seeing her, saying whatever it was she was going to say, still hovered over her. At least she wouldn't have to deal with it until tomorrow.

She stood in front of the pantry and wondered what Curtis might like for dinner. It was one of the things she enjoyed most about being home—taking care of him. He and Laura had done so much for her, and she'd missed him. He was obviously feeling better, since he wasn't anywhere in the house, and she assumed he was working the office and tending to whatever needed handling. She glanced out the window above the kitchen sink just in time to see him step around the front corner of the motel and point toward the house. He was talking to someone behind him.

Dakota rounded the corner and seemed to look directly at Jessie.

Dakota? Instinctively, she ducked to the side, then peered through the window once more, still trying to stay out of sight. What was Dakota doing there?

Before Jessie could even guess, Dakota moved down the steps and started across the gravel lot toward the back door of the house. Her strides were long. She carried herself with characteristic assurance, but her eyes were hidden behind dark glasses, her expression veiled. Her mouth was set.

Her mouth. Jessie felt the heat of it on her own, then fought a full response as the arousal from the night before threatened to reignite. She snapped herself back to here, to now, to what was about to happen.

Dakota was almost to the steps of the back porch.

Jessie looked down at herself. She wore old, faded blue sweat pants and an oversized, threadbare New England Patriots football jersey she'd snagged in the breakup from Shelly for its comfort. No bra. No shoes. And no time to do a damned thing about any of it.

A loud knock rattled the door.

Jessie was frozen in place. Was there a way out of this? Could she simply pretend she wasn't there? Curtis had clearly told Dakota she was, though, and she might have seen her before she'd moved away from the window. Besides, her car was parked right outside, next to the house.

Dakota knocked again.

It was possible for someone not to hear a knock, right? She could be in the shower. But she wasn't. She was standing right there, a mere eight feet from Dakota with only a wall between them. If she moved six inches to the left, Dakota would probably be able to see her through the small window at the top of the door. Jessie sighed and ran her hands through her hair, trying to make it look like she hadn't rolled out of bed an hour earlier. She opened the door. "Coach Scott," was all she said in greeting.

Tension crackled between them.

Dakota's head dipped slightly, but she didn't say anything.

Jessie couldn't tell where she was looking. The tinting on Dakota's sunglasses was too dark. Her bare feet? Her ratty sweats? Her breasts? Her nipples tightened at the last thought. Her face heated with embarrassment.

Dakota cleared her throat. "I, uh…" One hand went to her hip, the other to the back of her neck. "I wanted to make sure you were okay."

Of all the things Jessie might have expected, this was not one. "You what?"

"When you weren't at school today, I just..." Dakota scratched beneath her ponytail.

Jessie remembered how thick and lush Dakota's hair had been the night before when she'd freed it from its band to dry it in front of the fire. She'd wanted so badly to touch it, to feel it, to bury her hands in it where it fell around Dakota's shoulders. She couldn't think about that now.

"You know," Dakota was saying. "It was late when you left. And dark. And wet. And...you know...you were upset."

Mr. and Mrs. Wilson, an older couple staying at the motel on a visit with their grandkids, came around the corner of the office on their way to their car. They smiled and gave Jessie a cheerful wave.

Great. If she stood here in the open doorway long enough, half the world could see her in her SSA—Secret Single Attire. She returned a weak smile and wiggled her fingers at the couple. "Can you come in?" she said to Dakota with resignation.

Dakota stepped through the doorway and removed her glasses, positioning them on top of her head. She squinted slightly against the late afternoon sunlight streaming through the windows. Her eyes were bloodshot, obvious sleeplessness bruising the tender flesh beneath them.

I'd look the same if I hadn't gone back to sleep. "May I get you something?" she asked, remembering there was such a thing as manners. "Coffee? Or I have herbal tea."

"Coffee would be great." Dakota scanned the kitchen. Her gaze returned to Jessie and held. She seemed to be searching Jessie's face for something.

Jessie squirmed inwardly, still self-conscious of her appearance, what she was wearing, and what she wasn't. She moved toward the counter and lifted the carafe of the coffeemaker. "This is from this morning. It'll only take a minute to make a fresh pot."

"No, that's okay. Don't bother. Just nuke it. It'll be fine." Dakota's tone was distracted.

Jessie looked over her shoulder to find Dakota still staring at her. *What does she want?* She filled a cup and placed it in the microwave. She wasn't going to argue. She wanted to get on with this, whatever this was.

"Are you?" Dakota asked.

Jessie tilted her head, confused. "Am I what?"

"Are you okay?" Dakota said. "I mean, you look okay, but… you didn't fall or anything, did you?"

Something wasn't right. Granted, Jessie didn't know Dakota well at all, but her usual confidence, her cockiness, seemed shaky. Jessie could tell she was trying to hold it in place, but it kept slipping, just a little. She wondered what was underneath. "I'm fine. Nothing happened to me last night." *Nothing but that kiss.* She motioned to the dinette. "Would you like to sit?"

Indecision passed through Dakota's eyes, but she pulled out a chair. "Okay."

The microwave dinged, and Jessie retrieved the cup. "Cream or sugar?" she asked.

"Black's good."

Jessie joined Dakota and slid the coffee across the table. And there they were, all social amenities dispensed with and ready for…

"I'm sorry—" Jessie said in the exact instant Dakota said, "I don't—" They both halted.

Jessie laughed nervously. "Go ahead."

"No. That's all right. You go." Dakota gave a little smile, but it seemed forced.

Jessie wondered about the contradiction, then took the invitation at face value. "I just wanted to say I'm sorry for last night. For blurting out who I am. I mean, I planned to tell you, but not like that." She hesitated. Did she really mean this next part? "And for the kiss," she said finally. "I shouldn't have—"

"I kissed you," Dakota said flatly.

"I know, but I should have stopped it sooner. I shouldn't have let it happen at all."

"Why did you?" Dakota's gaze was intense, her expression inscrutable.

Is she mad? Jessie looked away. She had no intention of admitting to the crush she'd had on Dakota so long ago, or to her current curiosity about being close to her. And the truth was, she hadn't seen it coming. She squared her shoulders and looked directly into Dakota's questioning expression. "I was so busy watching you for signs that you remembered me or had figured out for yourself that I was Jackie's sister, I missed the signals. Normally, I'm better at that, but you caught me off guard."

Dakota had shown no interest in actually drinking her coffee, but she tapped her fingertips against the side of the mug as she studied Jessie.

Why is she here? Jessie wished she'd simply say what she wanted. She held herself still, refusing to allow Dakota to make her fidget.

"I didn't know Jackie had a sister." Dakota's stare never wavered. It was unnerving.

Irritation prickled beneath Jessie's patience. "Yes. I'm clear on that."

"Why didn't I know that?"

"I think we covered that last night," Jessie said flatly.

"Oh yeah." Dakota nodded, as though remembering. "Because I'm a self-absorbed Scott who doesn't care about anything or anyone but herself. But really. Why didn't I at least hear about a kid sister who was left behind?"

Jessie felt a twinge of remorse for her blunt words the previous evening. Maybe she should try to answer Dakota's questions. After all, Dakota had come over to check on her—and pump her for information, it seemed—but still… She sighed. "I don't know. Maybe because you were gone those first few months immediately following the accident, when most of the talk was going on. And I was younger. I was still in junior high when you and your friends were seniors. By the time I hit high school, you were gone."

Dakota studied her. "Why is your name Weldon, not Brogan?"

"I was married," Jessie said reluctantly. She didn't intend to share her whole life story. "The divorce from Shelley wasn't final when I…" She let her answer trail off along with Dakota's gaze.

"Why are you here?" Dakota asked, clearly not caring about the unfinished response.

Jessie lifted an incredulous eyebrow, her defenses rising with it. "I live here. You came to see me."

"No. Why are you in Clearwater Springs? I mean, obviously you left. Why did you come back?" Dakota asked, though she sounded as though she was trying to figure out the answer for herself.

There were so many ways to respond to that. *To heal my heart. To take on this town that I've felt for so long stole everyone from me. To reconnect with Curtis. To let go of the past. And apparently, to make peace with you.* She wasn't about to share any of that with Dakota, though. "It's personal."

Dakota nodded slowly. "Right. Personal." She rested an elbow on the table and rubbed her eyes. "Then why didn't you keep it that way? Why'd you have to tell me you're Jackie Brogan's sister?"

Jessie flinched at the sting of Dakota's tone. She leaned back in her chair and folded her hands in front of her. She tried to think of a lie, just a small one to get them through the moment, but the only thing that came was the truth, a truth she hadn't fully realized until she opened her mouth to speak. "I've always wanted you to know there were consequences to what happened that night. There were a lot of things said back then, and I don't know what's true, but—"

"So you don't mean consequences to what happened. You mean consequences for what *I* did. And you don't know if I was joy riding, or drunk, or high on something. You don't know if the police buried the results of a tox screen, or didn't bother doing one at all because of my family, like your mother told everyone." Dakota's voice rose. "I, of all people, know there were consequences. I don't need you, no matter who you are, to tell me that."

"I didn't mean—"

"Yes, you did." Dakota's expression hardened. "You meant the same thing everyone else means when they have something to say about what happened. But you know what? Nobody knows what happened. There were only three people out there on the road that night. One of them is dead, and the other two can't agree. So what makes you or anyone else think—"

"All I'd like to know is if there's any truth to those things that have been said." Jessie's own temper flared.

"Why? So you can know for sure it was my fault? You think, after all this time, I'm going to say? 'Oh yeah, since you're Jackie's sister, sure I'd be happy to tell you I was drunk. I'd had a whole fifth of whiskey and couldn't even see the line down the middle of the road, much less someone standing in the dark on the side.'" The pulse in her neck pounded visibly. "Is that what you thought I'd say?"

The words hit Jessie like a hammer. "Is that the truth?" she asked. Somehow, though, she knew it wasn't. It didn't fit with who Dakota had seemed to be. None of the things Jessie's mother had said did. Jessie's mother had needed someone to blame, though, and once Jessie had heard the whisperings of what Drew had said, she did too. She'd only been thirteen and needed something to hold on to other than a devastating possibility.

"Why should I tell you?" Dakota scoffed. "Is it going to make you feel better somehow to finally know it's okay to blame me, to hate me? That it's legitimate?" She was on her feet, shoving the chair beneath the table. "It's not my job to make you feel better."

Jessie's anger ignited fully. She rose to meet Dakota. "My sister's dead, and has been for a long time. My mother died when I was fifteen, having never recovered from losing Jackie."

Dakota folded her arms tightly across her chest. "Oh, now I killed your mother, too?"

"I didn't say that. I'm just trying to figure out how…" *Oh, my God!* What had she been about to reveal—that she was trying to make peace with losing everyone she'd loved as a child so she could let herself love and be loved now? *Speaking of personal.* It'd taken a lot of hours in therapy to even admit that to herself. She wasn't about to blurt it out here.

"You implied it," Dakota yelled. "And I'm not taking it on. I have enough to deal with, and now, apparently, I have you. I've spent my entire adult life trying to forget everything that happened that night, and I resent the hell out of you showing up here now just to make me remember it all."

Jessie went rigid. "Trying to *forget* it?" Tears of rage filled her eyes. "What happened that night devastated me *and* my mother. She never recovered. Other than Jackie's funeral, she spent months in bed, too depressed to function. After that, she only went through the motions of life. She was an empty shell. I'd lost my sister, and didn't even have a mother I could turn to. And *you've* spent your whole life trying to *forget*?"

"Welcome to the club of having a messed up family," Dakota yelled.

The back door opened, and Curtis stepped in from outside. "Ladies? Everything okay in here?" he asked cautiously. He looked at Jessie, concern shaping his features. "We can hear you all the way out front."

Jessie turned away, furious with herself for breaking down in front of Dakota. She slapped at her tears.

"I was just leaving," Dakota said, the jangle of her keys loud in the suddenly silent kitchen. "I'm sorry, Mr. Knight." Then, she was gone.

Curtis crossed to Jessie and took her into his arms. "Easy, Jessie girl."

She clung to him, overwhelmed by all the memories cresting over her, one right after another, of that night and the months and years that followed. She sobbed. Maybe Dakota was on to something. Maybe forgetting was the way to go.

Although, if the past eighteen hours were any indication, it didn't seem to have helped Dakota all that much.

Dakota stomped up the back steps to Drew and Selena's kitchen door. She'd known exactly where she'd find him as soon as she checked her watch after leaving the Triple M. He'd be in the kitchen with Selena, one of them preparing dinner while the other one sat at the bar keeping the cook company. It'd been their ritual for years. Sometimes it included Randy, others, just the two of them.

She hoped she could discreetly get Drew alone for a while. She was still so mad. She had to talk to him about what happened, about Jessie Brogan. She had to know if he'd known of her existence. She couldn't do it with Selena or Randy there, though. She'd never spoken of the topic with anyone but Drew or professionals, and with her emotions so raw and exposed, now wasn't the time to start.

"Anybody home?" Dakota asked as she pushed open the door and walked in.

"Hey, Dakota," Selena said over her shoulder from where she stood, chopping veggies on the cutting board. She stilled her hands. "Oh, wow. I was going to ask you to sit down and convince your brother that his day couldn't have been as awful as he thinks, but you look like yours was worse. I'm not sure I want you anywhere near him." Her gray eyes flashed with humor, and the laugh lines around her mouth deepened as she smiled.

"Thanks," Dakota said, drawing out the word. "I can always count on being cheered up when I come here."

Drew chuckled, his own eyes sparkling with amusement. He and Dakota had always looked quite a bit alike. All four of them did—Crystal, Drew, Dakota, and Tina—the same coloring as their mother, their father's easy grin. Drew had a rugged look to him, though, his face tanned and weathered from working the ranch all his life. "What's up, little sister?" Drew asked, disregarding Selena's remark about Dakota's appearance.

Dakota shrugged. "I just thought I'd stop by and mooch some dinner." She sniffed the air. "Lasagna?"

"It'll be done in about a half an hour," Selena said, her tone casual, but Dakota knew she didn't buy it. She knew Dakota too well.

Dakota slid onto an empty stool beside Drew. "So what's up with you?" she asked him.

"Oh, just one of those days, running around putting out fires, but never actually getting anything done. You know the kind."

Dakota nodded, but that hadn't been her day today. If there'd been any fires she should have put out, they'd have burned the school to the ground. She'd been too distracted to notice.

Selena slid a small bowl of cucumber slices across the bar to her.

Dakota frowned. "What? I don't get a whole salad?"

"They're for your eyes," Selena said, then turned back to her task and started cutting up a tomato.

"My eyes?" Dakota asked blankly.

Selena turned back around. "They'll get rid of all this puffiness and those dark circles." She motioned toward Dakota's face with her knife.

Dakota glanced at Drew.

He lifted a shoulder. "I'd do what she says. She's usually right."

"How can eating cucumbers make your eyes look better?" The question came out as a grumble.

"You don't eat them," Selena said. "You—"

The back door opened.

"Ready, Selena?" Randy stepped into the kitchen. "Hi, Dakota."

"Hey." Dakota poked at the cucumber slices suspiciously.

"Ready for what?" Drew asked.

"Oh, my gosh." Selena wiped her hands on a dish towel. "I completely forgot. Give me just a minute." She rushed from the room.

"What's up?" Drew asked Randy.

"I'm thinking about redoing my bathroom," Randy said, crossing to the bar. He gave Drew a light kiss. "Selena said she'd go with me to look at some tile and paint samples." He watched Dakota play with the vegetables. "What's that?"

"Cucumber slices," Dakota said, still perplexed. "They're for my eyes, apparently." She looked at Randy to see if he understood.

He squinted slightly and cocked his head. "Nope. No idea."

"Okay, I'm ready," Selena said, hurrying back into the room with her purse.

"What about dinner?" Drew asked. "I thought we were going to eat together."

"When the timer goes off, take the lasagna out and let it stand for five minutes. The salad's finished and ready for dressing." Selena ran her fingers through his hair, then kissed him. "I won't be long. And this will give Dakota a chance to talk with you alone about whatever's upsetting her." She smiled at Dakota and kissed her cheek.

"I still don't know what I'm supposed to do with these," Dakota said, flicking at the cucumbers.

Selena hesitated, then grabbed her by the hand. "Come here." She pulled her off the stool and into the living room.

The two men followed.

"Lie down." Selena directed Dakota to the couch, then leaned over her. She ran a cucumber slice over and around each of Dakota's closed eyes, then laid it over one. She placed another slice over the other eye. "Now, just lie there and relax until dinner's ready. You'll feel better."

"Bye, baby," Randy said, obviously to Drew. "See ya later, Dakota."

"Yeah," Dakota said. "See you." As the burn in her eyes began to subside, she heard the kitchen door close.

The room fell silent.

"I don't trust them," Drew said finally. "They're up to something."

"Like what?" Dakota asked, relaxing into the sofa.

A pause. "I don't know," Drew said, clearly thinking. The soft whoosh of the cushion as he lowered himself into the recliner was the only sound. "Oh, no."

"What?" Dakota tensed.

"A surprise birthday party," Drew said, the words tumbling out. "I'll bet that's what they're up to."

"What's wrong with that?" Dakota asked. "They love you. You should let them do it."

Drew scoffed. "It's not going to be just me. It's your birthday too, remember. And it's our fiftieth, so you know it's going to be a big deal."

Dakota groaned.

"You look ridiculous, by the way," Drew said. "You know that, right?"

"It feels good," Dakota couldn't help admitting. "There's something to this cucumber thing."

Drew grunted. "What'd you come out here for, anyway?"

Images and emotions from her encounters with Jessie returned in a rush, along with her anger. She'd managed a whole five minutes without thinking about any of that. She huffed out a breath and laced her fingers behind her head. "Did you know Jackie Brogan had a sister?"

Drew's astonishment was evident in his silence.

Dakota could feel his stare. "I didn't either," she said without waiting for an actual answer. "But she's here. In town. Working at the high school."

"At the high school?"

"She's an English teacher." Dakota found it easier to talk without being able to see Drew. "She took a long-term sub position for Jim Anderson."

"Jeez," Drew said quietly. "Well, I guess we all grow up. She was just a kid when it happened."

It took a second for Drew's meaning to sink in. Dakota swiped the cucumber slices off her eyes and sat up straight. "You knew about her?"

Drew looked dazed, as though he were gazing into the past. "Only because she was with her mom at the funeral. I never talked to her."

"Why'd you seem surprised when I mentioned her?"

He turned to Dakota. "I was just shocked you were bringing up anything about that night. How long has she been back?"

Her earlier anger flooding back in, Dakota tossed the cucumbers back into the bowl Selena had left on the coffee table. "How would I know? I didn't even know she existed. Why didn't you ever tell me?"

Drew studied her incredulously. "You really want to go there?"

"Yeah, okay, so I've never wanted to talk about it," Dakota said, jolting to her feet. "But this…" She paced the room. "*This* is important. How could you let me just run into her?"

"I forgot about her." Drew's voice rose in defense. "Like I said, she was a kid. We were seniors that next year, then went off to college. I guess by the time I came home, her mom had died, and *she* was gone, so I never thought about her again. So did you just see her name on the faculty list or something?"

"Oh, no. It couldn't be that easy." Dakota stopped pacing and ran a hand over the back of her neck, trying to ease the tension headache coming on. "No, she doesn't go by Brogan anymore. She goes by Jessie Weldon." She shot a glance at Drew.

"Ooooh." He drew out the word. "So that's who that was."

Dakota did a double take. "That's who who was? What are you talking about?"

"Over the summer, Berta met this new woman in town." Berta—Roberta Stevens—was a ranch hand that had worked for Drew at The Ghost Rider for quite a few years. She flirted with Dakota off and on, but neither was the other's type. "Went all gaga over her, but no one knew who she was." Drew met Dakota's eyes. "I mean, we didn't meet her, but no one recognized the name Jessie Weldon."

"She was here all summer?" Dakota asked.

Drew shrugged. "I guess. She and Berta went out a few times, maybe around the end of June, early July."

June? What was that? Five months ago? *How did we not run into each other?* And staying at the Triple M all that time? No, not at the Triple M—not at the motel—*behind* it, in the house where the owner lived. Curtis Knight. *What's the connection there?* And she'd dated? Berta? Dakota remembered the touch of Jessie's lips, the taste of her mouth, the soft curves of her body. A spark of jealousy flickered to life in Dakota's gut. Her mind reeled. But no, she couldn't go there. This *wasn't* Jessica Weldon. It was Jessie Brogan. *It's Jessie.* And she represented everything Dakota had tried so hard to forget.

"So how'd you come across her?" Drew asked, pulling Dakota's attention back to him.

She flopped into the chair at the other end of the coffee table. "I had to talk to her about one of my players."

Drew rolled his eyes. "You're still doing that?"

"No. I'm not, but that's a different conversation." *Sort of.* "My player's going to get extra help from Ms. Weldon and is on academic probation."

Drew nodded. "Nice."

"Anyway, we have to interact over that, and I kind of started noticing I like her."

"You mean you're attracted to her?" Drew quirked an eyebrow in evident interest.

"Yes, but I didn't know who she was then," Dakota said in her own defense. "And last night, she came to my house."

"What was she doing there?"

"I don't know. Just listen, okay?"

Drew settled back in his chair. "Listening."

"She came to my house, and she told me she used to live there…in that field. In those shitty little cottages. Remember those? And I still didn't get it, even though I knew that's where Jackie lived. There were a bunch of them. You know?" She looked at him for confirmation.

He nodded.

"And I told her about Mom." Dakota buried her face in her hands. "Christ, why did I tell her about Mom?"

"What about Mom?" Drew asked, his tone gentle.

"About those times we spent all night looking for her, wondering if she was dead." She felt Drew's next question creep up her spine and slither around her neck. She lifted her gaze to his. "No, I didn't tell her that sometimes I wished she were." *Thank God.* She pushed to her feet and began to pace again. "And I kissed her. And *then…*" She punctuated the word with a thrust of her fist. "That's when she told me she's Jackie Brogan's sister."

"Wow," Drew whispered.

"Wow? That's all you have to say?"

"No." Drew watched her. "But you're not going to like the rest."

"I don't particularly like wow," Dakota said with a glare.

"I think it might be good for you that she showed up."

Dakota couldn't believe what she was hearing. And no, she didn't like it. "How do you figure?"

"It's opening you up," Drew said. "You haven't said this much about anything to do with the accident in the entire thirty years since it happened, much less all at once. It's been eating you up, keeping it all inside. You need to get it out."

"You don't know what you're talking about."

"I know you." His voice softened. "And you've been feeling guilty this whole time for something that wasn't your fault."

A knot tightened in Dakota's stomach. "I don't know that it wasn't."

"You don't know that it was, either." He crossed to her. "You didn't see what happened, so why can't you take the word of someone who did?" He ran his hand down her arm, stroking it gently the way he did when he was testing the waters to see if she was open to comfort.

Her eyes burned again as they brimmed with tears. "She said she wanted to make sure I understood there were consequences to what happened that night." She choked on the words. It was no wonder she never wanted to talk about this. "Like I don't fucking know that. Like I don't know that Jackie Brogan died. That her mother lost a daughter." A sob wrenched free from her throat. "And now, I know that some little kid lost her big sister." Her heart felt like it was being torn into pieces. "God, Drew, can you imagine if we'd lost Crystal back then? What would we have done?"

Drew stepped close and wrapped her in a hug.

She didn't reciprocate, but she didn't resist either. She wanted the closeness—needed it—but, like always, didn't feel she deserved any comfort where this topic was concerned.

"But we didn't. And it wasn't our fault Jackie's little sister lost her. Why can't you accept that?"

Dakota slumped against Drew's chest and felt his arms tighten around her. "I don't know." She clutched his shirt. She did know, though. It was because of what had happened the one time someone had said it out loud, the morning after at the hospital. Jackie's mother had gone into hysterics. Her eyes had gone wild, and she'd thrown herself at Drew. It'd taken two deputies and an orderly to pull her off, and Drew had to have one of the lacerations from the accident re-stitched while Jackie's mother had been sedated.

It'd terrified Dakota. All of a sudden, she'd been hurled back in time to when she was seven in that moment with her own mother when she'd feared for her life. She hadn't told anyone because she was afraid they'd send her mother away, and afterward because she couldn't say the words. Following the incident with Jackie's mother and Drew, Dakota had sunk into a corner and cried uncontrollably, until she too had been sedated. When she'd awakened, she learned that her father had made arrangements for her to go to a private inpatient clinic to get help with her recovery from the trauma of hitting and killing her classmate. Had she stayed in Clearwater Springs for that summer, had she been able to attend Jackie's funeral, she would have known about Jessie Brogan. Maybe she would have been prepared for the possibility of her showing up one day. *Maybe*.

"I think it's time, Dakota," Drew whispered in her ear.

Dakota snaked her arms around his waist and hung on. She shook her head against his shoulder. "I can't."

"You already are, Kota Bear." He kissed her temple. "It's already started. Let it come out."

"I can't cope with her." Dakota sobbed. "It's too much."

Drew settled into the recliner and pulled her into his lap, still holding her tightly. "You don't have to." He began to rock. "Just deal with her as much as you have to professionally, but you don't have to seek her out. But let all these feelings out. Let go of the guilt. Believe me when I say it wasn't your fault. Let's finally talk about it…when you're ready."

Dakota burrowed into him. He was so solid, so strong. He'd always been her rock. Could she talk about it, just to him? She felt herself beginning to calm. Only him. Not Jessie Brogan.

He stroked her back, soothing her. "Just me," he whispered.

Maybe. She swallowed hard. *Maybe just him.*

Chapter Eight

Jessie watched the clock. As the second hand ticked away a minute, then another—and another—she grew tenser. It was one week to the day since Dakota had first walked into Jessie's classroom to discuss Melinda Jenson, but everything between them had changed in that short amount of time. Neither one of them was who the other had thought her to be.

Dakota had believed Jessie to be just another substitute teacher that filled in when needed, a newbie to Clearwater Springs, and perhaps a woman to win over with her charm. Jessie had thought Dakota was still nothing more than an entitled rich kid—albeit grown—that did whatever she wanted in life with no consequences and no regard for anything or anyone she left in her wake. But now, Dakota knew exactly who Jessie was, and Jessie knew Dakota had definitely been affected by what she'd done so many years ago—and, clearly, still was.

In addition, now there was even more between them that felt unresolved. There was still the bare truth of the night that linked them, whatever that truth was. There were angry words. And there was the kiss and the feel of their bodies pressed together, the knowledge, presumably on both their parts, of an undeniable attraction between them, that Jessie, at least, had no idea what to do with.

The fact remained, however, that they had to work together. They had Melinda's best interest and academic well-being to keep under consideration as well as that of the other students Dakota had referred to. Maintaining a professional relationship was imperative, regardless of anything else.

When Jessie heard Dakota's voice in the hallway, she straightened, steadied herself, and pretended to be absorbed in something on her computer screen. She waited until Dakota and Melinda were all the way in the room and Melinda had taken a seat before looking up.

Dakota hovered between the door and Jessie's desk.

"Coach Scott," Jessie said in greeting. She smiled politely, but her heartbeat quickened with anxiety.

"Ms. Weldon," Dakota said, shifting from one foot to the other. "Mel said you were going to go over parts of speech with her for her vocabulary tests. Is it okay if I sit in?" Her manner was courteous and respectful, but gone was the cocky, flirty Dakota.

Good. That absence will make things easier. But Jessie felt the slightest twinge of disappointment too. "Of course," she said, collecting the week's vocab folder and moving toward Melinda's desk. "It will help you quiz Melinda for the test on Friday."

"All right. I'll just sit over here and listen." Dakota settled across the aisle from Melinda.

Ian rushed through the doorway. "Sorry I'm late," he said. He was breathing hard, his eyes a little frantic.

Jessie had noticed he wasn't there, but in the midst of her nerves and apprehension about what the dynamic between Dakota and her would be, she hadn't considered he was actually late. "Mr. Langston. Take a seat."

He looked at her expectantly.

Of course, he expected something, some kind of reprimand or consequence. She'd stressed her list of rules so strongly, how could he not? "And don't let it happen again." She tried to sound stern, but her attempt was feeble. She wanted this moment behind her.

Ian looked from her to Dakota, then to Melinda, a question in his expression. Then he sat and opened the notebook he'd been sketching in on Monday.

To Jessie's astonishment, without a word, Melinda took him a sandwich, some chips, and a fruit cup, then returned to her desk. Ian didn't look up, but she saw him stare at the sandwich. Jessie tried not to look surprised. *What on earth did I miss yesterday when I stayed home?*

The period went fairly quickly. Jessie spent most of the time reviewing the parts of speech, specifically using the SAT vocabulary words for the week, covering what they were and what functions they served. Melinda nodded occasionally, acknowledging once or twice that she'd heard it before at various times in her schooling but had forgotten most of it. Ian worked in his notebook, and Dakota sat nearby, never uttering a word. It was all a bit surreal.

As soon as the bell rang, Dakota jumped up and started toward the door. "Thank you, Ms. Weldon," she said, her manner gracious yet official.

"You're most welcome," Jessie said in a similar tone as she returned to her desk.

"See you at practice, Mel." And with that, Dakota was gone.

Jessie sighed with relief, but that twinge of regret flickered in her heart again. She could live with it, though. Seriously, what had she expected?

"Thank you, Ms. Weldon." Melinda's voice cut into Jessie's thoughts. She'd gathered her things and was also leaving.

"My pleasure," Jessie said with more enthusiasm than before.

Melinda paused at Ian's desk and looked at what he was working on. "That's awesome," she said quietly.

"Thanks," Ian said in his usual dismissive tone. Then he looked up at her. "And thanks for the…you know…the food."

Jessie watched the exchange with interest. She couldn't help but wonder what had changed between them. She remembered seeing Melinda with the boys Ian had been avoiding and tried to imagine how they all might be linked. She kept coming back to a nagging thought of the bruise on Ian's face and the fight the vice principal had told her about. The image of Melinda slapping the one boy's arm replayed in her mind. Every school had cliques—the jocks and cheerleaders, the nerds and geeks, the druggies, the poor kids—and all schools dealt with bullying. Was that what was going on here? And was Melinda somehow involved in that and the change in her manner due to guilt?

Melinda lifted a shoulder. "Sure. No problem." She turned to leave. "See you tomorrow."

Ian nodded, his gaze following her. "Hey," he said after a moment.

Melinda turned in the doorway.

"How come you're being so nice to me all of a sudden?" The question seemed sincere, even if a little suspicious.

Jessie was wondering the same thing.

Melinda considered him as though weighing the pros and cons of really telling him, then glanced at the floor. "Can't someone just decide to be a nicer person?"

He hesitated, then said, "I guess." He shifted in his seat and closed his notebook. "See ya."

"Mr. Langston," Jessie said as he rose. "May I see what you were working on today?"

His step caught before he changed direction and moved toward her. "You said drawing was okay on Monday."

She smiled. "It is. I was so impressed with what you showed me, though, I'd like to see what you did today. If you don't mind."

The apprehension in his expression eased, and he seemed to relax.

Jessie wished her own tension was so easily alleviated.

He opened the notebook and held it out to her.

Her breath caught.

Looking back at her from the page was a dog, scrawny and scraggly. He'd been hunched over a ripped garbage bag, evidently scarfing up its contents, and was now looking cautiously behind him at the artist. The detail in the sketch was astonishing, from the tiny, yet legible, labels on the cans and boxes spilling from the opening in the bag, to the intricate knotting of the dog's matted fur, to the complexity of the look in his wary eyes—fear, warning, and maybe, just maybe, a tiny spark of hope. The dog reminded her of Ian in a way, of herself when she'd been younger and growing up in hard times. She'd never been *that* skinny, and neither was Ian, for that matter, but she'd seen the look in the dog's eyes in Ian's and was sure it'd been in her own at times. A chord struck in her heart. She tore her gaze from the picture and looked up into Ian's face. "That's amazing." Her voice was only a whisper.

Ian held her gaze for the very first time. "He hangs around the trailer park where I live. I don't know where he came from." He flipped the notebook around to study the sketch himself. "My grandpa says he might be part wolf."

Jessie remembered what Curtis had said about Ian coming to live with his grandfather about a year earlier. "You live with your grandpa?" she asked softly.

Ian nodded, his focus still on the dog.

Jessie wondered if he saw himself there as easily as she could see her child self. She waited, hoping he would fill the silence.

He did. "I don't have parents," he said haltingly. "I mean, I do, but…" He swallowed hard. "They'd rather have drugs instead of me."

His stare bore into the page, but Jessie could tell he was no longer seeing it. He'd shifted to something in the distance, maybe the past. A sheen of moisture glistened in his eyes. Then he flinched. His hand began to tremble ever so slightly. He'd said too much.

Jessie recognized the signs. She had to help him, give him a way back without embarrassing him. A student from her fifth-period class entered the room.

Panic shone in Ian's eyes, and he swiped at them. He started to bolt.

"Mr. Langston," Jessie said firmly but casually.

He jerked his head up to look at her, his expression that of a frightened animal.

"You're a very gifted artist." Jessie simply began to speak, hoping to hold his attention, to guide him back to the present. "You mentioned that you aren't in the art classes because of your grades. I'd like your permission to talk to the art teacher, to show him some of your work, and see if he'd be willing to let you in. Would that be okay with you?"

He focused on her, met her eyes. "Uh…They won't…I mean, do you think?" He was back from whatever dark place the earlier conversation had taken him.

Jessie allowed herself an inner sigh of relief. She knew if he'd run, if he'd gotten out the door, she'd have lost him. "I can't promise anything. I don't even know the art teacher, but I'd like to try."

Excitement lit Ian's face. "Yeah," was all he said. Then for the first time since she'd met him, he smiled.

Jessie warmed at the sight. This kid had touched her somehow, had called out to her. Maybe it was because his situation reminded her of her own years ago. Her parents hadn't left her exactly, at least not in the same way, but she'd had to make her way through her teens and the rest of her life without them like Ian was having to do. She remembered asking Laura once why she and Curtis had done so much for her and recalled Laura's response. *We saw ways we could help, so we did.* It was so simple.

Jessie had felt that way and done the same when she could over the years, but something about the pull to Ian felt stronger. Maybe it was just being back in Clearwater Springs, living with Curtis again, reigniting all the memories from that time in her life, of Jackie, of her mother, of Dakota. Whatever it was, she saw ways she could help, so she would. She could see about getting him into an art class to develop his talent, and she could look into what it might take to start an internship program like she and Curtis had been talking about for kids like Ian. Even if Ian wasn't interested in it, there were no doubt plenty of others who might be.

And maybe, if I keep myself busy all the time, I can put everything with Dakota behind me. The lure of that old crush. The anger and painful stab of learning she was nothing more than a resented reminder of everything Dakota had tried to forget. The lingering, visceral sensation of that kiss on her lips.

Maybe.

❖

Dakota sank into her desk chair and blew out a breath. Okay, she could do this. The face-to-face with Jessica Weldon had gone fine. Professional. To the point. Focused on Mel's work. They could be colleagues. In fact, that's all they were. Even in the past, they'd never known each other. Dakota had never even known *of* her.

Something tugged at a memory in the recesses of her mind. She searched the past. No, she *hadn't* known of Jessica Weldon or Brogan, or… *It's Jessie.* Dakota felt their lips touch. She slammed that door.

Damn it! Don't go there. Professional relationship only. And what did that mean? Working with Jessica Weldon to bring Mel's grade up and referring a few other players to her for extra help, and that was all. Dakota turned to her computer and pulled up Nancy Avery's grades. She'd spend her fifth period prep checking every one of her girls' quarter grades, both volleyball and basketball players, and take care of any other issues before they became urgent like Mel's. She intended to stay on top of the eligibility question from now on.

When she'd finished, she had three more students that were hovering right around the 2.0 GPA mark. One wasn't in any of Jessica's classes, but from what Dakota had experienced of her, she didn't think that would matter. She'd talk with her about it tomorrow. It would probably help them move past any residual awkwardness to have something else work-related to discuss.

There was still what Drew had said to consider, however. Was he right? Was Dakota opening up to deal with everything she'd buried so deeply regarding the accident and its repercussions? And was it because of Jessie Brogan? She supposed the latter was irrelevant. If she were going to talk to anyone about it, Drew was the best option. Even when she'd worked with therapists, trying to let go of her guilt and resentment from that night, she'd only ended up feeling worse about herself. Drew had been there, right at her side. He'd seen it, felt it, knew what she'd gone through on that road. He wouldn't judge her. If all that was true, though, why had she never been able to accept what he said had happened? Was she merely too afraid of hurting more people?

Dakota paused and leaned back in her chair. *That* was a question she'd never asked herself before. Maybe she was ready to let some things bubble to the surface. If she did, though, what else might come up? That question terrified her.

Her cell phone began to vibrate and skitter across her desk.

She picked it up and glanced at the screen.

Crystal's picture smiled back at her.

"Hey, Crys, what's up?"

"Nothing earth-shattering. I just wanted to talk to someone with some sanity. Got a minute?"

Dakota heard the soft New Age music in the background that Crystal played in her office. She let out a short laugh. "I'm not sure how sane I am today." Jessica Weldon was making her nuts. "I'll do my best, though. What's going on?"

Crystal paused. "We're going to have to get back to that statement. It sounds intriguing. But first, I want to pick your brain."

Dakota groaned. "Is this foundation business? You know I'm no good at all that. That's your thing."

The Scott Foundation had been created forty years earlier by their aunt when she'd gotten the idea and asked her father for a portion of the Scott assets to support it. Crystal had loved working with her and started putting in countless volunteer hours at an early age, and after receiving an MBA in her early thirties, she was hired as CEO. Their aunt still served as president, but Crystal ran the operations and events. In the beginning, the endowments had gone to local causes and community projects—and still did if needed—but as the foundation grew, so did its reputation. Now, they received requests from all over the country.

"I know, but humor me, okay? Pretend I'm complaining about Paul and need some ideas about how to get him to roll the toothpaste from the bottom instead of squeezing it in the middle."

Dakota chuckled. "Can't help you there. I'm a squeezer too. I don't see the point of the roll thing. It's not like it stays rolled up anyway."

"Well then, it's fortunate I'm not really asking about that," Crystal said with an edge of impatience. "Can we move on?"

"Sorry." Dakota resigned herself to the subject at hand and settled in. "Let me start over. Hi, Crystal. How may I serve you this afternoon?"

Crystal laughed softly. "Much better."

Dakota felt her shift into administrator mode.

"We're coming up on that time of year to present the endowment."

"And? I don't hear a dilemma." Dakota relaxed. It felt good to be talking and thinking about something other than Jessica Weldon. "Usually, you're all over this. You zip right through it and have money winging out into the world to do good in a flash."

"I know." Crystal sighed. "That's the problem. I'm having trouble finding something that gets me excited."

"What do you mean? You shouldn't have to find anything. Don't people and groups send in applications or requests or something? They're supposed to contact you, right?"

"We have gotten a lot of requests. Some of our usual ones for continuing funding for past projects that we'll probably shift over to ongoing support. And there are some new ones." Crystal hesitated as though thinking. "I don't know. I feel like I want to do something different this year."

"Like what?" Dakota balanced a quarter on the back of her knuckles.

"That's why I called you," Crystal said in the tone she used when she was delegating. "Is there anything going on in the world of athletics, either at the high school level or college? You still have a lot of connections with the NCAA. I thought maybe you might have heard of something that fits with our mission statement."

"Hmm." Dakota flipped the quarter and caught it. "Not that I can think of off the top of my head, but I can check around."

"Would you?" Crystal asked. "I'd appreciate it."

"Sure. But, you know, Crys, the right one will show up or might be sitting on your desk right now. You and the board always end up supporting great programs that have an impact on a lot of lives."

"Thanks, Dakota. I appreciate that." Crystal's voice softened into a more personal lilt. "Even if you did refuse one of the family seats on the board," she added dryly.

"When's the deadline?" Dakota sidestepped the dig.

Crystal rattled off the date and a few more pertinent pieces of information, then her tone changed to one of big-sisterly concern. "Why are you doubting your sanity today?"

The sudden change in topic caught Dakota off guard. Anxiety tightened her throat. She dropped the quarter, and it rolled under the desk. Should she tell Crystal about Jessie Brogan?

Crystal was like everyone else. She'd always had questions about what had happened and how Dakota coped with it—hers born out of love, not idle gossip—but Dakota had never shared anything with her, either.

Once she opened the door, it would be open for everything else Crystal had held back over the years—all the questions, all the emotions. She'd respected Dakota's boundaries, but Dakota knew she was like the tide being held back by a floodgate. As soon as the sluice opened, Dakota would be drowned. As much as she loved Crystal, she wasn't ready to face it.

With Drew, she didn't have to start from scratch. She could begin with the present. She wouldn't have to describe every detail of that night, because he had been there with her, seen them for himself. She wouldn't have to dredge up all those old, raw emotions because he'd been there to hold her while she cried.

"Oh, just work stuff," Dakota said, hoping that would suffice. "You know, my best volleyball player on academic probation. A couple more barely staying eligible. Stuff like that."

"That's not good," Crystal said sympathetically. "What are you going to do?"

"They're getting extra help. I think it'll be fine." And here she was again, one question away from Jessica Weldon—dangerously close to Jessie Brogan. There was a part of her that wanted to share everything with Crystal, all the present day stuff, that is. She'd love to be able to tell her sister about this strong, intelligent, attractive, sexy woman she'd met, about her coming to Dakota's house, about the kiss that had lit up every erogenous zone in her body. She wished that was all there was to it, no tie to the past, no link to the worst experience of her life. She couldn't, though. If she brought up *that* woman, Crystal would, of course, want to know who she was, where she'd come from, how Dakota had met her, and then they'd be right back where they were now.

Loneliness crept into Dakota's heart, born of keeping secrets, keeping parts of one's self sealed off from others. She'd felt it before, during those years she'd stayed away from Clearwater Springs, away from her family. She'd thought she could put it behind her when she'd come home, thought she could reconnect with Drew and Crystal—Tina, not as much, but maybe a little—and close the distance she'd created with them. She finally realized the distance had never been physical, and the only way to close it was to deal with the root of it.

Then maybe she could let Crystal and Drew back in. Maybe she could explain some things. After all, they'd been affected by everything, too, along with the scars they all shared from their mother's mental illness. They'd been through so much together, and then Dakota had just shut them out.

And what about Jessie? Dakota had been awfully hard on her. Was she entitled to something? Some information? Maybe not Dakota's feelings, her conflict, her nightmares, but some basic facts about her sister's death that weren't tainted by accusation and gossip? Dakota chilled and her breath caught in her throat at the thought.

No. She doubted she could ever talk to Jessie about that night, and she couldn't talk to Crystal now. Drew had been right, though. She could talk to him, and all of a sudden, she knew it had to be soon. If it weren't, she'd lose herself in this loneliness.

And that realization terrified her.

Chapter Nine

Jessie woke, bathed in sweat, her breath ragged.

Sweet and holy mother of all things sacred and sugary. What the hell?

She still felt the softness of Dakota's hair between her fingers, the heat of her mouth on her breasts, the strength of her fingers thrusting inside her. She'd been on the precipice of orgasm when the car alarm went off outside, the short, sharp blasts of the horn in sync with the pulse of pleasure between her thighs. She moaned and threw back the covers. She needed air.

As her skin began to dry in the chilled morning and her breathing evened, she ran her hands through her hair. She was still groggy enough to wonder about the feel of Dakota's. Its thickness. Its texture. Its caress on her bare stomach as Dakota moved lower.

It'd been a long time since she'd had a sex dream starring… anyone, really. Had the last one been that gallery owner from the art show she and Sandy went to in New York a few years ago? That one was hot. Surely, she'd had one since then, though. *Ah, yes.* She smiled as she remembered. There had been the one with that actress from the cell phone commercial. *That* had been hot, *hot.* She'd always remembered her very first one, though. She'd been in junior high, and it'd starred none other than this morning's leading lady. It hadn't actually been a sex dream, but probably the closest thing Jessie could have conjured at the time. Dakota had kissed her and held her tightly, pressing Jessie hard against a wall. Jessie had awakened wet, the sensitive flesh between her legs swollen. It hadn't been the first time she'd touched herself, enjoyed her own fingers, but it *had* been the first time she'd reached a climax, her initial discovery of the full pleasure her body offered. And that body now raged with need for release.

Dream Dakota's gotten much better. She'd learned some moves.

Jessie closed her eyes and caressed her abdomen, making lazy circles over her damp skin. What if Dakota wasn't good in bed? Everyone's crush, everyone's fantasy, wealthy, successful, charming, gorgeous and sexy—and lousy in bed. Wouldn't that be ironic? Jessie's mother would consider it poetic justice.

Jessie winced. *One should never think of one's mother when about to masturbate.*

But a dream Dakota who was bad in bed didn't serve Jessie's purposes at the moment. *Besides, who fantasizes about bad sex?*

She trailed her fingers up to her nipples, thinking of Dakota's mouth—mmm, that warm, soft, skilled mouth—sucking and licking them into stiff peaks. She squeezed them, rolled them, felt every sensation shoot directly to her center. She pressed her legs together.

"Uh-uh. None of that." Dakota's voice was hoarse with desire as she sat at the foot of the bed, watching. "Open." Dakota leaned closer.

Arousal surged through Jessie's lower belly. She spread her legs wide. The cool morning air whispered across her hot, wet folds.

Dakota's breath.

She groaned and pinched her nipples harder. She slid one hand down her torso, dragged her nails through the soft curls covering her mound, touched a fingertip to her clitoris. She gasped.

Dakota's tongue.

She stroked, lightly at first, but the orgasm that had abated with the interruption of her dream rushed back in, threatening to claim her. She held it at bay, wanting the fantasy a little bit longer. She closed her fingers, capturing her clitoris between them.

Dakota's lips.

She stifled a cry of release and lifted her hips, pressing her need into her hand.

Dakota sucked her in, slipped a finger inside her. "Come for me, Jessie."

And she did. Hard. Fast. Shatteringly. She curled onto her side, her thighs clamped around her hand, her body jerking with every spasm of pleasure. When her orgasm finally subsided and she caught her breath, she flopped onto her back.

What had she done now? *It wasn't enough that I kissed her?* An odd sense of guilt welled up inside her. Why was she having sex dreams about Dakota, fantasizing about her? She was done with her. She'd confronted her, said her piece, and was moving on.

Even if that were true, though, she was an adult. She could have sex dreams about anyone she wanted. She didn't have to feel guilty about it. But she remembered that feeling after Jackie's death, when she still wanted to think the best of Dakota, wanted to believe she was what Jessie had always thought she was, but her mother had said Dakota was to blame. She'd said the Scotts could cover up anything because of who they were in Clearwater Springs. That Dakota should have been punished but had gotten away with it only because she was a Scott. Jessie had been so confused, but her mother's accusations were all she heard. Her idol, her crush, had vanished for the whole summer. Dakota's father had issued a statement to the paper saying she was recovering from the trauma of the accident and receiving counseling at a facility recommended by her doctor.

Then one day, she'd appeared on the doorstep of that horrible little cottage where Jessie and her mother lived, where Jackie had lived—and she'd apologized.

Everything about the scene had stunned Jessie into abject shock—the unlikelihood of Dakota Scott, returned after months and standing on *her* doorstep; the implausibility that her mother had dragged herself from the sofa bed to answer the knock; her own mortification that *this* might be how Dakota became aware of her existence. Jessie had shrunk into the shadows of the hallway, staying only close enough to hear. As much as she'd always wanted to forget that day, the memory washed over her, and she let it come.

"Hello, Mrs. Brogan."

Jessie heard Dakota's voice before she saw her standing at the front door. She was thinner, and her face was drawn, her cheekbones sharp beneath the skin. Jessie gasped in surprise. Never would she have guessed that Dakota Scott would be on her doorstep, not in this lifetime. But what *was* she doing there?

"I, uh…" Dakota's voice was thick.

Jessie couldn't see her mother's face, but she saw her stiffen and knew the instant she realized who was speaking to her.

"What the hell do you want?" Her tone was harsh. "You have some nerve showing up here."

Dakota drew in a sharp breath. "I…uh…" She faltered. "I just…wanted…to say I'm…" She straightened, and her jaw tightened. "Mrs. Brogan, I'm so sorry. I—"

"You're sorry? You expect me to care that *you're sorry* for killing my daughter?" Jessie's mother swayed as her voice broke. "I don't care that you're sorry…*if* you even really are."

Dakota's face paled even more.

Jessie winced at her mother's cruelty. She wished she'd let Dakota talk.

"You're a Scott." Her mother's pitch rose. "Your father and grandfather bailed you out of this, whisked you out of town before the police report was even filed—the lie that it was. Then three months later, here you are. *Sorry.* What good does that do me? Does it bring my Jackie back?"

Dakota's eyes filled with tears. "I just wanted—"

"You Scotts think you can always get whatever you want. Well, not from me. You took my daughter," Jessie's mother screamed. "I don't know what happened out there on that road. All I know is that you and that brother of yours waltz around this town like you own it. You think you're entitled to anything you want, when girls like mine don't have a thing. You think you can do *anything* without consequences, and apparently you can in this crappy little town. But if there is a God, Dakota Scott, I hope you burn in hell for whatever happened out there. And it *wasn't* what that bastard brother of yours said." She began to sob. "My Jackie was a good girl."

Dakota looked stricken. She trembled and gripped the doorjamb to steady herself.

Jessie's mother slammed the door and crumpled to the floor.

Jessie ran to her.

"My Jackie was a good girl," she whispered through her tears. She gazed imploringly at Jessie. "She was a good girl. She wouldn't do that."

"No, Mommy, she wouldn't," Jessie said reassuringly. She knew Dakota was still on the other side of the door. She could sense her there, hovering, unsure what to do. She hugged her mother and held her for a few minutes, then helped her back to the sofa bed and drew the blanket up over her. She heard the slam of a car door, the roar of an engine coming to life, the scattering of gravel from spinning tires. Then, nothing.

Jessie's tears stung her eyes as she returned to the present. She hadn't thought of that day in so long, had locked the memory securely away. She could understand why it would resurface now—with being back in Clearwater Springs, dealing with all the memories that came with that, interacting with Dakota on a daily basis—but how could it still have the power to reduce her to tears? *It can't.* She wiped them away with the sheet on her bed. *Not if I don't let it.* She could remember without reliving the emotions.

After the day Dakota had shown up to apologize, Jessie could no longer look at Dakota as she once had, could no longer look up to her, idolize her, dream of her in that pleasurable, new way. When she did, it felt like a betrayal of her mother. While her mother had admitted she didn't know what happened that night, nothing she'd said was untrue. It was just that there were so many unanswered questions. And after Dakota's attempt at an apology, she'd gone back to how she'd always been—playing sports, winning championships, flashing that grin. To watch her, it was as though nothing out of the ordinary had happened. Then she'd gone off to college, even earned a spot on the 1980 women's Olympic volleyball team, though she was kept from playing by an ACL injury, became an NCAA coach, and seemed never to look back.

Jessie had never been sure what she expected Dakota to do. It was Jessie's mother who'd have nothing to do with the apology, Jessie's mother who'd been so cruel in her grief and sorrow. Was Dakota supposed to subject herself to that again or stop living her own life because of something she couldn't undo? She'd decided that was illogical, but thinking of Dakota in the same way still seemed disloyal to her mother. So she'd packed away all of the newspaper clippings she'd saved about Dakota, the pictures, that baseball—*that's where the baseball is*—into a box and put it all away. *Where is that box?* Maybe Curtis knew.

Absently, Jessie glanced at the clock. *Almost nine?* She leapt up and pulled on her robe. She'd wanted to give herself a little time to sleep in this morning, it being a Saturday and all, but she'd planned to be out the door by now. She had a lot on her agenda today. That damned sex dream had thrown off everything. As she made her way down the hall, she recalled its intensity, how vividly she'd felt Dakota's touch, the taste of her mouth. Had that been in the dream? No, that had been real, from the night at Dakota's house. The aftermath of the orgasm still thrummed through her. She smiled at herself in the bathroom mirror at the lingering pleasure.

As for the dream itself, she was entitled. After all, she hadn't actually had sex with Dakota. It was no different than that actress or the gallery owner, except for the fact that she didn't have to face either one of them on a daily basis. But that was her own problem, no one else's, least of all, her mother's.

Dakota and Drew had started out early that morning, as they'd headed over to the east ridge. It'd felt good to be out in the open, breathing the crisp morning air as they'd crossed the pastures to the tree line, then made their way over the foothills to the base of the mountain range that bordered the east end of the ranch. They sat at the top of The Rock, as they'd named it as kids, gazing out over the landscape.

They'd left the horses grazing at the bottom and climbed the steep trail up the backside to the slab that jutted out over the edge of the ridge, leaving nothing but air beneath for about a hundred feet, where a sharp, rocky slope descended another thirty or so. The accomplishment was one Dakota was proud of with their fiftieth birthday right around the corner.

Drew leaned back on his elbow and took a bite of a sandwich Selena had packed for them.

Dakota tore open a bag of chips to go with hers. She gestured to the small lake nestled amidst a cluster of black oaks at the far end of the valley below. "Remember all the time we spent swimming there?"

Drew chuckled. "Yeah. Ada always used to say we had that big, beautiful pool at home, but we'd rather spend the entire day swimming in a mud hole."

Dakota laughed. "Well, Ada didn't know about the rock slide that plummets into it."

Drew shook his head. "If she had, we never would have seen it again." They shared a quiet moment in the memory, then he broke the silence. "What are we doing here, Sis?"

Leave it to Drew to cut to the chase. He'd actually been pretty patient, considering the amount of time it took to get there. "I've been thinking about what you said. You know, that I should talk about things." Dakota met his gaze. It was serious. "The past."

He arched an eyebrow.

She was nervous, scared even. She looked away.

"Any time, Kota Bear. Whenever you're ready."

She knew he'd used his nickname for her deliberately. It always softened her. "I don't know where to start," she said weakly.

He simply waited.

The varied songs of the birds tempered the silence, and a breeze touched Dakota's cheeks like a soft whisper.

She calmed. "You said you thought it was good that Jessie Brogan came back because it was opening me up."

He nodded. "What's coming up for you?"

She took a deep breath. The past week and a half, since her visit to Jessie at the Triple M, had been a hell of a balancing act. She'd managed to stay professional when they were around each other, but at other times, her emotions were all over the map. And not just about Jessie. "The nightmares are back."

"Doug says dreaming's always a good thing." Doug was the therapist Drew had been seeing off and on for years about any number of his life challenges, beginning right after the accident. "He says things can bubble up from our subconscious in dreams first, before we're quite ready to face them head on."

"Yeah, I know. Psychobabble," Dakota said with a smirk. "I've heard it all, too."

Drew gave her a sympathetic smile. "I know, but since Jackie's little sister's reappearance seems to have had an impact on you, it makes sense you'd be having dreams again."

Some of the dreams Dakota'd had since she'd found out who Jessie was—since the kiss—made it difficult to think of her as anyone's *little* sister. "They've mostly been of the scene itself. That's the most reoccurring one I've had over the years. The moment of impact, the crack, then Jackie's face against the windshield. The blood. The screech of the tires." She shivered even in the warmth of the late morning sunshine that caressed her face. "You remember all that?"

"Yeah, I do," Drew whispered. "I had dreams about it for quite a while too."

"You did?" Dakota was surprised. "How'd you make them stop?"

Drew shrugged. "I talked about them. I listened when people told me it wasn't my fault. I went out there and spent some time. Have you been out there in all these years?"

"Out where?" Dakota asked in astonishment. "You mean to…" She faltered. "To Brogan's Bend?"

"It helped me a lot. It was hard at first." Drew's eyes went distant. "Then one day, I finally let go of the guilt."

Dakota stared at him. "What did you have to feel guilty about? I was the one driving."

He met and held her gaze. "I felt guilty that I *wasn't* the one driving, that it was you," he said quietly. "I should have been, Kota Bear. It was my car. I've always wanted to tell you how sorry I am for that, but you wouldn't—"

"You don't have anything to be sorry about. You had that beer at Stevie's. You couldn't have driven. That was always something we were good about." Dakota looked out across the valley again. "And then we got that damned call about Mom." Anger rumbled up from deep within, and there was the other guilt that always ate at her. "If we hadn't been racing home for the billionth time…Why couldn't we have just had a normal mom?" There, she'd said it, right out loud in front of God and everyone. Well, in front of God and Drew, anyway.

Drew sighed. "The million-dollar question." He pulled the straw off the side of a juice box and stuck it into the hole at the top. "You know how Selena talks about our soul group?"

"Yeah." Dakota valued Selena's thoughts, even though sometimes they weren't conventional. She always found them worth thinking about.

"One time when she and I were talking about Mom and the family, she said that everyone in a soul group, at one time or another, has to be the one that the rest of the group takes care of, so everyone has the experience of being on both sides. This time around, it's Mom. Next time, maybe it's you or me, and she'll take care of us…like she couldn't do this time around."

Dakota looked into his eyes and saw her own pain at having their mother taken from her so long ago reflected back to her.

"I know you love her," he said.

"I do love her. That's the reason I came back. That and the rest of you." Dakota squeezed his hand before letting out the remainder of the words that had been fighting for freedom for so long. "But I hate that goddamned disease."

Drew brought her palm to his lips, then pressed it to his cheek. "Me, too."

They sat in silence for a long time as the morning gave way to afternoon.

Dakota let the image of Jackie Brogan from her dreams sit in her mind, allowed the anger and guilt from that night and at her mother's illness to be present, instead of shutting it away as she had always done. It tore at her, at first, leaving her insides feeling shredded and raw. She clenched her teeth and forced herself to sit still, to share the space with it, something a counselor had suggested more than once. She'd never been able to do it, though. Could she now? Her throat closed, and she felt the swell of her guilt, then the beginnings of the isolation it always brought.

She wasn't alone this time, though. She looked at Drew, and a strange feeling came over her, something new. It wasn't peace, by any means. After all, those images were still there. Jackie was still dead, and Dakota *was s*till responsible—that was the reality—but a sense of calm moved through her. Or, at least, she didn't feel the need to run, to hide, to shut herself down, and put on an act. She could breathe. That was good, right? Maybe this talking thing would be okay. She knew she was done for now, though. She needed time with everything she'd said, even if it really hadn't been much. "I think that's all I can do for right now, Drew," she said finally.

"Okay." He smiled. "That was good, though. Right?"

Her question. She nodded and felt the corners of her mouth lift. "I think it was, but don't say it too loud."

He chuckled. "Let's change the subject. Quick." He shifted. "How's the tutoring going with your failing players?"

Dakota grimaced. "That's not really a full change in subject, since Jessie Brogan is the one doing the tutoring, but I think it's okay. At least that subject doesn't have to do with that night." She took a deep breath and let herself move to the moment. "It's going well, I think. Mel's really catching on and actually seems to be enjoying it. Jessie…I mean, Ms. Weldon, is letting her use a story she wanted to write as the basis for some of the tutoring lessons. I think she's really a good teacher. She seems to be willing to use whatever's important to the kids to get them to learn."

"She sounds great." Drew finished his juice.

Dakota considered his comment. "I think she might be. You know, as a teacher."

"Right." He drew out the word. His lips quirked. "But I don't know. Maybe not just as a teacher. Berta was pretty taken with her when they were dating. I think she even started dotting her i's with little hearts."

Dakota knew he was joking. The idea of Berta—butch to the core—drawing little hearts for any reason was like something straight out of the old Far Side comic strip. She almost snorted a laugh, but the image of Berta with Jessie, holding her, kissing her, doing the things Jessie and Dakota had done in Dakota's dream only two nights earlier, choked out the humor.

Drew watched her. "Are you staying professional with her?"

Dakota felt herself blush. "In the way you and I talked about, yes. I'm not dealing with her in any way to do with her sister or the accident."

"But in other ways?" Drew knew the answer. They had that twin bond that meant he knew her better than anyone in the world.

"I told you I was attracted to her before I knew who she was, and we kissed." Dakota's mind flashed to that night, to Jessie's lips. *Not a dream.* Her body heated, rekindling the slow burn between her thighs that she'd been fighting with every memory of that night at her house and every dream since. "I'm having trouble forgetting that, but at the same time, I get mad being around her because it's—she's—such a reminder of Jackie. Never mind what she said about wanting me to understand there were consequences." Dakota shook her head. "That pissed me off. What the hell does she think I am? A sociopath?"

Drew looped an arm around her neck and pulled her against him. "It doesn't matter what she thinks," he said against her hair. "What matters is that you might be finally coming back to us. And if it took her showing up to crack you open, then I'll buy her a nice gift when she leaves. Try not to let her get to you."

Dakota nodded, her cheek rubbing against the softness of his shirt, but her thoughts lingered on Jessie. *Easier said than done.* "I should head back," she said, patting his chest. "I need to get over to Shady Acres." She got to her feet and dusted herself off.

"The assisted living place?" Drew looked up in evident surprise. "You're still visiting Dodger?" He began shoving their lunch trash into his backpack.

Dodger was the nickname given to Gloria Fisher, the previous, long-standing girls' PE teacher Dakota had replaced ten years earlier. She'd also been Dakota's teacher in high school as well as her volleyball coach. She'd earned the moniker way back when, due to her obsession with the Los Angeles Dodgers baseball team.

"Yeah," Dakota said, wadding up her sandwich wrapper and stuffing it into the potato chip bag. She handed it to Drew. "I try to get over there a couple times a month. She likes me to play the guitar for everyone."

Drew squinted at her in question.

Dakota shrugged. "I still know the few songs I learned in sixth grade. She doesn't seem to mind that they're kids' songs."

He smiled, his eyes sparking with laughter. "You're a good girl, Dakota Scott."

"Yeah. Just don't let it get around." Dakota turned to make her way to the trail to where they'd left the horses. She felt Drew's gaze on her. She looked back at him. "What?"

"Will you let me say it?" He stood, his weight shifted to one foot, the backpack dangling from his hand. "I've always needed to say I'm sorry."

She studied him. She saw every bit of the man he'd become, but in his eyes, she saw the teenage boy. "There's nothing for you to—"

"Please, Dakota. It's my journey too." He sounded so vulnerable.

In an instant, Dakota was standing outside the Colby Cottages, waiting for Jackie Brogan's mother to answer the door. She'd gone to apologize. As weak of an offering as it was, it was all she'd had. At the time, she'd thought she was there for Jackie's mother. It wasn't until years later she realized she'd been there for herself. Everyone else had told her it wasn't her fault, that she could forgive herself, but she'd needed to hear it from Mrs. Brogan, from the one person she'd hurt the most, other than Jackie herself. She hadn't understood at the time what she was asking of the poor woman. All she knew was the pain of Mrs. Brogan's words, the agony of her refusal. And now Drew was asking for the same thing. She wouldn't deny him what Jackie's mom had denied her.

His eyes shone with tears. "Dakota, I'm so sorry I had that beer. I'm so sorry you were the one driving." He wiped his face with his free hand. "It should have been me. I need to know you forgive me."

Dakota went to him. She wanted to tell him he didn't do anything, that there was nothing to forgive, but she knew what he needed to hear—what she'd needed to hear all these years. She wrapped him in her arms. "It's okay, Drew," she whispered in his ear. "I forgive you. And I'm sorry I never let you say that before now."

She'd had no idea he'd been carrying that all this time. Had she been willing to talk, been willing to listen, she would have, but she'd shut him and everyone else out when she'd shut herself down. She'd done the same thing to Drew that Mrs. Brogan had done to her. She could understand Mrs. Brogan's reaction to the girl who'd killed her daughter showing up at her door, but Drew was the most important person in Dakota's life. How could she have done that to him?

She'd opened up to him today, though, shared with him for the very first time, and that had allowed him to ask her for what he needed. *That counts for something, doesn't it?* And there, standing on top of The Rock, looking out over the expanse of so much beauty, she knew her world was different, her life was different. She'd taken that first step that she'd never been willing to take before.

Now, she was ready to face her past.

CHAPTER TEN

Jessie knocked on the door of the camp trailer. When Ian hadn't shown up for his last detention period the previous day, she'd checked with the office to find he was absent from school entirely. Odd, since he'd seemed perfectly healthy on Thursday. She'd told herself it would be fine to wait and talk to him on Monday, but she was too excited to tell him about her conversation with the art teacher. She'd looked up his phone number only to discover there wasn't one, then jotted down the space number at the trailer park and added the stop to her list of scheduled visits on Saturday.

When Curtis had told her Ian lived with his grandfather out at the trailer park, Jessie had pictured at least a singlewide mobile home in the main area, not a thirty-two-foot camping trailer set up in the overnight section.

She glanced around. Although this portion of the park was designated for short-term use, most of the units appeared to be pretty established. A number of them had large barbecues set up outside, rather than smaller, more portable grills, and one even had a screened-in porch built on to the side. Wooden steps with handrails led to many of the doors, including the one Jessie stood in front of, instead of the little stools that could easily be thrown inside when it was time to move on. There were a few units that looked as though they were actually there for a temporary stay, but Jessie supposed most people who were camping in the area would check into the actual campground in the state park up in the foothills.

Most of the individual sites here had large trees that in the summer time would provide lush shade to keep the area cool. Some of the occupants had planted small patches of grass, and on the gentle curve of the pot-holed road that dissected the two rows of campers and trailers sat a cement building with the words *Shower* and *Laundry Room* painted in black on the side. It wouldn't be a horrible place to live. The Colby Cottages had provided no shade, no grass, and certainly no laundry facility. This was a step up from where she'd lived as a kid.

"Can I help you?"

The rich, baritone voice startled Jessie from her musings. She spun around to find an older man standing at the corner of the trailer, carrying a grocery bag. He wore faded blue jeans with a frayed denim work shirt tucked at the waist, and the deep creases etched into his face told a story of a hard-lived life. His light blue eyes—Ian's eyes—were sharp and held wariness—also like Ian's.

"Are you Mr. Reynolds?" Jessie asked.

He eyed her, obviously sizing her up. He gave a single nod. "Isaac."

She smiled and extended her hand. "Jessica Weldon." Her official name for an official call. But then, this wasn't really an official call. She softened. "Jessie."

He shook her hand. His grip was firm, but there was also a gentleness to it. "Are you another one of those social workers? I swear, we never see the same one of you twice."

"No," Jessie said. "I'm a teacher at the high school."

Isaac's expression remained cautious. "Is he in more trouble?"

"Oh," Jessie said in surprise. She forgot that many parents automatically assumed calls or visits from teachers were a bad thing. In all fairness, she supposed most of the time they were. "Not at all." For the first time, she considered other meanings Ian's absence the previous day might have. "I mean, not that I know of. He wasn't at school yesterday, and I wanted to talk to him about an art class I said I'd try to get him into."

Isaac visibly relaxed. "An art class?" His lips twisted in the hint of a smile. "He'd like that. He sure has some talent, that boy."

"Yes, he does," Jessie said, settling into the shift in energy.

"Would you like to sit, Ms. Weldon?" He motioned to two green plastic chairs arranged under an awning that stretched out from the roof of the trailer.

She almost reminded him to call her Jessie but wanted him to be comfortable. She smiled. "Thank you. I'd love to."

He gave her that single nod again, but this time with an accompanying look that clearly indicated he'd decided she was okay. "Let me just put these groceries inside. I'd invite you in, but two bachelors live here. Ain't no place for a lady." He was back in the amount of time it took her to chuckle at his joke. He took the chair beside her. "You must like my grandson to come all the way out here. And on a Saturday, no less."

Jessie raised an eyebrow. "I do like Ian. I think underneath his tough guy act, he has a lot going for him. I don't have him in a class, but he seems intelligent, and he's a gifted artist."

Suspicion returned to Isaac's eyes. "I thought you said you were his teacher."

"I said I'm *a* teacher. I also supervise morning detention. That's where I met Ian."

"He said he didn't have to go early anymore," Isaac said with a challenge. "It ain't like him to lie."

"He didn't lie." Jessie held Isaac's gaze. "On the first day, he asked if he could serve his detention in my classroom at lunch instead of in the morning. I okayed it."

Isaac pursed his lips. "That was nice 'a you. He helps Jenny Perkins with her little one in the morning before school." He inclined his head down the road. "She has to leave for her job at the deli before her mama gets home from her nightshift. He and Jenny are just friends, but he loves that little boy."

Jessie's heart warmed at Ian's kindness. "See there," she said softly. "How could I not like a teenage boy who would do something like that every morning?" She meant it, while at the same time hoping to lighten the conversation again.

Instead, Isaac seemed to grow more serious. "He's in some kind of trouble at school, you know."

"You mean for the fight he got into a couple of weeks ago?" Jessie shifted in her chair to face him more.

He gave her a long, measuring look, as though trying to decide something. "You're on his side, right?"

Jessie considered her answer carefully. She'd always had good instincts about people, and she'd honed them even sharper over her two decades of teaching. Everything in her said Ian was a good kid. "Yes, Isaac, I am. What's the matter?"

"I ain't sure, and he won't talk to me about it. It started with little things. A sprained finger. A limp from dropping something on his foot, he said. Then his back and shoulder hurt for a while, and finally that fight a few weeks back and that God-awful bruise on his face that's just now almost faded. I think whatever's going on, he finally got sick of it and fought back. That's when he got detention."

Jessie listened, remembering the three boys in the hall that Ian had avoided that first day. "Do you know who he fought with?"

Isaac shook his head. "When I asked at the meeting with the vice principal, he said it was being handled, that I didn't need to be concerned."

"Was that the last thing that happened?" Jessie asked, wondering about Ian's absence the previous day.

Isaac hesitated, clearly reluctant to say more. Finally, he sighed. "Yesterday, he left for school, came back an hour later with a busted lip, a bloodied nose, and a few bruised ribs. He cleaned up and spent the rest of the day in bed."

Jessie gasped. "Did he see a doctor about his ribs? Could they be broken?"

"I've lived a hard life, Ms. Weldon. I know broken ribs, and I know bruised ones. These are bruised, and there ain't nothing a doc can do about bruised ribs." Isaac leaned forward in his chair. "What has me worried is it keeps getting worse. Plus, Ian made some noise about not going back to school."

"He *has* to go to school, by law, at least until he's sixteen." Jessie knew the absurdity of her statement. No one could *make* a kid past the age of about ten go to school if he absolutely refused.

Isaac let out a sharp laugh. "My daughter left with him when he was three, and I'd guess he's been having to make his own decisions since then. I hadn't seen him since the day they vanished until the social worker called last year and asked me if I'd take him in. Said my daughter was in prison and he needed a place." He rubbed the stubble on his chin. "I never thought they'd let him stay with me once they saw where I live. But they said my roof was sound and I have enough to put food on the table. Said he'd be better off with a family member than not." He leveled a steady gaze on Jessie. "I love my grandson, Ms. Weldon, but I ain't fool enough to think I can *make* him do what he doesn't want to do… what, maybe, he's afraid to do. And if he doesn't go to school, they *won't* let him keep living here."

"May I speak with him?" Jessie asked. "Is he here?" She glanced behind her at the window of the trailer.

"He's down at the reservoir." Isaac's tone was skeptical. "I don't know that he'll tell you anything, though, since he wouldn't tell me."

"Maybe I'll just talk to him about the art class. Maybe finding out he can take it will be enough to keep him in school for now. That will give me some time to check into what might be going on." Jessie stood. "Can you tell me where the reservoir is?"

"Thank you, Ms. Weldon. I can't tell you how grateful I am. Ian's a good boy."

Jessie smiled. "Yes, he is."

She followed his directions down the road through the overnight section and around the curve that led back up to the main road. When she crossed it and found the path through the bushes on the opposite side, she understood Isaac's chuckle when she'd mentioned driving. She continued just past the large bump he'd described, then split off the trail to the left to the chain link fence and followed it until she came to the opening—a hole that had been cut with bolt cutters, most likely—not ten feet away from a

No Trespassing sign. What the hell was she doing? *I could come back later when he'd most likely be home. Maybe around dinner time.*

She didn't want to wait, though. She felt a driving need to connect with him now, to see for herself that he was okay. She ducked through the fence, scuttled through the oleander bushes on the other side, and came out in a shady, wooded area. She could hear the sound of machinery, pumps maybe, and followed it. After about twenty feet, she rounded the trunk of a large tree and almost fell right over the top of Ian.

He leapt up, turned, and stumbled backward, ending up in the water up to his mid calves. His eyes were wide.

"Mr. Langston," Jessie said in surprise, trying to capture her teacher persona. "I'm sorry. I didn't see you."

He stared at her while he caught his breath. "Ms. Weldon? What are you…?" He wrapped his arms around his middle in a subtle motion.

If Isaac hadn't told her about his bruised ribs, she would have missed it. "I wanted to talk with you about a couple of things. Your grandfather told me where I could find you, but I'm not really the trailblazer type." She laughed. "Are you all right?"

He nodded and splashed his way back onto the shore. He still looked a bit shaky.

"I'm surprised you didn't hear me coming, tromping through all the underbrush," Jessie said lightly.

"I, uh…" He gently rubbed a spot on his side. "I must've fallen asleep."

"May I join you?" Jessie asked.

"Sure." Ian still watched her, his customary wariness shaping his expression. "I guess."

Jessie eased down onto a blanket spread out beneath the trees and settled beside a backpack, an old rusty fishing pole, and what she assumed was a tackle box. A jar of wiggling worms sat off to the side. "Have you caught anything?" she asked.

"Naw." Ian knelt opposite her on the blanket. "It's the end of the month. They stock it at the beginning. There's probably not much left."

Jessie took in the greenery around them, the chirping birds, the sound of the breeze through the leaves of the trees. "This is nice. Do you spend a lot of time out here?"

"Till it gets too cold." He shrugged, and the look in his eyes told her he could do this all day.

She couldn't blame him. Even with the couple of moments of connection they'd shared, she was sure he wasn't used to anyone, particularly authority figures, seeking him out for anything other than him being in trouble. She was happy to dispel that. "Well, you must be wondering why I'm here." She smiled. "I have some good news for you." She retrieved the notebook he used for his drawings from her bag and handed it to him. He'd given it to her so she could show the art teacher his work. "Mr. Eldridge was very impressed."

Ian held it tentatively.

"He'd very much like to work with you," Jessie went on, "and has agreed to let you into his sixth period class. We checked your schedule, and we'll need to rearrange some things."

"Sixth period's Advanced Art," Ian said with evident wonder.

Jessie nodded, still smiling. Now that she was here, she was glad he and his grandfather had no phone. She wouldn't have wanted to miss this look on his face. "It is. Mr. Eldridge said with your skill, you won't have any trouble at that level. He said there will probably be some terminology and some other mediums for you to learn, but other than that, you'll fit right in."

Ian lowered his gaze to the notebook again, then lifted it back to Jessie. He still looked skeptical. "What about my grades?"

She admired his concern for the rules. "Mr. Eldridge said as long as you don't cause any trouble in his class and stay off the suspension list, he'll overlook that. I'll be happy to help you get your English grade up, though. And I've even been known to pass a few math tests in my life." She thought of the detention he'd just served as well as what Isaac had told her about some kind of trouble he was in. If whatever that was blew up, it would ruin his opportunity for this chance, but she didn't want to taint this moment for him by bringing up any of that.

He gave a weak smile at her humor.

"I can tutor you, if you'd like to maintain your place in the art class legitimately."

"Okay." He brightened, the doubt leaving his expression.

Jessie had known he'd want that. That way, no one could take this from him. Her heart ached at the thought of how much loss this boy had suffered at such a young age. "Okay then," she said, widening her smile. "We'll work out those details."

A grin finally broke free. "Fuckin' a," he said, then immediately, his eyes went wide. "I'm sorry," he added in a rush. "I didn't mean to say that."

"It's okay." Jessie laughed. "We'll chalk it up to the heat of the moment." She returned to her bag. "I have something else for you, as long as I'm here." She held out a brand new copy of the graphic novel of *A Game of Thrones* and a paperback of the actual novel. "Now you can return Richard's to him."

He froze, then drew back ever so slightly.

Jessie wiggled the books at him. "Go on, take them. They're not going to bite."

He reached for them, then eased down, sitting cross-legged. He stared at the books in his hands. "I just really wanted to read it," he said finally, the words barely audible.

She was glad he hadn't bothered with a denial. He was clearly beginning to trust her. "I understand," she said softly. She remembered how hard it was to grow up without the things all the other kids had, even the unnecessary ones. Maybe especially the unnecessary ones. The books and movies and games that everyone was talking about, that she'd had no way of joining in on, leaving her isolated and alone. "And now, you have your own copy, but you do need to return Richard's to him."

Ian looked sick. "How do I do that without…If I get into any more trouble, I'll get suspended."

Jessie realized what he was getting at. If he returned the book the *right* way, face-to-face with an explanation and an apology, he could end up back in Vice Principal Thornton's office and get suspended. Then there went the art class she'd just dangled in front of him, like a piece of steak in front of that scrawny dog he'd drawn, only to be snatched away before he could even taste it. She sighed. "Can you think of a way that wouldn't jeopardize anything?"

"If I just left it on his desk where I took it? You know, without saying anything?"

Jessie studied him. "And no more stealing?" she asked, her tone firm.

Ian shook his head. "I promise."

"Is there anything else that needs to be cleared up before a fresh start?"

Ian hesitated.

Jessie paused long enough to give him the chance to bring up whatever else was going on. When he didn't, she resigned herself to what they'd accomplished so far being enough. She'd do some poking around on her own before asking him about it directly. "All right, then. Go see your counselor first thing Monday morning, and she'll give you your new schedule that incorporates your art class, and we'll go from there."

He lifted his gaze to hers, his expression a mixture of disbelief and gratitude. "Thank you, Ms. Weldon. I…" He looked away. "Thank you."

"It's my pleasure, Ian. I'm happy to help an aspiring artist," she said brightly in an attempt to alleviate his evident discomfort. "When you're rich and famous, I'll expect an autograph."

He laughed, then returned his attention to the books in his hands. "Is the actual book different from the graphic novel," he asked, the change in subject obviously deliberate.

"I don't know. I've never read the graphic novel," Jessie said, going with the shift. "How about if I read it and you read the novel, and then we'll talk about it?"

Ian nodded. "Okay."

By the time Jessie was back in her car and on her way to her last stop, it was mid-afternoon. She'd stayed longer with Ian, chatting with him about the basics of *A Game of Thrones*, impressing him with her willingness to reach into the jar of worms and bait the hook, then awing him with a beautiful cast of the line out into the middle of the reservoir. She'd sent him home with two good-sized catches he and Isaac could fry up for dinner. The look on his face had been priceless.

She was glad to be able to give him that kind of time. What she would have given to have had a teacher do that for her when she'd been so lost and felt so alone. Maybe it was the fact that she hadn't, though, that made it so important to her to offer it to Ian. Who knew how these things worked? She just knew she'd never forget this afternoon with him.

She smiled as she checked her side mirror before moving into the left turn lane at the entrance to Shady Acres Assisted Living.

Before she'd gone to see Ian, her morning had been filled with stops at various locally owned businesses to speak with the owners about the possibility of their participation in the student internship program she wanted to start. She'd been pleased with the amount of interest she'd found, but almost all of them had brought up the same concern as Curtis—financial backing for the additional costs. When she'd proposed the idea to the superintendent of the Clearwater Springs School District, he'd told her there was no room in the budget for such a program, but that if she could find funding somewhere else, he was sure the board would give the green light on the project.

"It sounds like a win-win all the way around," he'd said.

Many of the business owners had suggested asking the Scott Foundation for financial assistance, but she couldn't imagine herself going, hat in hand, begging for money from the Scotts. If the kiss with Dakota hadn't already flipped her mother over several times in her grave, surely the mere idea of asking them for funding for *anything* would shatter her eternal slumber. Jessie was confident she could find backing elsewhere. She'd get on the Internet tonight and research grants and endowments for programs like this one. There had to be some.

Jessie was greeted warmly by Regina Melville, the managing owner of the facility, and escorted into her office. She gave her presentation, which she could do in her sleep by now, highlighting the benefits to both the businesses and the community as well as the obvious advantages to the students, and received the reactions she'd grown accustomed to—surprise, enthusiasm, questions about the logistics, financial concerns, and, finally, the suggestion of the Scott Foundation. She smiled, answered the questions, added Shady Acres to the list of interested participants, and thanked Regina profusely. The beginning stages of this project were going better than she could have hoped.

When they stepped from Regina's office, Jessie paused and offered her hand. As they shook, the melody of a familiar song, one of Jessie's favorites as a child, touched her ears. She tilted her head. "'Puff the Magic Dragon'?"

Regina laughed. "Yes. Sometimes the family members of our residents or community members come in and provide entertainment. We get all kinds of things."

Jessie listened to the story of Jackie Paper. The voice singing it was a rich alto. "I love this song."

"You're welcome to stop by the dining room and listen for a while," Regina said. "We always like the community to know what we provide."

They followed the music down the corridor and through the wide double doors to the dining hall. Thirty or forty residents were scattered among the tables, some in wheelchairs, one group playing cards. A couple moved in a circle, dancing to the children's song.

Jessie smiled. When her eyes landed on Dakota seated on a stool on the small stage at the front of the room, she couldn't help but laugh. *Dakota Scott, singing "Puff the Magic Dragon" to a group of senior citizens?* It was something she couldn't have conjured in her wildest imagination.

As Dakota played the final chord, she looked directly at Jessie, then immediately broke into "The Purple People Eater."

Jessie leaned against the doorjamb, mesmerized. She shouldn't be, especially considering she was still having flashes of dream Dakota from that morning. She should leave, keep things professional, keep her distance. She couldn't do those things if she was mesmerized. There was something about Dakota in this context, though—outside of school, completely separate from their past, so casual and having fun. Jessie couldn't take her eyes off of her. If they'd met now for the first time, could things be different? Would they have been different? Would they have gone out for coffee, then dinner? When they'd kissed, would they have continued kissing into the early morning hours, instead of Jessie breaking it off and running out into the rain soaked night? Could they have been something to one another other than a painful reminder of a long ago shared tragedy?

She caught herself. All irrelevant questions. They were who they were, nothing could change that. She straightened. "I should go," she said briskly. She turned to Regina. "Thank you again for your willingness to be part of the internship program. I'll be in touch as it progresses."

"Oh!" Regina said, sounding surprised. "Why don't you wait and speak with Dakota." She waved toward the stage. "She's one of the Scotts, you know."

"Yes, I know," Jessie said politely. "But I don't have anything close to a formal proposal to present yet."

"That's okay. Let's just run the idea by her and see what she thinks." Regina waved at Dakota again, who nodded to show she'd seen the gesture.

Dakota had finished singing and was putting her guitar in its case. She smiled their way.

Was that a hesitation, a flinch, Jessie saw? Of course it was. She was undoubtedly no more eager to talk to Jessie than Jessie was to talk to her. Hadn't they agreed on that, albeit unofficially?

She started toward them, her trademark relaxed, cocky saunter forcing Jessie to look away.

"Dakota," Regina said, beaming. "That was wonderful, as always."

Dakota gave a sheepish grin. "Well, it was definitely as always. I'll agree to that." She turned her attention to Jessie and leaned in, conspiratorially. "I only know five songs, so I play the same ones every time I come," she whispered. "Fortunately, most of the residents don't remember. I think the staff is about to run me off, though."

"Not a chance," Regina said. "We appreciate all community involvement. And you sing your five songs very well." She winked and laughed. "Have you met Jessica Weldon?"

"Yes. We work together." Dakota tipped her head to Jessie.

"Coach Scott," Jessie said in acknowledgement.

"Of course, how silly of me," Regina said. "Jessica has just presented an intriguing proposal for a student internship program to enable high school students who aren't college bound to learn marketable skills in their areas of interest."

"Really?" Dakota rested an arm on the end of her guitar case. She looked at Jessie. "That does sound interesting."

"It's in need of some funding, however," Regina said, hurrying on. "Is that something the Scott Foundation might be open to?"

Dakota's eyes lingered on Jessie, an intensity brightening the deep green—or was it simply the shade of the sweater she wore?

Jessie remembered those eyes in her dream. Dakota above her, gazing down at her as she slipped her fingers—She startled back to the moment, but not before her body responded to the memory.

Dakota looked to Regina. "I don't have anything to do with the foundation," she said pleasantly. "That's my older sister's domain. But I'm sure she'd be happy to listen to the details." She glanced back at Jessie.

Jessie's cheeks were warm. Arousal throbbed between her thighs. *Damn it!*

"She did say she was looking for something new and different this year. You should get in touch with her." Dakota flashed her grin. "If you ladies will excuse me, I need to get going. Thanks, Regina, for letting me play rock star."

Regina hugged her. "Any time, you know that. It's the only thing that keeps Dodger under control."

"Always a pleasure," Dakota said to Jessie.

Jessie admired her easy demeanor, her ability to appear exactly how she wanted. She only hoped her own manner conveyed equivalent coolness. She knew Dakota wasn't masking desire, though. She knew exactly how Dakota felt about her. Dakota had told her in no uncertain terms. She simply nodded in agreement. Better that the encounter end.

As she watched Dakota stride down the hall, though, she thought of Ian, his bruised ribs, the trouble his grandfather had referred to. She remembered the three boys Ian had avoided that first day she'd met him. They were athletes. Dakota would most likely know who they were. And she obviously knew about the fight Ian had been in because she'd made the comment about him being trouble. Would she be willing to put their personal issues aside and tell Jessie what she knew, if anything?

Jessie could probably get some information from Vice Principal Thornton. Then she wouldn't have to ask Dakota for help. She could talk to the football coach as well, though she hadn't made any points with him in the last conversation they'd had. He'd approached Jessie for the same reason Dakota had when Jessie first started the substitute position, but he hadn't taken as well to her suggestions for his players as Dakota.

No, Jessie could do this. She could talk to Dakota, even if it was uncomfortable. It wasn't as though Jessie was asking for herself. It was for Ian, after all.

Chapter Eleven

Dakota shoved her guitar into the backseat of her Jeep and slammed the door. *What the hell? That woman was in town for five months before I ever met her, but now I can't even go visit an old friend without running into her.*

Wasn't it enough that she saw her every day at school, sometimes twice if they ran into each other in the teachers' lounge? She'd also seen her earlier in the week coming out of the grocery store, fortunately before Dakota had gotten out of her car, so she'd avoided her by waiting until Jessie had driven away. It'd still had the same effect as always, though. In fact, in some ways, it was even stronger, since she was able to watch her without the distraction of social amenities and trying to pretend they were simply colleagues. She'd been drawn in by the way Jessie moved, the sway of her hips as she'd rounded the end of her car, the infectious quality of her smile as she'd greeted the kid collecting carts and how he'd grinned back at her. Dakota had been riveted, remembering how that mouth had felt beneath hers, how inviting and welcoming it'd been, until, all of a sudden, it wasn't.

She wanted more, even though she didn't. She wanted to be close to Jessie again, even though all she wanted was to be as far away as possible. She wanted to see her in *that* way every single day, while at the same time, never wanting to see her again. Was she losing it?

That day in the parking lot, after Jessie was gone, Dakota had realized she was unconsciously squeezing her legs tightly around her pulsing center, her hand resting high on her thigh, itching to take over. And today, when she'd leaned in close to Jessie to make the joke about how few songs she knew... She shouldn't have inhaled. The light fragrance of peaches that always hovered around Jessie made Dakota want to taste her. The underlying scent of outdoors and a hint of...fish? Who knew what that was about. But being close enough to Jessie to take all that in had set Dakota on fire. She'd wanted so badly to be pressed against her, to hold Jessie close, that her nipples had tightened at the mere thought. And with that surge of desire, as always—even if in a dream—came the anger. Why, if she had to be this attracted to someone, did it have to be someone who brought up so much other crap as well?

She's opening you up. Drew's words drifted back to her. And maybe that was why Dakota had to be so attracted to her. If it'd been just anyone, she could easily walk away and forget all about her. The Universe was cruel sometimes. What better plan to get someone to deal with their shit than to wrap it all up in an irresistible package? *Christ.* Well, she didn't have to deal with it right now. She yanked open her car door. Before she could climb in behind the wheel, though, she heard that voice.

"Coach Scott?" Jessie called from a distance. "May I speak with you for a minute?"

Dakota squeezed her eyes shut and grimaced. *And you still won't call me Dakota.* "Yes, Ms. Weldon." She ground out the words as she turned to face her. "What can I do for you?"

Jessie picked up her pace, then broke into a jog, covering the space between them. Her silken hair lifted in a fluid motion, her full breasts undulated with each footfall, the muscles of her hips and thighs strained beneath the denim of her jeans.

Dakota gave an inner eye roll. *Really, Universe? Enough already. I get it.*

Jessie stopped in front of her and smiled. "I'm glad I caught you." She took in a long breath. "You really sounded good in there." She waved in the general direction of the facility. "How often do you do that?"

"Thanks." Dakota softened. It wasn't Jessie's fault she made Dakota crazy. She had no control over whose sister she was or all the things she brought up for Dakota. She had no idea how she made Dakota ache. "I try to make it out here a couple of times a month."

"That's nice of you. They seem to really enjoy it."

"Dodger hounded me for months to get me to do it the first time, but then, it was so much fun, I kept doing it." Dakota shrugged. "I guess it's a small way of giving back. Most of the people in there were part of my childhood."

The corners of Jessie's mouth lifted slightly and her eyes went tender. "That's sweet."

Dakota fidgeted. "Yeah, well…I'm sure that's not what you wanted to talk to me about."

"No. No, it isn't," Jessie said, regaining a look of focus. "I wanted to ask you if you know anything about the fight that Ian Langston was in a few weeks ago. The boy in my classroom at lunch with Melinda?" she added quickly.

"I heard about it," Dakota said, thinking back. "What of it?"

"Do you know who he fought?"

Dakota hesitated, wondering where Jessie was going.

"I saw an interesting exchange between Ian and three boys in letterman jackets the first day I met him. He looked like he was avoiding them, and they seemed…I don't know…threatening."

Dakota raised an eyebrow. "Threatening?"

"Yes. When Ian left my room, they were waiting at the end of the hall and stared at him, until he went the other way. Melinda was with them. I could ask her if she knows anything, but I just thought…"

Dakota remembered the time she'd seen almost exactly the same interaction between Ian, Justin Byrd, Alex Damian, and Dale Simpson. But Ian had said nothing was going on there. "I know who they are," she said guardedly. "You think there's more to it than just the one fight?"

Jessie pursed her lips. "I talked with Ian's grandfather today, and he said Ian's come home with a variety of injuries over the past couple of months. Then yesterday, he left for school, only to return an hour later pretty beaten up. He might even have some bruised ribs." A light wind kicked up and blew Jessie's hair across her face.

Dakota wanted to tuck it back behind her ear, just to be able to touch her. Instead, she folded her arms across her chest. "And you think it's these boys you saw that are bullying him?"

Jessie stiffened almost imperceptibly, but Dakota caught it. "I realize, Coach Scott, that sometimes coaches like to think athletes are above certain—"

"Don't go there, Ms. Weldon." She emphasized the name for effect. "I'm simply trying to get information and determine exactly what it is you're saying." In fact, Dakota wasn't the kind of coach Jessie had been about to refer to. Yes, she'd asked for favors on grades and such, but when it came to her athletes bullying other kids, she didn't stand for it. "I stress to my athletes that their roles at the school and in our community are the same as professional athletes. They're role models, and they're to behave as such. Anyone found abusing that role faces the consequences. And I hold all of our athletes to that."

Jessie looked contrite. "I apologize. And I'm glad to hear that, because I think something's going on between Ian and these boys, and it seems Ian's the only one who's had any consequences."

"What do you mean?"

"Ian is in my detention, but none of the other boys are."

Dakota shrugged. "Yours isn't the only detention."

"No," Jessie said, her tone dangerously close to condescending. "But the other one is after school, and if the boys are on the football team—and they look as though they would be—they wouldn't be able to do the after school detention because of practice."

"They are." Dakota nodded. "And no, they wouldn't be assigned the after school detention."

"So why is Ian the only one who got detention, since all four of them were in the fight?" Jessie asked, clearly trying to hold back her temper. "Never mind that Ian has been told repeatedly that if he gets into any more trouble at all, he'll be suspended."

Dakota fought back a grin. As clichéd as it was, Jessie was cute when she was all fired up, as long as she wasn't fired up at Dakota. She remembered Jessie's John Wayne imitation and had to cover a laugh with a cough. What she was saying, though, was important. She was right. Ian shouldn't have been the only one to serve consequences, and it made the entire athletic department look bad. "Let me check into it, ask a few questions, and see what I can find out."

"Thank you, Coach Scott."

"Is that it?" That was it for Dakota. She was done. This whole love/hate thing she had going with Jessie, the fluctuating emotions, one minute wanting to tell her off, the next wanting to touch her, kiss her, take her right there on the hood of her car, was exhausting.

"Yes." Jessie looked like she wanted to say more, but she didn't.

Dakota climbed into her Jeep. "Okay, then. I'll look into it on Monday." She pressed the button to start the engine. "I'll let you know as soon as I find out anything." She glanced at Jessie for acknowledgement to make sure she wasn't being rude, then pulled the door closed. She needed distance.

After picking up a deli salad on her way home, Dakota stretched out on her couch to enjoy it. She'd considered going out to the ranch house for dinner to avoid being alone with her thoughts, but as she sat in the quiet of her house, she realized the quiet was exactly what she needed. There was a lot to process from the day. There was Drew's confession at the top of the list. That was something she never would have guessed. If only she'd... *God, I've been such an ass.* She was glad, though, she'd finally given him the peace he'd needed.

Dakota's own revelations, ones she'd seldom, if ever, let herself say out loud, had felt good. It'd been surprisingly easy, though Dakota knew it was all in the timing. Other times she'd tried, it'd practically choked her.

Now there was also the fight Jessie had brought up and the questions that went with it. When she'd heard about it, Coach Allen had said Ian had jumped the other boys in the locker room following an altercation during a basketball game in their P. E. class. At the time, Dakota didn't think much of it. Teenage boys came with a lot of wildly flowing testosterone. Fights happened. Now that she thought about it, though, and had seen Ian in the hall that day, she had to admit, the story didn't make any sense. She stabbed a forkful of salad and shoved it into her mouth.

And Jessie… Had Ian asked her for help? Dakota doubted it. He'd be too proud, or stubborn, to ask for help. She understood completely. So Jessie had noticed all this and was going to bat for the kid. Dakota admired the kind of teacher Jessie seemed to be. It made her want to do better. And what about what Drew said, that she sounded great not just as a teacher? *Well, no denying that.*

What was Dakota supposed to do with it, though? Images of Jessie that afternoon, her cheeks flushed, her hair gently blowing around her face, her eyes so animated as she spoke. Dakota could have simply leaned down and kissed her, taken those soft lips for her own. *Mmmm, wouldn't that be nice? Mine to kiss any time I want.* She gave herself a brief moment of indulgence, then called herself into check. *That doesn't help anything.* She had all the rest to deal with.

As scattered as her thoughts were, one had lurked in the back of her mind all afternoon. *Have you been out there?* Drew had asked the question almost casually, as though he expected her to say yes. *Sure, I go out once a month or so and have a picnic in the spot where I killed someone.* He'd said it'd helped him, though, to let go of the guilt. Why would that be? Dakota tried to figure out the connection, but what did she know about how the mind and emotions worked? She'd spent most of her life running from them. Maybe it was time to stop.

After only three more bites, she dropped her fork into her salad and tossed the bowl onto the coffee table. She glanced outside. It was dark. Without giving herself a chance to back out, she grabbed her keys and headed out.

She drove for hours, hitting every back road around Clearwater Springs except Hightower. She'd even deliberately avoided it twice, not ready to face whatever awaited her there. Finally, at eleven o'clock, she made herself turn at the junction where the highway met Hightower. She was still about ten miles from Brogan's Bend. God, she hated the name, especially now that she knew Jessie. It seemed so dismissive when she knew someone could be hurt by it.

Eight miles. She kept her speed down, taking the curves slowly. She remembered how fast she used to take them, knowing the pattern of the road like it was part of her.

Six miles. A mailbox beside a gravel drive that led into the trees. That was new.

Four miles, Three. Two. Nothing else was different. All just the same as it had been then. Around the final curve, and there it was.

Dakota braked to a stop. She stared.

It was beautiful.

She held her breath, expecting something to change, but nothing did. The trees reached high into the sky, each branch fringed in moonlight. The meadow on the other side looked like the setting for a fairy tale cottage where dwarves might live. Rocks and trees lining either side made the road seem sleek, like an iced sled run. It didn't look anything like what she'd made up in her mind all these years, nothing like a Dead Man's Curve or Kamikaze Corner. Just a bend in the road that people traveled every day on their way home.

She got out of her car and leaned on the door, taking in the scene. It was so quiet, only the soft whoosh of the air moving through the trees and an occasional hoot of an owl. Had it been this quiet that night, before the roar of an engine, the screech of tires, the shattering of glass? She closed the door and walked up the center of the road, her hands in the pockets of her down vest. She turned in a full circle in the exact spot where it'd happened. She didn't have to guess or even think about it. It still haunted her dreams.

But she didn't *feel* anything. *Shouldn't I feel something?*

She walked to the other side—where Jackie had been—and into the trees. Where, exactly, was she standing? Dakota looked up. She startled. Her gait caught. A shadow in the moonlight.

"Don't worry. I'm not a ghost." Jessie's voice.

Dakota took a deep breath, steadying her nerves, then groaned softly. Jessie was the last person she wanted to see—again, today—but she couldn't curb her curiosity as to what she was doing out there. She made her way to the base of the tall rock Jessie sat on and looked up at her, uncertain what to say.

"Come here often?" Jessie asked, with a hint of humor.

Dakota knew, though, she was serious as well. Dakota would love to know the same thing. "No, never. It's my first time since…"

"Oh, that's right. You've spent your life trying to forget." Jessie looped her arms around her drawn up knees and looked out across the road.

"How'd you get up there?" Dakota looked around for a path.

"The back of the rock is sloped. You can walk right up."

"Mind if I join you?"

There was a pause before Jessie said, "Okay."

Dakota settled next to her and dangled her legs over the edge. Why hadn't she known Jessie was there? Then it hit her. "Where's your car?"

"At home," Jessie said. She pulled her bomber jacket more tightly around her.

Dakota looked at her, surprised. "You walked all the way here from town?"

"Well, from the Triple M." Jessie leaned back and gazed up into the branches of the trees. "I like to walk. It clears my head."

Dakota wondered what the smooth skin of her throat would feel like under her lips. "Still, that's quite a walk." She looked away.

"Three point seven miles," Jessie said decisively.

Dakota chuckled. "I see. But then, three point seven miles back, too."

"Yes, sometimes that's the questionable part after sitting out here on a hard rock for a while." Jessie's tone was light, maybe even friendly. "But you know what they say. The way home is always easier."

Dakota wasn't sure she agreed, but for the sake of argument, she nodded. "So the Triple M is home?"

"Ever since Curtis and Laura took me in after my mother died," Jessie said, tucking a lock of hair behind her ear, as Dakota had wanted to do earlier. "I lived there the last few years of high school, then left for college. Curtis and Laura are my sense of home, so that's where I went when I finally came back."

Dakota thought of her own family—big and loud and full of drama—and couldn't imagine being alone at such a young age. Or even now, for that matter. Her own guilt reared up at the part she'd played in that for Jessie. "So...do you...come here often?" She asked, changing the subject.

Jessie cut her a sideways glance.

"If you don't want to say, that's fine." Dakota didn't know if she'd violated a boundary. It was hard to tell where the lines were between them.

"I'm just surprised you want to know. Last time anything about this place came up, you were pretty adamant about not wanting anything to do with the subject." Jessie smiled softly. "But I don't mind. I suppose I do come here relatively often. I started in high school at times when I missed my family a lot. It always helped me feel closer to my father and Jackie. I've only been here a few times since I've been back, but it's still nice."

"I've been afraid to come here," Dakota said without meaning to, but she kept going. "I think I was scared that if I did, it'd happen all over again. I'd see it all again, which is stupid, now that I think about it, since I've been seeing it over and over in my head all these years."

Jessie didn't say anything. She didn't even look at Dakota. She simply slipped her hand over Dakota's where it rested on the edge of the rock, squeezed it gently, then eased away.

Her touch was soothing, with the bare whisper of a thank you, and it spread through Dakota like a healing balm over a raw and jagged wound. Dakota remembered what Jessie had said, that she wanted to know that Dakota understood there were consequences to that night. Did she mean she needed to know Dakota was affected by what happened? And was that *all* she needed? Like Drew, just one simple thing?

"I think I've never worried about that because I've never really known what actually happened that night," Jessie said finally. "Even when I'm out here and I look at the road, I don't know which way the car was going or where on the curve it took place. I don't know where Jackie's body ended up. I've always wondered."

Dakota took in Jessie's profile in the dappled moonlight that shone through the trees. Her features were composed, expressionless. There was no trace of Jessica Weldon, the teacher. In that moment, she was simply Jessie Brogan, the girl who'd lost her sister, and Dakota was simply Dakota, the girl who'd taken her.

"Do you want to know?" Dakota whispered. This was something else she could give Jessie, wasn't it? She could do it, right?

Jessie didn't answer for several minutes.

Dakota waited, knowing how important that answer was, because once Jessie knew the details, she could never unknow them. This place might never be the same for her. Jessie's long deliberation of the question told Dakota she knew the importance of the answer as well.

At length, Jessie turned to her. "Yes."

Dakota stood and held out her hand.

Jessie took it, but didn't let go once she was standing.

Dakota led her down the back slope of the rock and out to the road.

As they reached the pavement, Jessie lagged, stretching their arms out between them, but still not releasing Dakota's fingers. Her eyes were wide as she stared into the night.

"Are you sure you want to do this?" Dakota asked.

Jessie nodded, her lips tight. "Just give me a minute."

While she waited, Dakota glanced down the road in the direction from which she'd been coming the night of the accident. Was she sure *she* wanted to do this? Could she now that she'd offered?

"All right," Jessie said. "I'm ready."

Dakota tightened her grip, then led them down the lane to the entrance of the curve. "We were coming from this way. From town. We were coming from Stevie McCall's house. Remember him?" As soon as she asked the question, she felt like an idiot. *How irrelevant can that be?* Who cared if she remembered Stevie?

Jessie seemed to have had the same thought, since she said nothing, her expression expectant.

"I had been speeding, but I'd slowed down for the previous curve. I swear." She looked at Jessie for acknowledgement.

Another slight nod.

Dakota moved back the way they'd come, then stopped. "And it was right here. I don't know where she came from." Drew's version flashed in her mind. *No.* Jessie had asked to hear what happened, so she was going to hear what Dakota knew, not what other people thought. "I *hadn't* looked away. At Drew. At the radio dial. My eyes were on the road. And suddenly, she was just… right here…out of nowhere." Her voice faltered. She wanted to do this—for Jessie and herself—but it was all coming at her now. She struggled to slow it down, struggled to breathe. "Drew yelled something. Look out, I think. Right as I hit the brake. But it was too late. There was a huge thump, and the car jerked, then the loud crack of glass as she hit the windshield. And then that crackle, when the cracks spider-webbed through the glass. It seemed so loud." As she spoke, the image that had haunted her for so long flooded her mind once more—Jackie's face, broken and bleeding, against the shattered glass. *Shit! Here come the feelings.* The shock, the terror, the regret, the guilt. She started, and her heart pounded. "It was like she could see me, see who killed her. I don't know if she could. Or if she was maybe still alive." Dakota's voice broke. She felt Jessie's arms come around her and realized she'd stopped seeing the present.

Jessie still didn't speak. She only held her tightly.

Dakota forced herself to focus.

"Can you go on?" Jessie whispered. "I want to know it all."

"Yeah." Dakota wanted to swallow the word, but steeled herself for the rest. "Then she was gone," she said, relieved that the image had vanished also. "And the car went into a spin. It skidded all the way around, then slammed into that tree." She pointed to the one that had dented in the driver's door and trapped her inside for the few minutes it'd taken Drew to come to his senses and drag her out over the console.

Jessie followed her gesture, the tree holding her attention for several minutes, as though she was trying to picture the scene. Then she returned her focus to the road. "Where was Jackie?"

Dakota inhaled deeply, then walked off the pavement and into the trees and underbrush. "We found her over here."

Jessie followed.

"She was thrown pretty far." Dakota stepped between two rocks and stared at the ground. A shiver ran through her.

Jessie stopped beside her. She looked back to the point on the road where Dakota said Jackie had appeared, then back to her feet. She knelt. At length, she ran her fingertips over the dirt, then pressed her palm against it. Then the other. She bowed her head. Her shoulders began to shake.

Dakota stood frozen in place, struck inactive by uncertainty, then instinct took over. She squatted and ran a gentle hand over Jessie's back.

Jessie turned and leaned into her. She gripped Dakota's vest and buried her face in the hollow of Dakota's shoulder.

"Jessie, I'm so sorry," Dakota said, her breath catching in her throat. "Maybe if I'd swerved sooner. Or braked harder. Or…" She squeezed her eyes shut.

"Dakota." Jessie pressed her fingers to Dakota's lips. "Shhh." The audible caress came through a choked sob.

The sound of Jessie whispering her name—not Coach Scott—touched something deep inside Dakota. She broke apart, walls she'd so carefully constructed crumbling to dust. Tears spilled down her cheeks. Her strength failed, and she dropped the remaining distance to the ground. She encircled Jessie in her arms and leaned against the rock behind her, bringing Jessie with her.

Jessie hugged her tightly as they both cried.

Dakota felt like a huge block of ice was melting inside her. She'd never felt such relief and comfort in tears.

Chapter Twelve

Jessie had no idea how long they'd been lying there. She'd cried herself out in Dakota's arms, her own wrapped around Dakota's waist, and Dakota had seemed to do the same. After their tears were spent, though, neither one had moved. Neither had spoken. They had simply lain under the trees, under the stars, in the quiet.

The entire night had been dreamlike, from the time Jessie had seen Dakota's car pull to a stop, watched her get out, taken in her movements, her facial expressions as she'd walked up the road. She'd known the instant Dakota had seen her by the catch in her step, and had been astonished when Dakota had asked if she could join her. She'd almost made a snide remark when Dakota had said she'd never been out there before, but she was glad she hadn't. She'd somehow sensed that whatever brought Dakota there tonight was important. So she'd shared something important to her as well. There had seemed something magical about the scene. As they'd begun with a little light banter and some small talk, then proceeded to more serious topics, Jessie felt she would have told Dakota anything, and, clearly, Dakota had felt the same. Even now, Jessie felt as though they were in a protective bubble that had somehow stopped time, suspending them simultaneously in the present and in the past.

Jessie knew she should get up, or at least say something, but she didn't want to. She wanted to stay right here, in this moment.

She now knew the details she'd ached to know for so long about what had actually happened that night. The things she'd wondered about every time she'd come out to Brogan's Bend, every time she'd thought about it. Exactly where the car had come from, where Jackie had been—where she had died. Now she knew it all. Now, though, she wanted to know more. She wanted to know about Dakota, how she felt, and, in truth, how she'd survived that night all these years. True, she'd shut herself off from it all. She'd distanced herself. But still…

The muscles of Dakota's shoulder moved beneath Jessie's cheek, and Dakota brought her hand up to stroke Jessie's hair. The caress was feather light, like in Jessie's dream.

How had she known what Dakota's touch would feel like?

Dakota began a gentle massage of Jessie scalp, rubbing her temple, combing her fingers through Jessie's hair. She slipped her hand beneath the fleece collar of Jessie's jacket and slowly stroked the sensitive skin of her neck.

Jessie closed her eyes and sank into the sensations, the emotions. This was the touch she'd waited for all her life but had found only in her imagination. It'd been the touch of many fantasy women, mostly faceless, occasionally even Dakota, for which she'd chastised herself and called it ridiculous. But here it was, and it was everything she'd known it would be. Not only sexually. Yes, her body was definitely responding to each stroke of those fingers, to each tiny circle of her pulse point, but more than that, it called to her deep in her soul—and her soul was answering.

"You awake?" Dakota whispered.

Jessie didn't want to speak. She didn't want to break this spell. "Yes," she said, just as softly.

"You're shivering."

Not shivering. Trembling. She couldn't help but notice, though, that the temperature had dropped. Her upper body was supported by Dakota's torso, warmth radiating between them. Even through her jeans, however, where the side of one leg met the bare earth and the other fell victim to the night air, she could feel the chill. "It's a little cold."

"Do you want me to drive you home?"

"I'm not ready." Jessie tightened her hold on Dakota. She immediately regretted it. She hadn't intended to be out here this late, and surely, Dakota hadn't either. She probably had a lot to do the next day. "But if you need to go, you don't have to—"

"No. I'd like to stay here with you longer…If that's okay." Dakota's voice shook slightly. "I have a sleeping bag in the Jeep we could wrap up in, if you want."

Jessie lifted her head and looked into Dakota's face. "That would be nice."

As Dakota jogged back from her car, Jessie met her on the far side of the road, leading the way between two trees and down to the edge of the meadow. "There's a great spot down here that's out of sight from the road," she said, stepping up onto a large flat rock and crossing it. "It has to be getting about that time of night when everyone's drunk enough to start daring their friends to come out here. They never make it this far."

Dakota chuckled. "You know all the ropes."

Jessie smiled over her shoulder. "It doesn't happen as much as it used to, but it has once or twice since I've been home." She sat on the rock's edge, then slid off the short drop to the ground below.

"Yeah, I heard." Dakota jumped down beside Jessie. "The morning after we…after I…the night you were at my house." She took in their surroundings. "You must have spent a lot of time out here to know this place so well."

"Yes," Jessie said, taking her own survey of the area. "That tree over there…" She pointed. "It has the coolest shade to lie in and read in July and August. And if you cross the meadow, beyond that grove, there's a little stream when you get thirsty. But I think whoever bought the land a little way down the road must own that acreage too, because now there's a fence you have to climb to get to the water." She glanced at Dakota.

Dakota wasn't looking in the direction Jessie had been speaking of, but rather, directly at her, amusement in her eyes. "You climbed a fence?"

Jessie flushed, not from the question, but from Dakota's direct attention. She felt like she was twelve again. "I was thirsty."

Dakota smiled. "And where's the best place to sit on a night like tonight?"

Jessie quelled the fluttering in her stomach. *Has there ever been a night like tonight?* "Right here," she said, pointing to their feet. "It's invisible from the road. We can see the whole meadow and watch how it changes as the moonlight shifts. And right beneath this little overhang…" She patted the rock. "There's a small mound that can be a nice pillow if you want to rest your head."

Dakota still watched her, but something Jessie couldn't identify had replaced the amusement. "Right here it is then," she said softly. She unhooked the bungee cord from around the sleeping bag, and unzipped the entire thing, making it flat. She draped it over her shoulders and opened her arms. "Come on," she said.

When Jessie had stepped in beside her and Dakota had wrapped an arm around her, they sat simultaneously. Their backs were covered, but the cold night air met their fronts.

"This won't work," Dakota said, clearly already seeking a new plan. "Stand up a sec."

Jessie did, stifling a laugh at Dakota's take-charge manner.

Dakota rearranged the bag around her, then splayed her legs wide and patted the fabric in front of her. "Sit right here." She looked up at Jessie. "Is that okay?"

Jessie wondered. Was it? Wasn't this still Dakota Scott, no matter what they'd shared tonight? *It's not a good idea. I should go home.* The protest was weak, though, the thought fleeting. She lowered herself to the ground between Dakota's thighs, her back to Dakota's chest, and drew up her knees.

Dakota closed the warmth of the sleeping bag around them, encasing them in their own snug cocoon.

Jessie relaxed into the comfort, the rightness of the moment. They weren't finished. She could tell. She'd learned a lot, but she still had questions. She let her mind wander to find them. There was always the looming one about Dakota's brother's statement, the one Jessie was never sure she could face. Anxiety quickened her pulse. Tonight seemed no exception. Besides, wouldn't Dakota have mentioned that if there were any truth to it? Even that consideration was too much, though. Maybe she could summon the nerve to ask sometime later. She let it skitter away.

She remembered the first time she'd seen Dakota, that basketball game she'd gone to with Jackie. She'd asked Jackie if she knew her. Jackie had laughed and said, "Everyone knows Dakota Scott." That's when *she'd* learned Dakota's name. But now, she wondered about the reverse. "Did you know Jackie?" she asked, breaking the silence that had closed in around them.

"I knew who she was," Dakota said without hesitation. Evidently, her thoughts had returned to that subject as well. "But I didn't really know her. I don't think we ever had an actual conversation. We never had any classes together or anything, since she was a year behind me."

Dakota's voice was low in Jessie's ear, her breath light across her cheek. It called Jessie even closer. She leaned her head back against Dakota's shoulder. "No," she said, thoughtfully. "She wouldn't have been in the same classes as you. She hated school and didn't do very well."

"I do have one really vivid memory of her, though." Dakota shifted slightly, bringing Jessie more snugly against her. "I mean, aside from the other one."

"What's that?" Jessie was curious that something else about Jackie would have stuck with Dakota all that time. She felt Dakota's head lift, as though she was looking out across the landscape or maybe at the stars.

"Do you remember Rochelle Bassler?"

"I think so," Jessie said. "She was a cheerleader, right?"

"That's her. And when we were all little, she was spoiled rotten and bossy and mean as a cornered bobcat. One day at school, word got around that she'd challenged Jackie to a fight over something that happened at lunch. I don't know what. Anyway, Rochelle was always challenging kids to fights, but no one ever showed up because if you did, you also had to face all of her friends, including a few boys. But Jackie…" Dakota let out a low chuckle. "She not only showed up, but she made short work of Rochelle's entourage of bodyguards by scattering them with a big stick, then went after Rochelle, who'd made a mad dash for home. Jackie chased her all the way. We all followed, of course. She stood outside on the front porch, screaming for her to come out and fight, until Rochelle's mother came to the door to find out what was going on. And Jackie told her. Every bit of it. And went on to tell her just what her sweet little girl was like at school and how mean she was." This time Dakota actually started to laugh.

Jessie smiled.

"After that, Rochelle started to change. I don't know if it was the fear and humiliation from what happened and everyone knowing about it, or if her mother had something to do with it, but by the time we all hit high school, Rochelle was a fairly decent human being."

Jessie sat with the story for a moment, picturing it all. "I can see Jackie doing that. It would have taken a lot to get her to that point, though." *Unless.* "How old was she? Do you remember?"

"Hm. Let's see, I was in fifth grade. I remember because the only reason I was there to see it all was that I was going home with a friend to work on our state reports. So that would have put Jackie in fourth. How old is that? Nine?"

"Yes. Nine." It made sense. "That was the year our dad was killed. Jackie was really angry for a long time. Maybe always." She felt Dakota go still.

"I'm sorry, Jessie." Dakota said, pressing her cheek to Jessie's hair. "I didn't mean to bring up something else that would hurt you. I thought it might help to hear something I remembered about Jackie."

"It did. It *does*." Jessie found Dakota's hands in the folds of the sleeping bag and squeezed them. "Don't be sorry. I've grieved my father's death. I don't actually remember a lot about him. I was pretty young when he died."

"How old?" Dakota asked.

"Six, just barely. It was three weeks after my birthday." Jessie thought about some of the things Jackie had said about their father.

"Jackie told me a lot about him, so I have her memories. But I always wished I'd had *him*."

Dakota nodded. "Yeah. That's a tough age to lose a parent. I was six when my mother first started changing. We didn't know what it was at the time, but all of a sudden, there were days she wasn't herself. Hell, when it all started, she was always around just us kids, so when she began acting out her delusions, at first, we all thought it was a fun game. Until it got more serious."

"Where was your father?" Jessie asked quietly.

"He was getting his veterinary practice going. He worked a lot of hours. He'd always intended to set up a practice here, and he came back to Clearwater Springs with Mom when Crystal was two. He got to work and never stopped. Meanwhile, they had three more babies that my mom took care of, in addition to running the ranch house and all the social and community responsibilities of being a Scott. It all got to be too much for her." There was a long pause before Dakota continued. "Then, Drew almost drowned. The doctors said later that was probably the final event that caused her psychotic break."

Jessie didn't know what to say that wouldn't sound trite. Dakota had most likely heard every reaction a person could have to such a tragic story. Before Jessie could find any words at all, Dakota went on.

"Can I tell you something I've never told anyone?" Her voice held a tremor.

Still holding Dakota's hands through the padded fabric, Jessie pulled Dakota's arms more tightly around her and turned her head to press her cheek against Dakota's. "If you want."

"I went with her one day. My mom. She wanted us to pick flowers. It was after her moods had gotten darker, and she'd become more unpredictable. Crystal had told me and Drew not to go anywhere with her alone, but Dad had said she was just going through a rough time and to try to help her. So I went." Dakota shuddered. "And when we were in the field of wildflowers, she changed. She started saying I wasn't really her daughter. That I'd stolen her daughter and taken her place. And she started shaking me and screaming at me to give her daughter back. I was so scared. I thought she was going to kill me. She shook me so hard, I lost my balance and fell down an embankment, over a bunch of rocks. By the time I got brave enough to climb back up, she was gone. When I got home, she was in the kitchen and told me to wash up for dinner. She didn't remember any of it."

"Oh my God, Dakota." Jessie sat up and twisted around to face her.

Dakota stared into the distance, tears streaking her cheeks.

Jessie could tell she wasn't finished. She cupped Dakota's chin and turned her head until their gazes met.

"I was too scared to tell anyone," Dakota said, resting her hands on Jessie's hips. "Crystal poured mercurochrome and stuck Band-Aids all over me, and demanded to know what happened, but I said I just tripped on my own. I knew if I told, they'd take my mother away. And it'd be my fault because I didn't listen to Crystal."

Jessie's heart broke at the pain in Dakota's eyes.

"But then later, they took her away because she almost killed Tina." Dakota took in a huge gulp of air. "And if I'd told Crystal what'd happened before, then she couldn't have almost hurt Tina, so that was my fault, too."

Jessie rose to her knees and took Dakota in her arms. "No, no, no." She rocked her. "None of it was your fault. You were just a little girl."

"I love my mother," Dakota said, grabbing onto Jessie as though she were drowning. "But I…I *hate* her. I wished…*she'd*… died that night instead of Jackie."

Then it hit Jessie—a memory. The night of the accident, a few hours before the police had come to the door, she'd been lying in bed, reading, and she'd looked out the window at that big house on the hill—and all the lights were on. "That's why you were on this road that night, isn't it? You were racing home to help find your mother?"

Dakota buried her face in Jessie's hair and began to sob.

"Shhh. Shhh. It's okay," Jessie whispered in Dakota's ear. "It's all okay." As the torrent of Dakota's tears began to ebb, Jessie eased them both to the ground and rearranged the sleeping bag around them again. She held Dakota, cradling her head against her breasts and stroking her back.

Finally, Dakota's breathing evened, and Jessie knew she was asleep.

So this is the reality of what it's like to be a Scott. Not all those fairy tale fantasies she'd made up. Not all the bitter beliefs of entitlement and having it easy her mother had conjured. This haunted woman in Jessie's arms was a true Scott.

From that first day Dakota had shown up in her classroom, Jessie never would have fathomed how much raw torment had been buried deep beneath that cocky façade. Even the night at her house, after Dakota had shared that snippet about life at the Ghost Rider Ranch, she'd bounced right back with flirtation and an actual kiss with all this churning below. *How did she do it?* Everyone does what they need to in order to survive, she knew. She'd done her share of burying things and trying to outrun them.

She'd wanted to know that Jackie's death had affected Dakota, had had an impact on her. She'd wanted her to know there were consequences, and now, *she* had learned of consequences she'd never have been able to imagine, intricately tied to so many other things. Whatever had made her think that once she'd gotten her answers, she could be done with Dakota? She felt more connected to her than ever.

Dakota stirred against her. "That feels good," she murmured.

It was only then that Jessie realized she'd slipped her hand beneath Dakota's down vest and was caressing her back through the soft knit of a thin sweater. She slowed her fingers.

"Don't stop. Please?"

Jessie made a tentative circle. Then another. "How are you feeling?" she asked, trying not to notice the play of muscle beneath her hand.

Dakota sighed. "To be honest, raw, drained, and not just a little bit embarrassed."

Jessie smiled, touched by the sincerity. She would have expected a joke or dismissal. Maybe they'd moved past all that, though. God knew, something should be different after a night like tonight. "There's nothing to be embarrassed about. You've been holding a lot in all these years. I don't know how you've done it."

"I'm sorry if it was—"

"It wasn't anything you need to apologize for. I think we both needed tonight," Jessie said, not wanting anything they'd shared ruined by regrets or after thoughts. "Can we just see where it all settles?"

Dakota raised up onto her elbow and gazed down at Jessie.

Jessie's hand slid down from Dakota's torso to her hip with the motion. She kept her other arm looped around Dakota's shoulders.

"I think Drew's right," Dakota said, staring into Jessie's eyes.

"About what?" Jessie whispered.

Dakota ran her thumb across Jessie's lower lip. "He said you're—"

"Dakota!" A deep voice boomed through the quiet night.

They both jumped.

"Jesus Christ!" Dakota said. "Who the hell was that?"

Jessie slapped a hand to her chest to steady her heartbeat, then laughed. "It sounded like God."

"Dakota! You out here?"

Dakota stood and peered over the edge of the rock they were beneath. "Who is that?" she called.

A bright light shone in her face. "It's me. Hank. You okay?"

"Hank? What the hell?" Dakota covered her eyes.

"Sorry." The light swiveled to the side.

Dakota climbed up onto the rock. "What are you doing out here?"

"Dispatch got several calls about your car being out on this road tonight," Hank said. "I thought when the last one came in four hours after the first, maybe I should come on out and check on you."

Curious, Jessie rose and looked up to where the other two stood.

A thirty-something, broad-shouldered man in a sheriff's uniform met her gaze. He wasn't anyone she knew. She had little to do with the police. "Oh. Sorry, ma'am. I didn't mean to interrupt—"

"You didn't, Hank. It's fine." Dakota reached down and helped Jessie over the ledge. "You didn't interrupt anything. This is Jessica Weldon," she said, not missing a beat. "Jessica, this is Sergeant Hank Woolf."

"It's nice to meet you, Sergeant." Jessie extended her hand, feeling her cheeks heat. She knew what he must be thinking.

He shook it, then turned back to Dakota. "Well, if everything's okay here, I'll be on my way." He seemed as embarrassed by the whole encounter as Jessie was feeling.

"Everything's good," Dakota said. "But thanks for checking."

"All right, then. I'll be seeing you." Hank walked away, switching off his flashlight as he reached the road.

When the patrol car engine started up and he pulled away, Jessie and Dakota began to laugh.

Dakota smirked. "Gotta love small towns," she said, with a shrug. "I think that's our cue to call it a night."

"I agree." Jessie smiled. But something had changed between them. Maybe everything. As she'd said, they'd let it all settle. "I want to do something first, though."

She crossed the road again to the spot where Dakota had said they'd found Jackie's body. She reached behind her neck and started working the clasp of the gold chain she'd worn for years. She shivered at the brush of Dakota's hands over her skin as Dakota lifted her hair out of the way. Her fingers slipped, but she managed the clasp and removed the necklace. "Will you hold this?" She held the gold ankh out to Dakota.

Dakota took it without a word.

Jessie knelt and began scooping away the loose topsoil, then tried digging her fingers into the more packed dirt beneath. It was moist from the recent rains, but still presented a challenge.

"Here, try this," Dakota said. She handed Jessie a Swiss army knife with an opened blade and spoon.

Jessie laughed and took it. "Thank you." Within minutes, she had a hole about eight inches deep. She took the necklace from Dakota and pressed it to her lips. "Be well, Jackie," she whispered. "Walk in peace in your new life, wherever that is." She placed the pendant in the hole and carefully covered it.

Dakota touched her shoulder. "Can I ask?"

Jessie swiped away a single tear. "Jackie liked the ankh. I'm not sure why. I looked it up, and it's the symbol of future life or life after death. She started drawing them and cutting out pictures in the last couple of years she was alive." Jessie got to her feet. "I bought that one in her memory when I was in Egypt eleven years ago, and I've always wanted to give it to her somehow. I was going to bury it at her gravesite, but that didn't feel right when I went to do it. This feels right."

Dakota tenderly finger combed Jessie's hair behind her ear and simply nodded.

As Dakota maneuvered her Jeep into the parking area behind the Triple M, she killed the lights, then the engine. She looked down at her hands on the steering wheel. "I'm not sure what to say about tonight, Jessie."

"You don't need to say anything, if you don't want to." Jessie studied her profile.

Dakota turned to her. "I do want to." She reached across the space and draped her hand over Jessie's headrest. "I don't know if I have words to tell you how much it means to me—"

The back porch light of the house came on and the door opened.

Jessie sighed in exasperation. Who would have thought there could be so many interruptions at four in the morning? She opened her door. "It's me, Curtis. I'll be in in a minute."

"Oh, okay, Jessie girl." Curtis waved and stepped back inside.

"He's a light sleeper," Jessie said with an apologetic smile.

Dakota laughed. "Is it just me, or does it feel like we're in high school again?"

"I was never out this late in high school," Jessie said innocently, and it was true, she *never* was. She met Dakota's eyes, a slightly darker green than usual under the dome light. "Thank you for telling me everything that happened that night. I don't know why, but it's always felt incomplete, not knowing, like I could never put it all fully behind me. Maybe now I can."

Dakota took Jessie's hand and ran her thumb over her knuckles. "I think it helped me, too, to be out there and go over it all again. And the rest of what I told you? I've never…" She shook her head. "That was something."

Jessie laced her fingers through Dakota's. "Yes, it was. You've been through a lot. Be gentle with yourself, Dakota."

Dakota looked at their linked hands and tightened her grip, then returned her attention to Jessie's face. "I like it when you say my name."

Jessie liked it too. She remembered all the times, when she was little, she'd said Dakota's name out loud just because she liked the way it sounded. This was different, though. So very different. Now, she liked the way it felt on her lips. "I like *saying* your name. Dakota," she whispered.

Dakota closed her eyes.

A comfortable silence stretched between them.

"Well," Jessie said finally. "Good night, Dakota Scott."

Dakota lifted Jessie's hand and kissed it. "Good night, Jessie Brogan."

As Jessie stood on the porch and waved at Dakota backing out of the lot, she couldn't help but wonder what tomorrow would bring for them. A new beginning? Or the close of a very old story.

CHAPTER THIRTEEN

Early Monday morning, Dakota pulled into her parking spot beside the gym. Everything was so familiar, the same buildings, the same trees, the same indications that the planet was spinning and life would go on as usual. It was the exact same place she'd been coming to at least two hundred days out of each of the past ten years, and yet, her world felt brand new.

She'd needed much of the day Sunday to process everything that had happened Saturday night—to process and to sleep. When she'd gotten home after dropping Jessie off at the Triple M, she'd literally fallen into bed, exhausted, emotionally drained, and so confused. When she'd finally awakened at two in the afternoon, feeling like a wrung out dish rag, she'd spent the rest of the day at home alone, thinking back over everything that had taken place.

It'd been one hell of a long night. When she'd originally left her house with the thought of revisiting the site of the accident, all she'd meant to do was drive down Hightower Road, possibly stop for a few minutes and look around, and she hadn't even been sure she was going to get out of the car. Once she had, it seemed as though someone else had taken over. She'd faced every memory of that night so long ago. She'd seen, confronted, and relived everything that had happened, and she had Jessie to thank. Had Jessie not asked her to tell her exactly what had occurred, Dakota knew she never would have dealt with so many details.

And the emotional connection they'd shared, the depth to which she'd *felt* Jessie, was something she'd never experienced before, with anyone. What was that?

As she'd pondered the question, she'd realized it'd started well before Saturday night. It'd begun the very moment Jessie had challenged her to do the right thing where Mel was concerned, challenged her to be better. In fact, Dakota realized it was that connection between them that had caused her to rise to that challenge. Initially, it'd felt simply like an attraction, but she had to wonder. The strength of her shock and anger when she'd found out who Jessie was, the intensity of her resistance to being around her, belied the degree to which she hadn't been able to get Jessie out of her mind after they'd kissed. The conflict between wanting Jessie, to be near her, to be *with* her, and never wanting to see her again was all so over the top.

The things they'd shared out at Brogan's Bend, the things she'd told Jessie…What had she been thinking? And yet, then again, it didn't feel like it'd been her, at least not the person she'd known herself to be for so long. At least the Dakota that had told Jessie so many of her dark secrets about the accident, her mother, and her hatred of her mother's illness was much smarter than she was, because that Dakota had known, without a doubt, the right person to tell.

The most confusing question, though, was what *made* Jessie that person, and what did it mean? Could Dakota trust it? She'd told Diane far less, and Diane had vanished like a magician's assistant. Jessie had listened, though, to everything Dakota had confessed, and she hadn't run screaming into the night. She'd stayed. She'd held Dakota. She'd said none of it was Dakota's fault. Did she really mean *none of* it? Or did she still blame Dakota for Jackie's death? After spending the rest of that evening, and on into the night, pondering those dilemmas, this morning, Dakota hoped they could look for the answers together. She didn't know what she wanted with Jessie, but she was sure she didn't want it to be over.

For the time being, though, there were things she could take care of, questions that could be answered. In addition to all the thinking she'd done about Saturday night, she'd also spent some time going over what Jessie had mentioned at Shady Acres about the trouble Ian was possibly having with several of the football players. The first item on her agenda this morning was to catch Mel before school. Mel always stopped by the locker room first thing on Mondays to drop off her practice uniform, cleaned for the week. Dakota had been intrigued that Jessie thought maybe Mel knew something about what was going on, and she wanted to find out for herself.

Then, depending on what she learned from Mel, her next stop was a conversation with Gary Allen, the football coach. She'd been on the panel that had interviewed and hired him several years earlier, so she had a friendly and respectful rapport with him. If there was something going on and he had any knowledge of it, she was sure he'd be willing to discuss it.

As she climbed from the Jeep, she checked the parking lot, halfway hoping to see Jessie's car, but she knew Jessie parked in the faculty section at the front of the school. Dakota had always parked here, at the end of the student lot, because it was so close to her office. She saw Mel turning in off the main road and waved, then went about opening up the locker room and turning on the lights and heat in the gym. On her way back, she shot a hello at several more of her players passing through, then caught Mel's attention. "Can I see you for a few minutes?"

"Sure, Coach," Mel said, closing her locker. "What's up?"

"In my office?" Dakota kept walking, but caught Mel's quizzical expression. By the time Dakota had reached her desk and sat down behind it, Mel was in the doorway.

"Is everything okay?" Mel asked.

Dakota smiled. "I'm sure it is. I just wanted to ask you about something. Come in, please. And close the door."

Mel hesitated, then turned her attention to her friends waiting below. "I'll catch up with you guys." She waved, then did as Dakota said.

Dakota waited until she'd settled in the chair across from her.

Mel grinned and leaned forward. "Is this about the scout from UCLA?"

An old friend of Dakota's was a recruiter for the women's volleyball team at the University of California Los Angeles, and she'd arranged for him to come take a look at one of her senior players. She'd also suggested that he check out Mel as a possibility for the following year. "No," Dakota said, sorry to disappoint her. "It's about the kid in Ms. Weldon's room with you at lunch. What do you know about him?"

Mel looked surprised. "Ian Langston?"

"Yeah, Ian." Dakota glanced at the wall clock. They didn't have a lot of time.

Mel shrugged. "I don't know. Not a lot. He's really good at art. You should see some of his pictures. And he likes *Game of Thrones*."

"Ms. Weldon says he's having some trouble with some lettermen." Maybe this was pointless. Dakota doubted Mel would know anything about it. She wasn't the type to stand by and watch someone get bullied, especially not when Dakota stressed integrity to her players as strongly as she did. On the other hand, she did have to jump Mel for calling Ian a loser that one day. Maybe those talks didn't do as much as Dakota thought. Maybe they couldn't as long as she was being hypocritical when it came to grades. But she was fixing that. "Do you know anything about it?"

Mel averted her gaze, then returned it to Dakota just as quickly. She leaned back in her chair. "Um…I don't know…He got in a fight. I know about that."

Dakota watched her closely. A little color had drained from her face. "Ms. Weldon said she saw you with the boys he fought with, and they were acting threateningly toward Ian." She gave Mel a hard stare and waited. She let Mel squirm. "Come on, Mel. Don't make me drag this out of you. If you know something, spit it out."

An expression that held a mixture of dread and relief moved over Mel's face. She sighed. "Some of the guys have been hassling him." She looked at the floor.

"Who?" Dakota wanted Mel to say the names she already knew so there'd be no ambiguity.

Mel did, though she still didn't make eye contact.

"So they've been bullying him since the fight?" Dakota asked.

Mel's jaw worked as she shook her head. "No." Her answer was barely audible. "It's been going on since the beginning of the year. I think it even started over the summer."

"And you've just stood by and let it happen?"

"I wasn't there," Mel said, a plea in her eyes. "I just hear about it after."

"But you knew."

Mel flinched. "Dale's my boyfriend's cousin. I couldn't—"

"I don't care if he's your grandma," Dakota said with a snap. "You're a leader in this school. Other kids look up to you. You don't just stand by and let someone get picked on and beaten up."

Mel looked sick.

Dakota tapped a finger against her desktop, weighing what she was hearing. "Did you know it happened again Friday? He might have some bruised ribs this time. And it could have been worse."

Mel's eyes widened. "Is he okay?"

"No, he's not okay." Dakota scoffed. "Didn't you hear me? His ribs are bruised. Does that sound okay to you?"

Mel's eyes were filled with tears, but she didn't say anything.

"And knowing all this, you sit in Ms. Weldon's classroom every day, pretending to be his friend?"

"I couldn't...I didn't...I wanted him to know I'm not like them." Mel squeezed her eyes shut. A tear slipped from beneath one lid. "I'm sorry."

Dakota sighed. She hated making her players cry. "Well, all right. I'm going to be talking to Coach Allen, so you might get some backlash on this."

Mel nodded. "Okay."

"And you'll be running laps in practice *and* class for the next two weeks."

Mel jerked her head up. "But I'm not off the team?"

Dakota remembered her allusion to such a consequence in one of her lectures about sportsmanship and being role models. She frowned. "No, you're not off the team, but in addition to being on academic probation, you're now on probation with me, too.

You'd better fly right from now on. If you hear anything else about Ian, you come to me immediately. And you're benched for this Thursday's game."

"What?" Mel's voice was a squeak. "What if that scout comes this week?"

"Then I guess you'll learn a hard lesson," Dakota said, turning to boot up her computer and send Coach Allen an email to see when he could meet. "Now, get to class."

Jessie felt someone watching her, that prickle at the back of her neck, that tingle down her spine. Ian and Melinda had been working quietly at their desks for the past twenty-five minutes, and Jessie stood at the front of her classroom, writing notes for fifth period on the white board. Curious, she turned to find Dakota standing in the doorway. Warmth flooded her heart and body at the sight.

Dakota wore her characteristic tailored jogging pants with a snug fitting Stanford University sweatshirt, her long auburn hair in a braid draped over one shoulder, those brilliant green eyes gleaming with something Jessie couldn't quite identify. Excitement, maybe, with a bit of appreciation? Was there even a hint of desire?

Suddenly, Jessie was with Dakota again on Saturday night, feeling the length of Dakota's body against her, Dakota's arms wrapped tightly around her. Her heartbeat quickened. *At school? Really?* She forced herself to settle.

Jessie had gone straight to bed after Dakota had dropped her off early Sunday morning, but she hadn't been able to sleep. She hadn't been able to stop thinking about everything that had taken place, or stop feeling all of the emotions it'd brought up for her. The shift that had occurred between them during everything they'd shared was visceral. Dakota was no longer someone she only thought and dreamed about. She was no longer merely a crush or a fantasy. Jessie had now touched her, felt her—even kissed her—and Dakota seemed somehow to have made her way under her skin. *It's ridiculous.* The only real difference was that Jessie now had more information about what had happened with Jackie, about the impact it'd had on Dakota, about Dakota's life. It felt like so much more, though.

Dakota flashed a grin in her usual manner, but even that somehow was different. It in itself was the same, but there was a sincerity in Dakota's eyes that was new.

Jessie couldn't help but smile in response.

Dakota arched an eyebrow, pointed to herself, then at Ian, who was hunched over a notebook working on a writing sample, then crooked a thumb behind her.

Intrigued, Jessie shifted her thoughts. "Mr. Langston," she said into the quiet room. "Coach Scott would like to see you in the hallway."

Ian looked up, Jessie's own surprise reflected in his expression.

She pointed to Dakota, still hovering in the doorway.

With obvious uncertainty, Ian rose and left the room with Dakota.

Melinda's gaze lingered on the empty doorway. Jessie finished her notes, then returned to her desk just as Dakota and Ian came back into the room.

Ian looked relaxed, almost happy.

Dakota wore a self-satisfied expression as she approached Jessie. "Hello, Ms. Weldon," she said, her lips quirking in a quick smile.

Jessie felt a light blush heat her cheeks. *Twelve again? This is absurd.* "Coach Scott," she said, as she always had, but she knew their customary greetings were now a formality, simply appropriate behavior in front of students.

Dakota leaned close. "How are you today?" she asked, lowering her voice.

"I'm fine." Jessie needlessly straightened a couple of books on her desk. She cleared her throat. "I'm well. Thank you." Why did she feel awkward all of a sudden?

Dakota stared at her, the same question apparent in her eyes.

Jessie sighed. "I'm sorry. Everything feels so different," she whispered, hoping Dakota would understand.

Dakota nodded. "I get it. It is a little strange, but we can get through it, right?" She glanced over her shoulder toward Mel and Ian.

Jessie compelled herself to calm. "Of course."

"Besides, I'm here about the other topic." Dakota tipped her head in Ian's direction. "I think we got everything cleared up."

When it registered what Dakota was talking about, Jessie blinked. "All of it?"

"Yep. It seems the grandpa was right. There's been an ongoing situation since the middle of summer between the boys you saw and Ian. Mel confirmed that."

Jessie listened, amazed at how quickly Dakota had taken care of the matter.

"When I spoke with Coach Allen, he said he thought it was just a boys-will-be-boys kind of thing," Dakota said, keeping her voice hushed. "We straightened that out, and he called the boys in. Long story short, they'll be serving a month's detention with you starting tomorrow, and they won't be bothering Ian again. We'll also probably lose the football game this Friday, since they're all first string, and they won't be playing."

Jessie couldn't hide her shock.

Dakota shrugged. "It seemed only fair since I pulled Mel from Thursday's volleyball game for knowing about it all and not saying anything."

"Ah," Jessie said, comprehending Melinda's mood. "That explains something she muttered when she came in today. And what's the thing about a scout?"

"She's worried a recruiter might be here this week to check out a couple players," Dakota said, even more quietly.

Jessie had to move closer to hear her. Their shoulders touched, making Jessie remember more. "You're going to let her miss a scout?"

"He's not coming until next week," Dakota whispered, "but she doesn't know that. It'll do her good to sweat a little."

Jessie smiled at Dakota's handling of the situation. "What about repercussions for Ian? What if—"

"There won't be any," Dakota said, her expression going hard. "The boys have been warned to stay completely away from him. If anything happens to him, they'll be held responsible and face expulsion from the team and suspension from school."

"What about their friends or other athletes?"

"If *they* bother him again, if their friends or other athletes bother him, if *friends* of other athletes bother him…if the dog of another athlete's friend even nips at his heel…the original three will be held responsible. So they know it's in their best interest to make sure Ian's life is sunshine and daisies from this point on. And I told Ian to let me or you know right away if there's any more trouble of any kind."

Jessie laughed, then softened, touched by the sincerity—and speed—with which Dakota had dealt with the problem. She was sure she would have gotten a lot more run around had she attempted it. "Thank you, Dakota," she said quietly.

Something flickered in Dakota's eyes. "You're welcome," she said, her voice slightly hoarse.

"I think I owe you."

"Don't be silly," Dakota said, hooking her foot around the leg of a nearby desk and pulling it over. She sat on the top.

Jessie stifled a smile.

"That isn't necessary. But if you did owe me," Dakota went on, "how would you repay me?"

A number of ways Jessie would *like* to repay her came to mind, a few from her recent dream. *I have to get a grip on this.* She was sure there was no innuendo in the question, just humor. "A nice home cooked dinner, maybe?" Jessie said, pulling from way down the list.

"Really? I'm listening." Dakota looped her arms around her drawn up knee. "Usually, I have to drive all the way out to the ranch house for that."

"Well, you'd still have to drive over to the Triple M." Jessie kept an eye on Ian and Melinda, making sure she and Dakota hadn't captured their attention. "And Curtis would most likely be joining us."

Dakota squinted, as though considering other options. "How about if you come over to my house? That way, I wouldn't have to drive, we'd have a chance to talk some more…maybe have a glass of wine. And you could make me a home cooked meal there." She shrugged. "You know, if you really wanted to repay me, which isn't necessary, as I said."

Was Dakota flirting with her? Asking her out in some strange way? The flutter of anxiety in her stomach surprised her. *No, this would be just a thank you. For helping Ian.* And maybe the clearing away of anything that might still be lingering from the past. She couldn't date Dakota. Could she? "When might this unnecessary repayment work for you?" she heard herself ask.

"Oh, I don't know." Dakota looked at the ceiling. "Maybe tomorrow night. At seven." She met Jessie's gaze. "That will give me time to get cleaned up after practice."

Jessie hesitated. Was this a good idea? *Probably not.* Even with everything that had changed between them, with all they'd shared, Dakota was still Dakota Scott, and Jessie was still Jessie Brogan. If Jessie's mother were alive today, she'd be outraged at the mere idea of Jessie spending time with Dakota—for any reason. Maybe not, though. It'd been a long time. Maybe even her mother would have been able to put it all to rest by now.

The image of her mother crumpled at the door of that horrible cottage they'd lived in, sobbing and clinging to Jessie, flashed in her memory. Her mother's words. *The Scotts think they can get away with anything,* and *My Jackie was a good girl* rang loudly in her ears. Whether or not her mother might have moved past it all by now was moot. She'd died heartbroken and bitter, and that would never change. What about Jessie, though? Could *she* move past it completely? Even if she couldn't, she could allow herself this one dinner with Dakota.

"Okay," she said with feigned certainty. "Tomorrow night. Seven o'clock."

Chapter Fourteen

At 6:58, the doorbell rang.

Dakota had gotten home a little bit later than she'd anticipated; she'd rushed through her house, picking up and straightening; jumped into the shower; blow-dried her hair; and was now hooking gold filigree hoops through the holes in her earlobes that normally held small diamond studs. She'd stopped herself from putting on perfume because this wasn't a date, although she had to admit, it kind of felt like one.

It was just a dinner, an evening, some time with Jessie during which she could try to sort out what it was she was feeling. Definitely not a date.

She checked herself in the mirror. Chocolate brown, linen pants—not as dressy as the wool slacks she'd started with, but nicer than jeans. A rich green cotton blouse—comfortable, yet stylish. And bare feet—because, after all, she was at home. Only a touch of mascara and no lip gloss, because…Not a date. She fluffed her hair to frame her face and shoulders, then set out to answer the bell.

"Right on time," she said, swinging open the door.

"I waited in the car for a few minutes," Jessie said.

And then some more words that sounded like *wah, wah, wah* to Dakota's overloaded brain. She was busy taking in the gold ring around Jessie's lush brown irises, brought out by the copper colored V-neck sweater beneath a brown suede tailored blazer.

Snug dress jeans hugged the curves of her hips, tapering down into soft leather ankle boots. *Beautiful. Casual. Mouth-watering.* Dakota's pulse leapt, sending a throb of arousal to her center. She was attracted to Jessie before, but with so much of her guard down now, could she even speak? Jessie saved her from having to try.

"I wouldn't have taken you for the painted toenail type," Jessie said, looking at Dakota's feet. Apparently, she'd been conducting her own perusal. "Very nice." She brought her gaze back to Dakota's face, her smile shy.

Dakota rested her hand high on the edge of the door, going for her more confident stance, then tried for her cocky grin that had gotten her through so much. It helped. "A girl needs to feel pretty, even in the gym."

Jessie's smile widened. "I see." She waited a beat. "So…may I come in?"

Dakota flinched. "Oh, my God. Yes, of course." She leaned forward and took the casserole dish Jessie carried in one arm and the grocery bag that dangled from the fingers of the other. "I'm so sorry." She flushed with embarrassment. This wasn't like her. Sure, she'd been attracted to women, plenty of them, but she'd never gone mindless over one. She stepped aside. "Please, come in."

Jessie laughed softly as she passed through the foyer.

Dakota followed, then detoured to the kitchen to deposit the dinner items onto the counter. When she returned, Jessie stood, looking a bit awkward, in the middle of the living room. "Can I take your jacket?" Dakota asked.

"I'm a little chilly," Jessie said, pulling it more tightly around her. "I think I'll keep it on for now."

"Here, let me start a fire." Dakota crossed to the hearth and lit the teepee of kindling she'd set earlier. Now she was in her element. She'd done this many times for all types of company, not just women over for a romantic evening. She turned and rubbed her hands together. "So what do we need to do for dinner, oh mistress of the kitchen?"

Jessie stared at her, seemingly as speechless as Dakota had been a few minutes earlier. Her gaze was intense.

"Is something wrong?" Dakota asked.

Jessie gave a slight shake of her head. "It's just that I've never seen your hair down. Except for that one night when…and it was wet."

Dakota stepped toward her. "And?" She tilted her head and smiled.

"It's beautiful." Jessie's tone was low, throaty. "Maybe you should wear it like that in the gym, along with your painted toenails," she said much more lightly.

Dakota laughed. "All it would take is one dive for the volleyball or a bungled lay-up, and I assure you, it wouldn't be beautiful anymore. But thank you," she added, acknowledging the compliment.

Jessie took a deep breath. "Okay. About dinner." She turned and headed for the kitchen. "I made a creamy chicken and broccoli casserole that needs to bake for an hour and fifteen minutes. The salad and dressing should go in the refrigerator. And there's a loaf of French bread that can either go in with the casserole for the last twenty minutes or so, or we can broil it, whichever you'd prefer."

"Wow. That sounds delicious. When you repay, you really repay."

Jessie retrieved a large bowl holding the salad and a shaker bottle of what looked like homemade dressing from the grocery bag and found a place for them in the fridge. "Could you set the oven for three hundred degrees?" She left the bread on the counter. Her movements were easy, but she seemed on edge.

"Would you like a glass of wine?" Dakota asked, once the casserole was baking.

"Sure," Jessie said, leaning against the counter. She surveyed the kitchen, as though taking it in for the first time. "This place looks like you."

"It *looks* like me?" Dakota asked as she pulled two crystal glasses from the cupboard. "What does that mean?"

"It's classy and seems fancy on the surface, but if you look closely, it's down-to-earth and functional."

"Really?" Dakota poured their wine.

"Mm-hm. Your oven for example." Jessie gestured to the opposite wall. "It looks complicated with all those controls, but all you did to set it for the casserole was press two buttons."

"You're very observant." Dakota held out a glass to Jessie.

"Thank you," Jessie said, keeping her eyes averted. Her hand shook.

Dakota studied her. "What's the matter?"

"Nothing," Jessie said too quickly to be convincing.

"Then why are you trembling?"

Jessie cut her a sideways glance, then shifted to face her full on. She set her glass down. "I don't think I can do this. I should probably go. This was a bad idea."

"Do what?" Dakota asked, perplexed. "Have dinner?"

"Yes. Have dinner…with you…after…" Jessie's voice and gaze trailed away.

"After everything we shared the other night?" Dakota finished the sentence for her, surprising herself with her directness.

"Yes," Jessie said without returning her focus to Dakota.

"I thought the other night cleared out a bunch of stuff between us," Dakota said.

"I think it did." Jessie slipped her hands into the pockets of her blazer. "And maybe that's the problem."

"I don't understand." Dakota began to feel anxious. She could tell Jessie was about to leave, and she didn't want her to. She wanted this evening with her, whatever it brought.

"No," Jessie said reflectively. "You wouldn't."

"Well, then, explain it to me." Dakota wanted to touch Jessie, brush her thumb over her cheek, cup her chin and bring her gaze to meet Dakota's. She refrained. She could feel Jessie's anxiety. She was afraid anything at all would spook her to run.

"I can't," Jessie said. "It's too…personal. It's embarrassing."

"Embarrassing?" Dakota opted for humor and rolled her eyes. "How about this?" She picked up Jessie's wine glass. "We go sit on the couch and relax for a bit. Then I'll tell you something embarrassing about me first, so you don't feel so vulnerable." She started toward the door.

Jessie laughed, the tension broken. "I'd never pass up the opportunity to hear something embarrassing about a Scott, but I make no promises of reciprocation." She followed. "And give me back my wine. If there's going to be even a possibility of this being a two-way conversation, I'm going to need at least that glass."

Dakota held it out as a lure as she walked backward to the couch and sat. She didn't give it to Jessie until they were settled next to one another, looking into the fire. "See, now, isn't this nice?" she asked after a while.

"It is," Jessie said, before taking a sip, then leaning her head back.

Dakota did the same and relaxed into the moment. She could feel Jessie beside her, sense her warmth. She wished they were closer, their shoulders maybe touching, their thighs pressed together. But this was good. Jessie was staying, at least for now.

"Okay, I'm ready," Jessie said finally. "Tell me something embarrassing about you."

Dakota thought for a long moment, trying to come up with something funny about her as a child. Those were always cute and made points, but the only thing on her mind was the truth about the questions and feelings she had about Jessie, how hard it'd been for her to get ready tonight. She didn't want to share those things, though. She wanted to play it safe, in case all she and Jessie had was the past. She knew she couldn't expect Jessie to be honest, though, if she wasn't, and she really wanted to know what was troubling her. She sighed and shifted in her seat. "Okay, here goes."

Jessie kept her gaze on the fire and took another drink of her wine.

"I was so nervous about tonight," Dakota said haltingly, "that I changed clothes three times before deciding on what I'm wearing." She inhaled deeply. "I don't know what I feel about you, or why. I haven't been able to get you out of my mind since that first day I met you in your classroom, and even now, I can't stop thinking about you."

Jessie turned her head slowly to look at Dakota, her eyes wide.

"And I don't have any idea why I tell you the things I tell you…like this…and everything I told you the other night." Dakota finished in a rush.

Jessie glared at her. "Damn it, Dakota. Just when I want you to be superficial and arrogant, you decide to do something like this."

"Like what?" Dakota was at a loss. She'd expected Jessie to want to hear the truth, to want her to make herself vulnerable first.

Jessie sat up. "This! You go and get all sincere and honest."

Dakota blinked. "I'm…I'm sorry?"

Jessie thumped her wine glass down on the coffee table and covered her face with her hands. She slumped forward. "Fine," she said, straightening. "So we're going to do this? We're really going to talk about what we're feeling?"

"I thought that's what you wanted," Dakota said quietly.

Jessie looked over her shoulder at her. Her expression was wary. "Well, I don't know what I'm feeling, so I don't know how clear it's going to be."

Dakota let out a short and humorless laugh. "Did *I* sound clear just now?"

Jessie sighed. "I don't know what to do with you. When I came back to Clearwater Springs, I thought it would be easy. Or if not easy, at least manageable. I thought I'd spend some time with Curtis and re-establish my relationship with him that I'd taken for granted for so long and be able to bury all the old ghosts of the past. For most of my life, I blamed this town for the loss of my whole family, and I just wanted to be free of that."

Dakota didn't have to imagine what Jessie was talking about. She'd blamed this town for a lot herself and had neglected her own family relationships because of it, and mending some of that was the root of the reason she'd returned as well. Yes, on the surface, Drew and Crystal had asked her to come home, but underlying that, there was far more. She'd blamed this town and all its pressures for her mother's psychotic break. Then she'd blamed her mother for the accident that had killed Jackie. Then she'd blamed the accident for being the cause of her having to stay away, for her not feeling like anyone could or would ever love her because of how screwed up she and her family were. On one level, she knew it was all untrue, and she'd finally come home to face it all. It'd taken Jessie coming home, though, to break her open and bring it all to the surface. How could it have taken someone she didn't even know existed?

"Did you know I had a crush on you?" Jessie asked.

The question startled Dakota back to attention.

Jessie lifted her gaze to the ceiling and shook her head. "Of course you didn't. You didn't know about me at all." She settled back into the sofa and crossed her legs. "Here's the embarrassing part."

Dakota waited, astonished by this revelation.

"The first time I saw you, I was ten. It was at a JV basketball game I went to with Jackie. I couldn't take my eyes off you. Jackie told me who you were, and from that moment on, I idolized you. It started out as hero worship, but as I got older and all the hormones kicked in, it became a huge crush." Jessie rose and crossed to the fireplace. She kept her back to Dakota. "Then, after the accident, my mother hated you, but I still had those feelings, and they felt like such a betrayal. After she died and I graduated, I couldn't get out of here fast enough, but there was nowhere to go where all of this couldn't follow."

Dakota knew that story, too. *You can never get away from yourself.*

"And now, I come back…almost *thirty years later.*" Jessie turned and faced her. "And here you are again. And I realize I still have this stupid crush. And you're the one who can tell me what I've always wanted to know about Jackie's death and about that night, and about…" She swallowed hard. "About *you.* So I can't just ignore you and pretend you don't exist. Do you know how much I hate that? Do you have any idea?"

She did. She knew exactly. "Yes," she said flatly. "I know because I hate that you're the only one I've been able to talk to about that night. In fact, you make it impossible for me to keep it all buried. *You're* the one who somehow makes it all feel better…

makes me feel better…after all this time. And I don't understand why. I just know that when I'm around you, I feel like maybe I could be a good person. Not just someone who killed someone and hurt people and hates her mother. I mean, Jesus. Who hates their mother for something she can't help?"

"You don't hate her," Jessie said. Her tone had softened. "You told me you love her, but hate her sickness. That's different."

Relief welled in Dakota's chest, then almost immediately, it was replaced by irritation. "See, that right there." She pointed at Jessie. "When you say that, I feel it, like a four-ton weight I've been lugging around since I was a kid just lifted. But Drew's told me that, too." She stood and began to pace. "Why does it feel so different coming from you? I don't get it. When you first told me who you are, I just wanted to stay away from you. But then, I didn't because…You're so…I don't know…something."

Jessie watched her until she came to a stop in front of her.

Dakota looked into her eyes. The glowing embers of Dakota's earlier arousal sparked to life. "And then there's…"

Jessie's gaze dropped to Dakota's mouth.

A rush of desire overtook Dakota. Wet heat flooded her folds. "Yeah," she whispered. "There's that." She couldn't stop the memories of Jessie's kiss, the feel of her against her, in her arms, from filling her mind and senses. "What the hell do we do with that?"

Jessie's eyes darkened. She touched a fingertip to Dakota's lips. "I don't know."

Dakota sucked it gently into her mouth, then grazed it with her teeth.

Jessie hissed in a breath and closed her eyes. When Dakota sucked harder, Jessie jerked her hand back as though she'd been burned and twisted away.

Dakota moved like she was under some spell. She knew she should back off, put some distance between them. They needed time to figure out what was happening, to work through their confusion. *She* needed time. But she eased forward, closing the space between them until her body was softly pressed against

Jessie's backside. She dipped her head and nuzzled Jessie's neck through the lush curtain of Jessie's hair. Its silken caress against her face coaxed a quiet moan from her throat.

Jessie trembled, but didn't break the contact.

Dakota ran her hands over the curve of Jessie's hips. "Jessie," she whispered, tightening her grip. "I can't—"

Jessie spun around and kissed her. The kiss was hard and greedy, nothing like Dakota would have expected from Jessica Weldon. But this *wasn't* Jessica Weldon.

Dakota responded in kind, her own desperation igniting the need that had been smoldering in her belly since she'd answered the door earlier, since Saturday night, since their first kiss, since that first day in Jessie's classroom. She kissed Jessie long and deep, moved her hands up under her blazer and grasped her waist. She yanked Jessie to her as she felt Jessie's arms snake around her neck, Jessie's full breasts crush against hers. Her nipples strained and hardened under the pressure.

They kissed frantically, moving against one another, until they were both gasping for air. Finally, Jessie slid her hands to Dakota's shoulders and started to ease away.

Dakota panicked. She couldn't let her go. Not now. "No, don't," she murmured against Jessie's lips.

Jessie pressed her palms against Dakota's chest and pushed gently. "Wait," she said breathlessly. "Wait."

Dakota tightened her hold. "Please, don't—"

Jessie molded to her. "Shhhh. I'm not going anywhere. I just…just need air."

Dakota loosened her embrace but didn't let go. "You feel so good. I can't…I don't…"

"Shhh." Jessie ran her fingers along Dakota's collarbone. "Can we sit?"

Dakota took Jessie's hands in hers and led her to the couch. When they were seated, she pulled Jessie into her arms. *What is wrong with me?* She tried to relax, tried to let go of the anxiety she felt over Jessie possibly leaving. When she realized Jessie wasn't moving, was quietly lying against her, her tension began to ease.

At length, Jessie lifted her head and looked up at Dakota. She brushed her lips across Dakota's, reassurance in her eyes. She stood and slipped out of her jacket.

Dakota watched, letting her gaze travel over the hollow of Jessie's slender throat into the vee of her sweater, then over her breasts and down her torso. When she roamed back to find Jessie's face, Jessie was smiling.

Without a word, she lowered herself onto one knee beside Dakota on the sofa and urged Dakota onto her back. She covered Dakota's body with her own, slowly and deliberately, then claimed her mouth once more. This time the kiss was measured, probing—a physical exploration of Dakota's soul. Jessie's lips were full and swollen and hot.

There was more to this kiss than pure need, though. While Jessie's desire was still evident in the demand of her mouth and body and made Dakota hunger for more, there was also that connection between them from Saturday night that had grown stronger with each revelation they'd shared. Dakota couldn't think. All she could do was feel, feel Jessie—her body, her mouth, her hands, her heart, her very essence.

Dakota groaned and ran her palms up Jessie's back. She lifted her hips to press harder against her.

Jessie slipped her thigh between Dakota's legs and released a soft moan as she ground against Dakota's hip.

Dakota's orgasm built with each rotation, then ebbed as Jessie shifted her position. It felt so good. Dakota wanted to climax, wanted to feel Jessie peak and lose control. She wanted to touch her, maybe even taste her, but then, their first time would be over so quickly, too quickly. It'd all happened so fast, it was just now registering that Dakota was holding Jessie in her arms, kissing her, reveling in the pleasure they were sharing. She didn't want it to be over. If it were, what if *everything* between them was over? No, this was good just as it was. She buried her hands in Jessie's thick hair and devoured her mouth with her own.

Jessie seemed to be on the exact same page. There was no stroking of breasts, no unbuttoning of pants or blouse. There was just holding, pressing, kissing… Jessie's sensual exploration with her soft, warm lips of the sensitive spot beneath Dakota's jaw, and her languid trailing of the tip of her tongue into the open collar of Dakota's blouse. Dakota couldn't get enough.

A buzzing sounded. *A cell phone? An alarm?* It went on and on.

"What is that?" Jessie murmured in Dakota's ear. She ran the tip of her tongue around the rim.

Dakota groaned. "I don't know."

Jessie's hot breath tickled the lobe, and she tugged on the hoop with her teeth.

Dakota jerked as the pull shot straight to her clitoris. She thrust up into Jessie. She twisted her fingers into Jessie's hair. She coaxed her head back and nipped the pulse point on her neck.

Jessie cried out, then went still. "Could it be the oven timer?" Her breathing was ragged.

Dakota licked where she'd bitten and let the question register. "Mmm. Yeah. Timer."

Jessie looked down at her, her eyelids hooded, her gaze dark with arousal. She smiled distractedly. "I owe you dinner."

Dakota was torn. Her body raged with desire, with need, with the ache for release. And yet, somehow she knew there was more to all this. Whatever was between them, it wasn't merely sexual—although, God knew, that was definitely there. "Is that what you want?" She brushed Jessie's bangs from her eyes.

Jessie dipped her head and kissed Dakota lightly on the lips. Once. Twice. Then, slowly, a third time. "I think so," she said, pushing herself up and off of Dakota.

In the kitchen, as they toasted the bread in the broiler and dished up salads and plates of the amazing smelling casserole, they stayed close to one another. There was an occasional brush of hands or a soft peck to a temple or a cheek. The dinner conversation was casual and uncomplicated, about Mel, about Ian and his grandfather, about the annual, upcoming winter festival. After they'd cleaned up and Jessie had insisted on putting the leftovers into containers for Dakota to eat on throughout the week, they returned to the living room. Dakota stoked the fire; Jessie sat on the couch and watched her. Then they held hands. And when Dakota slipped her arm around Jessie, and Jessie snuggled into her, Dakota thought there could never be a more perfect moment.

Unless it was the one, later at the door, when they said good night.

The embrace was long, the final kiss lingering.

"Sleep well," Jessie said, everything about her tender and promising. She played with a lock of Dakota's hair. "I'll see you tomorrow at school."

"I can't wait," Dakota said with a smile that warmed her all the way down to her painted toes. She felt like a teenager again, her whole life stretching out before her, unmarred by tragedy. She'd just made out under the bleachers with the beautiful new girl and was now heading to bed exhilarated, turned on, and eager for more. Tomorrow hadn't looked this good in a very long time.

Chapter Fifteen

Jessie overslept—not so much overslept as she stayed in bed too long, thinking about everything that had taken place the night before.

When she'd gotten home, she'd set her alarm for the usual time. She'd considered taking out her vibrator for some much needed release after all of the tempting and teasing she and Dakota had done, but then she'd decided to savor the feelings, the sensations, the arousal, for a while. This morning, when the alarm had gone off, she hadn't been able to tear herself from the warm bed and even warmer thoughts of Dakota.

And now, she was running late.

She dashed into the kitchen, grabbed a travel mug from the cupboard, and filled it with coffee.

Curtis stood at the counter, buttering a piece of toast. "Everything okay?"

"Mm-hm," Jessie said, slightly breathless. "Everything's fine. Just running behind."

"Here." Curtis slapped some strawberry jam on the toast and spread it around. "Take this. I can make more." He placed it on a paper towel and handed it to her.

"You're so sweet. Thank you." Jessie rose onto her toes and kissed his cheek. "Have a good day." It could have been a morning in her teens, only she carried a briefcase instead of a backpack and Laura wasn't with them. Her heart swelled with gratitude for them both, and she mentally gave Laura a quick peck on the cheek as well, then shot out the back door.

In her car, she shifted into reverse and backed out of the parking lot, steering with one hand, while she took a bite of toast in her other. *Damn, I still need to call Sandy.* Jessie had told her about the dinner plans with Dakota, and if she didn't get a full report this morning, she'd be blowing up Jessie's phone with calls and texts by eight thirty. Jessie was actually surprised she hadn't heard from her already.

She pressed the Bluetooth connect button to her phone on the steering wheel, then said with a mouthful, "Call Sandy."

Sandy picked up at a half ring. "So what happened? I didn't call last night or this morning because, since I didn't hear from you, I figured you spent the night with her. Did you? Did you sleep with her? Is she as good as in your fantasies?"

"No, I didn't spend the night, and I didn't sleep with her. As for the fantasies… Based on what we did do, there's definite potential there. She's one hell of a kisser." Jessie licked a glob of jam from the crust before it dropped onto her slacks.

"What do you mean, you didn't sleep with her? After all this time and spending the whole night with her over the weekend just talking, you didn't jump her bones?"

"Nice, Sandy." Jessie popped the last bite of toast into her mouth and washed it down with a swig of coffee. In truth, when she'd first kissed Dakota, her hunger and need had been so strong, she'd wanted to rip every stitch of Dakota's clothes from her body. She could have easily jumped her bones and made a meal out of her in that moment, but then, something had softened between them.

"Hey, I've been married a long time. You're my only single friend. I count on you for vicarious experiences," Sandy said, her voice almost a whisper. "So if you didn't jump her bones, what did you do?"

An unexpected wave of giddiness hit Jessie. "We made out."

"You made out?" Sandy enunciated each word. "What are you, fifteen?"

Jessie giggled. "I feel fifteen. And there was something about last night…It was like the past three decades fell away."

"Explain."

Jessie waited for something to come. Nothing did. "I can't. It started out really hot, and I thought we might end up naked on the floor, with the whole thing over in five minutes. But then…" A horn tooted behind her, and she realized she'd been sitting too long at a stop sign.

"But then, what?" There was an edge of impatience to Sandy's question. "Jeez, woman, don't make me beg."

"Then…I don't know." Jessie turned left as she went back to the moment in which they'd paused, come up for air, and moved to the couch. "All of a sudden, it wasn't just animal lust anymore. Although, that was definitely still there. But I could feel everything she'd told me the other night, everything I now know about her and her family. I had all the answers I'd wondered about when I used to watch her and think about her, and it changed everything."

There was a long silence on the phone.

"You're fallin', girl," Sandy said finally.

"What are you talking about? I am not." But Jessie knew Sandy was right. She'd known it before Sandy even said it. That was crazy, though. There was too much between them that would never go away. They could talk about it now, share with each other how they felt about it, even comfort one another, but they'd never be able to be rid of it. "I know the reality of the situation and its complications. I'm just insanely attracted to her, like nothing I've ever felt before." Her center heated. Her clitoris began to throb. She could actually feel the pressure of Dakota's hip against it from the night before. She squirmed in her seat. *I should have used that vibrator last night, or this morning, or both. It might be a long day.*

"More than Kaitlyn Morris?" Sandy asked, referring to a short-term relationship Jessie had years ago that was based entirely on libidos and the exploration of fantasies.

Jessie had learned a lot about herself and her desires. It'd been hot, but nothing like this. "Exponentially."

Sandy whistled. "At least have some fun, then. If not for yourself, for me. But, honey, I think there might be more here."

"Well, we'll have to talk about it later. I'm at school, and I have to get my room open for detention." Jessie pulled into a parking space, grateful she wouldn't have to look at Sandy's theory now. She wanted some time to simply enjoy the memory of the previous night without deconstructing it.

"All right," Sandy said. "Call me tonight."

In her room, she started preparing for the day as students began trailing in. She tried to stay focused, but her mind kept wandering—or rather, her body kept dragging her thoughts—to Dakota, the night before, the conversation with Sandy. She could just have fun, couldn't she? Dakota seemed as attracted to Jessie as Jessie was to her, so Jessie saw no reason she would object. They were adults. They could talk about it and make a conscious decision.

You're fallin', girl. Sandy's words echoed in her head. She didn't have to be, though. She could manage her emotions, apply reason. Besides, she suspected the largest part of her draw to Dakota *was* the long pent-up physical attraction and childish crush. Once those two things were explored and spent, there would probably be nothing there.

"Ms. Weldon?" The school principal sauntered into the room.

"Mr. Dansworth." Jessie snapped back to the moment and glanced around, checking that all the students were doing what they were supposed to be doing. "How are you this morning?"

He smiled. "I'm very impressed with a certain long-term substitute we've recently hired," he said, humor flashing in his eyes. "I've been hearing great things about you. Things that will carry a lot of weight if you decide to stay in Clearwater Springs and would like an actual contract for next year."

Stay in Clearwater Springs? Oh no, no, no. "Thank you. That's nice of you to say." Her face heated.

"I understand you have a new project in the works." He stopped in front of her desk and slipped his hands into the pockets of his slacks. "A community based student internship program."

"Yes, but I'm still in the fact-gathering phase to see if it's feasible." She'd actually been feeling discouraged about the whole thing once she'd started checking into possibilities for funding. She'd spent quite a bit of time on the Internet, looking up foundations and organizations that offered grants and endowments for such programs, only to discover that her timing was off. Most of them had already awarded their monies for the year and wouldn't be accepting new applications until spring or even summer. She could, of course, wait until the following year to submit requests and start the program the year after that, but she doubted she'd be in Clearwater Springs that long. Besides, it'd been Ian who'd been her inspiration for the project. It'd be a shame if he couldn't benefit from it.

Dansworth nodded. "These things can take time to get off the ground, but even the idea and the initial legwork is admirable. I just wanted to stop by and make sure you knew it hasn't gone unnoticed."

'Thank you." Jessie smiled.

"I understand there are some funding questions," he said, continuing his train of thought.

Here it comes.

"Have you spoken with Crystal Scott to see if the Scott Foundation would be interested?"

Jessie winced inwardly. And there it was—one of the most obvious pieces of evidence that there were still unresolved issues for her with Dakota and her family. She couldn't imagine sitting down with Crystal Scott and asking for money, even for a cause as good as this one. "No, but I've gotten that recommendation from several others as well."

"It's something to think about." Dansworth started toward the door. One thing that was nice about him, especially in meetings, was that he was a man of few words.

"I will. Thank you," Jessie said, but it wasn't as though she hadn't already thought about it. A lot. "And thank you again for your kind words."

He waved over his shoulder and disappeared around the corner.

Jessie stared after him, a little irked at the whole conversation. He'd basically offered her a permanent position at the high school, if she wanted it. But, of course, she didn't. She was only there temporarily to clean up her past. That was the plan, and she was sticking to it. She had a life in Boston to rebuild.

So what was she doing starting something like the internship program that was such a long-term project? It would need someone strongly committed to its success and to the students' lives it could affect to get it up and going. Then there would be upkeep to consider—screening for the best candidates, soliciting new businesses to participate over time, and securing continuing funding. All things she knew, but she hadn't considered the ramifications. She'd have to find someone she could trust to leave it with when she left. *Or...just postpone leaving?* No. What was she doing? Was she subconsciously sabotaging herself with this program? But why? Clearwater Springs wasn't her home. It never had been, and it never would be. An uneasiness rippled through her, but she held her ground. *No. It never will be.*

By lunch time, Jessie was sick to death of thinking about her dilemma regarding the internship program, the Scott Foundation, the anxiety it caused her when she tried to envision herself going to them for help, and the look on her mother's face if she were alive to witness that. She had to completely slam that last door when her thoughts returned to Dakota and another round of reminiscing about kissing her, lying on top of her, and further images of things that hadn't happened yet. By the time Dakota was due to arrive, Jessie's body was humming with desire again.

Melinda came alone, though.

Jessie had wondered if this day would ever come. Now that it had, she was a tad disappointed. She couldn't help but wonder where Dakota was and what she was doing—and about the timing. "Finally not afraid to be alone with me?" she asked Melinda with a teasing lilt.

Melinda blushed but smiled. "You're not as scary as I thought you'd be. Actually, you're pretty nice."

Jessie laughed. "I must be slipping."

When Ian appeared, they settled into what had become their routine. Melinda broke out lunch for her and Ian; Jessie went over the corrections she'd made on each of their prior assignments; and they all got to work. Jessie had taken to bringing a lunch from home as well, but she'd been in such a rush that morning, she hadn't had time to make one, so she began grading papers. After a while, she became aware of whispering and looked over at the two teens.

Melinda had moved across the aisle and was sitting, facing backward, in the desk in front of Ian. Ian was looking through some papers she'd given him.

"Are you two plotting an overthrow?" Jessie asked to get their attention.

Melinda looked up, her eyes wide.

Ian turned in his seat. "Mel wrote some stories she wants me to draw pictures for."

"Really?" Jessie crossed to where they sat, intrigued by the idea of them working together.

"They're nothing important," Melinda said, taking the pages back from Ian. "Just some stories I wrote for my little brothers and sister. I thought if they had pictures to go with them, maybe I could send them to one of those sites where they'll turn them into an actual book, and I could give them to the kids for Christmas."

"May I see?" Jessie asked.

Melinda bit her lower lip. "Sure," she said, handing them to Jessie.

Jessie quickly read through the set clearly meant for a toddler. There were only one or two short sentences per page. The story was about the fat froggie folks. She smiled at the end, when Francie Froggie, the older sister, took all the little froggies to the bug museum. The second shorter story looked to be at about a first grade level, and the longer third one was about a superhero named Jet Black, whose super power was manipulating the inky shadows of the night. "These look great. Very imaginative," Jessie said. "Are you going to do the illustrations?" she added to Ian.

Ian shrugged. "Sure. It'll be fun."

Melinda broke into a grin. "Thanks." She turned to Jessie. "Ms. Weldon, will you read through them and correct any mistakes and see if the stories could be better?"

Jessie smiled. "I could do that." She took in the two students in front of her who'd started out not even glancing at one another, from two completely different worlds, and yet, now here they were, working on a sweet project together and, maybe, becoming friends. All it'd taken was a willingness to see each other differently than before. She thought of herself and Dakota and wondered if they'd end up friends when everything was said and done. *Friends with benefits, perhaps.* She could hear Sandy's cackle in her mind.

The afternoon classes went by quickly, and after school, Jessie found herself seated at her desk going through Melinda's stories with interest. She had a highly evolved imagination and had clearly developed each story specifically for the individual child for whom she'd written it. Jessie could feel the love that had gone into each tale. She made some comments to strengthen Jet Black's character arc and some technical corrections on all three. She was surprised when she looked at the time to find it was going on five thirty. She wondered if Melinda was still at volleyball practice. Jessie was excited to tell her what a great job she'd done.

And, as a perk, I could see Dakota in her element.

Jessie walked down the hall and looked out the door. A number of cars dotted the student parking lot, including Dakota's. She smiled.

When she entered the gym, all the sounds and smells of her ancient P. E. classes swarmed around her—the echo of shouts and bouncing balls, the squeaks of rubber soles on the wood floorboards, the tangy scent of sweat, and whatever that uniquely-gym smell was that unified *all* gymnasiums. She watched as Melinda set up ball after ball for Dakota to spike over the net—*That's what it's called, right? Spiking?*—for the players on the other side to try to return. Few came back over.

She let her gaze roam freely over the tight shorts that hugged Dakota's ass and thighs. The muscles of her legs and arms strained with each leap into the air, each slam of her fist into the ball. Jessie moaned inwardly at the memory of those hard muscles beneath her, her body moving against them, the night before. She shivered at the recall of Dakota's strong arms around her, holding her tightly.

"All right, twenty laps," Dakota yelled. "Since you're obviously not here to play volleyball, you can run. We have a match tomorrow, ladies. *Somebody* better show up for it."

Jessie hid the quirk of her lips behind a pretense of scratching her cheek as the team ran past her and out the door. She'd seen, felt, even held, the real Dakota, the one who could be scared and vulnerable, the one who was soft. *This* Dakota was a façade, much like that of her own.

"Hey, Ms. Weldon, what are you doing in the gym?" It was Melinda, standing in front of her, her expression curious.

Jessie snapped her attention back to her reason for being there. "I finished your stories and wanted to tell you how good I think they are."

Melinda grinned. "You really think so?"

"I do," Jessie said softly. "I made some suggestions in the Jet Black story that we can talk about, if you'd like. And then there are some corrections, just technical things. You've come a long way with that, too."

"Jenson, hit the track." Dakota's voice boomed in the quiet gym. "*You* owe me a lot more than twenty."

Melinda seemed unfazed. "Thanks, Ms Weldon. See you tomorrow." Without acknowledging Dakota's interruption, she jogged out the door, her stories in hand.

Jessie was sure Dakota's athletes were well acquainted with this side of her, and, in fact, counted on it for what they needed.

Dakota picked up a towel from the bottom bleacher and wiped her face. She flashed a grin, but not before raking her gaze down Jessie's body and back up again. "You look nice," she said.

That wasn't what her expression said, though. It said, *You look delicious, edible.* It said, *If we were anywhere else, I'd devour you.*

An ache of need flamed between Jessie's thighs, and she felt her nipples harden beneath the sheer fabric of her bra. She was grateful for the thickness of the sweater she had on.

"To what do I owe this unexpected pleasure?" Dakota was coming toward her, her leg muscles bunching and flexing as she walked.

Jessie glanced away. "I brought something to Melinda," she said, refocusing on Dakota's face.

Dakota stopped in front of her as she dried the back of her neck. "So you didn't come to see me?" A rivulet of sweat trickled down toward the vee of her T-shirt.

Jessie wanted to catch it on the tip of her tongue, go in after it between Dakota's breasts. *Christ! Why didn't I use that vibrator?* All that sweat. All that shiny, slippery skin. All those taut muscles. All that...Dakota. "No. Not technically." She tried to answer, but she wasn't sure she even remembered the question. Something about seeing her?

Dakota arched an eyebrow. "Not technically? But...a little bit?"

Jessie flushed. This was ridiculous. What did she think she was hiding? Dakota knew the effect she had on Jessie. It certainly wasn't a secret now. She smiled. "Yes, of course. A little bit." She held up her thumb and forefinger about a half an inch apart.

"If that's all, I'm going to have to up my game." Dakota grew more serious. "What are you doing tonight? Do you have plans?"

"Yes. Hot ones." Jessie wanted to follow up with, *tailing you home and finishing what we started last night*. "Dinner with Curtis and grading papers," she said instead with a smile.

"Do you think Curtis would mind if I stole you for another evening?" Dakota draped the towel around her neck.

Jessie wanted to take the ends and pull Dakota to her, pull her mouth to hers. She was painfully aware of where they were, though, in the middle of the gym where Dakota taught her classes, at the school where they both worked, with students who could return at any moment. She forced herself to take a step back. "Actually, Curtis has a lady friend who hasn't gotten to see him as much since I've been home. I'm sure neither would mind if I were stolen more."

Dakota grinned. "Perfect. How about dinner at my place again?"

Jessie could barely contain her relief that Dakota hadn't suggested a restaurant. *That w*ould be her personal version of

Dante's second circle of hell, the eternal dwelling place for those overcome by the desires of the flesh. "Am I bringing it again?" she asked, only half joking.

Dakota chuckled. "No. I think I can manage something tonight."

"When?" Jessie heard the lust in her voice and wondered if Dakota had.

"Give me an hour and a half," Dakota said, walking backward, away from Jessie.

Jessie wanted so badly to follow her. Maybe they could sneak a kiss under the bleachers. *Right. Like I'd be willing to stop after a kiss.*

Dakota took hold of a wheeled basket and began collecting volleyballs. "That gives me time to get everyone out of here and do a quick fix-it project when I get home, before I clean up."

"Do you want some help here?" Jessie asked.

Dakota paused, then blew out a long breath. "No. I think you should leave before I do something highly inappropriate for the setting."

Ah. Dakota was feeling it too. *Good to know.* "Well, if you're sure." Jessie turned and sashayed toward the door, putting a little extra swish into her hips. She heard Dakota groan. She smiled and threw her a finger wave over her shoulder. "See you soon, Coach Scott."

Before Dakota could respond, the doors flew open and the team burst back into the gym.

It wasn't long before Jessie found herself parked in front of Dakota's house. It hadn't been an hour and a half, maybe not even an hour, but the Jeep was in the driveway, so Dakota was home. Jessie had quickly regretted her last little taunt. It'd had the desired effect on Dakota, but it had also fully ignited the burning need in Jessie as well. She'd tried killing time by calling Sandy, who hadn't answered, tried working, but couldn't concentrate. She'd even tried simply allowing herself to imagine the night ahead, but had been driven even crazier with her own desires. So…here she was, early and as excited as a sailor on a long awaited shore leave.

She rang the doorbell. No answer. She rang it again. Maybe Dakota was in the shower. She tried the knob. It turned easily. "Hello?" she called quietly. She stepped inside and listened. Not a sound. No running water. No music or TV. She glanced down the hallway and could see, just barely, into the master bedroom at the end. Then she caught a movement through the living room, out on the patio. Dakota stood on a step stool, balancing something—a rain gutter, maybe—at the edge of the roof.

She wore a pair of sweat pants over her shorts, but Jessie knew exactly what was underneath—at least down one layer. And there were those arms again, stretched above her head. She held the gutter with one hand and fastened something with the other. The hem of her T-shirt hung slightly above her waistband, revealing a peek of her bare stomach.

Jessie's breath caught. She wanted her lips there, her hands cupping Dakota's ass. She cleared her throat, as much to call herself into check as to alert Dakota to her presence.

"Hey," Dakota said. "You're early."

"I couldn't wait." Jessie let her gaze linger on that thin strip of Dakota's stomach. She felt Dakota watching her.

"I'm almost done. This came down in that last storm, and I didn't get it back up," Dakota said, sounding *almost* casual, but Jessie caught the tremor in her voice. "We're supposed to get more rain this weekend."

Jessie didn't comment. She couldn't. All she could think about was how Dakota's lips, throat, collarbone had tasted the night before and wonder if that thin strip of stomach would taste different.

"Help yourself to whatever you want. There's beer, wine, and soda in the fridge. And, I think, some juice."

Jessie met her eyes. "Whatever I want?" The words echoed in her mind, reverberated in her body. She moved to the base of the step stool and slipped her hands beneath Dakota's shirt. She pressed her lips to Dakota's stomach, right above her navel. She licked unhurriedly. She moaned at the salty taste.

Dakota gasped. Her muscles clenched. "Jessie. Wait."

Jessie moaned against her skin. "I can't," she whispered. "Oh my God, this must be what it feels like to be a teenage boy. I have to have you, Dakota." She inched the waistband down and flicked her tongue into Dakota's navel.

"Okay, okay," Dakota said in a rush of air. "Let me put this down."

Jessie eased off long enough for Dakota to get off the step stool and set the gutter on the patio table, but she never broke contact. As soon as Dakota was facing her again, she slid her hands up her torso and over Dakota's breasts. She squeezed as she pressed her mound against Dakota. "Kiss me."

Dakota groaned as Jessie's fingers closed around her nipples, then she claimed Jessie's mouth. She thrust her tongue in deep as she wrapped her arms around Jessie and crushed her to her.

Jessie answered with as much hunger and need. She found the front clasp of Dakota's bra, undid it, and filled her hands with Dakota's bare breasts, the hard nipples stabbing into her palms.

Dakota walked her backward, into the house, but they only made it to the dining room.

Jessie bumped into a chair, then spun Dakota around and coaxed her down onto the table. She extracted Dakota from her bra and shirt, then was up and over her before Dakota was fully down. She sucked one of Dakota's nipples into her mouth and squeezed the other between her fingers.

Dakota cried out, her fingers thrusting into Jessie's hair, gripping tightly. She held Jessie's mouth in place and arched into her.

Jessie sucked with a greed she'd never felt before. She straddled Dakota's thigh, insinuating one of her own into the apex of Dakota's. She began to rock. Her clit ached, pounded with need, screamed for release.

Dakota thrust up into her. "Jessie. Oh God, Jessie. I'm going to come."

Jessie slowed. "Nooo. No, no, no," she murmured around Dakota's nipple. "I'm so not finished." She made a grinding rotation with her hips, then eased off. Her body raged in protest.

Dakota released a long whimper. She panted, squeezing her eyes shut. "Jessie."

"Shhh." Jessie moved up her torso and kissed her parted lips. She slipped her tongue inside, her fingers still teasing one nipple.

Dakota sucked her tongue, then her lower lip. She melted into a slow, languid kiss, but her hips still pumped against Jessie.

As their mouths worked against one another, Jessie shifted her weight and slid her hand down Dakota's stomach and into her pants. Beneath her shorts. Beneath her underwear. Into the triangle of soft hair. And finally, finally, finally, into the wet heat of her folds.

They groaned together.

When Jessie's fingertips grazed Dakota's clitoris, her own surged in response.

Dakota thrust against Jessie's hand.

Jessie broke their kiss. "I want to taste you. I want my mouth on you." She dipped a finger inside Dakota and felt her clench around her in response.

"Wait," Dakota said, gasping for air. "Take a shower with me. I'm all sweaty. It won't—"

"I want you sweaty," Jessie said, running her tongue over Dakota's stomach. "I want to touch you and taste you the way you were when I saw you in the gym." She tugged at Dakota's pants. "I want to taste you just the way you are. I want you to come in my mouth, Dakota."

"Oooooh." Dakota's voice was rough, gravelly. She lifted her hips.

"Will you do that, Dakota?" Jessie whispered as she slid the clothes down Dakota's legs and off her feet. "Will you come in my mouth?" She opened Dakota's thighs wider.

Dakota gasped. "Yes."

And that was all Jessie needed. She pressed her mouth to Dakota's center, moved her lips over her clit, tongued her opening. Dakota tasted musky and savory, smelled of an earthy, primal scent. Jessie couldn't get enough.

A guttural, animal sound tore from Dakota's throat. She stretched back on the table, thrusting upward, giving Jessie more access.

Jessie buried her face deeper between Dakota's legs, licking, sucking, circling her clit. She nipped at her labia.

Dakota's fingers twisted into Jessie's hair and pulled her hard against her need. She cried out with each pass of Jessie's tongue.

Jessie moved faster, the pulse in Dakota's swollen clitoris driving her.

Dakota writhed beneath her. Her legs tensed. Her hips lifted off the table.

"Come for me, baby," Jessie murmured against Dakota's hot, wet flesh.

Dakota cried out and lurched upward. She thrust hard and fast against Jessie's mouth.

Jessie held on tight, riding Dakota's orgasm all the way through, never easing up. When Dakota's thrashing slowed, Jessie slipped two fingers inside her and began to stroke.

Almost instantly, Dakota came again.

Jessie kept her fingers moving, her lips sucking, her tongue caressing, through Dakota's last spasm.

Dakota's hands fell from Jessie's hair. "Jesus Christ." Her voice shook. Her body quivered. She moaned softly.

Jessie pressed one last tender kiss to Dakota's clit, then moved up beside her on the table. She slipped an arm beneath Dakota's head and cradled her. She kissed her forehead, her temple. When Dakota curled into her, she caressed her back. She wanted to hold her like this forever.

But no. That's not what this was. This was just fun. Right? The hot, sensuous scratching of a long-standing itch, and there was still more to come. After tonight, and maybe a few more times, it was sure to be out of her system…and Dakota's…and that would be that.

For now, though, there was no harm in holding her.

CHAPTER SIXTEEN

Dakota drifted back to awareness. She had no idea how long she'd been asleep. Had she merely dozed off for a couple of minutes, or had she been asleep for a couple of hours? She had no way of knowing.

The side of her face pressed into something soft. Her body curled into something warm. Not some*thing*. Some*one*. Jessie. It all rushed back to her, and the sensations in her body, the satiation of her desire came into sharp focus.

Jessie's lips brushed her forehead. "Welcome back." Her tone was low and husky.

Dakota opened her eyes to find her head resting on Jessie's arm and her face enticingly close to Jessie's throat. It took only the slightest shift for her to sprinkle three light kisses across it.

"Mmmm. Do that again, and your time of respite will be over."

"Pshh. What did you do to me?"

"What I've been wanting to do to you for some time." Jessie ran her hand lazily down Dakota's back. She teased the dimple at the top of her buttocks.

Dakota's clitoris began to waken. "Oh, no-no." Dakota reached behind her and took Jessie's hand. She brought it to her lips. "I think it's my turn to do some things I'd like to do."

"You didn't like what we just did?" Jessie asked, a smile in her voice.

Dakota rose onto her elbow, instantly aware of the hard surface of the table beneath her. She took in the length of Jessie's fully clothed body—*even her boots are still on*—then glanced down at herself, completely naked. *What the hell?* This wasn't the way things usually went. She was always the one to take charge, to be on top, so to speak. What had happened? Now that she thought about it, the same thing had happened the night before. Jessie had completely topped her then too. And who was she to complain? "I loved what we just did. *And* I have some other ideas…." She climbed off the table, still holding Jessie's hand.

In the master bathroom, Dakota started the shower. She still held Jessie's fingers, intertwined with her own, and looked back at her as she tested the water temperature.

Jessie's gaze was fixed on her, her eyes smoldering with need. She stood perfectly still.

With sudden awareness, Dakota realized Jessie hadn't climaxed when she'd been taking Dakota—or the previous night either. Or, at least, Dakota was fairly sure she hadn't. As passionate as Jessie was, Dakota doubted she was the quiet type. So while Jessie had so delectably fed Dakota's hunger, her own still raged. The thought made Dakota ache all over again. Without a word, she stepped close to Jessie and bent her head to kiss her. She ran the tip of her tongue over Jessie's lips, then between them, slipping inside.

Jessie moaned into Dakota's mouth. She reached for the hem of her sweater and started to raise it.

Dakota grasped her hands and stilled them.

Jessie's eyes fluttered open.

Dakota held her in place and kissed her again.

Something softened in the depth of Jessie's golden brown eyes, and she released the garment. She stretched her arms high above her and eased her head back to rest against the wall.

Dakota's body flamed. The thought of having this passionate, sexy, amazing woman to pleasure and satisfy, to make moan and scream with release, set her on fire. She took Jessie's mouth in a demanding kiss and inched the sweater up her torso. By the time she tore her mouth away, Jessie was gasping for air. Dakota slid the sweater over Jessie's head and off her arms, then dropped it to the floor. She stepped back and stared at Jessie's ample breasts, cupped and presented in a sheer amber colored bra, her nipples stiff and erect, begging to be touched.

Dakota couldn't breathe. She tentatively stroked the sides with her fingertips, coming close to the nipples, then trailing away. The fabric and the heat of Jessie's skin beneath it caressed her hands.

Jessie's nipples swelled even more. She whimpered and clenched her eyes shut. Her hips rocked.

Dakota ran her thumbnails over the taut points, and her clit hardened at the keen that came from Jessie. She broke free from her trance. She took Jessie's mouth in another fervent kiss as she reached behind her and unfastened the bra and tossed it to the floor. She kneaded Jessie's breasts, squeezing the nipples between her fingers as she did.

Jessie cried out and arched into her hands. Her arms dropped around Dakota's neck, and one leg came up around Dakota's hips.

Her tongue still probing Jessie's mouth, she opened Jessie's slacks and shoved her hand down the front of Jessie's panties. She slid her fingers over the hard swell of Jessie's clit and deep into her wetness.

Jessie clenched her legs around Dakota, Dakota supporting her weight against the wall. Dakota thrust into her three times, and Jessie came, screaming and bucking as she rode her hand.

Before Jessie could calm, Dakota dispensed with the rest of the clothing and moved the two of them into the shower. She pressed Jessie to the wall warmed by the steam and pushed into her again, this time more slowly, more gently.

Jessie moaned and met each stroke with a pump of her hips. Before too long, Jessie came again.

Dakota sighed with satisfaction. She wanted to pleasure Jessie all night, feel her muscles clamp tight around her fingers. She still wanted to taste her and feel her body once more against Dakota's. The way she felt right now, she doubted she could ever get enough of her.

They washed each other, Jessie taking her teasing time between Dakota's legs where new arousal continued to build, and Dakota reveling in the feel of Jessie's full breasts and sensitive nipples under her hands and mouth.

"Take me to bed," Jessie said finally, her breath fanning Dakota's ear as she moved against her.

Dakota nuzzled her neck. "Gladly." They hurriedly toweled each other off, then kissed and groped their way into the bedroom. "Do you want a fire?" Dakota asked, gesturing to the hearth in the corner.

"No." Jessie sprawled on the bed, braced on her elbow. "I don't want anything that's going to take you more than this far away from me." She patted the comforter beside her.

Dakota grinned and flopped onto her back where Jessie had indicated. "I like a woman who knows what she wants."

"Well then, you're *really* going to like me in a few minutes." Jessie ran a fingertip around Dakota's nipple.

"Mmmm. I already *really* like you." Dakota brushed Jessie's hair away from her face, then cupped the back of her head and brought her lips to hers.

Jessie responded eagerly with a tenderly heated kiss. She slid her leg across Dakota's thighs and sat up, straddling her.

Dakota inhaled as she took in every inch of her. She ran her hands up Jessie's bare legs to the patch of dark gold hair at the apex, then stroked its softness with her thumbs. "You look gorgeous up there."

Jessie sucked in a sharp breath and lifted her hips slightly. "And *you* look gorgeous down there." She leaned forward and rubbed her breasts across Dakota's.

Dakota moaned at the resurgence of the ache in her nipples.

"Do you have any music in here?" Jessie asked as she trailed kisses along Dakota's neck.

Dakota hissed at the sensations and pointed to the nightstand. "Up there. Push the green button." She felt Jessie shift, then the piano rendition of "I Will Remember You" began to play through the surround sound.

"Very nice," Jessie whispered. She hovered over Dakota, supporting herself on her hands. Her breasts hung free.

Dakota couldn't resist. She cradled their weight, then thumbed the nipples.

Jessie arched backward and closed her eyes. Her thighs tightened around Dakota's hips.

Dakota gently squeezed one nipple between her fingertips while she ran her other hand down Jessie's abdomen to cup her sex.

Jessie quivered and released a shuddering breath. She raised onto her knees and let Dakota caress her slowly, lightly.

Dakota tightened her grasp on Jessie's nipple, feeling it grow more rigid. She wanted to suck it, to feel it swell in her mouth, but she'd wait for Jessie to tell her to do it. Somehow, she knew she would. She ran a fingertip along the slick seam of her folds.

Jessie cried out softly but remained still.

Dakota moved to the other nipple and squeezed, feeling it harden and grow. Her own arousal was building, her own breasts aching for Jessie's mouth. She pressed into Jessie's hot, wet center, one finger then just the tip of a second.

Jessie trembled, her breath coming in shallow puffs, pressing firmly into Dakota's grasp. She opened her eyes. Her darkened gaze pinned Dakota.

"What do you want, sweetheart?" Dakota murmured.

Jessie's muscles clamped around Dakota's fingers, and her eyes clenched shut again. She groaned. Her answer was clear.

Dakota pushed deep into her and rolled her nipple, pinching softly.

Jessie keened. She arched and rocked her hips before claiming Dakota's mouth in a hungry kiss.

Dakota thrust into her in a slow rhythm, taking her more fully with each of Jessie's moans.

Finally, Jessie broke the kiss with a gasp and gripped the back of Dakota's neck. She pulled her firmly against her breast.

Dakota sucked the nipple in hard and fast while she palmed the other one in quick, tight circles. She was deliberate, but kept her pace almost languid, thrilling at the feel of Jessie's increasing need, the tightening of her arms that held Dakota against her, the thrusting of her hips that pulled Dakota into her more deeply. Finally, Dakota pressed her thumb to Jessie's clitoris and began slow, easy circles.

Jessie stiffened and arched her back. She moaned with each pass around her swollen clit, with each caress and suckle of her nipples, with each stroke of Dakota's fingers inside her, but she held herself still, letting Dakota pleasure her fully.

And Dakota did—slowly, calculatingly, thoroughly. Her own need increased with every passing moment. When Jessie's body finally went completely rigid and she crushed Dakota into her at every point of contact, when she finally screamed and came hard around Dakota's hand, Dakota could barely fight back her own orgasm. She concentrated on Jessie's pleasure, coaxed every spasm, lured every quiver, from her. As Jessie began to calm, Dakota lifted her head and covered Jessie's lips with hers.

Jessie moaned softly into Dakota's mouth as Dakota let her fingers linger with two last thrusts, two final strokes, then slipped out. Jessie collapsed onto her, and Dakota took her into a gentle embrace.

Dakota's mind went quiet as she held her close. She realized there wasn't a thought in it. She could only feel the moment, and what she was feeling made no sense. She felt completely at peace, completely safe and secure, completely at home. A sense of home and safety she hadn't felt since she was a very young child. And she knew all of what she was feeling was Jessie. Jessie felt like peace. She felt like safety. She felt like home. How could that be?

Jessie moved against her. She grazed her nails across Dakota's stomach. "Are you okay?"

"Yeah," Dakota said, tightening her arms around Jessie. She wasn't at all sure it was true, but whatever was weird, Jessie couldn't fix. "I'm fine. Just getting a little hungry."

Jessie looked up. "That's right. You're cooking tonight."

Dakota laughed. "I never said I was cooking." The lightness of the topic settled her some. "I believe what I said was I could manage dinner. We can have pizza or Chinese. They both deliver. Or if you want to go out—"

"I don't," Jessie said quickly. She looped her arm around Dakota's waist and pulled her closer. "Let's do Chinese."

Dakota wondered if Jessie was avoiding any conversation about the first time she'd been there and they'd almost shared a pizza. Regardless, Dakota was glad. She didn't want to take the chance of ruining anything they might have started tonight. She placed the order, then offered Jessie some sweats to wear while they waited. She lit the fire in the living room, then pulled Jessie onto the couch.

Jessie sighed and draped herself across Dakota's lap, facing her.

Dakota snuggled Jessie into her. "Why don't you stay the night, and we'll both call in sick tomorrow?" she said jokingly. She kissed Jessie's neck.

Jessie leaned her head back, giving Dakota more access. "Why, Coach Scott, you have responsibilities tomorrow. Don't you remember?" She sat up straighter. "We have a match tomorrow, ladies," she said, deepening her voice. "*Somebody* better show up for it."

Dakota squinted. "Is that supposed to be me?"

Jessie giggled.

"Is that right? You're doing me?" Dakota asked playfully. "If so, it's worse than your John Wayne."

"It seems I am doing you, but that's a different topic altogether." Jessie settled once again into Dakota's arms. "That's the one that would certainly start the talk."

Dakota chuckled. "Oh, believe me, the talk has already started."

Jessie eyed her. "What do you mean?"

"Let's see." Dakota pretended to think. "Last Saturday, Hank found us snuggled together in a sleeping bag at three in the morning out on Hightower Road, and he's a worse gossip than Millie at the post office who lives right down the street. And I'm sure Millie's already spreading the word that this is the second night in a row your car's been in front of my house."

"Oh, God." Jessie buried her face in Dakota's shoulder. "This place hasn't changed a bit, has it?"

Dakota rubbed her cheek against Jessie's hair. "Sure it has. We now have one stop light and *three* fast food restaurants—if you count Burger Bob's, which is local, but still…. It's pretty fast and has a drive-through."

Jessie laughed.

"Oh, and I almost forgot." Dakota jostled her excitedly. "I hear there's a much sexier eleventh grade English teacher these days, because Jim Anderson…Well, nice enough guy, but I don't know how hot he'd look in my sweats."

Jessie considered her. "It doesn't bother you to be talked about?"

Dakota waited for the absurdity of the question to hit Jessie.

When it did, Jessie closed her eyes. "I'm sorry. How could I be so—"

"Hey, you're not so anything." Dakota ran her fingers through Jessie's hair. "Except…a beautiful woman, an amazing lover, an inspiring teacher, and as I mentioned before, so much sexier than Jim Anderson."

Jessie tilted her head back and laughed. Then she grew serious. "How do you stay so unaffected by things?"

Dakota met Jessie's gaze, and all of her defenses came crashing down. She felt the ache in her heart that always accompanied that vulnerability.

Realization passed through Jessie's eyes. "But you *are* affected. I know that. So…it's an act, isn't it?"

Dakota frowned, then cleared her throat. "Would it be okay if we didn't talk about any of that tonight? Can we just be with each other and enjoy the evening?"

"Yes, of course." Jessie cuddled in close again. "Let's just leave the world outside."

The doorbell rang.

"Except for the Chinese food, of course," Dakota said with a laugh.

After they'd eaten, Jessie insisted on clearing the table and putting away the leftovers. When she returned to the dining room, she was stark naked. "Did you mean it when you said you like a woman who knows what she wants?"

Dakota's abdomen clenched with a flood of arousal. "Absolutely," she murmured, taking in every sensuous aspect of Jessie's voluptuous body.

"Good, because I know exactly what I want right now." Jessie closed the distance between them and slid onto the table in front of Dakota. She lay back and dipped a finger between her legs. She touched the wetness to Dakota's lips.

Dakota groaned and sucked it in.

"That's right, baby. I want your mouth." Jessie lay back and opened her thighs wide. She gasped as Dakota began to feast.

Dakota followed the team into the gym to begin their warm-ups before the match. She'd been on a high all day, remembering and reliving as much as she could while teaching classes, every detail of the previous night, but her lack of sleep was beginning to catch up with her. Jessie had stayed until almost four, and even then, she'd left mostly due to the concern that they might fall asleep and get caught by the sunrise—and Millie.

Dakota was hoping the excitement and tension of competing against Mountainview, their biggest rivals, would give her a second wind. It wasn't a good day to have Mel sitting the bench, but she thought the rest of the team would rally. If not, it was only one loss, and for an important lesson learned. When the buzzer sounded, signaling the start of the first game, she noticed Mel scanning the bleachers.

Mel had taken her consequences stoically and had come clean and apologized to Ian of her own volition. Ian, for his part, had been gracious. There seemed to be a friendship growing there. Mel had even given her second string replacement a much-needed pep talk and some pointers during Tuesday's practice. Dakota considered easing Mel's mind about the scout several times, but had held off on principle. Maybe it was time. She leaned down and tapped her shoulder. "He's not coming until next week."

Mel turned, her eyes wide and excited. "Really?"

Dakota nodded and walked away. She watched the first serve, then an impressive volley. The first game went relatively well, with Clearwater Springs taking the game point. The second one, not so much. Mountainview came back with a vengeance. As she traded out her first string setter who'd twisted an ankle, she caught Mel looking into the stands again. "I told you he isn't here. Pay attention to the game and support your team."

"Sorry," Mel said. "I was just waving at Ms. Weldon."

Dakota faltered. "Ms. Weldon?"

"Uh-huh." Mel pointed to the top of the bleachers behind them.

Jessie sat on the highest bench, holding a cup from the refreshment stand. Her hair shimmered under the bright lights, and a Clearwater Springs athletic jersey from a fundraiser the previous year stretched across those generous breasts. To keep herself from venturing too far into that thought, she wondered where Jessie had gotten the shirt. Maybe it belonged to Curtis.

Jessie sent her a small wave and a smile. Her expression revealed nothing but a friendly exchange between colleagues.

Dakota lifted her chin in acknowledgement, as she would with anyone else. Inwardly, though, the fire ignited. She turned back to the game, but had trouble concentrating. At the final buzzer, her bench emptied onto the court to celebrate the win with their teammates. Dakota grinned and gave them all a thumbs-up.

"Not bad, Sis. And without one of your strongest players," Drew said, slinging an arm around Dakota's shoulders. "They must have a good coach."

"Hey, thanks for coming." Dakota hugged Drew, then gave Selena a chaste kiss on the lips. "Were you guys here for the whole thing? The second game was a little brutal."

"Yeah, but your girls came back strong," Drew said.

Over his shoulder, Dakota saw Jessie in conversation with some students in front of her.

Drew followed her gaze. "Is that her?"

"What?" Dakota startled. "Who?"

Drew laughed. "What do you mean, who? You know who. Jessie Weldon."

"Uh, yeah." Dakota cut a glance to him, then Selena, then back to Jessie. "How'd you know that?"

"Well, hmmm." Drew stroked his chin in obvious imitation of their grandpa when he was thinking. "I haven't heard a word from you since Monday, when you told me you were having dinner with her the next night. And now, you blushed as soon as you saw her."

"I did not." She knew she had, though. Just a little.

"And now you're blushing more." Drew grinned. "You two have a good time?"

"Oh, yeah." Dakota nodded. "She came over again last night," she said in a hushed tone.

Drew's brow lifted. "Really." It wasn't a question. "So in all that time together, have you—"

"No," Dakota said sharply. She couldn't believe he was bringing that up here.

He pursed his lips. "That's a pretty big thing to leave out, since the two of you are talking so much."

"Honey," Selena said, a quiet reproach in her voice. She ran her hand up his arm.

"All right, knock it off. She's coming over." Dakota turned in Jessie's direction. "I'll fill you both in later."

"Good game, Coach," Jessie said as she approached.

The words sounded awkward coming from her, and Dakota doubted she'd ever said them in her life. "Thanks. The girls did great." She stepped back, opening a spot for her.

"Jessie, this is my brother, Drew, and his wife, Selena." She turned to the couple. "This is Jessie Weldon." She wanted to say Brogan, to let Jessie know they were aware of who she was, but it wasn't the time or place. Besides, she wanted to make sure there was no opening for Drew to bring up his version of what happened that night. Surely, he wouldn't, though. She knew him better than that.

"It's nice to meet you both," Jessie said, shaking hands with each of them.

"Likewise," Selena said. "Dakota tells us you've taken over Jim Anderson's classes."

"That's right. I..."

The conversation continued as Drew and Dakota eyed one another. Dakota knew he meant well, but why couldn't he let it drop? How could it matter after all this time? She knew why, though. Deep down, she knew it would matter to Jessie, and if they didn't talk about it now, along with everything else, soon it would be too late. It would become a deception between them, lying dormant, waiting to burst into the light at the worst possible moment.

Dakota had always been afraid to say it, though, especially since she wasn't even sure about the truth of it. How could she say it now—when she'd just found Jessie, when parts of her she'd thought died long ago on that back road were coming alive again, when there seemed to be even more at stake?

She didn't know if she could. But what would it cost if she didn't?

Chapter Seventeen

Jessie sat in the overstuffed chair beside the fireplace in Curtis's living room, grading papers. She'd always been careful not to think of it as her living room—in her teens, because she'd learned that nothing that felt like home lasted, and since she'd been back, because she didn't intend to stay. She loved being here with Curtis, though, the way they'd been able to reconnect and be family to one another.

It was Friday night, the first evening since Monday she'd been home, and she had a ton of work to catch up on as well as a phone call to make to Sandy. When she'd decided to leave Massachusetts after she and Shelly split up, she'd promised Sandy they'd talk just as much as they did living in the same city. More than that, however, she needed some time to herself to get her head on straight.

Being with Dakota, as hot and exquisitely hedonistic as it was, scrambled her brain. Or maybe *because* it was so hot and exquisitely hedonistic, it scrambled her brain. She'd always been a tad oversexed, or so she'd been told by a couple of girlfriends, and Dakota hadn't helped that. Jessie hadn't been able to get enough. Even when she'd come home in the wee hours of Thursday morning, she'd brought herself to two more climaxes fantasizing about her before getting ready for school. It was the confusion it caused her, though, that she really needed to get a handle on.

"You staying in tonight, Jessie girl?" Curtis asked from the doorway.

Jessie sighed. "Yes, and I'm looking forward—" She looked up and whistled.

He wore dress jeans, a western style plaid shirt, and a pair of dark leather cowboy boots.

"You sure aren't," she said with a wink. "You look great."

His cheeks dimpled, and he ducked his head shyly. "Margie and I are going dancing over at the Grange Hall."

Jessie smiled. "She's going to be the envy of all the other ladies."

Curtis chuckled, then seemed to linger. "I'm probably just an old fool."

Jessie caught a note of insecurity beneath his usual joking manner. "You most certainly are not. Any woman would be honored to have your attention."

"You think?" He looked at her questioningly, then came into the room and sat on the sofa across from her.

She could tell there was something on his mind. "Do you want to talk about it?"

"Would you mind? I mean, it might be kind of odd, like talking to your dad about dating."

Jessie set her stack of papers on the floor beside her. "Curtis, it *is* talking to my dad about dating. And I'm happy to. I want my dad to be happy."

He seemed to relax. "I really like Margie," he said without hesitation. "I mean, I've always liked her. You know, I've known her for a long time, but recently, I've started…You know?"

"Yes," Jessie said softly. "I know. And I can tell she feels the same way."

His eyes brightened. "You can?"

Jessie laughed. "Only a blind person wouldn't see the way she lights up when you're around. And even then, a blind person would be able to feel it."

"Really? Because I haven't been sure."

Jessie shrugged. "Maybe that's because you never get to see her right before you walk into the room."

"Mm." He nodded, his expression serious. "But, you know, I'm seventy years old."

"And?" Jessie raised an eyebrow.

"And…you know…I've had a long and wonderful love."

"Is that what you're concerned about? That Laura might not approve?"

Curtis looked down at his boots. He seemed so much like a little boy in that instant, it melted Jessie's heart. "I just don't want her to think…"

Jessie shifted from the chair and knelt before him. "Curtis."

He lifted his gaze to her.

"Laura would never want you to be alone, unless you wanted to be. She'd want you to be happy."

He looked uncertain.

"You know what she told me about you once?" Jessie asked, suddenly remembering the conversation.

He tilted his head.

"She said you have so much love to give and are such a wonderful husband, it would be a crime if you were ever alone."

"Aw, shrimp." He scoffed. "You're making that up to make me feel better."

Jessie laughed. "I am not. It was right after Mrs. Julian died, and Frank was left all alone. We were talking in the kitchen."

He considered her, the twinkle back in his eyes. "And it would be all right with you, if Margie and I were more than friends?"

Tears sprang to Jessie's eyes. "Oh, Curtis, absolutely. And if I'm in the way, being here—"

"You are never in the way," he said sternly, taking her hands in his. "Get that right outta your head. This is your home, if you want it to be."

She nodded and wiped her cheeks.

"Well, now all that's taken care of," Curtis said matter-of-factly. "How have you been. How's that internship project of yours going?"

Jessie groaned inwardly, then brought him up to speed.

"I know this might be a touchy subject given the history and all, but the Scott Foundation—"

"Yes, I know." Jessie held up her hand. At least Curtis understood. "I've had that suggested quite a few times."

"Didn't you say that you and Dakota Scott have cleared the air some?" he asked, taking his turn as the voice of reason.

Cleared the air? Is that what we're doing? That seemed to be what they'd done last Saturday night out at Brogan's Bend, and maybe even on Tuesday at Dakota's. But nothing about Wednesday night had cleared up anything for her. "What about my mother? You know how she felt about the Scotts. I just can't bring myself to go to them for anything, however irrational it might be."

"Your mother." Curtis shook his head. "I've never said this out loud before, but I'm going to say it now because I think it's important for you to hear." He leveled his gaze on her. "Your mother was a bitter woman, even before Jackie's death. Jackie's death was a tragedy, for all of us who loved her, but I think your mother wanted someone to blame. After your daddy died, she let it turn her sour. And the Scotts…Well, they have all that money, and the big house and ranch up on the hill, and it was the twins in the car…But we all have our troubles, and the Scotts are no exception. In fact, I wouldn't trade every trouble I've ever had for theirs."

Jessie wondered exactly how much Curtis knew about Dakota's family's troubles.

"You were such a little girl when all that happened, Jessie," Curtis said, continuing his train of thought. "And I know how much you wanted to be there for your mother, to be what she needed you to be, but I'd hate to see you base your decisions today on back then. Especially if you and Dakota Scott are finding…" Curtis blushed. "Well, you know."

She didn't know, at least, not about that. But the rest of what he was saying, she'd thought of before. She knew her mother's bitterness and how much she'd needed someone to blame for her life. "Thank you," she said, squeezing his hands.

He smiled and nodded.

"And now, you should get going, or Margie's going to think you stood her up," she said teasingly.

He stood. "And thank you too, Jessie girl." He stopped in the doorway. "Oh, and if I don't come home tonight, don't worry about me."

Jessie grinned. She remained on the floor, thinking about what Curtis had said as she listened to him moving around the kitchen. Was he right? Was she still reacting as a little girl? Suddenly, she remembered the baseball Dakota had tossed to her that day. "Hey, Curtis?" she called to him.

"Yep?" he said, poking his head back into the room.

"Do you remember some boxes I left here when I went off to college?"

"Sure. They're up in the attic with some things of your mother's and Jackie's. We kept it all in case you wanted it someday. I can get them down for you tomorrow, if you want."

It seemed silly to have him climb all the way into the attic for one childhood artifact. "That's okay. I just wondered where they were. I don't actually need them."

"Okay, then I'm off to trip the light fantastic." Curtis did a little turn, then a step.

Jessie laughed, remembering when he and Laura had taken a ballroom dance class. "As I said, Margie will be the envy of all the ladies."

Jessie pondered her conversation with Curtis for a long time after he left. The house was quiet, silent except for the ticking and quarterly chimes of Laura's grandfather clock and the crackling of the fire. The fact that he had felt comfortable talking with her about Margie and had asked if she was okay with them becoming more than friends touched her deeply. And what he'd said about her mother and the Scotts and her making her decisions based on her mother's feelings...She couldn't go so far as to apply it to Dakota—after all, she didn't even know what was going on between them—but could she apply it to the internship program? That was just money, and it could help a lot of local teens learn valuable skills. It didn't make any sense not to utilize a foundation that was known for its support of the local community.

Her stomach twisted at the thought. She knew it was an intellectual versus emotional battle, and the emotional in this case was unfounded. What if she simply made herself do it, powered through that first phone call to see what happened? She could even place it now, after hours, when she wouldn't have to talk to an actual person and could get away with leaving a message. She picked up her phone and stared at it.

After finding the number online, she prepared the message she'd leave in her head. *Hi...No...Hello.* More professional. *My name is Jessica Weldon, and I'm a teacher at Clearwater Springs High School.* Not completely accurate, but not a lie either. *I've put together a proposal for a student internship program that would benefit local students who are interested in vocational skills rather than the college track.* She'd written out most of it as part of the proposal itself, but she didn't want to read it. She wanted it to sound more natural, like she hadn't deliberately planned to leave a message. Once she felt confident with what she'd come up with, she dialed.

One ring. Two rings.

"Crystal Scott."

Shit! Jessie almost hung up, but remembered caller ID. Damned technology. *Who works at eight o'clock on a Friday night?* She glanced at the stack of papers beside her chair. *Whatever.* "Yes, uh, hi..." *Great opening.* "Is this the Scott Foundation?" A reasonable question given that it wasn't a secretary that answered and the manner in which Crystal had. She remembered the picture of the four Scott children on Dakota's mantel and Crystal leaning on Drew.

"Yes, it is," Crystal said. "I'm the CEO. May I help you?"

"Well, I was calling to leave a message in hopes of setting up an appointment to speak with you about a proposal I've put together." Jessie felt her momentum returning. "But I can call back on Monday," she added quickly.

"Oh, no need. As long as we're on the phone," Crystal said. "Where are you from?"

"I'm from here…Clearwater Springs. I mean, I'm here now."

"Oh." Crystal sounded surprised. "Your number isn't local, so I thought… Is your proposal for a local program?"

"Yes."

A pause. "Are you the one working on the student internship program through the high school?"

Jessie rolled her eyes, remembering Dakota's words. *Gotta love small towns.* Of course Crystal would have heard about it with all the people who'd suggested the Scott Foundation. "Yes," she said. "Yes, I am. My name is Jessica Weldon, and I'm a teacher at Clearwater Springs High School." Finally, something she'd actually prepared.

"Great. I've heard a little bit about it, and I'd love to hear more. It sounds like something we'll be interested in."

Jessie's insides flip-flopped with a bittersweet reaction. She was excited to learn that the program might be able to be implemented, and Crystal hadn't said she'd missed this year's deadline—but she was asking for help from the Scotts. She might as well have reached into her mother's grave and killed her again. She clung to Curtis's words from earlier. "That's great," she forced herself to say.

"Let's see," Crystal said, not missing a beat. "I'm out of town tomorrow, but I'll be back Sunday. Could we meet in the afternoon? Say at three?"

"Sure, that will work." Jessie jotted it down on a magazine cover, but she was certain she'd remember. "Where are you located?"

"Oh, yes, that's another thing." Crystal sighed. "Our office has a broken water pipe, and repairs are being done. That's why I forwarded all the calls to my cell, and I forgot to switch it back after hours. Anyway, I'm working out of my home office. Would you mind meeting there?"

"Not at all," Jessie said. "Wherever is convenient for you."

"Do you know where the Ghost Rider Ranch is?"

Jessie tensed. "Yes. Yes, I do." She instinctively looked out the front window up to the hill. It was a different view from the one she'd grown up with, but there it was—the Scott mansion.

"Fantastic. If you just buzz at the gate and give your name, you'll be let in. I'm very much looking forward to our meeting, Ms. Weldon." Crystal brought the call to a close.

"I am as well, Ms. Scott. Thank you." Jessie felt more than a little bit blindsided when she hung up. *That was a nasty trick by the powers that be.* She dropped onto the couch. Well, she'd wanted to force herself to make that first phone call and see what happened. So *this* is what happened.

It would be all right. It was a good program. It needed funding. The Scott Foundation had funding and supported a lot of things in this community. Hell, even her mother had probably benefited in some way at some point from the Scott Foundation, unbeknownst to her, Jessie was sure. Jackie could have even benefited from something like the student internship program, if she'd lived.

If the Scott twins hadn't killed her. It was her mother's voice. She'd awakened her. Jessie squeezed her eyes shut. No, it was only guilt—for going to the Scotts for money, for sleeping with Dakota, for never being able to fully get on board with her mother's accusations. Jessie finally knew what happened, though. Dakota had told her everything down to the smallest detail. It was an accident. Dakota wasn't drunk. She hadn't done anything wrong. The only thing left that Jessie didn't know was why Jackie was out there that night, and Dakota couldn't be expected to know that. Uncertainty rippled through her, but she stayed focused. *I'm not a child. I'm an adult. This is my life. These are my decisions.*

The more she repeated the mantra in her head, though, the more she thought about being a child. Not the child that tried so hard to be what her mother needed, but the child before that. The one who had a big sister that took her to football and basketball and baseball games, who'd looked out for her, who'd been there for her when their mother wasn't. The one that Curtis took fishing. The one that Dakota had tossed that ball to. She thought again of the box up in the attic, right above where she sat, possibly. She wondered about the ball. It seemed to be calling to her. *Crazy.*

She went to the kitchen and found a flashlight, then pulled the ladder from the storage closet and climbed up into the attic. It was dark and cold. She knew there was a light up there somewhere but couldn't remember where the switch was. She should have let Curtis find it for her tomorrow. There wasn't a lot up there—some small pieces of furniture, Laura's old sewing machine, a bookshelf, filled with books. *Interesting.* And along the back wall, several rows of boxes.

Jessie shined the light across the top of each. At length, she came to several with the name Nancy—her mother—scrawled across the top, beside them, two that read Jackie, and finally, her two. She opened the lid of one to find some clothes and books, neatly packed inside. The second was more haphazard, filled with some toys, a couple manila envelopes holding schoolwork from different grades, and there, in the bottom corner was the baseball.

She picked it up and balanced it in her hand. It was smaller than she recalled, but of course, she was bigger now. It was a softball, which made sense, but she hadn't remembered that. She thought of it sailing out into center field when Dakota had hit it and the two runners crossing home plate to win the game before it made it back to the catcher to tag Dakota out. And she remembered the grin on Dakota's face and the glint in her eyes when she'd tossed it to Jessie and the pure joy in her twelve-year-old heart when she'd caught it. She smiled at the memory. She tucked the ball under her arm and replaced the lid on the box.

As she rose to leave, Jackie's name caught her attention. She paused and ran her hand over the letters. She had no recollection of what Jackie had left behind, even though they'd shared a room. She opened the box and shined the light into its contents.

An old and faded Clearwater Springs baseball cap sat on top. Jessie picked it up and turned it over. R. Beckman was written inside in black permanent marker. Jessie opened an envelope to find some faded photographs, a few of her and Jackie, several of their parents, and one of all four of them in which Jessie was maybe three. She set them on the floor beside the ball. What looked like a hot pink fuzzy bunny foot peeked out from under the streamers of some pom-poms, and when Jessie tugged on it, not surprisingly, she pulled out a hot pink, fuzzy bunny. She laughed out loud.

Mr. Whiskers, named for his long neon green whiskers which were now bent and smooshed against his chubby cheeks, had been Jackie's most cherished possession. He'd been her present from their father on her seventh birthday. The only time she'd let Jessie cuddle with him was once when Jessie had fallen and skinned both her knees. She hugged him to her chest now.

With one hand, she rummaged through the remainder of the box, finding mostly books toward the bottom. As she started to pull several out, she heard the phone in the kitchen ring. She tossed them back in, replaced the lid, and scooped up the pictures and the softball, then hurried down the ladder. By the time her feet hit the floor, the call had gone to voice mail.

The warmth of the house alerted her to just how cold it'd been up there, and she quickly closed the access door and put away the ladder. She really needed to get some work done. She settled Mr. Whiskers comfortably on her bed in hopes of making up for all those years stuffed in a box underneath some pom-poms, and tucked the pictures in the drawer of her nightstand. The ball she took with her back to the living room for no reason she could determine. She simply wanted it with her. She sent Sandy a text, saying she'd call tomorrow, to receive one in return reminding her that Sandy and Bethany were at a fundraising event for Bethany's work anyway. With a sigh, she started grading vocabulary tests.

An hour and a half later, when she was finishing up her second period papers, her phone chirped, signaling an incoming text. She checked the screen.

Still awake? It was Dakota.

They'd finally gotten around to exchanging numbers sometime Wednesday night.

Who wants to know? She added a smiley face.

Your back door girl.

Jessie looked through the kitchen at the door. She could see the shadow of the top of someone's head through the high window. *Really?*

Come see for yourself. Smiley.

When Jessie opened the door, she found Dakota standing on the porch, her hands behind her back, grinning ear to ear. She laughed. "You look very pleased with yourself."

Dakota dipped her head. "I am." Her hair was down, framing her face and shoulders. Her eyes were bright with mischief, and her mouth…Mmm, her mouth.

Jessie no longer had only a kiss to think about when she looked at Dakota's mouth. Now she knew exactly how good it felt kissing, sucking, tasting every inch of her body. She shivered at the memory. "I thought you'd be at the football game tonight."

"The football game ended thirty minutes ago."

"I see." Jessie chuckled. She was enjoying this playful side of Dakota. "So what's behind your back?"

"I come bearing gifts." Her grin grew wider.

"Gifts?"

"Mm-hm." With a flourish, Dakota brought her hands from behind her. In one, she held a brown paper bag. With the other, she extended a single white rose.

Jessie smiled, warmth touching her cheeks and heart. She took the flower. "It's beautiful."

"The white rose is associated with new beginnings—and some other stuff like virginity, purity, and chastity, that probably don't apply to us, especially after Wednesday night. But a single rose of any color means simplicity and gratitude. I wanted to thank you for the time we spent together this week." Dakota's expression changed to one of sincerity. "All of it."

Jessie was speechless. Whenever she thought she had Dakota Scott all figured out, she threw her for a loop. All she could do was answer with the same degree of authenticity. "It's meant a lot to me too. You…You're something I never expected."

Dakota's gaze was intense. It held Jessie, pulling her in like a tractor beam.

Jessie wanted so badly to slip her arms around Dakota's neck and kiss her. She cleared her throat. "What's in the bag?"

Dakota shook her head slightly, as though clearing it. She grinned again. "Two world famous chocolate malts from Burger Bob's."

Jessie laughed. "One of our three fast food restaurants."

"Exactly," Dakota said.

"If there are two malts, does that mean you're staying?" Jessie asked, not sure if that was a good idea. She still hadn't gotten clear where Dakota was concerned. "Or is one for Curtis?"

"I happen to know that Curtis is at the Grange with Margie Newman, dancing up a storm. And they looked pretty cozy, so I'd be surprised if he isn't home late." Dakota nodded thoughtfully. "I think I'd better stay and take this other malt off your hands."

"You said you were at the football game," Jessie said, stepping aside and gesturing her into the kitchen.

"No, you said I was at the football game. *I* said the football game ended a half hour ago."

Jessie closed the door behind her. "I can tell I'm going to have to take you literally."

Dakota looped her arms around Jessie and pulled her close. "You can take me any way you want, darlin'." She took her mouth in a slow, luxuriant kiss.

Jessie encircled Dakota's waist and melted into her. When the kiss finally ended, she drew in a steadying breath. "Do you have spoons and straws in that bag?"

Dakota grinned again. "I've got everything you need, baby."

Jessie let out a throaty chuckle. "You certainly do."

When they were in the living room, each indulging in a thick, delicious malt, Dakota lay back on the sofa. "Seriously, I don't mean to interrupt." She nodded to the stack of papers beside Jessie. "I can't seem to stop thinking about you. I just wanted to see you. I won't stay long."

"I've been thinking about you, too."

"Yeah?"

"Yeah."

"Hey, what's that?" Dakota asked, glancing down beside Jessie. "Is that a softball?"

Jessie retrieved it from where it'd gotten wedged between the chair and the cushion. She held it up. "It is." The hat flashed in her mind, and her curiosity peaked. "Did you know someone with the last name of Beckman in high school?"

Dakota cocked her head. "There was Ron Beckman. I didn't really know him, though. He was only here for a year. And he was a jerk. Why?"

"Oh, I just came across the name and wondered." Jessie shrugged dismissively, regretting she'd let the question slip out. She didn't want to talk about Jackie tonight. Besides, if he'd been in Clearwater Springs for such a short time, he couldn't have been that significant to her. "It's not important."

Dakota took the softball. "Is this Curtis's?" she asked, clearly more interested in it than anything to do with Ron Beckman. "I've never seen him play. Is he in the city league?"

Jessie watched her toss the ball in the air, then catch it. *Am I going to tell her?* She waited to see. "No, it's mine." *I guess I am.*

"Yours?" Dakota looked closely at it, then, read, "Property of Clearwater Springs High School." She gasped. "You *stole* it?" she asked in obvious mock outrage.

Jessie laughed. "I didn't steal it. Someone gave it to me."

"Well then, they stole it." Dakota set the ball on the couch and took another spoonful of her malt. "Who gave it to you?"

Jessie smiled at her, remembering, once again, every detail of that day. "You did."

Dakota's next bite stopped midway to her mouth. "I did? When?"

"A long time ago," Jessie said, drawing her feet up beneath her. "I was twelve, and you were sixteen. It was after a game. You were the last batter, and you hit that ball way into the outfield and brought in the winning runs. Afterward, a bunch of people were outside the locker room, and when you came out, you tossed the ball to me."

Dakota was staring at her, seemingly rapt. "And you kept it all this time?"

"Not exactly. I kept it for a while. Actually, I cherished it. Remember I told you I had a huge crush on you?"

Dakota nodded.

"I kept it until after the accident, until you went away to college." Jessie picked at a thread on the arm of the chair. "But my mother kept doing all the stuff she did, and saying all kinds of things. And it got too confusing. So I put it away in a box and forgot about it. And at some point it got moved here. I just found it again tonight."

"Did you forget about me, too?" Dakota asked.

Jessie tried to meet her eyes but couldn't. She shook her head.

Then Dakota was there, shifting her over, in the chair with her, holding her.

Jessie rested her head on Dakota's shoulder.

"Shhh." Dakota squeezed her more tightly.

Jessie hadn't realized she was crying. When had she started? And *why*? "Maybe that's us, Dakota," she said softly. "Maybe as long as we keep each other put away somewhere, or stay far apart, it's okay. All of it. My crush. The accident. Jackie's death. My mother. Your mother. But when we're together…" she searched Dakota's face, "like this, and like the other night…I don't know what to do with you, Dakota. I don't know what I feel. And I can't figure it out."

"Can't we just see this through together and find out where we end up? This is helping me, and I think it could help you too."

"It is helping me," Jessie said, trying to sound reassuring. "I mean it did. I'm so grateful that you told me everything that happened that night."

Dakota flinched ever so slightly and averted her gaze. Then she was back just as quickly. "Then let's keep going. Together. Because if we can get through all this crap, maybe we could have something. I think I want that, Jessie, and I don't want to lose you before we even know."

Jessie's mind was muddled. Could she be hearing correctly? Was she saying she felt something for Jessie? She nestled her head in the hollow of Dakota's shoulder. Maybe she didn't have to figure it out now. Maybe Dakota was right. If they could get through all this together, maybe they could have something with one another.

They sat in the chair, intertwined, cuddling, and talking, until the clock chimed twelve. By then, they were both laughing again, and when Dakota's lips met Jessie's as they stood at the back door saying good night, their kisses held the promise of something, even if they didn't know what.

And when Jessie went to bed that night, she slept with an old Clearwater Springs softball, a hot pink fuzzy bunny, and a single white rose.

Chapter Eighteen

Dakota sat in the library with her mother. It'd always been Vivian Scott's favorite room in the ranch house and where she spent many hours in the colder months of the year.

Dakota tried to keep her regular visits on Saturdays, usually in the late afternoon or evening, but she'd taken her varsity team to a tournament in Riverside the previous day and hadn't gotten home until late. Sunday afternoons were quiet around the ranch, since most of the employees had the day off, so Dakota and her mother had taken a nice long walk and stopped by to see Drew, Selena, and Randy who were barbecuing. Now, they were enjoying a cup of tea, as much as Dakota ever enjoyed tea.

She swallowed a mouthful of the new lemon grass and ginger blend her mother had wanted her to try and set down her cup. She felt the weight of her mother's stare. "Mama, you've been looking at me weird all afternoon. Did I grow a second head or something?"

Her mother's eyes sparkled with amusement. "Something's different about you today," she said after another perusal of Dakota's face. "There's something new."

"There's nothing new," Dakota said, avoiding the most obvious topic. "Things are going well, but everything's pretty much the same as usual. The job's good, the team's doing great… That's about it."

"No. It's nothing like that. This is…" Her mother gasped. "You've found the one. I know it. I can see it in the spark in your eyes. You look exactly like Crystal did a week after she met Paul. And Drew, he's had it twice. And me and your father, of course, when we first met. It's your turn."

"No, Mama. Nothing like that." She'd known she should have pushed Jessie out of her mind every time she'd crept in. What was she supposed to say? *Yeah, Mama, I met this hot and incredibly sexy woman who made me come eight times the other night.* She could share something like that with Drew—although she hadn't—but not with her mother. Besides, how could Jessie be *the one* with all the complications between them?

She'd thought a lot about what Jessie had said, that maybe they'd be better off staying away from one another. That everything would be okay then. Even if it were true, though, Dakota knew she couldn't do it.

"Honey, if you've found her, or if she's found you, there's nothing you can do to deter the inevitable." She patted Dakota's hand.

If Jessie had found *her*? Dakota tried to imagine Jessie, pragmatic, in charge, as regal as the queen herself in her classroom, succumbing to a notion as romantic and magical as *the one*. Although, the woman Dakota had spent four out of the past eight nights with wasn't any of those things—well, except maybe the in-charge type on Wednesday. The Jessie she'd been getting to know, and know very well in some ways, could be uncertain, and vulnerable. She was honest, though, and pretty damned brave. She'd faced every conversation they'd had, every topic they'd explored, head on. She had more courage than Dakota. "How can you still believe in the one when Dad's with Rowina?"

Her mother frowned.

Dakota hadn't meant to ask the question. Or maybe she had. She could be mean sometimes, especially when her mother dealt out words of wisdom. It was that love/hate thing, a therapist had explained to her once. She immediately regretted her dig.

"I demanded the divorce *because* he's the one for me. I can't support him the way he needs to be supported by the woman who loves him. I wanted him to be able to be with someone who could. It doesn't mean I don't love him and he doesn't love me. We'll be together again." Her mother didn't sound mad, only factual. She seemed to understand Dakota's occasional snip.

"I'm sorry, Mama."

"It's all right, dear," her mother said with affection. "This time around has been difficult for all of us."

Dakota sighed with resignation. How could a perfectly lovely afternoon turn so quickly?

"Tell me about her," her mother said.

Dakota stiffened. *No.* The last thing she wanted to do was talk about Jessie with her mother—with anyone, really. Not yet. She wanted to keep her all to herself for a while. She even regretted Drew knowing a little bit, and that was unheard of. He kept pushing her, though.

Dakota's cell phone rang, and she'd never been so thankful for an interruption. It was Crystal's ring. "Hello?" she said when she answered.

"Hey, Dakota." Crystal sounded winded. "Can you do me a huge favor?"

Dakota glanced at her mother. She looked tired. Their visit was probably coming to a close soon anyway, especially since Dakota had no intention of talking about Jessie being *the one* or otherwise. "Probably. What's up?"

"I have a three o'clock appointment, and I was running a few minutes late getting back to town anyway. But I've blown a tire. I have to wait for a tow. Could you go out to the ranch and meet our potential client and entertain her until I get there?"

"Entertain her?" Dakota laughed. "Like with my juggling act?"

"I don't know," Crystal said, sounding frustrated. "Get her something to drink. Show her around the ranch. Just be your charming self."

"Why don't you call her and reschedule?" Dakota supposed she didn't mind doing it. She'd do almost anything for Crystal. She'd wanted to try to touch base with Jessie this afternoon, though.

"I could, but I'd rather not, if I can help it. She wants to talk about funding for a program she's putting together, and I'm kind of excited about the little bit I already know of it. There was something odd about the phone call, though. For one thing, she made it at eight o'clock on Friday night—not exactly business hours—and she sounded reluctant for some reason. I'd like to get our initial meeting established."

Dakota fidgeted. She felt like such a misfit when it came to foundation business, but Crystal hadn't asked her to do that. She'd only said to be charming. *That* Dakota could do.

"Please, Dakota." Crystal slipped a note of desperation into her voice.

"All right. Sure. How long do you think you'll be?" She'd still have time to talk to Jessie, if Jessie was even available.

"I'm about a half hour out, and Triple A said they'd be here in thirty minutes." Crystal still sounded rushed, but she always did when it came to her work. "Ms. Weldon won't be there until three, so you won't be stuck with her for long."

Dakota's pulse leapt. "Ms. Weldon?"

Her mother's expression shifted with evident interest.

"Yes," Crystal said. "Do you know her? She said she works at the high school."

"Uh, yeah. We've met a few times." Apparently, she'd be talking to Jessie after all. If her mother hadn't been scrutinizing her so closely, she would have broken out in a grin.

"Great. How soon can you get there?"

"Already here," Dakota said. "I've been with Mom."

"You're a lifesaver. Thank you so much, Dakota." Crystal sighed heavily. "I'll get there as soon as I can."

"No worries," Dakota said, meaning it. "I'll just be my charming self, as you put it, and she won't even notice the time."

Crystal chuckled. "I have no doubt. See you soon."

Dakota's mother had seemed as ready for their visit to conclude as Dakota, or maybe she simply sensed that Dakota's mind was now someplace else, and had curled up with a book and an afghan in front of the picture window in the library. Dakota notified the aide on duty that she'd no longer be with her mother and of her mother's whereabouts in the house, and headed to prepare for Jessie.

Most of the staff was gone for the day, including Ada, so Dakota brewed some coffee and heated more water for tea, not sure which Jessie preferred, then looked for some cookies or biscotti to serve with the drinks. When security announced Jessie's arrival, she went out to the front veranda to wait.

An odd feeling came over her as she watched Jessie's car move up the long drive from the front gate. A fluttering in her stomach. An irrational concern about what to do with her hands. She slid them into the back pockets of her jeans, then planted them on her hips. Finally, she tried folding her arms across her chest. *Am I nervous? What's up with that?* When Jessie came to a stop in the circular drive in front of the house, Dakota moved down the steps to greet her. She saw Jessie hesitate at the sight of her. She opened the driver's side door and held out her hand to help her out.

Jessie gave her a curious look, then smiled and slipped her fingers over Dakota's palm. She gripped the handle of a briefcase with her free hand. "Do you greet all your family's guests this way?" She straightened.

"Crystal told me to be my charming self," Dakota said, but she couldn't get her mind to focus on anything other than how beautiful Jessie looked. It wasn't that she wore anything fancy, on the contrary. Basic black slacks enhanced her shapely hips and legs, while a royal blue sweater hugged her upper body in all the best ways. *God, she can fill out a sweater.* A multicolored scarf adorned her neck and shoulders, and dangly earrings of three two-toned gold strands with small crystals on the ends, drew Dakota's thoughts to how soft and plump the lobe felt between her lips. She cleared her throat. "She had a flat and is running late. She sends her deepest apologies and hopes you won't mind waiting."

"Will I be waiting with you?" Jessie's tone was playful, but held a note of tension as well.

Dakota grinned and bowed. "I am at your service, my lady."

Jessie gave a sultry laugh. "Okay, but you'll have to stop saying things that get my imagination going."

"Fair enough." Dakota nodded, calling her own responses into check. "Would you like to come inside and have some coffee or tea?"

Jessie turned in a half circle, scanning her surroundings, then looked up at the three-story house in front of her. "I've always wondered what this place looked like."

Dakota cocked her head to one side. "I can give you a tour."

Jessie considered her. "Just a cup of coffee for now."

When they were settled in the living room, Jessie dipped a biscotti into her drink and took a bite. Her gaze moved over every detail of the lushly furnished room.

Dakota was so used to not noticing much of anything in the house she'd grown up in, she couldn't help but wonder what Jessie saw. She decided to stay on a less personal topic. "So are you asking Crystal for funding for that intern program Regina was talking about at Shady Acres last week?" *Was that only a week ago?*

"Yes." Jessie placed her cup in its saucer and set both on the occasional table in front of the sofa. Her hand fluttered up to adjust the edge of her scarf.

"You seem nervous," Dakota said, intrigued. "I've never seen you anything but confident, when it comes to work anyway."

"I am," Jessie said bluntly. She met Dakota's eyes, then looked around the room again. "I feel kind of like I'm in the enemy camp."

The words stung. Even with everything they'd shared, Jessie still viewed her as the enemy?

Jessie pressed her lips together and closed her eyes. "I'm sorry. That was insensitive."

"Hey, no." Dakota held up her hands. "If that's how you feel. If nothing else, we've been honest with each other through everything."

"I didn't mean to hurt you, Dakota." Jessie touched Dakota's hand.

Dakota wanted to tell her she wasn't hurt, wanted to pretend, but she couldn't. She lifted a shoulder. "I'll be fine. I'd rather know what you're thinking and feeling, even if it hurts." She glanced around the room at some of the things Jessie had taken in. "Would you like to see the rest of the camp? You know, check to see how we treat our prisoners, if we're following the Geneva Conventions? It might put your mind at ease," she said in an attempt to lighten the mood.

Jessie didn't smile, but she did look thoughtful. "You know what I'd like to see?"

"What? Anything," Dakota said, happy to be off the previous topic.

"Your room." Jessie slipped her hand into Dakota's. "The room that was yours when you lived here."

Dakota hadn't been in that room for years. She'd gone into it once right after Diane left. She wasn't sure what she'd been looking for, but she hadn't found it. Diane had asked to see it, and Dakota had lied, telling her it'd been made over into a guest room, but she wouldn't lie to Jessie. With everything Jessie had shared—the Colby Cottages, her crush, the story of the softball—she deserved to see Dakota's old room. She nodded, then looked up at the slam of the front door.

Jessie jerked her hand free from Dakota's.

In seconds, Crystal hurried into the room. "I'm so sorry, Ms. Weldon," she said as she strode across the Persian rug, her hand extended. "Thank you for waiting. I'm so eager to hear about this program."

Crystal and Jessie shook hands and exchanged pleasantries.

"Dakota, could you please show Ms. Weldon to my office? I'll be right there," she said to Jessie, not waiting for Dakota's response.

"Well, I guess some other time," Jessie said, once Crystal was gone.

Dakota knew she was referring to seeing her old bedroom. "I can wait," she said without hesitation. She really wanted to spend some time with Jessie today. What could seem more natural than maybe going out for something to eat straight from there?

"Oh!" Jessie's pleasure with the suggestion was obvious in the tenor of that one word. "That would be nice."

Dakota smiled. "I'll be right here."

At the conclusion of the meeting, Jessie followed Crystal down a back hallway on their way to where Dakota waited for her. It was a different route than that which Dakota had taken escorting her to Crystal's office. Jessie had recurring dreams about houses like this one that seemed to go on and on, with new rooms materializing at the opening of a door, and halls and staircases that could just as easily lead to the center of a labyrinth as to nowhere. Her counselor had told her they represented the exploration of new opportunities in her life. Did the reality of such a situation mean anything?

The presentation of her proposal had gone well. It had turned out to be more of an informal conversation, with Crystal asking questions that hadn't occurred to Jessie, but they'd come up with the answers together as they'd brainstormed. By the conclusion, it'd felt as though they'd been working together forever, and the future of the program and its funding looked promising. Jessie still felt somewhat squirmy, if she thought much about the money coming from the Scott Foundation and actually being *in* the Scott mansion, and she knew she was going to have to find a way to put her mother's opinions and old accusations to rest when it came to the internship program.

As for her involvement with Dakota, that was a different topic entirely. She had no idea how to approach that. Even with Crystal, Jessie had lied and said she and Dakota had some things to discuss regarding Dakota's players Jessie was tutoring. She had no idea if Dakota had shared anything with Crystal about who she was. It was all so complicated. She really should stay away from Dakota *and* her bedroom—childhood and otherwise.

"Here we are," Crystal said as they magically appeared back in the living room from what Jessie would have thought to be the completely opposite direction from when she'd left.

Dakota stood at a wall of glass, staring out into a darkened afternoon and rivulets of rain trickling down the enormous picture window.

"Thank you again for contacting me about this program," Crystal said to Jessie. "I'm so excited about it, and as I said, I think the board will be too. It's exactly what we've been looking for."

"Thank you for your time and interest," Jessie said. "I'll have the formal written proposal to you by the end of the week."

Crystal smiled. "Perfect. And now, I'm going to go find my husband and say hello, then start thinking about dinner, since its Ada's day off. If you'd like to stay and eat with us when you're finished with Dakota, we'd love to have you. Our brother and his family and our younger sister, Tina, and her fiancé will be here too, as well as our mother. You could meet everyone."

The image of herself surrounded by the entire Scott clan overwhelmed Jessie. She forced a smile. "Thank you. That's such a nice invitation," she said, trying to keep from looking at Dakota for her reaction. "I do have plans, so maybe another time?"

"Of course." Crystal excused herself, and it was Jessie and Dakota alone in the large room.

"How'd it go?" Dakota asked from the window.

"Great, I think. There's still all the official approval and red tape to get through, but your sister seemed to think it will be fine." Jessie stepped up beside Dakota and gazed out what she realized was a sliding glass door set into the wall of windows. There was a balcony outside, and below that, a swimming pool surrounded by lush landscaping. In the distance, tennis courts occupied the top of one hill, and another house, a smaller one, was nestled in a grove of trees just below it. Jessie felt like she was in a hotel rather than a home.

"That's Tina's place," Dakota said, following Jessie's gaze.

Jessie nodded.

"Still want to see my old room?" Dakota asked. A non sequitur, but a welcome one.

"I do."

Jessie had seen the main staircase leading to the upper floors in the grand foyer when she'd come into the house, but Dakota led her through a formal dining room, into the kitchen, and up a much smaller set of stairs to the second floor. About halfway down the long hall, she stopped at a set of double doors and opened one. She motioned Jessie through.

The room was enormous. A king-sized bed sat nudged into a built-in headboard of shelves and cabinets. Across from it stood an entertainment center in light wood that matched the large desk and dresser in the corner and held a big screen TV, stereo system, and several shelves of books. A sitting area was perfectly situated for a view of both the TV and the panoramic scene outside the wall of windows.

The most interesting aspect of the room, however, was the presence of all the personal items still on display. Old pictures of Dakota and Drew, and a few with Crystal, peppered the top of the dresser and some nooks and crannies of both the headboard and the entertainment unit. One long shelf built into the wall held trophies of various kinds. A baseball mitt occupied the end. A couple of books sat on the lowest part of the headboard, as though waiting to be picked up at bedtime. It gave the room a lived-in appearance, and yet, paradoxically, there was no true sense of someone there. Despite the detritus of effects, the walls were bare.

The empty feeling made Jessie shiver. "Wow," was all she could find to say.

"Not what you expected?" Dakota moved farther into the room.

Jessie crossed to the array of trophies and noted the years—all from Dakota's teenage days. She scanned some of the book titles. "Is all this stuff from high school?"

"Mostly. I've told my mother and Ada I don't want any of it, but they say it's here when I'm ready." Dakota drew in a deep breath and moved to the window, taking the same stance she was in when Jessie had returned to the living room. She looked like a caged animal staring longingly out at freedom.

"Why don't you live at the ranch?" Jessie wasn't sure if she was crossing a boundary. *Do we have any boundaries, with everything that's between us?* "I mean, you said Tina has a house here, and Crystal actually lives in the mansion. And Drew, doesn't he live somewhere out here, too?"

Dakota shrugged. "Too many ghosts. Too much past," she said flatly. She sounded far away.

Jessie stepped up behind her and put her arms around Dakota's waist. "Is this hard for you? We don't have to stay."

"It's okay." Dakota slid her hands over Jessie's and pulled the embrace more tightly around her. "It feels kind of nice being in here with you."

Jessie pressed her cheek to Dakota's shoulder and felt Dakota relax into her arms.

They stood together in a comfortable silence, each with her own thoughts, but linked by something invisible and intangible.

Finally, Dakota shifted and coaxed Jessie around to face her. She held her close.

Jessie nestled against her. She wanted to say something, words that would bring them still closer together. She wanted to crawl inside Dakota but wasn't sure what the next step was.

Below in the circular driveway, a pickup truck pulled up and Drew and Selena and another man got out. But Jessie stayed fixated on Drew.

Dakota's hands moved up Jessie's back and began a gentle caress through her sweater.

Her tension eased under Dakota's touch. *Drew.* What was she going to do about Drew and what he'd said that night so long ago? It couldn't be true. *Jackie wouldn't do that.* And it really was what *he'd* said. Dakota hadn't said it—back then or now. Dakota had told her everything that had happened that night, and she hadn't said *that*. And she would have, if she'd thought it was true. *Right?* Could Jessie let it go? Accept that it was only Drew's perception? And did it really even matter? It was all so long ago. Since Friday night, Dakota's words had played over and over in her mind. She wanted to see if she and Dakota could have something. A part of her wanted the new beginning that single white rose promised.

She lifted her face to Dakota's. "Can I be with you tonight?" she whispered, pushing Drew from her mind. "Can I come over after your dinner with your family?"

"I'm not having dinner with my family." Dakota kissed Jessie gently on the lips. "I thought you had plans."

Her mouth was so soft and tasted of coffee and cookie. "I wanted to have plans…with you."

Dakota kissed her again, more insistently. She moaned quietly. "Then let's go have plans."

And for right now, that was enough.

Chapter Nineteen

Dakota inhaled Jessie's scent, savored her taste. She circled her clit with her tongue, once, twice…three more times, then moved down to slip inside her.

Jessie released a primal groan. She tightened her legs around Dakota's neck and shoulders and thrust against her mouth.

Dakota looped her arms around Jessie's hips, grasping her thighs and splaying them again. She pressed her to the bed and held her firmly in place, then buried her tongue in her sex.

Jessie's upper body thrashed against the mattress, but she was at Dakota's mercy.

And Dakota took full advantage. She licked and sucked and probed and teased with excruciating slowness, drawing all the sounds she loved from Jessie.

In the three and a half weeks since that first time they'd been together, Dakota had learned so much about her. What pleased her. What drove her wild. What brought her orgasms raging from her depths. And Jessie had learned all the same things about Dakota. So it was only fair this morning that it was now Jessie's turn after she'd awakened Dakota, her mouth working Dakota's nipples, her fingers deep inside, taking her God damned sweet time letting her come. Their sex was hot and passionate and frequent, almost always starting in lustful need and finishing in tender caresses that—if they'd talked about it—would be called lovemaking.

They hadn't, though. It was as though all of the talking of that first week and a half about everything that had taken place in the past had become too much. It seemed they both needed a reprieve, a moment to catch their breath. Or maybe it was that they'd already covered everything they could, up to the one thing still left beneath the surface. Dakota knew it was up to her to bring that up, and yet, she couldn't make herself do it. She was terrified to risk everything she'd found with Jessie. If she were going to do it, it should have been right in the beginning, before the stakes got too high.

"Dakota. Oh, God, Dakota." Jessie's voice was hoarse with need.

Dakota still thrilled at the sound of her name from Jessie's lips. She didn't understand why it had such an impact on her, unless it was because it'd taken Jessie so long to be willing to call her anything but Coach Scott. Dakota sucked her clitoris, pulling a cry of pleasure from deep within her.

Jessie found Dakota's hair and twisted her fingers into it. "Oh, God, Dakota," she screamed as she came.

Dakota smiled against Jessie's oh-so-sensitive, pulsing flesh as Jessie's climax flooded her mouth. "I love waking up with you," she murmured as Jessie began to calm.

It took a while for Jessie to answer. "Happy birthday," she said when she did.

Surprised, Dakota lifted her head and looked up the length of Jessie's body. "How'd you know it's my birthday?"

Jessie smiled. "Crystal told me. And Melinda mentioned it. And—"

"All right, all right." Dakota moved up on the bed and curled around Jessie.

Jessie ran her fingers over Dakota's lips and cheeks, wiping away her own wetness. "It's a small town. The real question is why didn't you tell me."

"I don't know. I started to a couple of times, but it felt awkward." Dakota cuddled Jessie against her. "Like you'd think that you had to get me a present."

"What would be wrong with me getting you a present?" Jessie traced Dakota's collarbone with the tip of a finger. Her breath caressed Dakota's neck. "Are you afraid I'd get you some ugly sweater you'd have to wear?" Her tone was playful.

Dakota chuckled. "No," she said without a doubt. "I know you'd never get me anything ugly."

Jessie trailed her hand down Dakota's chest, between her breasts. "I do have something for you, if you want it."

"You didn't have to do that." Dakota hugged her.

"Do you want it?" Jessie sounded tentative.

Dakota crooked a finger beneath her chin and tipped her head back to meet her eyes. "Of course, I do. I want anything that's from you."

"Okay." Jessie sat up. "Do you remember that night you brought me that white rose, and you said you wanted to work everything out between us and see if we could have something?"

Dakota nodded uncertainly. *Where's she going with this?*

"Do you remember what I said?"

Dakota thought back. "That maybe we were like the softball. Maybe it would be better if we stayed far away from one another." She didn't like this. How could this be a birthday present? She raised up on an elbow. "Jessie—"

Jessie pressed her finger to Dakota's lips. "My present is to take that back and to say, yes. I want to see if we can have something, too. My present is me, if you still want that."

Dakota was stunned, exhilarated, speechless. Jessie hadn't really shared much of any consequence since that night. She'd asked to see Dakota's room at the ranch house, but had said very little about it. It was as though she'd simply shut down some part of herself. Seeing Dakota was apparently fine, sleeping with her, and even those gentle, tender interludes, as long as they didn't talk about them, were fine. And now this. Dakota could tell from the small waver in Jessie's eye contact, the slight quaver in her voice, that this was huge for her. She rose up and kissed her. "Oh, Jessie, I soooooo want it. I want you."

Jessie draped her arms around Dakota and searched her face. "You're sure? I still have things to work out, like being around your family and trying to figure out how to get my mother's voice out of my head. I know those things hurt you."

Dakota cradled Jessie. "I'm sure." And she was. She knew she wanted a real chance with her more than she'd ever wanted to be with any other woman, but then her own fear clutched at her throat. If she and Jessie were going to try to move forward together, she knew she was going to have to come clean with everything. She clenched her eyes shut. *Damn it! Why couldn't Drew and I have just seen the same thing that night?* That, all by itself, would have made this the best birthday ever.

It was still pretty damned good, though.

They stayed in bed another couple of hours, holding each other, snuggling, and finally making love again. Then Jessie made hash browns and omelets, and they went back to bed to eat them. Dakota would have loved to have spent the whole day and night there, but Crystal was making a birthday dinner for the whole family.

"Come to the ranch with me for dinner," Dakota said, setting a plate on the nightstand. "We don't have to stay late. Then we can come back here and pick up where we left off." Jessie had been working with Crystal quite a bit since their initial meeting about the internship program, and they seemed to be getting along well, so Dakota thought she might have a chance of getting Jessie to agree. And if she and Dakota were going to be together, even in the beginning stages, Jessie would have to meet the rest of them at some point. Why not sooner rather than later?

"I can't," Jessie said. "Today's the day I told Curtis I'd cover the motel so he and Margie can go visit her sister." Her eyes sparkled at the mention of him. "He's so cute all in love, and he's really nervous. I can't disappoint them."

"No, of course not," Dakota said, trying not to let her own disappointment show.

"I can come over afterward." Jessie lay against Dakota, their bodies fitting together perfectly. "I'll be finished at ten."

Dakota perked up. "That sounds doable. Maybe I'll be waiting right here."

When Jessie left with the promise to return with more birthday surprises and an extra special present she assured Dakota they'd both enjoy, Dakota was alone with nothing but her thoughts and worries. How was she going to do this without screwing everything up? *I'm an idiot. I should have told her everything all at once.* She almost wished Drew was the kind of person to take matters into his own hands. Then it would all be over by now—one way or another. But Dakota knew it had to come from her.

❖

Jessie chatted with a couple of other teachers from the high school as she stood by the fire and sipped her wine. The crowd kept growing as more people arrived, and she was surprised by a few who were on the guest list, herself being one of them. She didn't think Selena and Randy knew about the intimate side of her and Dakota's relationship, but she could be wrong. She knew Dakota told Drew a lot, and maybe she was almost as close to his wife and partner. She even wondered if they might know who she really was. Whatever it was they knew, it was enough that she'd been invited to the surprise birthday party they were throwing for Drew and Dakota.

Jessie watched Selena, Randy, and Crystal working right alongside the catering staff as they set out food, checked on the bar, and made sure the DJ had everything she needed. They'd clearly done this before. The living room was dimly lit by only one lamp and the firelight, and some of the ranch hands were in charge of driving all the cars off to some distant point on the property, so as to keep the party a secret until the final moment when Drew and Dakota walked in, expecting a cozy, family dinner. Someone named Roland had the earlier task of sneaking into Dakota's garage and disconnecting something in her car engine, so Drew would have to go pick her up. The whole bunch of them were pretty devious.

A ripple of envy, an age-old longing for her family, for home, for a sense of belonging, wriggled through Jessie.

"More wine, ma'am?" a young waiter asked as he passed by.

"No, thank you" Jessie said. "I'm fine." She was fine, for the most part, but her gift to Dakota that morning, her decision to fully embrace a new beginning with her, had her nerves humming and her body slightly trembling. It'd, in fact, been the invitation to this party, along with her decision to attend, that had given her the final push to let go of everything from the past and actually be with Dakota—or at least try. She needed to work on being here at the mansion again, and this time with Dakota's entire family.

"Okay, everyone." Randy raised his hands and clapped them together to get the crowd's attention. "They just passed through the gate, so let's quiet down and hide as best you can."

Jessie moved with Coach Allen into the corner near the fireplace, stepping into the shadows.

A hush fell over the room. The sound of the front door opening, then closing, was followed by Dakota's voice. "Hey, where is everyone?" Two figures moved into silhouette in the doorway. The lights came on.

"Surprise!" The chorus of voices shattered the silence.

Dakota jumped back, her hand flying to her chest.

Drew laughed. "I told you they were up to something."

"Happy birthday," came from various parts of the room. A few party horns blew.

Dakota was laughing now too, a huge grin stretching across her face. She hugged a few people, shook hands with others. When her gaze landed on Jessie, her eyes went wide. "You knew?" she mouthed. She squinted and pointed a finger at her.

Jessie waited her turn as Dakota and Drew made the rounds—the Scott twins in all their glory. She curbed her mother's sarcastic voice in her head.

At length, Dakota reached her. "I can't believe you knew about this." She hugged Jessie to her. In the celebratory atmosphere, it didn't seem unusual. "And you lied to me."

Jessie kissed her cheek. "Sometimes you have to lie around birthdays and Christmas. Get used to it."

Dakota beamed. "I plan to get used to a lot of things with you." She winked.

Jessie smirked and stifled an eye roll. *Who winks at people? Really?*

"Jessie, it's good to see you again." Drew stepped up beside them. "Thanks for coming."

"She's here for my birthday," Dakota said before Jessie could respond. "Not yours."

"That's only fair." Drew clamped an arm around Dakota's neck. "You should have at least one person here."

Jessie laughed. "Thank you, Drew. And happy birthday."

"If you'll excuse Dakota for a little bit longer," Drew said, dragging her away. "We need to mingle for a while, or Crystal will hang our hides out to dry."

Jessie wandered out onto the balcony that overlooked the pool. When she'd seen it before, it was still lit by daylight. Now, however, the pool light glowed a gorgeous blue and landscape lighting lit the surrounding greenery. It was beautiful. She remembered how she used to imagine parties like this taking place here from her bedroom down in the town. Now that she knew the truth about many of those nights and that it was one of those very nights on which Jackie was killed, it no longer seemed romantic. She didn't want to think about it.

"Hey, Jessie, how's it going?" Berta's familiar voice helped distract her.

She turned and smiled in greeting. "Hi, Berta. I'm well. It's so nice to see you."

Berta was dressed casually in black jeans, a silver button-up shirt with thin black stripes, and black leather boots. "I'm glad. You look great."

"Thank you," Jessie said. "So do you." It was nice they'd ended things on friendly terms. Clearwater Springs was too small for things to be awkward with someone she once dated. Her time with Berta had been enjoyable, but there hadn't been that necessary spark for Jessie. "How's your family?"

Berta was close to her sister and nieces and nephews, and Jessie knew once they came up in conversation, she wouldn't need to say much. Berta grinned. "They're great. Bobby still asks about you," she said of her special needs nephew. "He has a huge crush on you."

They talked for a while on a variety of subjects. Jessie was thankful for the company, since she didn't know many of the other guests. Berta leaned on the balcony railing, looking out over the landscape, and Jessie stood beside her, taking in the chilly night air. Winter was definitely right around the corner.

"So…" Berta said, sounding nervous. "You and Dakota?"

Jessie hesitated, surprised, but then, with the gossip mill, she supposed most people knew how many nights her car was parked outside of Dakota's house. "Yes," she said quietly. It felt good to affirm it out loud. She turned to Berta.

Berta smiled softly. "I'm happy for you. Dakota's great. And she's one lucky woman," she said with a quick squeeze of Jessie's hand.

Jessie felt herself blush. "Thank you, Berta." She sensed Dakota's presence rather than actually seeing her approach.

"Hey, Berta," Dakota said as she stepped close to Jessie. "Jessie," she added in a similar tone to when she addressed her as Ms. Weldon.

"Hey, birthday girl," Jessie said with a smile. "Did you get all your mingling done?"

"Yes. I think Crystal is sufficiently impressed with my and Drew's social skills and has decided we can be trusted on our own for a while."

Berta laughed. "She'll still be keeping an eye on you." She glanced over her shoulder into the house. "If you'll both excuse me, I'll go check to see if anything needs doing." She met Dakota's gaze and patted her on the arm.

"Thanks, Bert," Dakota said.

Jessie sensed some unspoken communication between the two of them. "It was nice catching up with you," she said as Berta turned to leave.

When they were alone, Dakota grinned at Jessie, her eyes alight with pure happiness. "I can't believe you're here."

Jessie touched her arm. "Well, now that you've run off my company, you'd better stick around." She said it teasingly, though she wanted Dakota with her the rest of the night, and not just here at the party.

"I came out here to ask you if you'd like to dance." Dakota opened her arms.

It was only then Jessie noticed the soft music drifting out from inside. She set her glass on the railing and moved into Dakota's embrace.

They moved with the music without speaking, their gazes locked through one whole song. There was something slightly off about Dakota. Her eyes held their usual spark. Her moves had their natural easy flow, but there was an edge to her energy.

"Is everything okay?" Jessie asked.

Dakota pulled her closer, but was hesitant with her answer. "Can we go somewhere and talk?" she asked finally. "There's something I need to say."

Alarms went off in Jessie's head. Was this about them being together? Did Dakota not really want it? Jessie's heart felt like a fragile egg about to be crushed. "Of course," she said, hoping she sounded less frantic than she felt.

She didn't remember their walk up the stairs to Dakota's old room. It seemed as though suddenly they were just there. Jessie went to the window and looked out over the lighted driveway. She hugged herself for composure.

"Are you cold?" Dakota asked. "Do you want me to get you a jacket or a shawl or something?"

"No, Dakota. I just think I know what you're going to say. So can we get it over with?"

Dakota sat on the edge of the bed. "You do?"

"Yes." Jessie turned to her. "And it makes sense. Sometimes we think we want something, but then when we get it, we don't quite know what to do with it. And especially with everything that stands between you and me, both past and present… It's a lot to deal with. I understand," she said, trying to sound like she meant it. They were adults. This wasn't the end of the world.

Dakota blinked. "What? No." Dakota rose and came to her. "It's not that. I want to be with you, Jessie. I want you. It's…"

Jessie was confused. She cocked her head, looking up into Dakota's face. *If not that…* "Then what?"

Dakota took a deep breath. She looked scared.

"Go ahead, baby. What is it?" Jessie asked, but she realized she already knew. She tensed.

"You know how, when we were out on Hightower Road, you asked me to tell you everything from that night?"

Jessie's chest tightened. She averted her gaze. She couldn't answer.

"I didn't tell you everything," Dakota said, her voice trembling slightly. "I mean I told you everything I know, what I saw and experienced, but there's something else."

Oh, God. No. She was going to say it. The thing Jessie had convinced herself would be fine because Dakota had never actually said it. It was Drew who'd said it all those years ago. And Dakota would certainly know better than him because she was the one driving. And now, she was going to say it. "Dakota don't. Please?" Tears stung her eyes.

"Jessie, I have to." Dakota's voice broke. "If I don't, it's always going to be there between us, just lurking and waiting to…"

Jessie squeezed her eyes shut.

"When we came around that first curve, I didn't see Jackie, but Drew did." Dakota didn't touch Jessie. She turned to the window. "He saw her standing right at the side of the road. Just for an instant."

Then Jessie saw her too. "Dakota, please…"

"She stepped out in front of the car," Dakota said, as though Jessie hadn't spoken, as though she hadn't begged, as though her world—what she'd based her understanding of her world on—wasn't crashing down around her.

Jessie covered her face with her hands, felt her hot tears. She wanted to call Dakota a liar, wanted to deny what was being said, but deep down, she knew it was true. A part of her always had.

That's what hurt so badly. She whirled on Dakota. "Why now? After all this time when you've never said it. Why, now?"

Dakota paled. "I've always known it was true. Drew wouldn't say something like that if it weren't, but I was afraid to believe it because then I'd have to say it too." Dakota began to cry. "I was scared, Jessie. The morning after the accident, when Drew told your mother at the hospital, she lost it. She went berserk. She attacked him. I froze. All I could see, all I could feel, was the time with *my* mother, picking flowers…and I thought she was going to kill me. And I thought your mom was going to kill Drew. And then, when I found out about you, when I met you—when I fell in…" She choked on a sob. "I was afraid of *this.*"

Jessie looked at Dakota, tried to see her pain, tried to see that terrified little girl, that terrified seventeen-year-old. But all she could see through her own tears was Jackie, standing in the dark, waiting for a car—any car—and stepping out at that last second when it would be too late for it to stop. All she saw was Jackie making that decision to leave her behind, to leave her in that cold and lonely place that was their life. It was the very possibility Jessie had never been able to make herself face, and Dakota had just forced her to. Furthermore, Dakota had done the same thing Jackie had. She'd stood in shadows, waiting for that perfect moment when Jessie actually believed everything could be okay, that they could—maybe even had—overcome their tragic past, and then she'd thrown them in front of that same car. "You couldn't have just left it alone," Jessie whispered. "Why couldn't you just leave it alone?"

Dakota reached for her. "Jessie, I—"

Jessie recoiled. "No." She looked around her at the room they were in, the trophies, the books, all the fancy things Jessie and Jackie never had. And here she was, standing right smack in the world, in the very room, Dakota had come home to the next day, when Jackie had never come home at all. She knew her emotions were irrational, her anger misplaced. Dakota wasn't responsible for Jackie's choice that night, but Jessie was thirteen again—heartbroken, confused, lost. Then, she knew. They'd never be free from the past. *She'd* never be free—not if she were with Dakota. Suddenly, she had no air. "I have to go." She bolted for the door.

"Jessie, wait. Please." Dakota caught her and pulled her hard against her. "Please, don't."

Jessie began to sob. "Dakota, just let me go. Please. I can't be here in this room, in this house. I can't be with *you*. Don't you see? This is always going to be between us. No matter that it was Jackie's decision, that it wasn't your fault. And I *know* it wasn't. But it will *always* be between us."

"Dakota," another voice said softly. "Let me have her."

Dakota's hold tightened before she released Jessie and other arms went around her.

"Come on, honey. I'll take you home," Selena said gently.

As they moved into the hall, Jessie leaning heavily on Selena, they passed Drew on his way in to Dakota.

Jessie was glad Dakota had him, that he was always there for her. She knew how badly she'd just hurt Dakota by how much she herself was hurting.

What had she been thinking that morning when she'd told Dakota she wanted to see if they could have something together, that her birthday present to Dakota was herself? How could she have been so stupid as to think that could ever work? It'd taken the pain of the truth, that her big sister whom she'd counted on more than her mother—had deliberately left her behind, to bring everything to the surface, but she finally understood why she'd always felt so alone. And now that she did, with time, maybe she could actually be with someone and feel connected.

She doubted, though, it could ever be with Dakota.

Chapter Twenty

Dakota stared at her cell phone. It was something she spent a lot of time doing these days. She kept telling herself, *surely Jessie will call, or come over, or something.*

When Selena had returned from driving her home from the party, Randy following in Jessie's car, she'd said Jessie had seemed okay. Yes, she was upset, but she'd thanked Selena for her help, apologized for the inconvenience, and assured her that she'd be fine. The next day, Dakota had waited to hear from her so they could work things out. When she hadn't heard anything by noon, she'd called and left a message when Jessie didn't answer. Then she'd called again. And again. She'd sent a couple of texts, pleading with Jessie to talk to her. Finally, at around seven that evening, she'd gone to the Triple M, but when Curtis had answered her knock, he'd told her Jessie was asleep. When she'd called one more time later that evening because she couldn't stop herself, Jessie had finally picked up.

"Oh God, Jessie. Thank you for answering," Dakota had said. "I've been going—"

"Dakota, you need to stop calling." Jessie sounded stuffy. She'd obviously been crying.

Panic gripped Dakota. "Jessie, please, can we talk? I know if we could just sit down and talk, we could—"

"I have to sort things out. I have to think," Jessie said. She sounded exhausted. "Please, just give me some time and space."

Dakota's immediate thought was *how much time*, but she knew that was the antithesis of actually giving her time and space. "Okay," she said haltingly. "If that's what you need."

Jessie sighed. "It is. Thank you."

"So you'll…you'll call me or come see me when…you're ready?"

"Yes." There was a pause. "Good night, Dakota."

And that had been almost two weeks earlier.

Dakota had honored Jessie's request. No more calls. No texts. She hadn't tried to talk to her at school, not even to say hello. She'd stayed as much out of the main building as possible and confined herself to the gym, the athletic fields, and her office. But it was killing her.

She went from depressed and discouraged, thinking she'd never have the opportunity to clear things up, to pissed that Jessie would cut her off so cruelly and coldly, to waking up just knowing today would be the day Jessie would call and they'd talk and Jessie would…What? What would Jessie say? The night of the party, Dakota had been so scared and upset, she couldn't remember everything Jessie had said.

At first, Dakota had stayed at home when she wasn't at school, in case Jessie came by. After a while, she couldn't stand the emptiness of her house, the memories of Jessie in her bed, in her shower, in her kitchen, on her couch… She'd started spending most evenings at Drew's, or if not there, with Crystal, Paul, and her mother. All the while, in the back of her mind, she'd be wondering if Jessie was, at that moment, knocking on her door. Thanksgiving had come and gone the previous week, the first holiday they would have spent together. Dakota felt as though she was literally going insane.

The only thing that kept her focus was the varsity team making it to the playoffs.

The locker room door clanged open, and the clamor of teenage girls echoed off the metal lockers.

Dakota stuffed her cell back into her jacket pocket and turned her attention to the stats she'd pulled up for the team they'd be playing later in the week on her computer screen. She barely noticed Mel step into the doorway.

"Hey, Coach," Mel said, her customary enthusiasm seeming at about half wattage. "Can I show you something?"

Dakota looked up. "Sure. What's up?"

Mel came around the desk and opened a folder. She spread out some drawings of fat little frogs done in colored pencils, each corresponding to a page of text.

"What's this?" Dakota asked, genuinely curious.

"It's a story I wrote for my little sister, and Ian did some illustrations to go with it. Aren't they good?"

Dakota leafed through them, impressed. "They're fantastic. He's really got some talent." She started reading through the story, chuckling at the antics of the older sister frog with the little ones. "This is really cute."

Mel gave a half smile. "Thanks. Ian's working on two more for my brothers."

Dakota glanced up at her. "I'm thinking you should be a whole lot happier about this. Everything okay?"

Mel frowned. "Ms. Weldon's leaving."

"What?" Dakota must have heard wrong. Or the phrase meant something different from how it sounded. *Maybe she's just leaving to go home for the day.*

"She's leaving," Mel said again. "She's going back to Boston. I thought she was staying all year."

"Where'd you hear that?" Dakota asked, trying not to let her mind run wild.

"She told me and Ian today at lunch." Mel looked like she just lost her puppy. "She said she'd still work with us. She said we could call and send our work back and forth by email, but…" She shrugged.

Dakota didn't know what to say. She had plenty of words going through her head, but none that were appropriate to share with a student.

"Do you know why?" Mel asked. "I mean you and her…you know…"

"Well, no…we aren't…" Dakota searched for an answer even for herself. "I guess she doesn't like it here."

Mel only stared at her, seeming unsatisfied with Dakota's response. She left looking like a student losing a favorite teacher.

Dakota felt like she was losing a hell of a lot more than that.

Throughout practice, Dakota's emotions ran the gamut through hurt, devastated, abandoned, and mad as hell. When the last players had left, she wasted no time getting over to the Triple M. She wanted Jessie to tell her face-to-face. She pounded on the back door.

"Just a minute," Jessie called from somewhere inside.

Dakota turned and stared out across the parking lot, her fists planted on her hips. When the door opened behind her, she spun around. "You're leaving?"

"Dakota!"

"What, did you think I wouldn't find out before you snuck out of town?"

The shock in Jessie's expression melted into resignation. "Of course not. I was going to stop by your office today after school, but I had to meet with a parent."

Dakota glared at her. "So you were going to swing by and tell me you're going back to Boston on my way to practice? That's considerate. Thank you."

Jessie sighed. "No, I was going to see if we could meet for dinner or something so we could talk."

So now she wants to talk. It made Dakota want to tell her to go screw herself and storm off. This was what she'd been waiting for, though. Okay, not *this,* not being told Jessie was leaving Clearwater Springs, but for Jessie to be willing to talk at all. She clenched her jaw to keep from saying anything she'd regret.

"Can you come in?" Jessie asked, her demeanor softer than Dakota would have expected from the one curt phone conversation they'd had two weeks earlier. "Do you have time?"

Dakota was still mad, and she wanted to stay that way, because if she couldn't maintain her anger, she suspected this was going to hurt like hell. Without answering, she brushed past Jessie and into the kitchen.

"Would you like to sit in the living room?" Jessie asked.

"No. This is fine."

Jessie gestured to the table. "Would you like—"

"No, Jessie. I wouldn't like anything except to find out what the hell is going on? Why haven't you been willing to see me, for us, maybe, to have a conversation about whether you stay or go? This is out of left field for me. Until today, I didn't have any idea you were considering leaving, and I had to find out from a student, for Christ's sake."

Jessie pulled out a chair and sat. She folded her hands in front of her on the table. "You're right. I'm sorry. I haven't handled this well at all."

That caught Dakota off guard. She was expecting a fight—in truth, was ready for one—not an apology. Her defenses came tumbling down. "Don't go, Jessie. Please."

"I have to." Jessie's voice was barely above a whisper. "I can't stay here."

"Why? I thought we'd wrestled all the demons, for both of us. And if we haven't, we can keep doing it together."

"I thought so too." Regret tinged her words.

Dakota struggled to grasp her meaning. "But I'm still one of your demons?" A deep ache throbbed in her heart, and she realized that, at some point, she'd begun wanting from Jessie the forgiveness Jessie's mother hadn't been able to give her. She'd already gotten that, though, hadn't she—when Jessie had come to her, had been with her, had given herself to Dakota? Wasn't that what that was? Dakota had felt it. But it wasn't enough. She wanted Jessie, all of her. She wanted to be with her every day, to belong to her, to love her. Suddenly, she knew Jessie was *the one*. And now, Jessie wanted to leave. "Jessie, I'm sorry I—"

"It isn't you, Dakota. *You* aren't my demon." She shifted her gaze out the window. "It turns out my demon is this town. It took my entire family from me." She looked into Dakota's eyes. "And now, it's taken you."

"It's taken me?" Dakota balked. "No one's taken me. You're the one walking away."

Jessie studied her. "Do you remember how angry I was with you when you told me I was a reminder of everything you've been trying to forget all your adult life?"

A pang of guilt twisted in Dakota's gut. "I know I said that, but it isn't—"

"Hear me out, okay?

Dakota nodded, then pulled out a chair across from Jessie and joined her at the table.

"I didn't understand that at the time, but now I do." Jessie massaged her temples. "Deep down inside, I've known for a long time the possibility that Jackie stepped in front of your car deliberately. That she..." Jessie swallowed, as though the words trying to come out were choking her. "That she committed suicide. For the last several months before it happened, she was depressed and withdrawn. She hardly ever talked to me anymore. But it hurt too much to face that. I couldn't deal with the knowledge that she intentionally left me behind. She'd always said she'd be there for me, no matter what, and I believed her. And now that this is all out in the open and I don't have any choice as to whether or not I deal with it, that's all I can see when I see or think about you."

Dakota's stomach dropped. "Jessie, I tried to swerve. I couldn't..."

"I know, baby." The words were so soft, so tender.

Dakota's heart ached at the thought that this might be the last time Jessie ever called her baby. It might be the last time they ever spoke.

"I know it wasn't your fault. Or Drew's. Or even Jackie's. But I have to be able to put it all behind me. I can't do that here. And I especially can't do it with you." Jessie's eyes shimmered with a thin veneer of tears. "Believe me, I wish I could." She tentatively took Dakota's hand.

Dakota's throat closed with unspoken words and unshed tears. *How can something so right be so wrong?* She closed her fingers tightly around Jessie's.

"I have to go, Dakota. I can't see you every day. It hurts too much."

Dakota got that. She simply nodded and stood to leave. She didn't want to give up, but begging wouldn't do either of them any good, and she couldn't think of anything else to say. She could tell Jessie had made up her mind.

Outside, she got as far as the back steps before her legs went weak and she had to sit. She didn't know how long she rested there, watching the flashing *Vacancy* on the neon sign that read Midnight Moon Motel and gazing up at the stars mindlessly. When Curtis crossed the parking lot, coming from the office, and lowered himself to the top step beside her, all she could say was, "She's leaving."

He put an arm around her. "Yep," he said thoughtfully. "This town was never her home. I thought maybe you'd changed that, but it seems not."

"She helped me a lot." Dakota remembered the night they'd shared out at Brogan's Bend, the way Jessie had comforted and reassured her, how healing it'd felt when she'd told Dakota nothing about her mother was her fault, she'd only been a little girl. "I wish I could have helped her."

Curtis tightened his hold. "You did, Dakota. Trust me, you did."

Jessie finished putting the breakfast dishes into the dishwasher, then topped off Curtis's coffee as he read the weekly paper at the table.

"I'm sure going to miss you, Jessie girl." He took a swallow. "But I should be able to take off a few pounds once I'm back to my own cooking." He laughed.

Jessie curled into the chair across from him, drawing up one knee. "I'm sure Margie's going to have something to say about that. Once she moves in, you'll have home cooking every day."

"And what about you? Are you going to be okay all alone, once you're home again?" Curtis's tone was serious.

"I won't be alone," Jessie said, trying to keep things light. "Sandy's back there, and my other friends. Besides, I'm assuming it's still okay for me to come for a visit from time to time." She wasn't sure she would, but the comment made Curtis smile.

"You know you're welcome anytime," he said, closing his paper and laying it on the table. "You have to come back for the wedding, at least."

"I'd never miss that, Curtis. I'll definitely be here for it." She wasn't sure how she was going to swing that one. It wasn't until spring, though, so maybe it'd be easier running into Dakota by then. They'd maneuvered around each other at school since their last conversation, but Jessie's heart still ached whenever she saw her.

"Oh," Curtis said, bringing Jessie back to the moment. "I pulled those boxes out of the attic for you when you were making breakfast. They're in your room."

"Thank you. I appreciate that." One thing Jessie had made up her mind to do before she left was go through her, Jackie's, and their mother's things to see if there was anything else she wanted to keep and get rid of the rest. She didn't want any more of the past lingering around behind her. She intended to make a brand new start. When she went into her bedroom, though, to find them waiting for her, the job felt more daunting than she'd anticipated.

She set her mind to it and opened the first one, the one of her own in which she'd found the baseball. She decided fairly quickly not to keep the rest of its contents and moved on to the next. It was a good time to do this. She wasn't feeling particularly sentimental. Or maybe it was simply that she'd already taken the things that had any meaning to her—Mr. Whiskers and the softball.

When she got to Jackie's boxes, she went a little more slowly. At the books at the bottom, she paused. Several of them were diaries. She specifically recognized one with rainbows on the cover from seeing it on the upside-down milk crate that acted as a nightstand in their room. She opened it and startled at the first date. It was the year of Jackie's death.

Jessie inhaled sharply. She thumbed through the pages. Did she really want to do this? *I'm done with the past, remember?* One page caught her attention. It had a big red heart drawn on it with the initials RB and JB colored on it in sharp contrast. *Who was RB?* Jessie didn't recall Jackie ever having a boyfriend. She settled back on her bed and began to read.

She learned things about her sister she'd never known. Jackie was scared of never being good enough. She envied the popular kids at school and tried many things to become friends with them, including stealing for them from the drug store and, once she hit puberty, trading sex with the boys for acceptance. It was always fleeting, though. Her place in the in-group lasted only as long as she was willing to give what was asked of her. The entries held sadness and adolescent pain, until the initials RB began showing up, then finally, a name. Ron Beckman.

Jessie paused. *Ron Beckman?* The guy Dakota had said was a jerk. She picked up the baseball cap from one of Jackie's boxes and looked inside. There it was, in permanent marker. She looked at the cap again, this time with more interest.

According to Jackie's diary, Ron Beckman was the love of her life. He was her ticket into the world she wanted so desperately. *If he was all that, why do I not remember him?* There were poems about him, lots of heart drawings, accounts of his promises to marry her when he graduated and taking her with him when he went off to college, and a pregnancy scare Jackie wrote of in detail. The most interesting thing about that, however, was the lack of what R. Beckman felt about it. Then it came. In March, Ron told Jackie he'd been accepted to the University of California San Diego on an athletic scholarship, and she wouldn't be going with him. What followed was bone-chilling. Page after page after page of dark entries, rants of anger, self-hatred, and writings of death and self-destruction. There was so much pain, crying out to God, to her father, to her mother…And then, everything went calm, and a plan was formed.

As Jessie read the details, she sat up. It was spelled out to the letter—the bend in Hightower Road where their father had died, the time of night, sneaking from the house without waking Jessie or Mom, and then waiting, waiting by the side of the road in the shadows…

And then a paragraph to Jessie. Not a good-bye exactly, not even a paragraph *to* her so much as about her. *My little sister who's so much stronger than I am, who'd never do the things I've done. I'm sorry, Jessie. I can't be what you need me to be.* Jessie's breath caught, and tears blurred her vision.

The last entry, the day of Jackie's death…*I want to be with Daddy.*

Jessie put down the book and pondered those words. *I want to be with Daddy…Daddy.* Jackie was a lost child with nowhere to turn.

It took Jessie days to process all the information she'd gotten from Jackie's diary, during which time, she revisited Brogan's Bend, sitting on her rock for a long time, taking in the scene. She sat where Jackie's body had been thrown, lay where she and Dakota had lain. She thought of Jackie, Dakota, Drew, herself, pictured them…all children.

She went to the cemetery and put flowers on all three graves—Jackie's, their mother's, their father's—and spent an afternoon with them. Before she left, she accepted what Jackie had. Jackie couldn't be what Jessie needed her to be, and Jessie couldn't be what her mother had needed her to be. They were both too broken for this world, and Jessie couldn't have fixed that.

When she stood and walked away, she left something behind. She left the past.

A short time later, Jessie found herself at Dakota's door. She knew it was too late for them. She'd hurt Dakota so badly. She wanted her to know about Jackie, though, to be completely certain—once and for all—that she wasn't responsible in any way for Jackie's death. She knocked.

When Dakota answered, Jessie wasn't sure what to say. She hadn't planned anything. "Hi," was all she could manage.

"Hi," Dakota said coolly. She waited. Then, "Is there something I can do for you?"

Jessie cleared her throat. "I wanted to share something with you," she said. "May I come in?"

Dakota hesitated, her expression wary. "Sure. I guess."

It wasn't the greeting Jessie would have liked, but it probably was the one she deserved.

"I thought you'd be gone by now," Dakota said when they were inside.

"No, I'm having Christmas with Curtis and Margie." Jessie slipped Jackie's diary from her coat pocket and set it on the table.

"What's that?" Dakota asked.

"I was going through some old boxes Curtis has been storing for me for years, and I came across some diaries of Jackie's. This is the one that leads up to that night. I thought you might want to read it."

Dakota picked it up and studied the cover. "Is it important to you?"

"Not necessarily." Jessie nervously shifted from one foot to the other. "The part that's important to me, I'd like to tell you myself."

Dakota put the book back on the table. "Okay. You want to sit down?"

"Thank you." Jessie sat on the couch, Dakota, in the chair adjacent to it.

Dakota watched her expectantly.

Jessie steadied herself. Fortunately, she hadn't thought about how difficult this was going to be. If she had, she might not have come. She took a deep breath. "I was…seeing everything wrong all these years," she began haltingly. "Jackie was my older sister, and I saw her as bigger and stronger and someone I could count on, so I could never accept even the idea of her choosing to leave this world. She was supposed to be here for me, always."

Dakota cut her gaze to her feet, as though this was too personal for her to hear.

"The writings in there, though…" Jessie nodded to the book. "They're the writings, the thoughts, of a child. A frightened and insecure one. She took her life to be with our father because there wasn't anything here that made her feel safe. I don't think she'd felt safe since he died."

Dakota jerked her head up. "That's awful. She really must have been terrified."

"I know. She was only sixteen, and emotionally, probably much younger." Jessie relaxed a little with Dakota's understanding. "I wish I'd realized that before now."

"You couldn't have realized that back then. And even if you had, it probably wouldn't have made any difference. You couldn't have made her feel safe."

Jessie looked into Dakota's eyes. A wave of sadness washed through her. "No, I mean today. I wish I'd understood it sooner, today, before it cost me you."

"What do you mean?"

Jessie leaned back into the sofa cushion. "I've spent the past several days processing everything I read, everything that happened between me and you, trying to figure out what it all means, and I believe I've let go of it all. I've left the past in the past where it belongs. But it's too late. I've lost you. And, Dakota, I'm so sorry."

Dakota fidgeted with the drawstring on her jogging pants. "What if it isn't?" Other than the movement of her fingers, she remained perfectly still. "What if it isn't too late?"

Jessie felt something warm inside her, like the slight opening of the first bud of spring. "Isn't it?"

Dakota bit her lip, evidently either trying to say no more, or trying to work up the courage to go on. "Not for me," she whispered.

Jessie couldn't breathe. "Dakota," she said in an attempt to coax her to meet her gaze. "Are you sure?"

"If I say yes, will you stay? I can't go there, if you're not going to stay."

Tears of relief, of disbelief, stung Jessie's eyes. "Yes."

Dakota met and held her gaze. "Then yes, Jessie. I'm sure. I don't want you to leave. I've never wanted you to leave, from that very first day in your classroom and that stupid John Wayne impression."

Jessie laughed as she wiped the tears from her cheeks. "I've had you since then?"

Dakota nodded. "You've had me since then. It just took me a while to figure it all out too."

Jessie stifled a sob, one of pure happiness. "Can I touch you?"

In an instant, Dakota was on the couch, on her, kissing her, holding her. "God, Jessie, I love you. Stay with me. Be with me."

"Yes. Yes, baby. Yes." Jessie buried her face in Dakota's hair, kissed her neck. "I love you. I never want to be anywhere else."

Dakota stood and scooped her off the couch. She carried her down the hall to the bedroom. "I hope you don't have any plans tonight, or tomorrow, or the next day, or for the entire time I'm off for winter break, because I have some time with you to make up for."

"Okay, but if we're going to start making up for lost time, I have about thirty years *you* owe *me*. Starting right now." Jessie kissed her hard.

As she lay back on Dakota's bed, she felt the unmistakable comfort and safety of home. She felt the love promised in all the Christmas cards with pictures of a fire burning in the hearth and lights glowing in the windows. She felt like she belonged somewhere. She belonged here. It wasn't in this town, though, or in this house, or even in this room. It wasn't in the deep green of Dakota's eyes gazing down at her, or in her grin, or in the press of her body as she lowered herself onto Jessie.

It was in Dakota's heart that Jessie had finally found her home.

About the Author

Jeannie Levig is an award-winning author of lesbian fiction and a proud and happy member of the Bold Strokes Books family. Her debut novel, *Threads of the Heart*, won a 2016 Golden Crown Literary Society (Goldie) Award in the Debut Author category, and her second novel, *Embracing the Dawn*, was a 2017 Goldie finalist in the Traditional Contemporary Romance category. Her third novel, *Into Thin Air*, is a romantic intrigue and was released in January of 2017.

Raised by an English teacher, Jeannie has always been surrounded by literature and novels and learned to love reading at an early age. She tried her hand at writing fiction for the first time under the loving encouragement of her eighth grade English teacher, and in college, she received a bachelor's degree in English. She is deeply committed to her spiritual path and community, her family, and to writing the best stories possible to share with her readers.

Visit Jeannie at her website, www.JeannieLevig.com, or send her a note to say hi at Jeannie@jeannielevig.com. You may also find her on Facebook and Twitter. She'd love to hear from you.

Books Available from Bold Strokes Books

A Heart to Call Home by Jeannie Levig. When Jessie Weldon returns to her hometown after thirty years, can she and her childhood crush Dakota Scott heal the tragic past that links them? (978-1-63555-059-7)

Children of the Healer by Barbara Ann Wright. Life becomes desperate for ex-soldier Cordelia Ross when the indigenous aliens of her planet are drawn into a civil war and old enemies linger in the shadows. Book Three of the Godfall Series. (978-1-63555-031-3)

Hearts Like Hers by Melissa Brayden. Coffee shop owner Autumn Primm is ready to cut loose and live a little, but is the baggage that comes with out-of-towner Kate Carpenter too heavy for anything long term? (978-1-63555-014-6)

Love at Cooper's Creek by Missouri Vaun. Shaw Daily flees corporate life to find solace in the rural Blue Ridge Mountains, but escapism eludes her when her attentions are captured by small town beauty Kate Elkins. (978-1-62639-960-0)

Somewhere Over Lorain Road by Bud Gundy. Over forty years after murder allegations shattered the Esker family, can Don Esker find the true killer and clear his dying father's name? (978-1-63555-124-2)

Twice in a Lifetime by PJ Trebelhorn. Detective Callie Burke can't deny the growing attraction to her late friend's widow, Taylor Fletcher, who also happens to own the bar where Callie's sister works. (978-1-63555-033-7)

Undiscovered Affinity by Jane Hardee. Will a no strings attached affair be enough to break Olivia's control and convince Cardic that love does exist? (978-1-63555-061-0)

Between Sand and Stardust by Tina Michele. Are the lifelong bonds of love strong enough to conquer time, distance, and heartache when Haven Thorne and Willa Bennette are given another chance at forever? (978-1-62639-940-2)

Charming the Vicar by Jenny Frame. When magician and atheist Finn Kane seeks refuge in an English village after a spiritual crisis, can local vicar Bridget Claremont restore her faith in life and love? (978-1-63555-029-0)

Data Capture by Jesse J. Thoma. Lola Walker is undercover on the hunt for cybercriminals while trying not to notice the woman who might be perfectly wrong for her for all the right reasons. (978-1-62639-985-3)

Epicurean Delights by Renee Roman. Ariana Marks had no idea a leisure swim would lead to being rescued, in more ways than one, by the charismatic Hudson Frost. (978-1-63555-100-6)

Heart of the Devil by Ali Vali. We know most of Cain and Emma Casey's story, but *Heart of the Devil* will take you back to where it began one fateful night with a tray loaded with beer. (978-1-63555-045-0)

Known Threat by Kara A. McLeod. When Special Agent Ryan O'Connor reluctantly questions who protects the Secret Service, she learns courage truly is found in unlikely places. Agent O'Connor Series #3. (978-1-63555-132-7)

Seer and the Shield by D. Jackson Leigh. Time is running out for the Dragon Horse Army while two unlikely heroines struggle to put aside their attraction and find a way to stop a deadly cult. Dragon Horse War, Book 3. (978-1-63555-170-9)

Sinister Justice by Steve Pickens. When a vigilante targets citizens of Jake Finnigan's hometown, Jake and his partner Sam fall under suspicion themselves as they investigate the murders. (978-1-63555-094-8)

The Universe Between Us by Jane C. Esther. Ana Mitchell must make the hardest choice of her life: the promise of new love Jolie Dann on Earth, or a humanity-saving mission to colonize Mars. (978-1-63555-106-8)

Touch by Kris Bryant. Can one touch heal a heart? (978-1-63555-084-9)

Change in Time by Robyn Nyx. Working in the past is hell on your future. The Extractor Series: Book Two. (978-1-62639-880-1)

Love After Hours by Radclyffe. When Gina Antonelli agrees to renovate Carrie Longmire's new house, she doesn't welcome Carrie's overtures at friendship or her own unexpected attraction. A Rivers Community Novel. (978-1-63555-090-0)

Nantucket Rose by CF Frizzell. Maggie Jordan can't wait to convert an historic Nantucket home into a B&B, but doesn't expect to fall for mariner Ellis Chilton, who has more claim to the house than Maggie realizes. (978-1-63555-056-6)

Picture Perfect by Lisa Moreau. Falling in love wasn't supposed to be part of the stakes for Olive and Gabby, rival photographers in the competition of a lifetime. (978-1-62639-975-4)

Set the Stage by Karis Walsh. Actress Emilie Danvers takes the stage again in Ashland, Oregon, little realizing that landscaper Arden Philips is about to offer her a very personal romantic lead role. (978-1-63555-087-0)

Strike a Match by Fiona Riley. When their attempts at matchmaking fizzle out, firefighter Sasha and reluctant millionairess Abby find themselves turning to each other to strike a perfect match. (978-1-62639-999-0)

The Price of Cash by Ashley Bartlett. Cash Braddock is doing her best to keep her business afloat, stay out of jail, and avoid Detective Kallen. It's not working. (978-1-62639-708-8)

Under Her Wing by Ronica Black. At Angel's Wings Rescue, dogs are usually the ones saved, but when quiet Kassandra Haden meets outspoken owner Jayden Beaumont, the two stubborn women just might end up saving each other. (978-1-63555-077-1)

Underwater Vibes by Mickey Brent. When Hélène, a translator in Brussels, Belgium, meets Sylvie, a young Greek photographer and swim coach, unsettling feelings hijack Hélène's mind and body—even her poems. (978-1-63555-002-3)

A More Perfect Union by Carsen Taite. Major Zoey Granger and DC fixer Rook Daniels risk their reputations for a chance at true love while dealing with a scandal that threatens to rock the military. (978-1-62639-754-5)

Arrival by Gun Brooke. The spaceship *Pathfinder* reaches its passengers' new homeworld where danger lurks in the shadows while Pamas Seclan disembarks and finds unexpected love in young science genius Darmiya Do Voy. (978-1-62639-859-7)

Captain's Choice by VK Powell. Architect Kerstin Anthony's life is going to plan until Bennett Carlyle, the first girl she ever kissed, is assigned to her latest and most important project, a police district substation. (978-1-62639-997-6)

Falling Into Her by Erin Zak. Pam Phillips, widow at the age of forty, meets Kathryn Hawthorne, local Chicago celebrity, and it changes her life forever—in ways she hadn't even considered possible. (978-1-63555-092-4)

Hookin' Up by MJ Williamz. Will Leah get what she needs from casual hookups or will she see the love she desires right in front of her? (978-1-63555-051-1)

King of Thieves by Shea Godfrey. When art thief Casey Marinos meets bounty hunter Finnegan Starkweather, the crimes of the past just might set the stage for a payoff worth more than she ever dreamed possible. (978-1-63555-007-8)

Lucy's Chance by Jackie D. As a serial killer haunts the streets, Lucy tries to stitch up old wounds with her first love in the wake of a small town's rapid descent into chaos. (978-1-63555-027-6)

Right Here, Right Now by Georgia Beers. When Alicia Wright moves into the office next door to Lacey Chamberlain's accounting firm, Lacey is about to find out that sometimes the last person you want is exactly the person you need. (978-1-63555-154-9)

Strictly Need to Know by MB Austin. Covert operator Maji Rios will do whatever she must to complete her mission, but saving a gorgeous stranger from Russian mobsters was not in her plans. (978-1-63555-114-3)

Tailor-Made by Yolanda Wallace. Tailor Grace Henderson doesn't date clients, but when she meets gender-bending model Dakota Lane, she's tempted to throw all the rules out the window. (978-1-63555-081-8)

Time Will Tell by M. Ullrich. With the ability to time travel, Eva Caldwell will have to decide between having it all and erasing it all. (978-1-63555-088-7)

A Date to Die by Anne Laughlin. Someone is killing people close to Detective Kay Adler, who must look to her own troubled past for a suspect. There she finds more than one person seeking revenge against her. (978-1-63555-023-8)

Captured Soul by Laydin Michaels. Can Kadence Munroe save the woman she loves from a twisted killer, or will she lose her to a collector of souls? (978-1-62639-915-0)

Dawn's New Day by TJ Thomas. Can Dawn Oliver and Cam Cooper, two women who have loved and lost, open their hearts to love again? (978-1-63555-072-6)

Definite Possibility by Maggie Cummings. Sam Miller is just out for good times, but Lucy Weston makes her realize happily ever after is a definite possibility. (978-1-62639-909-9)

Eyes Like Those by Melissa Brayden. Isabel Chase and Taylor Andrews struggle between love and ambition from the writers' room on one of Hollywood's hottest TV shows. (978-1-63555-012-2)

Heart's Orders by Jaycie Morrison. Helen Tucker and Tee Owens escape hardscrabble lives to careers in the Women's Army Corps, but more than their hearts are at risk as friendship blossoms into love. (978-1-63555-073-3)

Hiding Out by Kay Bigelow. Treat Dandridge is unaware that her life is in danger from the murderer who is hunting the woman she's falling in love with, Mickey Heiden. (978-1-62639-983-9)

Omnipotence Enough by Sophia Kell Hagin. Can the tiny tool that abducted war veteran Jamie Gwynmorgan accidentally acquires help her escape an unknown enemy to reclaim her stolen life and the woman she deeply loves? (978-1-63555-037-5)

Summer's Cove by Aurora Rey. Emerson Lange moved to Provincetown to live in the moment, but when she meets Darcy Belo and her son Liam, her quest for summer romance becomes a family affair. (978-1-62639-971-6)

The Road to Wings by Julie Tizard. Lieutenant Casey Tompkins, Air Force student pilot, has to fly with the toughest instructor, Captain Kathryn "Hard Ass" Hardesty, fly a supersonic jet, and deal with a growing forbidden attraction. (978-1-62639-988-4)